Red Rum
Comes To Light

Red Rum Comes To Light

DEBRA GIBSON

Red Rum Comes To Light

Copyright © 2024 by Debra Gibson. All rights reserved.

Printed in the United States of America
ISBN 979-8-88945-477-9 (sc)
ISBN 979-8-88945-478-6 (e)

2024.01.11

Brilliant Books Literary
137 Forest Park Ln,
Thomasville, NC 27360,
United States

TABLE OF CONTENTS

Chapter 1 A sunny day, does not guarantee a good one. 5

Chapter 2 A bottle of chardonnay, a glass of solitude........................ 13

Chapter 3 In a black pot, the past is brewing........................21

Chapter 4 Grain of Salt........................ 33

Chapter 5 Happy Hour........................ 49

Chapter 6 Grains Taken Lightly........................ 59

Chapter 7 Hard To Swallow........................ 64

Chapter 8 Five of a Kind........................74

Chapter 9 In Vino Veritas........................ 86

Chapter 10 First Comes Love........................ 98

Chapter 11 Then Comes The Rain 103

Chapter 12 Time To Think 117

Chapter 13 New Millennium, New Face, New Friend 127

Chapter 14 Margarita Night........................146

Chapter 15 Proverbs 15:3........................165

Chapter 16 Red Twenty 180

Chapter 17 Beyond The Pale 192

Chapter 18 Taste Like Leukemia........................ 203

Chapter 19 Why Not?........................219

Chapter 20 Last Call........................ 230

Chapter 21 In Search Again 239

Chapter 22 The People VS. Tyler Walsh........................ 250

Chapter 23 The Re-incarnation of Love 264

Chapter 24 Your Prejudice Becomes You.................................... 278

Chapter 25 Third Time Around....................................... 288

Chapter 26 Know Thy Enemies 301

Chapter 27 Unfortunate Circumstances..................................315

Chapter 28 In the Black Pot, the Past Surfaces and Runs Overed 330

Chapter 29 Coming Full Circle.. 344

Chapter 30 Red Rum Comes To Light....................................365

Chapter 31 There's A Divinity That Shapes Our Ends....................... 383

*B*efore you judge, criticize and attempt to bring reproach on my justifiable actions, I ask that you lend me your eyes and ears and clear your mind of any prejudice or bias opinions; and give my words due process . . .

Red was the color of Gabrielle's palms as she slowly rose to her feet and stared at her hands. Her emotions were running high. She wasn't sure if she was in shock or just delusional. He was dead, but she couldn't understand why. There were other unreasonable deaths from people in her life, but this one appears to be personal and voluntarily cold. There was a loud crash behind Gabrielle that startled her weak, which brought more daylight into the condemned building. The police had knocked out some of the boarded up windows, as law enforcement officers enters from other parts of the building. Tears in her eyes, Gabrielle turns away from the bright light that is focused on her. She stumbles as she tries to walk, but didn't get far.

Detective John Mackey rushes up to Gabrielle, catching her before she falls. "Dr. Michaels, what happened, are you hurt? Get E M S in here now!" he yelled.

The room was spinning and she couldn't breathe. Gabrielle tries to pull away from detective Mackey in rage before letting out an emotional, soul-draining outcry. She then blacks out in his arms. Detective Mackey stares at the body on the floor, then his eyes gradually rises up at the other body hanging from the ceiling.

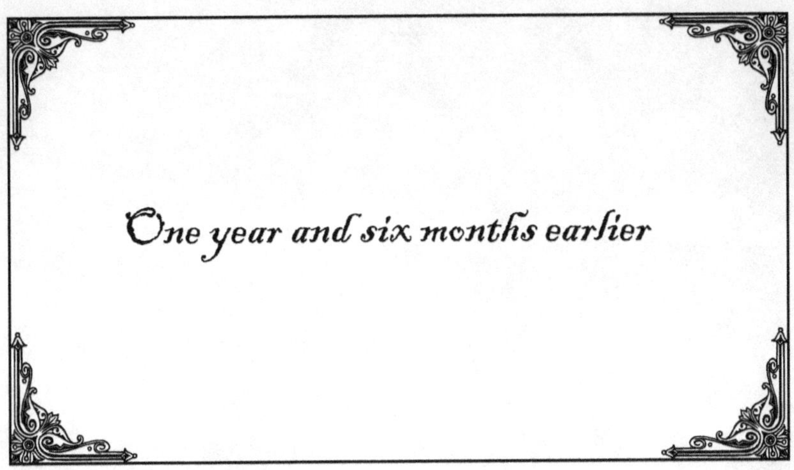
One year and six months earlier

CHAPTER ONE

A sunny day, does not guarantee a good one.

If you follow this particular rhythm of lively colored, radiate rays of the sun, it will probably lead you to 750 N Lakeshore Drive in Chicago, Illinois. There, you will find Northwestern University Hospital and at Lynn Sage Breast Cancer Center, a dull sunspot seems to have made its self comfortable. The waiting area at Lynn Sage Breast Cancer Center wasn't as crowded as it was last week. The nice arrangement of flowers and plants throughout the clinic offices seem to brighten the waiting rooms with hope. Attractive yet peculiar paintings were there to lose yourself in the moment and soft relaxing music to take your mind off your troubles. There was a variety of assorted magazines of your choice to read, magazines with topics such as: The hottest trends for the summer, The ten most moneymaking ideas, and How to lose ten pounds in ten days. Who cares? I'm sure these women waiting to be seen by a doctor have more important things on their minds, like do they have enough medical and life insurance coverage.

Dr. Michaels returns a folder back up front and stares out into the waiting area. She could imagine the exaggerating thoughts going through their heads. Dr. Michaels gave a brief smile to the medical assistant before returning to the back offices. A nurse in high spirits walked pass Dr. Michaels on her way to the waiting room. Just one more hour left before the entire staff calls it a day. Mrs. Susan Bayer was the next patient to be seen as the nurse calls her name. Doctor Rose Kessler calls Dr. Michaels into her office as she was walking by. However, Dr. Michaels have seen that same serious, have to give bad news expression on her face before. Dr. Kessler goes over some test results with Dr. Michaels before seeing the next patient.

Minutes later, Dr. Kessler and Dr. Michaels enters a small room where Mrs. Bayer was waiting which seem like forever, but patiently. Some small talk is made between the doctors and patient. Even in the brief moments of small talk, Mrs. Bayer couldn't help but stare at the folder Dr. Kessler held in her hands. In that folder held the welfare of Mrs. Bayer life and future. Being seriously sincere, Dr. Kessler gives Mrs. Bayer her test results.

"The mammogram and other extensive test confirms our findings to be accurate. Mrs. Bayer, you have breast cancer."

Mrs. Bayer tried to appear strong, but nodded her head in sympathy. Dr. Michaels felt every bit of the slow and gloomy passion of dull sadness that Mrs. Bayer was feeling, but had not quite totally registered in her head. This sadness Mrs. Bayer is absorbing is the kind of sadness that is in search of a sanctuary yet in desperate need of the yearning compassion of comfort, the kind of nurturing comfort a newborn baby receives in the arms of a mother.

In her quiet thoughts, Dr. Michaels could see herself reaching out her hand for comfort, a touch of hope. Dr. Michaels tries not to take each patient that is diagnosed with breast cancer personally, but with each case, even doctors are somehow affected one way or another. In need of a deep breath, Dr. Michaels kept her mind focused on her job and listens as Dr. Kessler goes over options.

The year was 1999, five months away from the new millennium. There was so much heighten current events and unbelievable chaos taken place in the U.S. at this time. The people of Illinois, Chicago particular, were trying to put together pieces of a puzzle to why a senseless, violent, cold-blooded act of a bizarre fatal shooting rampage across Illinois and Indiana took place. Mark Hale, a white supremacist leader, was the cause and reason of these senseless killings. Billy Smith, one of Mark Hale's followers was the murderer who committed these acts. Smith targeted minorities and when this three-day shooting rampage was all over, two people were dead and nine others were wounded. Among the two dead was former Northwestern University basketball coach Ronald Byrdsong. Hate, which seems to be the only endeavor, ended when police closed in on Smith and he shot and killed himself.

If that wasn't enough stunning, brick to the back of the head drama to comprehend, try the entire nation in mourning and disbelief of the tragic accidental death of a great man, JFK Jr. John Fitzgerald Kennedy, Jr., son of our 34th president died July 16, 1999 along with his wife and sister in law in a private plane crash. JFK Jr. was an American legend in his own time way before his passing. Americans felt as if they had been cheated by his death, that this country loss one of their future presidents.

If you attempt to ask yourself why such senseless killings and tragic deaths take place, it would only prolong the poignant grief, which can leave you subject to insanity. The mysterious ways some say God works only makes you wonder what other tragedies are in store for this great nation of ours.

You can be sure of one thing and that is, death knows no color. Death's nonchalant power has nothing to prove in this forever changing reality of life. More certain than the future of this world, death itself does not require an invitation or explanation. The only time we feel that death requires an explanation, from the department of government concerns primarily, is through an autopsy. Death, furthermore, is always questionable in the event of manslaughter, suicide, and far more than most, Murder.

5: 45 p.m. later that evening after the last patient was seen; Dr. Gabrielle Michaels was seen silently making her way out of the Lynn Sage Breast Cancer Center building. She walked peaceful, yet capriciously to a point of an unmotivated notion of utter calm. Amiable in good nature, she willingly makes way to her car that is always parked further from the other automobiles. This day however, didn't seem to be looking so good after all, but she refuse to dwell on it. Gabrielle was more than ready to let the downing affects of a workday melt away in a cool cocktail. Hopefully, the rest of her evening will be better. All she had to do first was, find her keys. This undoubtedly is a time delaying little game she involuntarily plays just about every other day. After two minutes of fumbling around in her purse, the keys were found hiding between her makeup case and a small pocket pack of Kleenex.

If Gabrielle were crazy, she would honestly believe that her keys had a mind of their own and deliberately hid themselves from her. The sound of her car alarm being disarmed is heard as Gabrielle opens her car door and elegantly slips herself inside. She closes the door and place the key inside the ignition, but did not proceed to start the engine. Closing her eyes, she begins her sacred well-being little ritual. Gabrielle takes a deep breath through her nose and slowly exhales out her mouth. She does this two or three more times then give her mind a few moments of peace. Peace, tranquility that feels like the sound of a colorful butterfly in motion as you capture a divine and almost intoxicating pleasurable affects of a mild sunset on a warm Country Time Lemonade summer day.

Gabrielle doesn't necessary think about the day she just endured. If it was a good day, then by all means. Just relax your mind for a minute; perhaps think about your evening ahead, the ocean, a rainbow, your kids, the love of your life, or the simple joys of life. It doesn't matter, whatever your thoughts can find peace in for a moment, just exhale any form of tension away. Gabrielle's thoughts seemed pleasing, but there were some negative vibes there. She gave a brief smile before starting the engine. *"So how are you feeling?"* she asked herself in thought. Gabrielle was about to answer herself in thought when the sound of a car horn came zooming by. She was slowly backing out in reverse, but quickly put on brakes. That only made Gabrielle think of the drive home traffic ahead. Slowly making her way out of the parking deck, a particular person came to mind. She drives around by the emergency room debating if she should stop in for a visit. After not much thought, Gabrielle decided not to stop by. She didn't want to seem as if she was crowding him. She would just look forward to seeing him later.

Ignoring traffic delays up dates on the radio, Gabrielle drives steady on Kennedy Expressway headed home to Des Plaines, Illinois. No point in listening to the traffic updates, there is always some accident or road construction holding up traffic somewhere anyway. If you do make it to your destination in good time, then you were safely guided by the roll of the dice sure luck. Sure enough, just as she thought, minutes into her drive home on I-94 express, there was road construction that had traffic slowly coming to a standstill.

The sun was still out and shinning, but was in harvest to set. Amazing bright blue skies so hypnotic, that if you stared long enough, you just might mistake it as a deep blue pool and pleasure yourself for a dip. Gabrielle slows her car down for traffic that seems to be backing up for miles. She reached in her purse for her cell phone knowing she probably has some missed calls. As she channels through her cell phone caller ID, a puzzled expression quickly ran across Gabrielle's face. She had three missed calls and one voicemail message and neither of the calls were from him. Trying not to focus on why, she listens to her voicemail message. The message was from one of her closest friends. Jillian liked to leave spiritual up lifting messages for her. Jillian's message gave Gabrielle a smile.

Traffic was barley inching along to the point of stop and roll, giving Gabrielle a pleasant thought and opportunity to call him. After one ring, his cell phone went straight to voicemail. She hated getting his voicemail when she calls, but left a message anyway. Her message was brief and in reference of getting together tonight. After leaving the voicemail message, she ends the call and tosses the cell phone over in the passenger seat. The thought of Mrs. Bayer somehow eased its way into Gabrielle's mind, bringing with it an overnight bag. Due to the inevitable situation at the moment, this thought could possibly dwell for a while. Traffic was now at a complete stop and with the air- conditioning comfortably running; Gabrielle couldn't help but think about her day. *"You have breast cancer."* That remark kept playing over and over in her mind.

Gabrielle didn't know what it feels like to personally hear news of that nature, cancer. Who would ever think a six letter word could hit you harder than stone and knock you to your knees. I guess it would bring the same affects for those who have to mentally digest the three letters, yet even powerful words of HIV or something worst as AIDS. Any illness can be a life changing and draining experience to endure. Looking at the world today and to witness all the life threatening illness's anyone can be exposed to or develop, makes you cherish each healthy day you live and thank God for each day given. You may thank God just to be able to get over a common cold, but how does one get over an illness like the *beast of cancer?* That's just it, you don't, or do you? Yes, there are survivors of cancer. These women proven to be stronger than death, only after going through hell, but do anyone ever really get over cancer?

Gabrielle remembers her mother asking that same question during her last days and fight with breast cancer. She wasn't there with her mother when she was given the sentence of death, death by cancer. Gabrielle was eleven years old then, just another ordinary day at school and in life for her.

She had know idea her mother's life was crumbling all around her. Thinking back, how could she have known. Children are always the last to know.

All Gabrielle did know was that her mother didn't feel well and wasn't her happy and playful self anymore. During her mother's illness, Gabrielle remembered her older sister Ivy taking over. Ivy took care of Gabrielle as if she was her own daughter. Her sister cooked, cleaned, helped Gabrielle with her homework, and even combed her hair. Where was Gabrielle's father you ask? Gabrielle remembered her father being sad only one day, but gone in and out of their home excessively. He seemed too busy with his music career and mistress. Gabrielle didn't find out about the other women until she got older.

If only she was older to realize and know what their mother was going through. Even if Gabrielle was old enough to know just what was happening, it wouldn't have been enough to actually save her mother. Her sister Ivy had this huge responsibility, including beginning her second year at Northwestern University of Law. Still till this day, Gabrielle doesn't know how her sister held it all together and had time to sincerely grieve for their mother. Gabrielle was told a year before their mother's death that she had breast cancer. A time when endless efforts to stop the spread of the *beast* failed and the body draining sickness of treatment that seemed to damn near kill her wasn't an option anymore, Janice Michaels died of breast cancer on Mother's Day in 1987 during the season of spring.

Spring represents the season of new beginnings of fruitful hope. Gabrielle however, can't say she ever had the pleasure to appreciate the season of spring since then. Her mother suffered through the hells of winter and when seasons did change to breathe a new chance of life and hope, spring seemed to take their mother away. Before Gabrielle's mother closed her eyes in death to breast cancer, it was as if her mother exhaled out that last bit of winter, to breathe in a dose of spring, only to never awaken again. Maybe it was the season of spring that saved her mother from any more pain and suffering. Gabrielle didn't hold spring accountable for her mother's death. Cancer, was positively guilty of that. Seasons may change, but cancer in most cases can stay the same. A doctor, yes, but forget about what Gabrielle has learned in the practice of medicine. When it comes to breast cancer, this is one illness Gabrielle knows personally from family, and this illness she calls the *beast,* seems to smile at her each time a woman is diagnosed with it.

The loud unpleasant sound of a car horn honking brought Gabrielle's thoughts back to the present. Traffic was moving again on I-94 express as cars zoomed pass her to get on with life. Thinking about her past didn't help her day. Gabrielle feels however, it's always good to think of her mother. Every childhood moment in the past was not all sad. She had good memories of her mother as well and that's what helps her deal with losing a love one to cancer.

Eager to improve her state of mind, Gabrielle reached over and turned up the volume on her radio. One of her favorite songs had just come on. Her eyes cautiously look over to make contact with her rearview mirror. Flipping up her right signal, she easily changed lanes. Dr. Michaels drove a 2000 black BMW 5 series. This BMW was bad, and she had a personalized tag to prove it. Her Illinois state license plate reads, 1Bad BMW. This bad BMW has leather and wood interior, CD player, sunroof, and all other sorts of neat gadgets. The inside was sleek and aspiring comfort. The outside was immaculate, and elegantly bold. This BMW with class is her baby, her pride and joy. It has been said, that a BMW is the ultimate driving machine. Gabrielle felt every bit of that exaltation every time she would shift gears.

It has also been said, that the type of car you drive defines who you are. At this current time in her life, Gabrielle is gratifyingly, undeniably, successful and wonderfully proud. Ahhh, driving is a pleasure. Actually, driving is like coloring. It requires you to stay within the lines. Gabrielle wasn't in a rush to get home, so she cruised the expressway enjoying her exceptionable ride.

Her fifteen-minute drive, thirty due to road construction delays, finally leads Gabrielle home. Gabrielle pulls into a parking lot at 901 Schaumburg Ave, Lake Vista mid-rise apartments. As soon as she opens the door to her lovely apartment, a healthy and sleepy looking white cat slowly makes its way to her. Gabrielle smiles, then places her keys, purse, and mail on a near by table, before lifting the cat off the floor. "Hello Jack, how was your day?"

The cat responds by meowing. Gabrielle sometime believes her cat can honestly understand what she is saying. Gabrielle has three loves in her life. Jack is the first love, and her BMW is the second.

Gabrielle walks with her cat into the kitchen and places him back on the floor. She opens up a can of food for him. Jack rubs up against Gabrielle's legs as she prepares his meal. As Jack feasted on fancy feast, Gabrielle makes her way into the living room. She picks up the remote and turns on the TV. Trying to catch up on current events from a local news station, Gabrielle looks across the room near the bar to see a red light flashing on her answering machine. "Oooh I have messages waiting." she thought. As Gabrielle makes her way over to the phone, the meteorologist was testifying about today's weather and current conditions. Make no doubt about it, it was a beautiful day in Chicago.

Gabrielle had three messages waiting for her. Just as her finger was about to push the black button, negative vibes invades her thoughts. She pressed the button anyway. The first messages was from her sister Ivy. The second message was from her other close friend Amber, she just wanted to know if Gabrielle was up for going out later. The third message was from Bryce, Dr. Bryce Monroe Whitney. The man she has been dating for two years and the third love in her life. Just to hear his voice put a warm smile on her face. However, as she listened to the message Bryce left, the smile of felicity would soon fade. "Hey Gabby, got your message, but I'm going to have to cancel tonight. I'm working a double at the hospital. I get off at 7 am and will be off tomorrow. Don't be upset. I'll call you later, love you."

Just as the message ended, the weatherman on TV just predicated a 100% chance of rain for tomorrow. This wasn't happening, she thought. Gabrielle felt sadder than the musical sounds of the legendary artist B.B. King, but refuse to allow her feelings to slip down that deep and grasp hold of roots known as the blues. One at a time, slowly she began to unbutton her blouse as she made her way to the bedroom. She opens the bedroom door and turned on the light. Gabriel just stood there in the entranceway of her bedroom thinking how the hopes of a lovely evening were just shot down.

Her cat Jack began to rub up against her legs and purrs. Jack circles her once before making a fast dash for the bed. After securing his spot for the night, Jack looks up and over at Gabrielle with a familiar "Looks like it's going to be just you and me tonight." expression on his furry face. *So how are you feeling?"* Gabrielle asked herself that question in thought. So in thought, she answered that question. *"I feel like the musical sounds of Sarah Vaughan with a glass of chardonnay."*

CHAPTER TWO

A bottle of chardonnay,
a glass of solitude

Gabrielle sat at the corner of her big elegant bathtub and turned on the hot and cold water. She watched as the water began to fill the tub. Her thoughts were all she had at the moment, jealous of disappointment and vulnerable to the friendship of loneliness. Gabrielle tempered her bath water with an aromatherapy solution hoping that this relaxing, carefree bubble bath will have the same effect to exfoliate her mood. She wasn't the type of person whose life is filled with stress. She wasn't the type of person egocentric, fake or common, more spiritual than religious. She wasn't the type of person to judge or constitute the trials and errors of the revelations of life, but always reserved the right to form an honest opinion.

What Gabrielle Delniece Michaels just so happen to be however, is a top honored graduate from Cornell University. Dr. Michaels is a fourth year residency in her specialty field of oncology at Northwestern University Hospital in which she is currently employed. Her lovely and almost condo worthy apartment is in a nice area of town in Des Plains, Illinois. Gabrielle won't deny her attractions to the finer things in life. What's wrong with wanting the good things in life? She worked hard and is a good person, so she deserves the best.

Friends would describe Gabrielle as pleasantly strange, fun loving with a wonderful personality. Never to a point of trying, Gabrielle has a personality that demands attention, a personality so attractive, that it blesses your heart just to be in her company. She is a lady, and not just any lady, but a young woman filled with life, youth, love, charisma, style, grace and soul. Believe me when I say, there is nothing ordinary about this girl.

If being smart, financially secure and having a strangely beautiful personality wasn't enough, Gabrielle's appearance just might make you envious as well. Gabrielle is a divine African-American woman with a fair light skin completion and shoulder length dark hair, hair that is her very own from birth, no hairweave. She was the type of female most dark skin sisters didn't appreciate. Her sister Ivy is just a touch of shade darker. Ivy has that caramel colored skin. Gabrielle and Ivy were two sisters' that are doing well in life. However, life wasn't always champagne and caviar, more like pimento loaf and Kool Aid.

Don't forget where you come from. Now blessed, without a doubt they wouldn't dream of it. Gabrielle and Ivy remember the hard times of insufficient resources of poverty and living in the rough projects of Chicago, day by day, living just enough and barely to make ends meet. There is nothing normal about poverty. You live the best way you know how and strive for a better life. Society thrives to believe that African-Americans lives for welfare and enjoys the comforts and support off the government. Opinions and reality can twist facts of the truth. Given the choice and opportunity, no one would choose the life of poverty, but sadly that's the life most African-American's are dealt.

Judging from the past and history of African-Americans, blacks were denied and weren't giving much of a great economical start for the future of success. This injustice equality of life still exists today, with racism and discrimination playing a major role in the economical success of black men and women. However, African-Americans can reverse society's negative stereotypical image of them, by standing up, speaking out and working to improve their own quality of life. Because one thing for sure, the government is not going to make blacks do better for themselves. Having goals, wanting and demanding a better way of life should come within.

Gabrielle and her family suffered and struggled through the ghetto life of poverty. Even when they managed to leave the projects, poverty seemed to still follow. Poverty is a coat, and in Gabrielle's family case, this was a coat they wore well. The power of poverty can keep you down as long as you allow it. These downing effects of poverty seemed to control Gabrielle's family, which later added the deep distress of grief to their lives.

Gabrielle and her sister Ivy have different fathers. Ivy is ten years older than her little sister. Ivy's father had moved out of state when Ivy was five years old. His uncle had a job for him in St. Louis. The job however, fell through and their mother lost contact with him. Their mother, only nineteen years old at the time, was left to raise little Ivy by herself. Janice's mother didn't approve of Ivy's father and gave Janice a hard time about getting knocked up and throwing her life away. Closeness wasn't something Janice and her mother shared and because of the situation with Ivy's father, they didn't get along too well. So Janice moved out of her mother's place to some well-known projects on Chicago south side.

Janice was on welfare, worked part time during the day and attended school at night to become a LPN. Four years later, she met Phillip Michaels, a jazzman saxophonist at a local nightclub. Janice was a true lover of music, everything from R&B to pop and was in love with contemporary Jazz.

She was out with some girlfriends when she met Phillip Michaels at a local Jazz club. If you have ever seen the movie **Mo Better Blues**, then you may recall these very words, *"Don't ever marry let alone go out with a musician. You will be inviting grief, pain, tears and heartbreak to your doorstep."*

A year later, they were married and Janice was pregnant with Gabrielle. Phillip Michaels was a good saxophonist and made somewhat decent money. Janice was now a nurse working at Cook County Hospital. With both of their income, it was enough to move them out of the projects to a somewhat better neighborhood.

Gabrielle was seven years old when they moved from Bridgeport Projects to a small two bedroom duplex house in Evanston. Despite the up's and down of poverty, Janice and her family still maintained their happiness and lived each day in impromptu through an up beat melody that seem to shine even through the rain. Those seem to be happy times then. Sooner or later however, all good times eventually come to an end.

When Gabrielle was nine years old, her father's Jazz career hadn't taking off as expected. He wasn't making as much money anymore. Change of management at the club and mismanagement of funds was affecting his income. It wasn't long before they were living just off of Janice's income.

Luckily, when Ivy turned nineteen, her father tracked them down. He owned his own construction company in Gary, Indiana for five years now. He also had much of the child support money that accumulated over the years. Janice used most of that money to pay for Ivy's education for law school. The little funds left over was used to help live off of. That remaining money helped in more ways than one and came at the right time too.

When Gabrielle turned eleven, their mother was diagnosed with breast cancer, and if that wasn't enough life changing discomfort to absorb, Janice and Phillip's marriage had begun to deteriorate as well. After being diagnosed with breast cancer, Janice immediately began treatment. Chemotherapy consumed her life and would cost her a lot of time off work. Gabrielle's father didn't help the situation by being unemployed. He only worked small gigs off and on from time to time. Leave the door open just a little, and depression will gladly invite itself inside. Phillip Michaels suffered from alcoholism. He had successfully been on the wagon three years before getting married. A A meetings seemed to keep him stable. However, all it takes is the complicated life of stress and one drink, that one drink alone can make you a born again alcoholic.

During the course of Janice's treatment, Gabrielle's father was romantically involved with another woman and was never home. Gabrielle wasn't aware of the circumstances of home life, only that her mother was ill. For almost a year in remission, Janice felt that somehow she had cancer beat. Sadly however, when Gabrielle turned thirteen the enemy had returned with a vengeance, and this time cancer was here to stay. Janice couldn't delay the inevitable anymore. So on the first day of winter, Gabrielle parents told her that her mother has cancer. Gabrielle didn't really understand all the aspects surrounding this deadly illness, but after she helplessly watched her mother close her eyes in death to the *beast* of cancer, she was more than willing to make a career out of helping save lives.

Gabrielle's father didn't stick around after the funeral. He felt that with Ivy's and their grandmother's help, Gabrielle was in better hands. Ivy had her degree and was practicing law, just starting out as a public defender actually.

Janice mother took her granddaughters in for a year, but soon died of a heart attack. Life didn't seem to be going well for Gabrielle and Ivy after their mother's death. They could have moved to Atlanta, Georgia to live with their only uncle, but Ivy was an adult, employed and remained in Illinois to raise her sister. A year after their grandmother's death, Ivy met her soon to be husband and was giving birth to her own daughter. Gabrielle lived with Ivy and her husband until she left for college to study medicine.

Gabrielle was certainly on her way to a rewarding life in medicine. It was uncertain at one point in her teenage years if she would attend college at all. Gabrielle began going through a rebellious stage. With help and a heavy hand from her sister, Gabrielle got over that adolescence, know everything, and won't back down attitude. Two years before Gabrielle left to attend Cornell University, Gabrielle's father was finally cleaning his act up and making a real life for himself. He got back on the wagon and vowed to remain there until death do them part. Phillip Michaels made a deal, signed a contract, and cut his first album as a solo contemporary Jazz artist. His first album was entitled, **GABRIELLE**. The album took off and went gold. With the success of his first album, three more successful albums followed.

Philip Michaels was definitely making a name for himself. He had the pleasure to play with some of Jazz legendary artist such as, Illinois Jacquet, Ramsey Lewis, and Wynton Marsalis, just to name a few. Phillip Michaels always had concert dates that lasted through Gabrielle's college years. Sure, Gabrielle heard about her father's success, but she would have no comment about him, nor was she looking to be saved by him. Gabrielle knew who her real family is. What Gabrielle didn't know was, that after her mother died, her father opened her up a savings account. Something else Gabrielle didn't know is, that even though her father didn't receive an invitation, Phillip Michaels was there and watched his only daughter walk across stage and graduate from Cornell University.

After learning that Gabrielle's residency would fortunately return her back home, Phillip Michaels attempted to make contact with her. He explained as much as he could in a letter about his enormity of improper and immoral ways in the past, along with a cashiers check of fifty thousand dollars. He wasn't trying to buy his way back into Gabrielle's life. That fifty thousand dollar check was a graduation gift from her savings account. Gabrielle was angry that her father left them after her mother died, but really hated the way he treated their mother during the time of her suffering with breast cancer. It was inexcusable however, Gabrielle was no fool and accepted the gift. The money wouldn't bring her mother back or make up for time lost. Gabrielle manages to put the money to good use. She donated some of it to breast cancer research and invested the rest in a Roth IRA savings.

Gabrielle and her father are on speaking terms, but not as close as he would like them to be. She gave him the opportunity to explain his estranged ways of the past. He explained to Gabrielle face to face how her mother was the true love of his life and when she became ill, he didn't know how to handle or accept the fact that the love of his life was dying. Gabrielle didn't know how to perceive his explanation or what to believe, because she didn't honestly know the kind of person her father truly is. She didn't know if her father was lying or telling the truth, but his eyes did seem truthfully sincere. Just to speak about her mother brought tears to his eyes. As a child, you view your parents in a commonly general way; loving, caring, and protective. Most parents are viewed as authority figures. Children however, cannot begin to grasp the intellectual qualities of an adult and their personality. Some adult themselves have a tough time dealing with the different stages of life. Even fully and mentally developed adults don't always make mature decisions. Life is about making choices and at some point in your life, you are bound to make more than a few mistakes. For Phillip Michaels, leaving his only daughter with her sister and their grandmother was a decision he still regrets, but knew it was the right thing to do. Janice never really knew her father and Gabrielle was glad to try and finally get to know hers.

There were other rough spots in Gabrielle's life, but so far, her life seems to be living up to what was expected. However, if there is a will, there's a way and life's unpredictable little challenges seem to make its way in everyone's life at one time or another. For Gabrielle's sake, trouble was settling in and all around her life and she don't even know it yet.

After a long hot bubble bath, Gabrielle slips into some comfortable clothes. Never to a point of full intoxication, Gabrielle drowned her soul in a bottle of Chardonnay while absorbing the sounds of Sarah Vaughan most of the evening, then tossed and turned most of the night. It was a mildly typical prelude to a depressing evening for Gabrielle, only to wake up to soggy skies. This is one of those days you wish the weatherman's accuracy was a little off, but wouldn't you know it, it rained all day.

Gabrielle woke up to gray skies and torrential rainfall. A rain cloud seemed to linger over Gabrielle's head throughout the day and followed her back to her front door of her apartment building. She quickly opens the door and hurries inside. "I hate the rain!" she professes. She lied. Gabrielle loves the rain. Its just not a good day for it, that's all. Despite the current down pour of rain, everyday was a delight to come home. The interior living of Gabrielle's spacious two-bedroom apartment is like a creative master piece of art; an ensemble variety of fine future, lucrative art, accompanied by a prestigious selection of ceramic and porcelain artifacts and figures. What home would be considered complete without crystal? Gabriel appreciates art and has good taste. She has several pieces of artwork stemming from eighteen century African-American to contemporary. Each unique painting is illustratively enchanting, yet curiously thought consuming to absorb from the naked eye. Her distinctive, delicate and peculiar personal choices in her art collection definitely make one goes hummm . . . Beautiful objects made Gabrielle's home very well to be proud. Lets just say, when it comes to the living space that Gabrielle calls home, she honestly consider charging visitors a fee for admission into her lovely condo worthy apartment. Those who honestly comprehend and appreciates the true essences of pure art, understands the beauty of life and living. Art, a skill acquired by experience is like a great bottle of wine, it only gets better with time.

After wrapping her umbrella back together, Gabrielle places it in a decorative pale beside her front door. Her fingers quickly punch in the codes to disarm her security alarm system. She then walks into the living room over by the bar to find one message waiting on her answering machine. Reluctant to hear more disappointing news, Gabrielle realized that her cat, Jack, has not greeted her yet. As she walked into the kitchen, Gabrielle called out for him, but there was no sight of him. The uneasy sensation of hunger settled in her stomach. She opens the refrigerator door to have a look inside. Just as she thought, not much and what she did have, couldn't possibly make a meal. Cheese, bottled water, yogurt, grapes, 2% milk, baking soda, OJ and a bottled of Clos Du Val Chardonnay were the contents in her fridge.

Jack then appears and innocently rubs up against Gabrielle's legs. She looks down pleased to see him. "There's my baby." Gabrielle lifts Jack up happily. The cat meows a few times before it squirms to get down. She places Jack back on the floor and he takes off to another part of the apartment. "Jack wait, don't you want something to eat?" There was no response or retreat from Jack. "I guess not." she said. Casually, Gabrielle walked to the bedroom and opened the door.

To her surprise, there laid Bryce across her bed with a clever smile.

There was a small table candle light dinner set up in the bedroom with a fancy bottle of wine, rose petals on the bed and floor that lead inside the bathroom. Her eyes glanced over at the open bathroom door to find a big bubble bath waiting with burning candles all around. With one red rose in hand, Bryce lifts it up to her. "I ordered Chinese. Is there anything else I can get for you?" There was a pleasurable smile on her face with serious hunger in her eyes. "Just you, just you." she whispered. Gabrielle slowly closed the bedroom door.

CHAPTER THREE

In a black pot, the past is brewing

"Document # 187436, People vs. Joseph Greene. Greene is charged with accounting fraud and embezzlement."

"How does the defendant plead Mrs. Jackson?" "Not guilty Your Honor. My client request bail."

"Your Honor the people request remand. Mr. Greene has more than an adequate amount of wealth, and no doubt a flight risk."

"Your Honor, the only way my client would be considered a flight risk, is if the plane would be traveling on ground. My client has assured me, he plans to be present for all court dates to clear his name of these false charges."

"If every accused criminal word could stand creditable Your Honor, there wouldn't be any use for such a word as bail."

"My client Your Honor, has been a great asset and given more than his share of contribution to this great city. His name alone should be creditable enough. However, his creditability as a businessman is on the line which brings us to his rights of innocent until proven guilty,"

"Your Honor-"

"And since we have not gone to trial yet Your Honor, the defense request bail in which Mr. Greene will gladly handover his passport. That is unless the prosecuting attorneys has granted themselves power as the judge and jury,"

"Your Honor-"

"By using clairvoyance to convict my client by what they have seen in the future Your Honor, and not by an actual trial."

It was 8:45 am and Judge England was looking a little irritable and one cup of coffee away from intolerable frustration. The prosecuting attorney was about to respond to the defense last statement when Judge England made his power of authority present.

"That will be quite enough counselors. Well now, if I knew I would be hearing arguments from you this morning Mrs. Jackson, I would have certainly brought some popcorn, and every since our first encounter, I've learned to take my Excedrin before court proceedings."

Judge England managed to muster a brief smile before continuing. "Ladies and gentlemen of the court. We have the pleasure to be in the presence of the great and profoundly noble Mrs. Ivy Jackson, one of Chicago's best public defenders. Well look at you now. Hear you hanging with the big boys down at Lambert, McGhee & Hewitt and it won't be long before you make partner. Well be that as it may, I will not allow you to turn my courtroom into a kangaroo courtroom, and since your client has given generous amount of contribution to the city, I doubt if he minds giving a little more. Bail is set at five hundred thousand dollars!"

Judge England strikes his gavel to confirm his ruling. Mrs. Jackson turns to her client. "Will that be a problem?"

"I was hoping for indemnity, but no."

"Good because he went light on you. Judge England is known for setting bail more than people make in ten years. He probably hasn't had his third cup of coffee yet." "How long before the actual trial? This partial lien is affecting my company. They may freeze all my assets."

"Don't worry Mr. Green. Call the office tomorrow and set up an appointment to come in and speak with your attorney. I'm substituting for Blake Tisdale until he returns from Washington. Until then, go home and relax, and try not to get accused of bilking any more laws before your trial."

After gathering papers and placing them into her briefcase, Ivy proudly walked out of the courtroom and immediately answers her cell phone. She listens to the caller as she walks out of the courthouse building.

"I'm aware of the ten o'clock meeting and on my way back to the office now. Reschedule my one o'clock. I also need you to obtain those statements from Tom Murphy's deposition. After the meeting, you'll be the first to know if we have to pull an all-nighter for the Murphy case."

Gabrielle's big sister Ivy Jackson, has made a respectable name for herself in Chicago. She is one of the top defense attorneys in the state, has been voted lawyer of the year twice in her career and has landed a respectable spot in Time Magazines "One hundred most influential people." Ivy Jackson prides herself in representing the innocent and wrongly accused. She hasn't lost a case since she began practicing law and with a strong adamant reputation like that, it's hard to over look her talent. Ivy holds good company with powerful African-American attorneys such as Johnnie Cochran and Donald Watkins. Many of Ivy cases are publicized, just like this one. She makes a few statements with the media before heading back to the office.

Mrs. Jackson is no doubt successful, prominent, willful and naturally true through and through, she's a bold believer in due process and justice for all, especially for her people. Lawyer or not, she's just good people. At this time in her life however, what Ivy Jackson really is, is hungry, hungry for a good murder case. She enjoys her status at one of Chicago's top law firms, but hasn't tried a murder case in almost a year. When Ivy was a public defender, she was assigned criminal cases all day long. Now that she's at this top-notch law firm, she handles mostly white-collar superficial crimes. Crimes that isn't worth her time, but since it's their dime, why not!

Ivy misses the in depth facts, theories and evidence of true crimes that's all ball up in a suspenseful slap in the face drama of a murder trial. Don't get Mrs. Jackson wrong, she doesn't wish death on anyone. Remember that saying, the only thing certain in life is death and taxes. Well, sad to say, but a great percentage of deaths is arranged or performed through acts of murder. Ivy knows this and continues to wait patiently for a murder case to fall in her lap. She will only defend the innocent. However, Mrs. Jackson knows people are not always who they appear to be. From her knowledge, there are five causes of murder: money, hate, jealousy, keeping someone quiet and just for the thrill of it, the sickest of them all. Regardless of the cause or reason, those who commit such inconceivable acts should by all means be brought to justice. In most cases and in more ways than one, to deliberately kill a human being, particularly any living soul or creature, is to commit Murder.

Funny how a miserable and dreary day can magically turn around into a flower blooming mystical night of enchanted romance. That one message waiting for Gabrielle yesterday was from her sister Ivy, a reminder of lunch today. The two sisters usually meet every Tuesday for lunch, but Ivy had to cancel their lunch yesterday. It was Ivy's turn to pick the restaurant and Gabrielle's time to buy. The time was 12:

15 pm as Gabrielle parked her car on the busy streets of Chicago. She fed the meter before she began her walk in search of the restaurant. Gabrielle felt glorious. It was partly cloudy, yet a beautiful day. The song "Breezing" by George Benson seem to be playing all around Gabrielle, mostly in her head, and with that song in mind, she gladly took a deep breath. Gabrielle spots the restaurant and continues to make a peaceful stride there. As Gabrielle makes her way to the restaurant, the melody in her thoughts slowly began to dissipate. Then like a sweater being place over your shoulders, an uninvited feeling eased its way over her.

Do you ever get the feeling that someone is watching you? Gabrielle does. As Gabrielle walks down the crowded sidewalk ready to meet her sister for lunch, that somewhat haunting feeling comes over her again, an uneasy feeling that someone is watching her. Gabrielle slowly stops walking and began to observe her surroundings. The people of Chicago continued with life as they walked by and around her. She extended her search out toward the street only to view people driving by in cars, trucks, taxies and buses, while others road bikes and scooters. Normal everyday life as usual was the city scene. Gabrielle brushes the feeling off and continues walking. Sometime the eyes of the beholder can be a heavy stare near or far, but who knows the true meaning behind ones watchfulness.

Gabrielle was headed north on St. Clair street in path of her destination. She usually calls ahead, but forgot this time. So naturally, this particular restaurant would have valet parking. Gabrielle walked in front of the restaurant and looked up at the name. The Capital Grille is the name of the restaurant she read as she entered the place. Upon walking inside the restaurant, Gabrielle was immediately greeted by a pleasant female hostess.

"Jackson, party of two." stated Gabrielle.

The hostess smiled before asking Gabrielle to follow her. Ivy was seated at a table near the bar and was delightfully enjoying her mesquite-grilled shrimp, when she looks up to see her sister headed her way. Ivy looks at her watch. The hostess hands Gabrielle a menu before leaving.

"Gee Gabrielle, I wish I could control time like you can." "Ok, point taken." Gabrielle takes a seat at the table.

"You do realize this is lunch rush hour, and it looks as if you have already ordered."

"Yes, I do realize it's lunch rush hour and no, just warming up with an appetizer."

"Probably the most expensive one I bet?" Ivy smiled. "You know it, and can afford it."

A waiter approaches the table and introduces himself to Gabrielle. The waiter then proceeded to ask Gabrielle would she care for something to drink from the bar. Gabrielle smiles before accepting his drink proposal.

"Why yes, I'll have a Cuba Libre please."

Ivy looks up from her appetizer at Gabrielle in objection, and then quickly interrupts them. "Excuse me, she's mistaken. She will have a 7up with a lemon wedge and two cherries and a glass of ice water."

Gabrielle laughs just a little before nodding her head to agree with her sister. "Yes, I do believe that does sound more refreshing."

The waiter smiles eagerly.

"I'll be right back with your beverages and would you like a refill ma'am?" "No, I enjoy staring at a glass of ice."

"Uh excuse my sister, she's non-compos mentis. That's Latin for not having control of the mind." The waiter walks away awkwardly confused.

"I do so have control over my mind." "Ivy you can be so mean sometimes."

"That's not being mean. That's speaking my truthful mind and I certainly hope you were kidding about your first beverage choice?"

Gabrielle smiles cleverly. "Maybe, maybe not."

"Well you are certainly in a good mood this afternoon." "Ahh, life is good."

Gabrielle glances over her menu before intriguingly staring through out the restaurant observing the atmosphere and scenery which is charming, contemporary, just typical business folks trying to enjoy a quick lunch. Gabrielle makes eye contact with the bartender. He smiles at her and Gabrielle returns the gesture with a warm alluring smile of her own. Ivy turns around to see who her sister is communicating with silently.

She offers Gabrielle one of her appetizers. "Have you decided what you are going to order, or are you going to flirt with the bartender through lunch?"

"He's quite handsome."

"I know, that's why I chose this place."

"Any-way, how's Wade and my girls?" Gabrielle easily ignored her sister's last statement.

"What, you don't think I can swing that guy?"

"Ivy, you love Wade and Wade loves you. He is what you might say uxorious, exceedingly devoted to one's wife."

Ivy settles back in her chair and let the thought of her uxorious husband slowly cook. "Well, he should be. I am after all the best thing that ever happen to him. Plus, I gave him two of the most beautiful and intelligent daughters a mother could have. By the way, my girls are fine, could be a little more appreciative toward their mother though."

"Jaclyn is nine and Meredith is seven, how unappreciative can children be?" "Have some someday, and you'll know."

The smell and attractive appearance of good food were paraded around as servers served other guest. That only inclined Gabrielle stomach to speak the incomprehensible language of hunger. Their waiter returned with Gabrielle beverages and refilled Ivy's glass.

"Are you ladies ready to order?" "Sorry, not me. How about you Ivy?" "Give us just a few more minutes please."

The waiter nodded his head and walked away.

Gabrielle reaches into Ivy's plate with a fork to try one of her mesquite-grilled shrimp.

"What's the verdict? "Delicious."

Gabrielle takes a sip of her lemon lime soda and then helped herself to another shrimp. Ivy quietly unfolds the newspaper that laid on the table next to her.

"Have you seen the news lately?"

"What on earth should I be concerned about now?"

Ivy slides the paper across the table for Gabrielle to read. Gabrielle eyes eagerly made their way to the bold black print in the Chicago Sun Times.

Attorney found dead hanging in his home.

Gabriel didn't give the bold heading much thought before adding her insensitive remarks.

"Yeah so, big deal. It's obviously an apparent suicide." "Maybe, but try reading the name of the departed."

Gabrielle stared back down at the newspaper again and her eyes expands. Her careless attitude grew seriously concerned. Her inquiring mind wanted to know more. Gabrielle silently read the story absorbing every word. When she finished, Gabrielle eyes slowly rose up to make contact with her sister.

"This couldn't be the same Stuart Elliott that defended Kenneth Harris and Rodney Peterson case?"

Ivy nodded her head yes before taking a swallow of her ice tea. "That's what the paper says."

Gabrielle thoughts went straight to an old high school friend that she knew not so long ago, but somehow would never forget.

"But he, wait."

"Now, I know what you are thinking Gabrielle, but I must say, this is more than likely a suicide."

"You know Ivy, I am not going to entertain my thoughts about this."

Ivy lifts up her glass of tea and quietly looks away before taking another sip. Somehow she knew her sister's opinion on the subject to remain silent was out of the question.

"But on second thought." "Ok, here we go." Ivy replied.

"Harris and Peterson's deaths happen over five years ago with no leads or arrests in the case, and now with Stuart Elliott's death, I believe Percy would say that justice has been served all the way around."

Their waiter had returned and asked were they ready to order. Ivy volunteered to order first and began her elaborate lunch order. Ivy knows good food and love for it to be prepared well. Gabrielle looked over her menu through the process of Ivy's intensive food order. For some reason Gabrielle thoughts were overwhelmed by the death of this attorney. Her eyes were slowly drawn back to the story in the Chicago Sun Times on the table. Meanwhile, outside sitting in a parked car, curious eyes were watching.

Gabrielle and Ivy enjoyed their lunch together and returned back to their professions. Finding it hard to keep her mind on her job, Gabrielle memories were filled with her teenage years, memories of a boy she loved and will always love internally until her heart beats no more. That evening at home, Gabrielle tried to catch the local news to find out more about Stuart Elliott's death. At this time, there wasn't much to go on and police were so far ruling it as a suicide. Gabrielle walked over to her cordless phone and picks it up. Someone other than Bryce was desperately on her mind. She wanted to call him, but sure he was aware of Elliot's death. Gabrielle placed the phone back down on the base. Before she could remove her hand, the phone rings. Gabrielle quickly answers the call. It was her friend Jillian.

Jillian who is always in a good spiritual mood called to speak about her day. It wasn't long before Gabrielle's other friend Amber called. Just the act of clicking over lines, dialing of a number and all three friends were now talking on line. As the evening winds down, so did Gabrielle's mood to communicate on the phone. Her last call was from Bryce who wished her a goodnight. A goodnight wasn't something Gabrielle expected tonight. She sat comfortably in a house robe sipping on a glass of wine reading old news paper articles. As she turned the pages of the newspaper, she came across a picture. Gabrielle stares broodingly at the picture trying to imagine what he was thinking at that very moment.

That particular picture in the newspaper wasn't a very good one.

Gabrielle closed the news article and began to make her way to her bedroom. She cuts off lights along the way as her cat Jack, follows her. She entered her bedroom and walked directly over to her beautiful armoire. She opened the cabinet and began to search through some clothes. As she slowly removed her arm, she brought out with her an 8x10 black and white picture. A song instantly came to mind and flows all around her. That particular song was "Angel" by Jon Secada.

There he was, all handsome and cute with an innocent smile on his face. That's how she likes to remember him. At least she knew at that moment that he was happy. Gabrielle makes her way over to the bed with the picture. She turns down the bed and slides under the covers. Gabrielle lifts up the picture, gives it a hug and places the picture on the pillow next to hers. After turning off the lamp, Gabrielle snuggles close to the other pillow for a peaceful nights rest. "Goodnight Percy." she whispered, before closing her eyes. Outside of Gabrielle's apartment however, sitting in a parked car, were those same pair of curious eyes, still watching.

Percy Renee James was proudly named after his grandfather on his mother side of the family. Percy James was a bright young man with proper dreams.

When it came to school, Percy wasn't like most statistics of African-American males. Percy wanted to do something with his life. He wanted to make a difference, be someone. His dream was to teach, teach history and not just American History, but Black History. Percy was proud of and believed in his heritage so strongly, that it was an honor and privileged to bare the brown skin that represents his race. Yet, that powerful dark skin continues to threaten and put fear into many white Americans, a fear that penetrates hate through their very soul. When it comes to racism in our nation: niggers, Negros, colored, blacks, or African-Americans take your pick, has come a long way, but still have very far to go.

Yes, Percy James wanted to teach black history and willing to teach this phenomenal, yet tragically amazing struggle of African-Americans, to any school, college, or university willing to have him. At the age of sixteen, Percy was already a mentor and was volunteering at the local Boys & Girls Club. Gabrielle and Percy lived in the same neighborhood at onetime when they were younger, but didn't actually meet until high school. While attending high school, Gabrielle lived with her sister in Evanston, Percy and his family lived on Chicago's Southside over near Cabrini Green projects. Both attended different high schools. So how did Gabrielle and Percy meet?

Well, they met at a basketball game. Percy and Gabrielle's schools just so happen to be playing each other in a tournament game.

Gabrielle was involved in various school curricular activities and was volunteering at the concession stand. Percy walked up to the concession stand with a friend who Gabrielle knew from around the way in Evanston. Business at the concession stand was a little slow, so Gabrielle was happy to see a familiar face. Sheldon Hayes was the acquaintance that Gabrielle and Percy shared. Sheldon was a little sweet on Gabrielle and was actually hoping to run into her at the game. Gabrielle remembered Sheldon as sort of the class clown in elementary, but with a good nature about himself. However, Sheldon wasn't Gabrielle's type and saw him no more than an around the way acquaintance.

Sheldon Hayes resentfully regrets ever bringing Percy to the basketball game that evening, because if he had known that Gabrielle and Percy would soon become boyfriend and girlfriend after their encounter, he would have gladly left Percy at home. When Sheldon introduced Percy to Gabrielle, there was an instant, thriving, have we met in another life attraction, an attraction so overwhelming and strong, that it could be defined as pure divine fate. From the moment Percy laid eyes on her, he would succumb to love her. Percy was mature for his age and not like most boys, he offered his hand to her. Gabrielle shook his hand softly with a warm smile. Both were intrigued by each other's subconscious and were almost ready to communicate telepathically if needed. Their need to communicate telepathically was due to Sheldon Hayes off the wall humor. Let's just say, Sheldon didn't appreciate being ignored as Percy and Gabrielle associated willingly sincere to one another. The two only talked a few minutes, but their brief encounter contrived to be a lasting impression for them both.

Sheldon practically had to drag Percy from the concession stand. Customers were beginning to pick up again during halftime. Sheldon and Percy hooked up with more friends during the game, which meant an easy escape for Percy. It wasn't long before Sheldon looked around and Percy was nowhere to be found. Sheldon already knew Percy ditched them and was probably back at the concession stand talking with Gabrielle. Needless to say, Sheldon was right. Percy spent the rest of the game getting to know a young girl that not only captured his heart and mind, but his very soul.

After the game Sheldon was nowhere to be found. He left without Percy. Percy didn't mind. He just called his brother to come pick him up. Percy waited in good spirits. When his brother did arrive, the first thing out of his mouth was, so who is she? That was the beginning of Percy and Gabrielle's relationship. Gabrielle was fifteen years old and Percy was one year older. Even though they attended different high schools, they saw each other almost everyday. Practically soul mates, their lives had a much more of a self-appointed personal meaning. It was believed that their friendship together was destined as husband and wife. Gabrielle and Percy spent most of their days together happily enjoying life as teenagers, and looked forward to life as adults.

Even on the seldom days they were apart, Gabrielle always felt she was with him spiritually, as he was to her. Sadly however, after only a year of being together, Gabrielle and Percy's relationship, their unbreakable bond of true friendship ended abruptly. Heartfelt enough to believe they were always with each other spiritually, Gabrielle felt she somehow abandoned Percy in the last few minutes of his life. Gabrielle was not there with Percy when a couple of Chicago police officers suffocated the last breath out of his body.

Percy had just left from visiting Gabrielle at her late grandmother's house in Evanston. He was driving his brother's car and was headed down town Chicago to N LaSalle Street to return his brother's car. Percy's brother Aaron, was the leader of a private organization called the Black Panthers.

The Black Panther Party was making an influential name for themselves in Chicago in which local authority didn't approve. Police still viewed the Black Panther Party Organization from what they represented in the past, which to them were militant political and social activist troublemakers. The Black Panthers were holding a meeting that night. Percy was only a block away from returning his brother's car when he was pulled over by cops. It was suppose to be a routine traffic stop, but somehow turned deadly. Officers Kenneth Harris and Rodney Peterson stated in their report that they were trying to subdue the subject into custody and that the subject continued to resist arrest, which lead to the alleged incident. The entire scene screamed of malice. Narcotics plagued the scene that lead to the arrest, yet angrily provoked the circumstances. However, when it was all over, there were no accounts of any actual witnesses, just the cop's word against a dead juvenile.

Gabrielle didn't notice when Aaron, Percy's brother came over to the house later that night, nor did she see him leave. However, Ivy was the one who had to tell Gabrielle that Percy was dead. Naturally, the thought of Gabrielle's soul mate not alive was inconceivable. She didn't believe Ivy and cursed at her for thinking such a thing. Ivy embraced Gabrielle with compassion, trying to offer her sympathy. Ivy assured Gabrielle that death is nothing to lie about or joke around with, and that Percy is really gone. Gabrielle's overwhelming reaction to Percy's death was expected and just like that, Percy was no longer apart of Gabrielle's life. It was a tragic ending to Gabrielle and Percy's future together.

Two days before Percy's death, Gabrielle and Percy had just celebrated their one year anniversary and lost their virginities together to each other. On the day of their anniversary, Gabrielle and Percy made believe they got married. Percy had a friend whose father is a deacon at a local Baptist church. That friend, who was bound to follow in his father's footsteps, willingly performed that innocent, yet not so creditable ceremony at that Baptist church. With just the three of them, Percy and Gabrielle exchanged vows and friendship rings sealed their deal of a notional marriage. Puppy love, maybe, but theirs was a love that could not be measured. They were young, in love, and vowed to be together forever.

Still till this day, just to think about what happen to Gabrielle's beloved Percy, brings tears to her eyes. Although Percy's life was ephemeral, he accomplished so much for someone so young. His purpose was cut short, but will carry on through the next sincerely qualified soul. Gabrielle believed that God had a special reason to call Percy. Just as God will remember a good man as Able, son of Adam, he will also remember Percy. As for Gabrielle, there will not be any tears tonight, just happy thoughts, good thoughts to promote healthy dreams, for Gabrielle knows that it is only through her dreams that Percy lives.

CHAPTER FOUR

Grain of Salt

Through the mist of a dream, you could hear laughter that echoes sweetly, yet timelessly from eternity. Slowly and softly, a gentle hand of love nudges her shoulder, a reminder that life must go on. As the sun quietly brighten Gabrielle's bedroom to aspire a new morning, she awakens with a felicitous smile on her face. She woke fifteen minutes before her alarm was to go off. Her approach to idealism through the mental essential nature of her dreams, has proven to be successful once again through the affects of nirvana.

Quite pleased with last night encounters, Gabrielle directs her eyes over to the picture laid up against the pillow across from her. "Good morning Percy." she said. Jack's alacrity responses for Percy. She looks down at the foot of her bed. "And good morning to you too Jack." Jack stood on all four legs to stretch. Seems like a good idea to Gabrielle, so she climbs out of bed and did the same. Turning off her alarm clock on the way to the bathroom, Gabrielle began to prepare herself for a brand new day. The outlook of the day seemed exceedingly promising. She only wondered would it last. I doubt if she would hold her breath, due to the ups and downs of evolution on everyday life. One last button to do and her outfit for work today would be complete. She placed the picture of Percy on her nightstand as she performed her routine of making the bed. Fond of pillows, she had plenty to go around. Gabrielle has a variety of shapes and sizes of decorative pillows that she believed was the real beauty to her sleeping accommodations, which made her relaxation a comfort zone. So she didn't mind the little extra time needed to prepare the bed to be just right. Without much thought, she takes the picture of Percy and returns it back to its safe haven. Leaving pictures of an old boyfriend around wasn't good for Gabrielle and Bryce's relationship.

Unfortunately, Gabrielle found that out the hard way. One night several months into their relationship, Gabrielle and Bryce had just finished making love, and usually at a time when a woman wants to be held, snuggled, or just talk. Anyway around it, it's one of those touchy feeling type of moment after the fact. Bryce came across that picture of Percy under his pillow while they were still in bed together. Let's just say, Bryce wasn't pleased in finding it. In fact, he was ready to smash it to pieces. Gabrielle learned her lesson and promised to get rid of it. Well not exactly, as long as the picture was out of sight, then Bryce's way of getting rid of it was taken care of.

After closing the doors to her armoire, Gabrielle makes her way to the kitchen and Jack anxiously follows her. Saying goodbye to Percy's picture was something unnecessary, nor would she ever dare to, being that she didn't get a chance to say goodbye to Percy before his life was snatched away unexpectedly. To ever bear part from his memory, to exclude him from her life would be emotionally unbearable.

A breakfast person was something she rarely took part of, but enjoyed the pleasure of sipping on a glass of OJ. Gabrielle pours Jack a helping of his favorite dry cat food then turned the small TV on in the kitchen to catch the morning buzz. However, the topic of every morning talk show or local news, was still the tragic death of JFK Junior. Gabrielle was one of the many people that empathized along with the rest of the nation about his untimely death; awful, just tragic the loss of such a great man. All the attention the media were delivering on the death of JFK Jr. was too much to take in and dwell on. Gabrielle changed the channel to a local new station.

"And in other news, an autopsy will be conducted to determine if the death of a Chicago attorney was suicide or if foul play maybe involved. The body of forty-three year old Stuart Elliott was found hanging in his home by his housekeeper. You may remember Elliot as the leading defense attorney in one of the year's most controversial cases back in 1990, when Elliott defended two former Chicago police officers, Kenneth Harris and Rodney Peterson on involuntary manslaughter charges against a juvenile, Percy James. Both police officers were acquitted of the charges. Peterson and Harris didn't find the same justice in the civil suit and would soon go on to meet their fate when both cops were shot and killed five years later after responding to a burglary in progress

call. Police still have no leads or suspects in those murders and considers it a cold case mystery."

The TV snaps off and Gabrielle lays the remote on the kitchen counter. She just stares at the blank TV screen. Her thoughts began to circle the past; weighing the facts that the repetitious loss of life somehow may or may not has probable cause to the present circumstances before her. "Could murders from the past, revengeful endeavors continue today after all this time to finally put an end to unreasonable justice?" she thought. "Could it be possible that all of this is somehow relevant?" Gabrielle hiccups out of the trance she was in and looks at her watch. "Damn it! I'm going to be late." she said. She grabs her purse and keys and hurries out the door.

As she took off on a mission to beat traffic, Gabrielle drove friendly, obeying all traffic laws, as opposed to the not so friendly, potential road rage, time bomb ready to explode, gotta get there now behavior of so many drivers. Gabrielle didn't hear her home phone ringing as she ran off this morning. However, it was the main person she wanted to speak with last night. He didn't leave a message, but somehow knew he would run into her somewhere before the day was over. As the day carried on, that same person made his way through the crowded Cudahy library off Lakeshore. It was Thursday afternoon and one place he knew he could find her.

In the reference section quietly reading, there she stood. To find her wasn't hard. She wasn't anything if not predictable. Haven't made her way to find a seat at a table just yet, she stood reading a topic that most inclined her. As he makes his way over to her, he knew it was time to resume the game, their game, the never-ending knowable battle of verbal chess.

"You know Dr. Michaels, you are the only person I know who enjoys spending their lunch hour in a library reading. Reading, is something my students are required to do." With her back to him, she didn't have to turn around to perceive just who was addressing her. She continued reading her material a few more brief moments before acknowledging his presence.

"Well professor James, you may have heard of the saying, the more you read, the more you know, the more you know, the smarter you'll grow."

"Yes, I believe I do."

She slowly turns around not once taking her eyes from the book. Blessed with a hearty smile, he stares at her with a great abundance of intellectual interest. Gabrielle looks up from the book to notice his captivated stare of interest in her profound thoughts. Just to see him was like looking at Percy as a thirty-four year old adult. Standing 5'11 with a physical fit body, he always appeared neatly groomed wearing expensive cologne. He sported a very low haircut with waves, sexy brown skin, deep brown eyes with moderate size lips and nose. He was handsome, but never the type to let it go to his head. After all, looks aren't everything. Him and Percy did look more alike than their other brother's did.

"Reading is your brain's vital stimulation and vitamins for growth and stop staring at me as if you are honestly concerned with what I have to say."

He shares another smile.

"Oh, but I am Gabrielle and always."

Now sharing eye contact, it was hard for her to keep a seriously mused expression. She finally gives in and welcomes his smile with a warm one of her own.

"Tell me Gabrielle, do you still read until your head hurts?"

"Oh I believe that's just the effects of absorption in the power of knowledge." "And the reading topic of choice of this week?"

She stares down at the book. "Major World Philosophers."

"Interesting choice, am I in there?" "You should be, but unlikely."

"I object, have you had lunch yet?"

"Ahh yes. I picked up a hotdog at Hot Doug's on my way here." "Sounds nutritious."

"Who eats healthy every single day of the week anyway?"

"Those who are discipline and seriously strive for good health to maintain a long life."

"Well you're going to die someday and if today is my day, then let me just say, that was one darn good hotdog."

He couldn't help but find humor in her last statement. Her personality was like a breath of fresh air.

"So how are you *feeling* Gabrielle? Oh, let me guess. You're feeling the sounds of Beethoven with a glass of Sherry."

"No, but close. I'm feeling the sounds of Mozart and a cup of tea actually." "That would be a Long Island ice tea in your case."

"Ha-ha, funny Aaron."

"So life is moderately good?"

"I can't complain and why are you here? If you don't mind me asking?"

"Well I tried calling you this morning before you left for work and can I not come to the library for some knowledge as well?

"Aaron, you have more than enough degrees, one I know in philosophy. There is nothing else for you to learn."

"Oh I beg to differ. As you said, the more you read, the more you know and so on."

Gabrielle had closed the book, giving Aaron her full attention. She was returning the favor with great depth of inquired interest.

"Mm-hmm, yes go on."

"There is always something new and exciting to learn everyday Gabrielle and in reference to your amusing behavior, I say touché."

She gives a cleverly witty smile with a slight turn of the head. Gabrielle then places the book she was reading back in its rightful place.

"Aaron, why on earth would you be calling me at that time of morning anyhow?"

"I'm sure you have been keeping up with the news lately?" "Yes, just tragic, what happen to JFK Junior."

"I agree, but I know you know what current topic I am speaking of."

Gabrielle tried to pretend as if the reason for his visit wasn't about the person she wanted to call him about last night, but this was the past speaking which undoubtedly included them both.

"Ok Aaron, yes I have been keeping up with the news. May I ask your where a bouts on that particular night or are you here to contrive an alibi?"

"Why on earth would I need an alibi?"

"Well for one, since the police has repeatedly questioned you in the murders of police officers Harris and Peterson, I'm sure they will want to know where exactly you were two nights ago."

"At home alone, watching our very own Chicago White Sox's play the Detroit Tigers."

"Can anyone confirm that Mr. James?"

Aarons retort in motion to respond sharply was delayed. He stops to think for a moment as his memory recapped that particular evening. A preoccupied expression was displayed across his face then the muscles in his face calmly relaxed.

"Why yes, yes someone can. Besides, Elliott's death hasn't been ruled a murder. There is a possibility he could have committed suicide and I was never formally charged with the murders of Peterson and Harris young lady."

"Yes, but that didn't stop the police from harassing the hell out of you."

"You're absolutely right, but they did manage to slack off some for a while. I guess this will give them a reason to start up again."

Gabrielle curiously drew a step closer to Aaron with half of a smile and another question in mind.

"So Aaron, just between the two of us, off the record. Did you have anything to do with the death of Stuart Elliot?" Gabrielle whispered.

"Normally if required, I would plead the fifth, but since it's you asking, someone who I consider a dear friend and should know me well enough to know if I'm capable in committing such an act. I have no grudge or hard feelings when I say, absolutely not."

Staring into his eyes, Gabrielle turns her head from one side to the other. In other words, she was honestly trying to seek out any bit of the truth that was beaming from Aarons dark brown eyes.

"Gabrielle Michaels." he uttered.

Aaron takes a step back and gives Gabrielle a hard stare. "You do believe me don't you?"

Head straight forward, gazing into the pupils of his sight, Gabrielle slowly draws a reassuring smile.

"Of course I do. I just needed to ask that's all."

"Good, because if I thought that one of the few people I can trust, didn't believe me, then well, all is lost. I myself would have to consider suicide."

"Oh Aaron, don't speak like that, not even in fun."

"Ok, but don't try to get me to feel any sympathy for the guy. He was the type of scum-sucking attorney that gives lawyers a bad name."

"Now I will allow that, but have you considered your options, if this guy comes up with a tag on his toe stating murder?"

"Not really, only the guilty worry, but by chance if the law comes knocking trying to pin such a rap on me, then I may need your sister to defend me. Her, Johnnie Cochran or those duty-bound students from Northwestern University. You see what they done for Gary Gauger, not that I couldn't defend myself since I do after all; have a degree in Criminal Justice."

"So my sister or Johnnie Cochran huh?"

"I want only the best. Do you think your sister would defend me if needed?" "I don't see why not."

Aaron gives a brief unsure smile of yeah right.

"Come on now Gabrielle. You and I both know Ivy doesn't exactly care for my company. Why don't your sister like me?"

"Ivy likes you. She just doesn't know you that well, that's all."

"We had one brief encounter nine years ago that started out good, but didn't end well."

"Well she was my guardian and just being protective."

"I didn't appreciate being threaten, but respected her wishes."

"Not completely you didn't. Anyway enough talk about my sister. I'm sure her ears are burning."

"So Gabrielle, what are your plans for the weekend?"

"Well, you know tomorrow is Friday and as you know, the ladies like to get together for cocktails."

"Ahh yes, a weekly and fashionably fundamental girls night out of social mixing, alcohol consuming, tons of fun, gratifying entertainment, which is just an excuse to dish the dirt."

"True, but also a time to unwind after a long work week."

"And I suppose the rest of the weekend is still reserved for him?"

Gabrielle was pretending to look for other interesting reading material, but cut a wary eye back over to Aaron's last comment. She turns back around to face him.

"Are you referring to who I think you are referring to, because him, just so happens to have a name."

"Why bother with names Gabrielle. Names are so personal, so-" "Oh shut up why don't you." Aaron utters a laugh quietly.

"And yes, the rest of my weekend are still reserved for Bryce." "What a pity."

"Don't hate, and why are you here again?"

"I think we established the reason for my visit Gabrielle."

"No, you've established a reason to bother me. By the way, since you are here. I'm still waiting for your answers to the meaning of life and the secret of happiness."

"Well Gabrielle, I can give you a short version to one of those questions now. Happiness, is a smile on a wave of peacefulness."

Gabrielle nods her head in agreement.

"Interesting, interesting. Although I believe happiness is a wave of love that showers down like a waterfall."

"Possibly yes, but whose to say that happiness can be found in a smile or in emotions of love, let alone some type of imaginative wave of life, because sooner or later, all waves must come crashing down."

A small frown evolved across Gabrielle's face. "Gee Aaron; you really know how to ruin good thoughts."

He smiles in reference to her comment. "I'm sorry. Then again no, no I'm not. There isn't always pain and disappointment in the truth. The reality of life just makes it so."

"Oooh, look at the time. Aaron you know I would like nothing more than to continue our little debate, but my lunch break is almost over. So until next time, we'll put this conversation on ice."

"As you wish."

Gabrielle throws her purse strap over her shoulder before walking away. After taking a few steps, Aaron calls out to her and Gabrielle responses by turning back around. He walked closer to her.

"About Stuart Elliott investigation, it's nothing to concern yourself with. I doubt foul play will contribute to his death. The media can make stories seem more potent than it really is. Until an autopsy proves otherwise, you must take what the media has to relate with a grain of salt."

"I'm not really concerned and will do. See ya around Aaron."

She smiles once more before peacefully walking off. During Gabrielle's and professor James little chat, neither one of them had no idea that not too far from them in a distance, a pair of dishonest eyes were watching and listening. As Aaron watched Gabrielle walk away, the image of her as the bright, vibrant, and adorably sweet teenager that grew into a well educated, sophisticated, beautiful and robust young woman came to mind. Their intellectual game of verbal chess has been going on for five years. So far, Aaron has been ahead, but Gabrielle manages to keep up and he admires her relentless desire to succeed in being the victor.

Aaron continues to smile with the warmest sincerity, simply long enough for Gabrielle to walk from his view. His smile then fades away. If you capture the stillness of his eyes, they would reveal the past. He can't help but think of his baby brother every time he see's her, yet a haunting ignominy also lingers deep within him. Aaron James is an influential black man that thrives authority. His ability to lead is distinguishably phenomenal and proven to be a force of nature to be reckoned with. His force of nature didn't just cause ripples in the water, but more like a mountain full of waves. Despite what the police viewed his organization to represent, many of his kind looked up to him. He had many followers of the Black Panther Organization, devoted members, all willing to sacrifice their very souls in their rock solid clinched fist salute belief.

Aaron knew his rights, not just as a black man, but also as a human being. Recognizing what past Black Panther Party leaders promoted, the New Generation Black Panther Party Organization purpose was to continue to make a stand for equal rights and end police brutality against all black Americans. It was more than an honor to carry on the legacy of the Black Panther Party Nation, it was his utmost duty. Aaron genuinely believed he was born to be a leader. Ask him who his hero is, and he would probably say Huey Newton and Bobby Seale. Malcolm X, Martin Luther King Jr., and Nelson Mandela also contribute to his list of respectable men he admired.

Due to the past history of the Black Panther Party, local police reserved their right to give their organization a hard time regardless in times of goodness. Just as in the past, the New Generation Black Panther Party continued to offer free breakfast programs and after school tutoring for inner city children and helped set up free health clinics. Sadly their generosity and good will for blacks through charity events only conspired cops to believe in a hidden agenda. Police venality belief in the Black Panthers Organization stood adamant. It didn't matter what good deeds the Black Panther Party performed, white cops disliked them and hated Aaron. Aaron was a leader to be cautious of; he was considered a smart nigger from white cops.

One would ask, why would the Black Panther Organization still be so active in this day and time? Their presences is still needed today and more than ever, simply for the none solving fact that two brothers name Prejudice and Racism continue to congest this hypocritical nation of ours. It has been stated, that political power comes through the barrel of a gun. However, the New Generation Black Panther Party strives and continues to promote and practice peaceful anti-violent demonstrations, all while carrying a loaded registered firearm.

Police brutality also continues to grow as well, brutality so dominantly powerful, that it brings forth repercussions of suppress anger and hatred, consequences sometimes resulting in death. On the night professor James younger brother Percy James died, their Black Panther Party Organization was holding a crucial meeting and was in heavy discussion over police brutality. Joseph Bolden a member of the Black Panther Party was severely beaten during a protest just two days earlier. It was suppose to be a peaceful protest, but the name Black Panther Party only meant bitter enemies to local police, especially white police officers. Conflict between the two enemies got out of hand that lead to several of the Black Panthers members being arrested.

Memory of that night of his brother's death always seems to play in slow motion in Aaron's mind. Aaron remembered being in a deep lecture at the Black Panthers Urban Headquarters located down town Chicago off N. LaSalle Street. When doors to the auditorium came flying open, it put members on alert. It was an unknown black man. He was quickly stopped and patted down. His business with the New Generation Black Panther Party Origination seemed urgent and in desperate need of attention. Some arguing erupted from the armed Black Panther members and their uninvited guest. Aaron noticed the commotion and asked the visitor could he be of some assistance. He then asked the man to come forward.

Accompanied by two Black Panther members, one on each side of him, the guest walked forward down closer to the stage. Stopping only a few feet from the stage, the unknown man looked up at Aaron with reasonable cause. Aaron looked deep into the man eyes. He appeared calm, but cautious to the man motives.

"Well brother, what is it? Don't be shy."

There was a sense of sadness in the man eyes. He didn't know Aaron personally, only from the media due to the Black Panther Organization strong influences and powerful protests. His son also attended the same school as Percy and recognized Percy that night.

"Aaron, you've got to go outside."

Aaron remembered hearing police sirens go by fifteen minutes ago, but had no reason to be concerned. It was of no importance to him.

"Brother, I can't be concerned, nor worried about every police siren that invades our lives. If we-"

"Aaron!"

The visitor demanded his attention. Aaron looked at the strange brave man oddly. "I said you have to go outside now, one block around the corner on Dearborn Street. It's your brother Percy."

Aaron looked hard at the man, but the thought of the police hatred for him surrounded his thoughts. Then he remembered his younger brother Percy did borrow his car and was suppose to be returning it. Aaron slowly backed away from the podium, but hurried down from the stage. He rushed passed the man as Black Panther members followed.

Wasting no time, Aaron and his men ran outside around the corner on Dearborn Street to his brother's aid. Due to the heavy police presence of law enforcement officers, Aaron slipped his gun to an important Black Panther member before rushing to the scene. Aaron broke through the crowd of people, but was forcefully stopped by police. He yelled out to the police that the person laying there is his brother and the police turned him loose. Aaron ran forward, but was dramatically taken aback, his baby brother lying lifeless on the cold streets. He shook his head no and ran to Percy's side.

Aaron raised Percy's head up trying to get his attention. Percy's head just fell over to the side motionless. Aaron called Percy's name a few times then listened for breathing. Aaron yelled for someone to call an ambulance then immediately began CPR. After trying to revive his brother with CPR, Aaron felt Percy's neck for a pulse. The ambulance had just arrived and police began to pull Aaron away from his brother. Aaron continued to pull away from the cops as he fought to stay. Police soon turned him loose, but there was nothing he could do. Percy was dead and Aaron knew it. Only after a few minutes of working on Percy, paramedics had just declared the current condition of this victim. There was nothing more they could do for him and pronounced the victim dead on the scene, time of death, 7:12 pm.

Anger, twisted with a high dose of adrenaline racing through his body and mind, couldn't begin to describe Aaron's behavior. Aaron's eyes looked around wildly at the many police officers around. "Who did this?" he demanded. Aaron cursed at the police and demanded an explanation. "You couldn't legally pin anything on me, so you kill my Brother!" Aaron looked out toward the crowd and asked for any witnesses. His search for the truth in a witness turned Aaron around in a complete circle. Then a man from the crowd motioned his head and eyes over to the cops responsible. He was passing by in his car when he witnessed the police trying to subdue Percy. Aaron eyes now full of dark anger, zoomed in on the cops responsible for taking his brother's life.

Officers Rodney Peterson and his partner Kenneth Harris were giving a report to their supervisor when Aaron charged at them, but was quickly stopped by members of the Black Panther Party. Police had already drawn their weapons and wasn't going to waist anytime taking him out as well.

"You're dead!" yelled Aaron. "Do you hear me? You both are dead men!"

Aaron was immediately taken into custody. He would soon be released within an hour. Percy's death provoked a small riot in the streets of Chicago. The people wanted answers and Aaron's family wanted justice and willing to achieve it by any means necessary.

Manslaughter charges were brought up against the two police officers involved in Percy James death. Police officers Rodney Peterson and Kenneth Harris pleaded not guilty to involuntary manslaughter, using excessive force on a minor and reckless endangerment charges, while the James family filed a very large wrongful death civil suit. As it may seem in most cases involving cops, the two police officers charged with involuntary manslaughter were found not guilty. That verdict provoked another small riot in the streets of down town Chicago. The James family was highly disappointed, but managed to strike oil in their wrongful death civil suit. It paid out the second largest settlement in Illinois history. Of course, no amount of money could ever replace the death of a love one.

Aaron tried for two years to get a judge to appeal the involuntary manslaughter case, but had no luck. He believed due to who he is and what his New Generation Black Panther Party Organization represented, that he didn't have a fighting chance. Percy's death somehow altered Aaron's personality. The unjust ruling in those two police officers manslaughter trial and the courts adamant irrational decision not to appeal the case is what really brought about a complete change in Aaron's character. His remarkable quality, that bright and intensifying loud voice burning deep within Aaron's soul seemed to slowly dim. He became more sullenly distant and his thriving passion for his Black Panther Organization wasn't as demanding or much of any real importance.

The not so obvious change that many people disregarded to notice was the quietly cold, violent and unpleasant nature that grew deep inside him. There was bitter animosity boiling inside Aaron that he managed to keep deep within his soul. Aaron was a walking volcano full of rage and revenge just waiting to erupt. Due to his high public status, Aaron remained peaceful and respectful to all in the public eye. He kept up his well prestige image in good sprits. Aaron managed to go on with life and concentrated more on his education. At the time of Percy's death, Aaron had two degrees; the first one was in political science, the other in business. He was now seeking a degree in criminal justice. Aaron continued to run Chicago's New Generation Black Panther Party Organization, just with less controversy and publicity. Gabrielle even took a keen interest in their organization. She started hanging out more at the Black Panthers meetings and their protests. She kind of latched on to Aaron like her big brother. For a long time Gabrielle blamed the police for Percy's death. Her and Aaron shared a common interest, their overwhelming pertinacious dislike toward law enforcement officers. However, Gabrielle's desired dedication to the New Generation Black Panthers Party would last only so long due to the proper influence from her sister.

For two months, Ivy empathized with her sister's feelings about losing a close friend. She understood her sister's anger toward the police, but wondered did Gabrielle fully comprehend the prejudice behavior she was forming. Ivy allowed Gabrielle to attend a few Black Panther meetings and one protest, other times when she wasn't allowed to go, Gabrielle would sneak out of the house to attend. Gabrielle eventually took her sister's kindness as a weakness in authority as a guardian. Gabrielle began skipping school, staying out late. She became disobedient, very rebellious. Ivy perceived and accepted Gabrielle's disorientation of behavior as a brief moderate stage of adolescence.

Then came coup degrace, the final blow. One night, not only did Gabrielle come home late on a school night, but she came home intoxicated. Ivy had enough of her sister's foolishness. After getting Gabrielle's condition under control and her into bed, Ivy asked her husband to keep an eye on their baby, while she pays the President of the New Generation Black Panther Party a visit. Ivy's husband had reason to be concerned because Ivy grabbed their grandmother's old brown pocketbook, which had black Betty, a .38 revolver inside.

Ivy drove down town to N. LaSalle Street to the Black Panthers Urban Headquarters. At 12:30 am, a social event was still carrying on. Ivy didn't want to enter the building. She gave her name and asked for Aaron's presence outside. After a few minutes two Black Panther members kindly escorts Ivy inside to their leader. As they made their way to Aarons location, Ivy noticed all the people, the loud music, the drinking and the smoking that had the familiar against the law hint to it, all contributed to this gathering. The two Black Panther members lead Ivy into a room where Aaron was surrounded by a small group of people. He was in one of his intellectual lectures. She listened patiently to the powerful words that Aaron spoke. When Aaron made eye contact with Ivy to acknowledge her presence, he excused himself from his guest.

Aaron walked up to Ivy with a warm trustworthy smile. Ivy did not return the gesture. "Mrs. Jackson it's a pleasure to see you." Aaron extended his hand. Ivy slowly extended her hand as they shook hands.

"I like some of what you said. I didn't agree with it all, but I like some of your words." Still holding her hand from their handshake, Aaron looked at Ivy holding her hand ever so softly.

"One day you will sister, one fine day all my brother and sisters will."

It was a moment somewhat out of the life of Malcolm X area, but sweet to encourage a real good first impression. Ivy then asked Aaron was there somewhere they could speak alone. Aaron raised his arm in the direction of his office and asked Ivy to follow him.

Once inside his office, Aaron shut his door, made his way over to his desk, and takes a seat. He asked Ivy to have a seat and Ivy declined.

"So what brings you out this late Mrs. Jackson? You know your sister has told me so many wonderful things about you."

"My sister is the reason for my visit, was Gabrielle here tonight?" "Yes, she was here."

"If I knew alcohol and smoking pot was apart of your lecture meetings, I would never have allowed Gabrielle to attend."

"Well this is not one of our lecturing meetings. This is a simple gathering." "With alcohol in the presence of a minor? Did you know Gabrielle came home drunk tonight? Her father is an alcoholic for Christ sake!" Aaron slowly stands from his seat.

"Hold on sister, I didn't give any alcohol to Gabrielle and wasn't aware she was drinking."

"Well she obtained it somehow, was Gabrielle with you the entire time?"
"No, I am only one person. My eyes can not be at two places at one time."

That remark drew a ferocious spark in Ivy's temper. She lifts up that pocketbook and pulled it close to her. Ivy somehow managed to let her anger subside.

"Do you realize the many violations you are in? How many problems I can cause for you and your organization?"

Aaron stares his visitor directly in her eyes. "I do."

"Well, I'm going to tell you this only once. Leave my sister alone. Gabrielle is not permitted to be around you or this organization anymore."

"Now hold on."

"No you hold on. You have your life or what it may seem to be your career profession, let my sister establish hers. Being apart of the Black Panthers Organization is not Gabrielle's future, and I won't allow it to be. A man of your stature, I'm sure you have no problem getting any and everything you put your mind to, but through the words of a Color Purple moment, Gabrielle, you flat out can't have, not now, not ever!"

"Sister what are you trying to say?"

"Let her go Aaron, or I will make more trouble for you and your organization than the police ever will."

Ivy turned around to leave, but stopped at the door.

"I know Percy was your heart and I'm sorry for your loss." Ivy opened the office door and walked away.

It was hard and upsetting for Aaron to turn Gabrielle away on her next and final visit as a teenager. He had to speak ugly to her and advised Gabrielle she was no longer welcome at their Black Panther Party Organization.

Years later while Gabrielle was in medical school, Aaron contacted her and explained his hostile behavior back then, but Gabrielle already knew her sister had something to do with it. At that point on, Aaron and Gabrielle kept in touch through letters and phone calls. He even came to visit her a few times. Aaron just didn't want Gabrielle thinking he was that cruel person back then that ran her away from their property. They bonded a close friendship and much respect for one another, a lasting friendship for years to come, all due to the fact that they shared a common history of interest, their love for Percy. Aaron closed the book Gabrielle was reading and placed it back in its rightful place. He looked at his Rolex watch and remembered there was somewhere else he needed to be, as he quietly made his way out of the library.

CHAPTER FIVE

Happy Hour

6:45 pm Gabrielle receives a rang from the intercom box in her apartment. "Yes hello."

"Hey girl, it's me. Buzz me in." "Hey Amber, come on up."

The door buzzer sounds and unlocks the front door entrance to the apartment building. "It's me." would be Amber Ella Carr Hudson, aka diamond girl. Amber has been Gabrielle best friend since the third grade. Just about every female has a close dear friend. All females usually have that one girlfriend that you separate from the rest of your gal pals and that you honestly believe is your sister than your own blood sister. This one of a kind close friend is a home girl that has your back, a confidant that you tell any and everything to, a best friend that keeps it real and tell you like it is at any and all cost. Well, that is what Amber would be to Gabrielle.

True to her word, this acute, sassy ball of fire may be diagnosed as 80 proof by volume, whirlwind of explicit charm. 5'6, petite with plenty of hair on her head, but doesn't mind sporting hair weave and is more than a handful. With a touch of that version said, Amber Ella Carr Hudson is an extraordinary young woman. This opinionated, bold and very frank African-American female is the essence of beauty and femininity. She's a professional when it comes to her career and business, but catch her in a bad mood on the wrong day, straight alley attitude from hell. Now with all that finally said, most people of this nature are nine out of ten times a front. Deep down she's a pussycat, quiet and reserved, just starving for attention and wants to be loved, but make no bones about it. Amber isn't anything if not Frank.

Her middle name comes from the late legendary Jazz artist, Ella Fitzgerald. Amber's mother loves the musical sounds of Ella Fitzgerald and listened to her music all during her pregnancy with Amber. Would you believe that the very moment after Amber was born, doctors and nurses drew serious attention to her? No, not for a medical emergency, but because as Amber began to cry, the medical staff swore she was belting out one of Ella Fitzgerald tunes. Her mother's only daughter, Amber was spoiled rotten. She has an older brother that lives in New York with their father.

Their father is one of few black plastic surgeons and their mother is a well-known interior decorator.

Amber didn't dare want for anything through her teen years. Coming from a somewhat low middle class family, they too had their share of financial difficulties like most black families. Five years after having Amber, her mother decided to go into her own business as an interior decorator and was financially supporting her husband through medical school. When both their careers took off, it assured proper dreams and bright educational futures for Amber and her brother despite their parents not so successful marriage.

Amber and Gabrielle has been tight since the third grade. They have had only one major fallout which was in the fifth grade over Jonathan Mitchell. Jonathan was the new kid at school who liked them both as a girlfriend, but Amber and Gabrielle didn't fight over him. The situation was resolved when they both agreed not to be his girlfriend. They made a promise then not to ever let a guy come between them again and that was that.

Graduating in 1998 from Loyola University with a MBA in Business Management, Amber holds a prestigious position at Ariel Capital Management L.L.C as one of their top executives. Her Husband Trey Hudson, plays pro-basketball. Well he did, he played two years for the Chicago Bulls 96-98. He was one of those guys you hardly ever seen until someone is about to foul out. He has since been cut from the team, which was ok with him because he manage to walk away with two championship rings. He now rides the bench for the Indiana Pacers. He was a great catch being that Trey Hudson is a real ladies man. Diamond girl, for Amber is a nickname that sort of latched on to her. She has always been fond of diamonds, what girls isn't and mostly because her husband showers her with them as gifts. Those gifts were usually after brief indiscretions possibly involving another woman, but Amber hasn't actually caught him cheating, yet. Amber knows if that day ever comes, his pre-nup allows her to be set for life.

As she makes her way up to Gabrielle apartment, two particular songs comes to mind, one is "That Girl" by Maxi Priest and Shaggy and the other song, "No diggity" by Black Street and Dr. Dre. Both songs describe her to the Tee, but don't try to imagine both songs at the same time, it will only confuse you. Now another nickname she goes by is Ella, and that is usually after she has said something indecorous, you know, unbecoming.

"Knock knock, coming in." "I'm in the kitchen Amber."

Amber makes her way to the kitchen and does a super model strut across the kitchen floor as if J. Alexander trained her himself, and now posing to show off her new outfit. "I don' believe it. That is the same outfit I was going to buy. Only She, department store right?"

"Yes, but I got an additional 25% off the ticket price." "And how on earth did you manage to pull that off?"

"Well, the one time I didn't have one of my creditable F.A.H cards, you know, fake as hell business cards."

"Um-hum."

"Well, after dropping the name of the owner of the store. I told the sales clerk that due to a bad experience on my last visit, that I was allowed 25% off of my next purchase."

"Let me guess, there was no bad experience on your last visit?" "Only if paying way too much for the last purchase counts."

Gabrielle shakes her head with a smile. "Amber, one day your under handed schemes are going to land you in so much trouble."

"Oh I don't think so, I have too many trump cards to play to ever allow that to happen."

"You're so right. So what's up girl?"

"Oh, if only all the people of the world was as beautiful as I am, the world would be a much better place."

"Yes Amber, I'm sure it would be. Any-way, have you heard from Jillian?"

"No, and she better not be running late trying to see about that psychotic bird of hers. Which reminds me, have you taken care of feeding your feline? Where is that evil rodent at anyway?" Amber immediately looks down around her legs.

"Don't call my cat a rat. Jack likes everyone. Well, everyone except you and he's under the bed sulking. Care for some grapes?"

"Girl I'm starving, don't mind if I do."

"He knows I'm going out for the evening when he sees me getting ready."

"Now you see, you know you don't need a pet like that. Does he check your clothes when you return to see if you've been taking care of another feline?"

"Don't be silly. Jack just prefers that I stay at home with him that's all."

"Prefer, oh he prefers. You see that's the problem. He's a cat. The only thing he should be choosy about is dry or can food, not your social life. The only person that should prefer that you stay at home with him, is your man. Leave the sulking to him." Interrupted by a ringing phone and forgetting she left the cordless phone over by the couch, Gabrielle walks into the next room to answer it. Amber follows and gladly takes advantage of the open bar.

"That was Jillian; she is going to meet us there." "She must be running late?"

"Probably so, starting happy hour a little early are we?" "You're low on Absolut."

"Thanks, remember that the next time you're at the liquor store." "Girl it has been a long week."

"Tell me about it. Hey, you like my new rock glasses?"

"It isn't the glassware; it's what's inside the glass that matters."

Amber lifts the glass to her mouth and swallows the remaining taste of vodka then reaches for the bottle once more.

"You might want to go easy on that. You're working on your second glass and I know five is your limit."

"Technically I've only had one, as you know this second drink is for Edgar Allen Poe."

"You know, he's the only deceased poet that still manages to consume alcohol after all this time."

"Well Edgar Allen Poe obviously needed a reason to drink and so do I. Although the man is responsible for me taking my first drink at such a young age."

"Yeah, I remember you said you were forced to take your first drink in the ninth grade, all because of an essay."

"Out of all the poet's listed on the blackboard in English class, I chose Poe to do my essay on."

"Why did you choose him anyway?"

"So many of the other students were choosing poets like Maya Angelo and Langston Hughes. My choice was the poet least chosen. So I'm thinking read a few of his poems, do some research on the guy and Bam! I'm done, easy A." Gabrielle laughs helplessly.

"My research found that Edgar Allen Poe was a true poet, but a drunk and his poems, my God! I couldn't comprehend his poems. His poems were psychologically frustrating. No wonder he drown himself in alcohol. You had to be on something to create such work. So that night trying to struggle with the meaning and aspects of his short life, through his words for the most, probably from a wine bottle. I was depressingly baffled and was driven to take a drink of my father's good brandy."

Amused with a smile, Gabrielle grabs the bottle of vodka and replaces the cap. "Amber, I just don't believe the words of Edgar Allen Poe drove you to take your first drink."

"It was not fully comprehending his words that drove me to take my first drink, and that's not the worst of it. I got a C on my essay. My first C ever. I was so angry, that I wanted to go find his grave, dig him up and beat the hell out of his remains!"

It's Friday, the weekend has begun and for most, it's a time to relax and enjoy life, a time to mentally unwind from a long and sometimes hectic workweek. People have many elaborate ways and remedies to relieve their lives from the hustle and bustle of everyday life. Although, some techniques in the principles of pleasure may dip into the extremes, some may loose sight of the essential reason for the weekend. Rest, in more ways than one should be the quality factor for the weekend, but what's a weekend without a little fun. Fun however, may not be on the agenda for the thousands of people that have to actually work or catch up on whatever. So their R&R or fun may have to come a little later when convenient.

For Gabrielle and two of her closest friends, the weekend in which they considers a personal holiday, has a remedy for relaxation that comes in a form of a liquid intoxicating agent poured into a glass of their favorite cocktail during happy hour. These good times are had on Friday's. It gives them something to look forward to at the end of the work week. This weekly social gathering is more of a girl's night out thang. Most of the time Gabrielle and her friends don't reach the bars or restaurants until after happy hour has expired. They usually go home from work to freshen up and change attire. Besides, happy hour is the price of drinks at the bar reduced and reduced drinks usually mean house brand. Liquor, if you are really serious about the quality of taste, accept no substitutes. Never the less, there is nothing wrong in saving a few dollars while you're getting your drink on, so to each their own.

These three friends mingle at a variety of bars and restaurants, but their main repetitious dwelling spot is at Miles Jazz Club, 1007 N. Rush Street. Miles Jazz Club is in the heart of Chicago nightlife cultural sectors, very laid back with contemporary Jazz and providing a piano bar with live entertainment. Miles's is a very popular chill spot for the sophisticatedly kool. Sometimes the ladies happy hour get together calls for them to fly off for the evening to another city for a change in scenery. Two weekends ago, Gabrielle and her friends were in Philly at a popular chill spot by the name of Warm Daddy's.

This weekend the girls will be at their regular hangout spot to regroup their habit while enjoying the carefree and comfortable atmosphere. Don't get them wrong, neither of the ladies suffer from alcoholism, although Amber's muse for drinking may come from Edgar Allen Poe. Never the less and always, their drinking and socializing are done in good taste. Gossip, always seems to be the topic of choice, however, generous amounts of intellectual topics swirls the table as well. Their informational investment advisor banks with E.F. Hutton and E.F. Hutton says . . . .

"That's absurd!" Amber could hardly contain her opinion, nor would she. "Whoever heard of relating breast cancer to chitterlings? So it's a black statistic?" "Girl how many white folks do you know that eat chitterlings?" asked Jillian.

"So like lupus only affects African-American females and HIV is a minority or homosexual disease?"

"Amber, I'm just stating what I read in an issue of the New York Times." Gabrielle replied.

"So basically it's another false misrepresentation about blacks as usual?" Amber takes a sip of her vodka martini.

"I don't know Amber, who's to say if these studies are really accurate."

"Gabrielle don't get Amber all worked up tonight. It's the weekend. Lets save that discussion for Margarita Night." said Jillian.

"Yes, because I feel my blood pressure rising, a condition I do not suffer from, but technically due to my race and statistics, will most likely develop someday."

Gabrielle and Jillian both found irresistible humor in Amber's devotedly proud behavior. "All that is, are statistical studies from racism. Just another negative way to degrade our heritage. I bet you never heard of caviar giving you breast cancer?" Amber vowed.

Trying to steal a pleasurable sip of her own drink, Gabrielle lowers her glass to respond to Amber's last statement.

"True, but with the limited health studies pertaining to our race, it's definitely something to consider."

"Something to consider." said Amber. "You honestly want us to worry our thoughts with such ridiculous anthropology. Here something to consider, with all the millions of dollars spent each year to develop cures, how about they develop a pill to cure Racism?"

"Girl what you talking 'bout, you know you can't cure racism, that's like trying to control the weather!" Jillian proclaimed.

"Yes, but-" Gabrielle thoughts were cut short.

"Ladies new subject please. Like I said, save it for Margarita Night. You're making the other race uncomfortable."

"Well Jimmy crack corn and you know I don't care." Blount and nonchalant were Amber's last remarks.

Jillian has always been neutral between the three friends, sensible, rational, a spirit up lifter, the calm after the storm. Ask anyone that really knows Jillian and they will tell you, she is one of the sweetest souls you could ever meet. Standing 5'8 and slender, she could be considered a potential model. She wears her hair cut low in a Halley Berry style, but favors a young Pam Grier. Jillian's sincerity toward people is true from the heart. She's a blessing to each child that she teaches, molds and inspires for the future from her third grade elementary class. A volunteer of a variety of organizations and a proud sponsor of the Make a Wish Foundation, Jillian Asbury is truly a good person.

She's a sweet person indeed, almost a shame that her life for the past year has been anything but that. A year older than her friends, Jillian met

Gabrielle and Amber for the first time in a home economics class their sophomore year in high school. You may say it was fate that they would become friends. After one group cooking assignment, they soon found out that Jillian's mother was Gabrielle's and Ambers third grade teacher, their favorite teacher of all teachers. So naturally they became instant friends.

Jillian followed in her mother's footsteps and became a third grade teacher, receiving a teaching degree from the University of Chicago. Happy with her career choice and a great love for children, Jillian looked forward to the future with a man she married three years ago. Their courtship of only six months didn't feel rushed, not even in the least bit because of the overwhelming love they seem to have for each other.

They say that's what being in love will do for you. It's a whole new world, you'll see your life in a brand new light, a light so abundantly bright, it makes your soul glow. A feeling like no other, this actual nature of being in love succumb your inner well-being. Being in love makes your heart beat a little healthier and your thoughts, although sometimes clouded due to daydreams, seems clear, your life generates happiness and is substantially content. Love is a bottle of wine and your wine of love tastes a tad bit sweeter, richer and flowers smells blessedly fresh, picked from the Garden of Eden. Well I'm sorry, but I didn't read that book because there isn't that much love in the world to not take the time to truly get to know your mate for life. Maybe if Jillian would have taken the relationship slow and honestly gotten to know Mr. Dennis Maxwell, maybe it would have saved her a tremendous amount of heartache, pain and regret, but as the saying goes, marry in haste, repent at leisure.

A year ago, Jillian and Dennis had just celebrated their three-year wedding anniversary. As in most newlyweds cases the marriage seem to be going well, blissful even. The only time Gabrielle and Amber did see Jillian was on their happy hour get together or on Margarita Night. Amber and Trey had been married a year and Gabrielle and Bryce had been in a Monogamous relationship for a year as well. The three couples use to dine out occasionally, go to various events. That was back when Trey was playing pro ball with the Chicago Bulls and they were able to get great seats.

Jillian's nightmare began one Friday evening right before their girl's night out get together. Also joining them that night was Rachel, another close friend theirs who they rarely seen because of her controlling husband.

In fact due to an unexpected problem, the girls were all meeting over Rachel's place. Rachel had changed her mind at the last minute, or should I say her husband changed her mind for her. He was working late and she couldn't find someone to baby-sit on short notice.

Jillian managed to get makeup on her blouse and wanted to go home and change. So since Rachel plans for the evening had been decided, the remaining three friends headed over to Jillian's place. It was around seven thirty when they arrived at Jillian's place when she lived over in the Highlands District. Jillian invited her friends inside because she would probably need more than a minute. Once Jillian opens the door to her place, she found a candlelight dinner for two set up in the dining room. How sweet, Jillian thought, Dennis was planning a surprise candlelight dinner for her. As Amber and Gabrielle investigated the dining room more closely, they found that someone has already begun to enjoy the romantic gestures before them.

Amber stated that something didn't feel right about this romantic scene and that she had a bad feeling. Jillian wasn't sure about the circumstances before her and began to search her place for answers. After calling out for Dennis and searching the kitchen, their bedroom door opens and Dennis walks out with just a towel around his waist. Words couldn't describe the expression on Dennis face to find his wife home with her friends standing in their dining room. You could imagine Jillian's surprise to hear the bedroom door open again only to see Dennis best friend, Rashad, walk out in Jillian's bathrobe, the same best friend that stood as best man at their wedding. Damn, now ain't that some La La? It's safe to say at this day and time, that when it comes down to the sexual preference of an individual, no one really knows what butters their bread.

That lovely surprise candlelight dinner Jillian was delighted to find, wasn't so lovely after all. In fact, the scene from that point got pretty ugly. Jillian was more than hurt, she was mortified. Gabrielle was embarrassed for her and Amber went off as expected. Needless to say, their girl's night out was canceled. Jillian threw Dennis and all his belongings out that night and Gabrielle and Amber stayed right there and helped her. Jillian immediately filed for divorce and assumed her maiden name. She had local movers remove the bed and had it taken to a dumpsite and burned. She closed and canceled their joint banking accounts and credit cards. Jillian did everything needed to erase any form of attachment or history between her and Dennis Maxwell. Bryce and Trey both stated on two different occasions that something was too perfect about Dennis. Jillian's cousin said that one of her friends thought they saw Dennis going into a gay bar on N. Broadway Street one night. All this time, Jillian's marriage was a fairy tale, a fairy tale ending in pure adulterated, makes you want to holler, drama episode from the Jerry Springer show.

At a low and critical point in Jillian's life, her girls had her back. They sympathized and even grieved with her because in actuality her marriage had passed away. Jillian's troubles didn't end right there because for almost a year now every three months, Jillian has been getting tested for HIV. Her doctor has advised her that HIV tests that often wasn't necessary. She has tested negative, but has since felt dirty, somehow mentally affected after finding out the truth. Brother's on the down low, men sleeping with other men. Those so-called men, don't realize that they put women lives in jeopardy when they live secret, reckless and double lives. Know this, and it applies to every human being. If someone takes it upon them self to cheat, have an affair, or commit adultery, they don't have respect for their body or themselves. So it's more than likely they will have the same amount of respect for you and your body. In other words, they will share and spread any illness or disease they may have on to you, whether they are aware of an illness or not.

Jillian has picked up the pieces to her life and has since tried to move on. It's hard though, because she doubts if she can fully trust another man completely. She has only been on one date since her life was turned upside down. Now okay and happily single as she puts it, Jillian smiles despite the past, but as the old saying goes, still waters run deep. If you stare deep into her eyes long enough, you can tell the true nature of her inner being. Like an unexpected sting from a bumblebee, she hurts and her heart still aches.

As the three women sit in Miles Jazz Club enjoying their version of happy hour festivities happily content, they didn't seem to have a care in the world.

They each raised their glass to christen the evening by toasting the good life. Meanwhile, across the room a pair of jealous eyes is staring.

CHAPTER SIX

Grains Taken Lightly

10:17 pm later that same happy hour evening, the remaining hours of Friday was leisurely unwinding to find closure for Aaron James. Comfortably relaxed in his favorite recliner with a bottle of Michelob in his right hand, he watched the ninth ending of a baseball game. Earlier that evening he attended a Black Panther Party social function. He didn't stay long, just long enough to represent his congregation while circulating his process of networking, but most importantly to show his face. After his brief noble appearance, he left. Aaron could have stayed out to seek other social activities of enjoyment elsewhere or go out on a date even, but found better peace at home alone.

Living in a very expensive brownstone in a predominantly white area of town, Aaron bought the home because it was considered too wealthy for blacks. In a neighborhood that seems to be full of rich and secretly racist white folks, Aaron didn't seem to mind. They didn't bother him and he didn't bother them, but that wasn't always the case. Of course, the other race didn't like the idea of a black man moving into the neighborhood, a leader of the Black Panther Party of all people. The one's that truly disapproved, tried to cause problems for him in the beginning by leaving nasty notes with racial slurs on his front door. Someone even threw a brick through his living room window, but when Aaron started having several members of his Black Panther Party organization stand guard outside his home twenty-four seven, all little misdemeanor crimes of hate seem to disappear.

Aaron eventually dismissed his men and haven't had any problems from his white prejudice neighbors. Aaron wasn't about to move because the other race didn't want to deal or embrace change in order to deal with blacks, niggers as they put it. Two neighbors moved away to other areas with less color. Shortly after that, a black family moved into the neighborhood. Once that happened there has not been another white neighbor to move away. Aaron figured they needed to stay in order to keep any more blacks from moving into their neighborhood. It's sad to think that African-Americans are stereotyped as a high risk and can be considered the less valuable economically depreciation of a neighborhood.

Plagues stimulating from the ghetto life of poverty, Aaron's family was no stranger to hard times. The future seemed about as bright as the flame from a cigarette lighter with chances of getting out of the ghetto very slim. Eventually the light from that cigarette flame goes out and statistics will prove that most black Americans use of that insufficient flame of hope will sadly be used only to smoke their life away on drugs.

Aaron stared briefly at the picture of his mother, father and brothers. Aaron however, always knew his family would succeed poverty. While most of his ghetto statistical communities will smoke their life away, Aaron dreams would advise him to make use of that smoke. Let your ambitions and determination to succeed take a hold of smoke and allow it to rise you to the top. That's exactly what Aaron dreams allowed him to do. His family did struggle to over come the statistics of ghetto life. It was a long road and it wasn't easy, only to be faced with prejudice racism. Difficult racism was something Aaron's family didn't need, especially when a curse seem to plague their family.

Aaron's parents were born in Hattiesburg, Mississippi. His mother Mavis Atkins, is a high yellow colored women cursed with beauty. A young man by the name of Clyde Tinker was just one of the many admires. He would come by and visit Mavis in hopes of making her his wife, but little did he know, Mavis's heart lies elsewhere. Another young man by the name of Baylock James, a dark complexion poor country boy with a good heart and a hard worker that worked on a farm, is where you could find Mavis's heart. He couldn't visit Mavis as much, but their love was sealed from the start.

Clyde Tinker was a hard worker and saved his money. On his eighteenth birthday, he asked Mavis to marry him. Mavis was flattered, but let him down easy. She told Clyde that her heart belongs to someone else. Naturally Clyde was disappointed. Clyde Tinker was a jealous man, an obsessed and evil hearted man. Clyde vowed that if his heart must suffer, then so would Mavis. One night Clyde watched Baylock James drop Mavis off at home for the evening. Clyde was able to talk Mavis into taking an evening walk. On that walk, he asked Mavis one last time to marry him.

Once again, Mavis had to let Clyde down easy. Clyde was disappointed again, but this time allowed his anger to be expressed. That night in the moonlight he told Mavis Atkins to her face, that if she marry's Baylock James, that he would place a powerful spell on their life together, that their marriage will be cursed and he would see it comes to pass. Mavis understood Clyde's bitterness, but paid him no mind. She took his threat with a grain of salt. Mavis went on to marry Baylock James and six months later, they moved to Chicago for hopes of a better life.

Baylock and Mavis had five children, five boys, Baylock Jr., Jesse, Aaron, Michael and Percy. Despite tough times ahead, Baylock and Mavis were happy. The couple was too happy to allow the plague of some curse to over come their future together, but a strong will of jealousy and bitter hatred of revenge can seek out happiness. On July 6, 1960 Baylock James Jr. was born, but died six days later of what doctors call Sudden Infant Death Syndrome. Saddened by his death; their loss didn't prevent them from having more children.

Blessed with four more boys, they looked forward to raising them. Sadly, two years after Percy was born, Baylock was struck and killed by a car walking home from work one night. It was a hit and run in which the person responsible was never caught. The family pulled together and tried to carry on. Mavis was devastated and would grieve her husband for years. The boys grew up without their father the best way they knew how. Jesse, the second oldest was the man of the house and wanted to help support their family. Jesse got involved in the wrong line of work. He started selling drugs at the age of sixteen. The family didn't approve and Jesse and Aaron argued constantly. Jesse James made a name for himself out in the hustling streets of the city that works. He was becoming Chi Towns very own version of New Jack City's Neno Brown. Eventually, he had to learn the hard way that there is no real successful outcome in that line of work. Jesse James is currently on death row at a state correction institute in Terre Pekin, Illinois for a double homicide.

The next to the youngest of the James boys is Michael James, an inspiring young star high school football player. Number one in the nation, his skills led him to sign a football scholarship with the University of Michigan Wolverines. Unfortunately Michael was at the wrong place at the wrong time and was struck by a stray bullet intended for someone else. Two years after his death, Mavis youngest son Percy also died. With the death of her husband Baylock and three of her sons dead and one on death row, it seemed as if Clyde Tinker's curse was proving to be true. When Aaron learned of the curse from his mother shortly after Percy's death, Aaron made a special trip to Mississippi in search of Mr. Clyde Tinker.

His search led him to Hattiesburg, Mississippi where he found Clyde Tinker living alone in his deceased parent's home. He also found Mr. Tinker's heart still plagued with envy and beating with bitterness. Aaron didn't have to give his name because Mr. Tinker already knew he was Baylock's son just by looking at him. Their conversation didn't last long because Clyde Tinker didn't have many kind words for him. He did however; admit to placing a curse on Mavis. Aaron left Mr. Tinker's home angry with justifiable criminal intent to do harm.

Aaron followed Mr. Tinker the next day. He followed him down town to a herbal medicine shop. When Clyde Tinker came out of the shop, Aaron went to comfront him again, but watched in horror as an out of control car runs over Clyde Tinker. The two men in the car didn't stop due to a local store they just robbed. Aaron ran over to help, but Mr. Tinker's longtime heartache ended that day. I guess what goes around comes around. With no time to waste, Aaron entered Mr. Tinker's home unlawfully. He found that Clyde Tinker did practice some form of black magic. He also found an old picture of his mother there. Aaron's unlawful search of this man's home also found pictures of their entire family. There was a recent newspaper article on Aaron as president of the New Generation Black Panther Party.

Aaron left Mississippi with very little answers. He collected all the pictures Mr. Tinker had of their family and took them with him. Aaron was concerned about that newspaper article Clyde had of him. That picture in the paper of him was circled in red. If there was a curse placed on the James family it died along with Mr. Tinker. When Aaron returned back home to Chicago, he assured his mother that Mr. Tinker's curse does not exist and that he was no longer around to pose any threat. Aaron told his mother that God is powerful than any curse. With the death of Clyde Tinker, the James family somehow felt safe. They were financially secure and tried to live righteously through God words. To ensure a full life, Aaron visit's a Buddhist Priest the first of every year. The Buddhist Priest blesses his soul, which wards off any negative spirits of forces that may linger and cause misfortune. So far, his technique seems to prove beneficial.

Flipping through channels on the TV, there didn't seem to be anything else worth watching on the tube. The TV stopped on a channel with presidential candidate Governor George W. Bush was speaking. When it came to Aaron's opinion on the republican candidate, in which he have many, one opinion seemed to float from his thoughts often, why waist a good ballot? WGN News broadcast of the eleven o'clock news aired thirty minutes late due to extra innings in the baseball game. His channel surfing was temporarily on hiatus as he finally committed to a single channel. Aaron took a swallow of his beer before giving the news his complete attention. The same topics seem to infiltrate the headlines. Then a more interesting developing story emerged, new information on a story recaptured his attention, information interesting enough to have Aaron sit up in his recliner.

"Police are now treating the death of a prominent attorney as a homicide. Stuart Elliott, a highly well-known defense attorney was found hanging dead in his home last Monday. It was believed that Elliott committed suicide, but an autopsy has ruled that out. If you have any information concerning Stuart Elliot's death, please contact Chicago's police department."

"I'll be damn." whispered Aaron.

CHAPTER SEVEN

Hard To Swallow

Rum, a popular alcoholic beverage distilled from a fermented sugar cane product, lingers unappreciatively in a glass on a kitchen counter for hours.

It was unfinished rum diluted with the flat watery base flavor of soda due to melting ice, which has contributed to the weakening effects of rums potent persuasion. Almost a shame to let such good liquor go to waste. Time has a majestic way of passing by especially when you're having fun, weekends are of no exceptions. Ponder this if you will, the way you spend your weekend may have a lingering impact on your mood come Monday morning.

After a gloriously filled Friday night with the girls, the next day Gabrielle spent the day with her loving man Bryce. That evening they dined at a favorite restaurant and that same night Gabrielle stayed the evening over to Bryce's place. Sleeping peacefully, Gabrielle awoke slow and mildly rested the next morning only to find herself alone in bed. She sits up and hears the shower going then lays her head back down on the pillow. He must have already gone running this morning. She thought. Curious of the time, her eyes made contact with the clock on his nightstand. The time was thirty-one minutes pass nine when Gabrielle heard the shower shut off. I could sleep here all day, she thought, but remembered plans she made with her nieces.

She sat up and eased her way out of his big wonderful bed then slips out of her nightie. Gabrielle took her time getting dress, but before she could put her blouse completely on, a pair of strong arms gently eased their way around her. She smiled as he hugged her body and kisses her neck. Bryce stood 6'1, 220lbs of muscular brown skin and yes, he has a nice ass. He also has stunning light brown eyes to go with his attractively handsome face and baldhead. Dr. Bryce Whitney is a total package.

"Good morning sunshine." "Good morning bright eyes."

His hands seductively slip their way underneath her open blouse to undo her bra. "You know Bryce; breakfast sounds good right about now."

"I'll make you some as soon as I finish mines."

Bryce turns Gabrielle around and kisses her softly, passionately, while his hands innocently began to remove her blouse. He continues to kiss her neck and shoulders. "Bryce, seriously, some OJ or apple juice."

His cell phones rings. He ignores it. "Aren't you going to answer that?" "Let voicemail answer it."

After the third ring, Gabrielle tries to go answer his cell phone and Bryce pulls her back to him. He places a finger underneath her chin and stares deeply into her eyes. "It's not important."

Bryce lifts her chin up some with his finger to bring her face closer to his and kisses her tenderly; a kiss so intimately soft, that the strong sincerity was felt in the pit of her stomach. He still manages to give her butterflies.

Looking into his eyes, she gently smiles before giving into his passion.

Drawn into his kiss, Gabrielle felt desired and compelled to just let go and be loved; then his pager goes off which totally ruined the moment. His pager was something he could not ignore because it was the ER. Bryce continued to try to kiss Gabrielle as she pulls away. He finally gives up by letting his arms drop down to his sides as if all is lost.

"You probably want to get that, since that is your work pager."

Gabrielle resumed the act of getting dressed and Bryce dives over onto the bed. He lays there for a few seconds before sitting up and grabbing the pager off the nightstand. As he checks the number that paged him, Gabrielle walks into his bathroom to freshen up. She could hear him talk on the phone as she tried to fix her hair. She then heard him click over to answer another call. She didn't pay the caller any mind because by that time, she was sipping on a glass of OJ in the kitchen. He joined her momentarily pouring himself a glass as well.

"They need me to come into work." "You're not schedule until three."

"Yes, but you know I am always on call. Should I go over the demanding requirements of my profession?"

"No, do I need to go over the demanding requirements of a relationship."
"Gabby, you are the one up and ready to run out the door."

"I have plans with my nieces later this afternoon, say like, after you were suppose to go in for work. I wasn't running out the door, but what does that matter now."

"It's not a life threatening emergency, they are just short of staff. I told them the earliest I could get there would be around eleven-thirty."

Wearing nothing but a towel around his waist, Bryce placed down his glass of OJ and walks over to Gabrielle. He removes the glass of OJ from her hands and pulls her close to him. "You know I don't like it as much as you do when I get called in, but it's my job, so don't be upset ok?"

He stares into her disappointed eyes with the deepest apologies. She know when he gets those pitifully sad look in his eyes, she could never stay mad. She slowly smiles accepting his apology. He then kisses her forehead. Still looking a little sad, Gabrielle pulls away first.

"Bryce, how do you feel about me, our relationship?"

An irritated somewhat mile let down of a disappointing expression immediately came across Bryce's face. "Not again Gabby."

"I mean I know you love me, but how true are those words?"

"Ok Gabrielle, there's obviously a few songs on your mind. So what main song is bugging you?" Without much thought Gabrielle answers.

"Well, it's a tie between Brownstone song, "If you love me" and "How deep is your love" by the Bee Gees." Bryce stares at Gabrielle deeply confound with intolerable patience's laced with compassion. Then he smiles because he knows this is just one of her many adorable qualities.

"Gabby, don't ask what you know is true. Must you continue to test me?"

"It's not a test, plus moods, feelings and life all one-way or another portray or reflects some type of song."

"I'm not going to get in a debate about this, so you win. What do you want to know?"

"I want to know what song comes to mind when you think of our relationship, your tremendous unconditional love for me. What song can reassure me of that?" Gabrielle walks up to him face to face waiting for his response. Bryce places his arm around Gabrielle and pulls her closer to him.

"Now let's see. This is tough. You really know how to put me on the spot." "It's not a trick question."

"Oh, I've got it."

"And that reassuring song would be?"

With a clever smile and cocky tilt of the head, Bryce released the name of the reassuring song. "Don't you know" by Luther Van dross."

Gabrielle smiles reassuringly satisfied, placing her arms around his neck. "Did I do good?"

"In more ways than one."

They began to kiss, but not long enough for him to reap the reward. Gabrielle pulls away first again.

"Now what, where are you rushing off to?"

He pulls Gabrielle back closer to his amazing body. "You have to get ready for your shift."

"Not until a little later. Now, where were we?"

Bryce leans in for a sweet kiss, but Gabrielle slowly turns her face to the side. "I'm a little tired, got stuff to do. I better go home now."

"Define tired?"

"Ahh let's see, work all night and drink of rum, daylight comes and me wanna go home."

He undoubtedly smiles at her unique reference.

"Are you sure Gabby because if memory serves, I believe you are quite fond of my extremely hard, firm and well endowed banana."

Bryce began to flex his physique and Gabrielle shakes her head with an honest smile.

"Well as you know Bryce, my devotion to hedonism has proven one thing for certain. Milk, isn't the only thing good for the body."

Bryce lifts Gabrielle up off the floor and carry's her back into the bedroom. He gently lays her body across the bed then romantically leans in for a kiss.

"Aren't you forgetting something?" she asked. "Oh yeah." he said with a naughty grin. "Mother may I?"

Staring at him with tranquility, yet seriously focus eyes, giving a half glare of a smile, she gives her answer.

"Yes, you may."

That last remark was followed by a tantalizing kiss and this time, Gabrielle did not dare pull away.

Bryce Monroe Whitney is a twenty-seven year old M.D. of emergency medicine at Northwestern University Hospital. He is the youngest of three other siblings in which all of their middle names are the same. Monroe is their mother's maiden name. Born with a silver spoon in his mouth, Bryce's family is somehow related or linked to Eli Whitney, the inventor of the cotton gin. This black history heritage connection however, is not how his family generates such wealth.

Bryce's father, Bernard Whitney holds a prestigious and successful executive position at Edward Jones Fidelity Investments. His mother, Eleanor Monroe Whitney is a Judge. His parents worked hard for many years to establish money, power and respect to ever allow the color of their skin or the ignorance of racism to stand in their way. Bryce has two brothers and a sister who each holds successful degrees from black colleges and universities. Their family represents the strive, pursuit and foreseeable opportunities of economic well-being, the equality of the American dream; and where there's financial wealth of success, you can best to believe you will find a Whitney.

Bryce' s views of the world on the other hand, were a little different. Well, not the same as his family as far as family values and pride of their roots were concerned. Bryce received his degree in medicine from Stanford University, his first choice in college to continue his education in the pursuit of becoming a doctor. It wasn't as important to him as it was to his parents to attend a black college or university as all of them. In the end of the debatable argument, the final decision was left to him. California is the state were he finished college and completed his residency and looked forward to making California his home, but a bad breakup with his former girlfriend and a offer from Northwestern University Hospital led him back home to the windy city.

Handsome in more ways than one, this fine young black doctor can satisfy any woman's appetite. Would you believe Gabrielle turned him down twice before finally agreeing to go out with him. It was her second year residency and first call to the ER for a consult on a patient. At the time, Dr. Whitney was the most eligible bachelor. He was professional when it came to his career and never dated or messed around with any of the nurses or female doctors at work. However, when Bryce saw Gabrielle with her boss for the first time, he was ready to drop the status of a bachelor.

Of course, Gabrielle found Bryce attractive, but Gabrielle had a rule, not to date or get involved with colleagues. Dating in the work place, people you have to deal with on day-to-day bases is just not reasonable. Not all on the job romances are the same. Some on the job relationships can work to their advantage, but for those dating catastrophes that doesn't, it can pose a problem if the affair doesn't work out. Besides, Bryce is a great looking guy. He could have his choice of any woman he wanted. Gabrielle already assumed he has slept with most of the female staff and fifty-five percent of his female patients. So naturally, she turned Bryce down flat the first time he asked her out after the consult visit. She turned him down again even though Bryce made a special trip over to the Lynn Sage building.

The third time Bryce asked Gabrielle out, well, he changed his approach a tad bit. Bryce caught Gabrielle just as she was leaving work and asked her would she like to go for a cup of coffee, no strings or commitments attached. Now a simple cup of java, she could do, especially on a cold winter day in Chicago. Coffee is the life support that mentally generates the bodies and souls of just about every hardworking American. Lucky for Bryce, Gabrielle is a coffee lover. They went to a coffee house in walking distances near by and wouldn't you know it, Gabrielle's assumption of him was all wrong.

Bryce was well-mannered and quite charming, a very modest individual and like a sip of rich quality coffee, he was warm and inviting. Gabrielle seem to melt into a cup of him and found his flavor quite soothing and relaxing. Their communicating over coffee, led to dinner and dinner to the two-year relationship that they are currently in, which seems happy. Their status as a couple remained low key and professional on hospital grounds. It was almost a year before anyone found out that the two were dating. It was love at first sight for Bryce, if there's really such a thing. Bryce didn't pressure Gabrielle, but stayed persistent on plans to live elsewhere with a reasonable climate. His plans of living in the fun in the sun state of California may have not worked out, but miraculously was able to find sunshine after all. Men know when they have found the one.

Always thrilled to welcome a visit from their favorite aunt, Gabrielle embraced her two nieces with a huge hug. Even though the girls are only two years apart, Gabrielle see's her childhood with her sister in them. Gabrielle looks forward to being blessed with her own children someday. Ivy's girls knows their aunt's life can become a little absorbed, but fortunately not busy enough to break plans with them. It was around three-thirty that afternoon when Gabrielle finally made her way over to Hoffman Estates, just another weekend at the Jackson home.

"Look Auntie Gabrielle, my kite has the little mermaid on it."

"Very pretty Meredith, I like it. What do you have on yours Jaclyn?"

"I couldn't find the one with rapper Tru on it, so I chose the Power Puff Girls." "Well I'm sorry you couldn't find what you wanted."

"Don't apologize Gabrielle, because the day my daughter marry's a rapper, she will be out of my home and finished with college. Hopefully by then, she will have had a change of heart toward this up and coming rapper."

"Hey sis, what's up?"

"Peace for the rest of the afternoon. You taking the girls to the beach?" "Yes, and we will fill up on ice cream and all the junk food we can." "Hooray!" yell the girls.

"No, I don't think so. They will have one scoop of ice cream after a sensible nutritious meal."

"Boooo." replied the girls.

"Sure, McDonalds sells brussels sprouts." "I'm serious Gabrielle."

"Ok, I understand." She then winks her eye and smiles at her nieces. "You girls go get your things together."

"Yes ma'am." said the girls.

Jaclyn and Meredith bolts out of the kitchen in a hurry. "No running please!" yelled their mother.

"So where's my brother in-law?"

"Wade is playing golf with a neighbor." "How are things going at O'Hara?"

"Fine, being one of very few African-American air traffic controllers has there days, but knowing I am gladly willing to bring a lawsuit against them for any cases of racial discrimination tends to up lift attitudes."

"Yes, that does seem to change racial views of prejudice behavior."

"How's life in the medical field?" "Always rewarding."

"Hey, you think I should buy an SUV?"

"Why would you want a SUV, are you tired of the Mercedes?"

"God no, Jaclyn likes when her father drops her off to school in his Land Rover. I think it's because a boy she likes at school told her he thinks Land Rovers are so cool." "Ivy, you're not a SUV person."

"I know, I even drove Wades Land Rover to work a few times." "Well just let Wade take the girls to school."

"He has his days and I have mine. I enjoy our time together when I drop the girls off. Work can have me coming home when they are already asleep."

"Hopefully it's a fashionably hip faze and she will get over it." "Since when does a SUV out ranks a Mercedes Benz?"

"Since your daughter classmate, who just so happens to be a boy, thinks so." "Well a Mercedes Benz can out top a Land Rover on any day of the week, including holidays."

Gabrielle cheerfully agrees.

Although an SUV is a vehicle she can imagine herself in someday, Gabrielle is more than satisfied with her BMW, which was a gift from her sister. As far as her sister's healthy eating habits for her children is concern, chicken nuggets from McDonalds seem be the closest form of good nutrition. Gabrielle did however, managed to give the girls one scoop of ice cream. Gabrielle and her nieces spent the rest of the afternoon flying kites at the beach. Somehow, people forget about the simple joys of life. With the complicated stress of everyday life, one may ask, when was the last time you took a deep breath?

The fruitful benefits in the simple joys of life are good for a healthy state of mind. The side effects of ignoring the simple joys of life are inexcusable regrets. These are regrets that clings to you when time, work, insignificant things, appointments, events and family appreciation have all backed up or passed you by to a point of no return; and at this point you may be too ill, in a none fixable predicament, or dead to resolve hope. This leaves behind a haunting question of thought, if only I. If only I took the time to call my mother, star gaze, fly a kite, go sailing, get lost in art, or actually stop to smell the flowers; then maybe life wouldn't feel so stressfully demanding. The key factor to this scenario is to truly enjoy life and the best part about the simple joys of life are virtually free; and kids, well that just makes it all worth it.

Gabrielle appreciates life and all the simple forms of it. She tries to avoid other peoples unpleasant mood swings views of it, but still manages to smile from the attitude of others. While flying kites with her nieces, Gabrielle receives a call on her cell phone.

"Hello."

"Well H e l l o Gabrielle." "Oh stop it Aaron."

"Stop what Gabrielle?"

"I hate it when you sound like Hannibal Lecter." "My apologies, do I hear children, where are you?" "I'm at the beach flying kites with my nieces." "Sounds fun."

"It is, if you appreciate the simple joys of life." "So how are you *feeling* Gabrielle?"

"At this very moment, I'm feeling the musical sounds of Louis Armstrong "What a Wonderful World" and because of my guests, with a glass of Kool-Aid."

Aaron smiles as he walks over to a near by window at his home. "Although, I can not say I was feeling so well a few hours ago." "Oh really, why not Gabrielle?"

"Well, I was at home and for some strange reason I began to experience dry mouth. Naturally, I took a sip of water, but to my surprise I began to experience an automatic reflux sensation, a gritty substance began to build up in my mouth."

"Gabrielle."

"Now, my guess would be that, the bit of information you told me to take with a grain of salt, wouldn't go down."

"Gabrielle."

"In fact, the salty after taste of Murder, was hard to swallow." "Gabrielle?"

"Yes Aaron?"

"May I speak now?" "Please, by all means."

Gabrielle began to distances herself some from her nieces.

"I am just as surprised as you are." "Are you?"

"This is the purpose of this call."

"It was murder, Elliott was murdered. Please tell me you had nothing to do with that?" Gabrielle whispered.

"I doubt this is the time to discuss this with the large consumption of excitement you seem to be having with your family."

"You are welcome to join us if you like."

Still looking out his window, there was a knock at Aaron's front door. "No no. You continue with your activities. We will talk later."

"Are you sure Aaron?"

"Yes, my plans for the evening have just become detained. We will talk soon. Goodbye Gabrielle."

"Bye Aaron."

A second knock rattles Aaron's front door once more before he had a chance to walk over and answer it. Aaron walks over to his front door and pauses, then takes a deep breath before opening the door.

"Good afternoon, Aaron James?" "Yes."

"I'm detective John Mackey; this is my partner detective Rodney Watts with Chicago police homicide. We were wondering if we could ask you a few questions about the death of Stuart Elliott."

CHAPTER EIGHT

Five of a Kind

Elmwood Park Illinois 11:20 am

Surveillance cameras observes a subject in view, zooms in and out, then willingly takes snap shots of a white male entering a shady commercial building across the street from them. The FBI has been investigating this particular group of individuals for two years now. They are members of the World Church of Masters Creator Organization. Their leader, Mark Hale was linked to a follower of their organization and the deadly shooting rampage a few weeks ago. This white supremacist group upholds their right to bear arms and strongly represent their white power superiority over all minorities. Their way of life is a form of hatred like no other with one rule of statement, One Nation, One Race.

"I see your fifty dollars and raise you fifty." "I'm in."

"I'm out."

"Me too, and going for cigarettes."

The service elevator doors open as the white male who walked in off the streets enters a lofty office. He holds the service elevator door for the member leaving out.

"Hey Patrick, you've been missing some good hands for assignments." "They're mostly low status. They save the priority cases for me."

The member just arriving walks over to a blackboard and writes his name on it. This particular member is pale looking and could use a tan. He stood 5'9 in height, thin, as was his face. He had brown hair and light blue eyes, a narrow nose with thin lips, your typically average looking white guy.

"Come on Jason, you in or out?"

"Oh I'm sorry Lou, am I keeping you from your soap operas?" "Screw you Jason!"

"Patrick you're late!" confirmed a voice from in the corner.

The member who just wrote his name on the black board, casually looks at his watch before making eye contact with the overseeing member. He then walks over to a tall file cabinet, opens a drawer and takes out the next file. After reading over the assignment, he looks at the picture then closes the folder.

"I'll just take this one." "Hold on hotshot!"

The overseeing member stands from his chair and walks from his desk.

"That's not the way it works. You want an assignment; you play the game like everyone else."

"Check with Mitch, he'll ok it."

"Don't need to, but you do. He wants you to phone him once you've arrived." "Looks like the poker Gods are smiling on me fellas. Five of a kind, read'em and weep Lou."

"There is no such God." Lou replied.

"Yeah whatever, Patrick I'll take that folder."

The member collects his winnings and Patrick walks over and hands the member the folder, as he makes his way over to a phone. He dials a number then places a hand over the receiver.

"Hey Jason, I'm aboard. I'll take second chair and assist."

The loyal member smiles. "Oh really, I'm flattered Patrick. Just as long as you remember, this is my assignment."

"Hello."

"Mitch, Patrick."

"Hey Patrick how you doing?" "Good."

"That's good. Something wrong with your watch buddy, is it busted or something?" "I lost track of time."

"Is that so?" "Yeah."

"Well regardless if Mark is your second or third cousin, I personally don't care, but if you want to continue to be apart of this organization, you take our rules seriously. As you know we don't play this particular card game too often, unless there's a special priority and you know Mark is kinda hot right now, so time is of the essences."

"So no special projects for me?"

"No Patrick. You're good, but not that good. Respect the rules. If you have a problem with that, come see me and stop giving Sam a hard time."

"Second." "What?"

"Mark is my second cousin."

"Whatever!" Click, was the sound heard as he hung up on the member.

In a house somewhere in East Peoria, Illinois, the evilest most vindictive pair of hateful eyes known to white man, stares motionlessly out a window. Sitting patiently in a unmarked car across the street, an FBI agent stares relentlessly right back.

"Mark, your cousin is something else."

This spiteful man staring out the window slowly draws from his cigarette. "How is he doing Mitch?"

"He's worthy, but his cocky wise ass attitude is not." "He's a good kid."

"He's a pain in the ass, what he is."

The cousin laughs. "Just give him time. He's just showing off."

The managing member walks over closer to his leader. "We don't need show offs Mark. We need by the book corporation."

"Don't worry about it. Since Patrick has been aboard, has his ability to clear an assignment let you down?"

"No."

"Then that's all that matters. I have a lot of plans for Patrick and at the tender age of twenty, his future looks bright."

"You honestly believe his talent for jobs is at a level four?"

"Yes and unlike Smith, he will prove to be the one. Patrick is a leader not a follower."

The white supremacist leader draws from his cigarette once more before staring back out the window.

"They're not going anywhere you know?" "I know. I just like fucking with them."

The leader then gives the FBI agent the middle finger unappreciatively.

On campus at Chicago State University, Professor Aaron James had just dismissed his class when he noticed an unwelcome guest that entered the classroom. Aaron kept his eyes on the visitor as he makes his way over to him. Judging from Aaron's facial expression, he was not pleased with the visitor. The uninvited guest proudly expands a huge smile across his face.

"Demarco what are you doing here?"

"Damn Aaron, can't a brother come visit his cousin?" "What do you want?"

"Lighten up professor. I could be attending classes here for all you know." "That's very unlikely; don't tell me they are enrolling ex-cons now?"

Aaron looks at his relative harshly before removing his reading glasses.

"Damn it Demarco! If you or any of your street employees are distributing any forms of illegal substances on this campus, I will call campus police." he whispered.

"Chill Aaron, slow your roll. Will you calm down?"

Aaron began to collect some papers and placed them in his briefcase. "I just wanted to talk to you."

"Haven't you heard of a phone?" "I was in the neighborhood."

"Well this isn't a good time. I have somewhere I need to be." Aaron walks pass his cousin.

"So you don't have time to talk?" Aaron stops and turns around.

"You want to talk, make an appointment with my office downtown and Demarco, don't ever come back out here again." Aaron walks out of the classroom as students began to make their way inside.

Mondays are not Gabrielle's favorite day of the week. Monday's are a drag, typically hectic, manic even and can be emotionally stressful. Did you know, that people are most likely to have a heart attack on Mondays than on any other day of the week? So far, Gabrielle's day has been going substantially well for a Monday. After enjoying lunch with Bryce in the hospital cafeteria, Gabrielle catches an elevator back to her working area. As soon as the elevator door opens to Lynn Sage Breast Cancer Center, she walks right into an acquaintance.

"Well if it isn't administration monitoring the halls." "Gabrielle, just the person I wanted to see."

"Hey Ross, what's up?"

The Director of Human Resources places a friendly arm around Gabrielle's shoulders as they began to walk.

"Do you remember our little project development discussion a few months ago?" Gabrielle nods her head yes.

"Good, because we are holding another meeting tonight to discuss final plans in getting the ball rolling and-"

"Say no more, just tell me the time and place."

"Tonight, 6:30 at Hyatt Regency Hotel on Wacker Drive." "Great, I'll be there."

"Excuse me, Dr. Michaels, am I right?" "Yes, Dr. Reynolds."

"Don't mean to intrude."

"It's perfectly fine, have you met Ross Thomas the Director of Human Resources." "No, I haven't."

"Ross, this is Dr. Reynolds, one of the hospitals anesthesiologist." The two men shake hands.

"Good to meet you Ross, I've seen your face before."

"Same here, well, I'm involved with a few projects developments."

"That's it. I've seen you on TV with your development plans for Project Hope." "Yes, that's right."

"Good thing you're doing. How's that coming along?"

"Actually, that's just what Gabrielle and I were discussing. The Partners are holding a meeting tonight at Hyatt Regency Hotel."

"I hear there are some big corporations that are opposing this development." "Yes, but we're hoping to work all concerned matters out."

"Hope it works out for you. Give me a call if you need extra assistances."

"Why thank you Dr. Reynolds. I just may take you up on that offer. Gabrielle, I've gotta go, so I will see you there tonight?"

"Absolutely."

"Great, it was a pleasure to meet you Dr. Reynolds." "Same here."

Dr. Reynolds business with Dr. Michaels was brief. They parted company and Gabrielle returned to her practice. She pleasantly looked forward to the rest of her workday, until she sees a patient whose outlook on life seemed less pleasantly inspiring. Mrs. Bayer was sitting in the waiting area with her husband and appeared motionlessly calm with grief stricken gloomy eyes.

It looks as if reality has sunk in and with the sad nature of cause, breast cancer carriers enough downers to spread around like vapors. Gabrielle's after work ritual will be needed after her shift is over.

There were a relatively high number in attendance of the Project Hope development meeting that night. City leaders, business men and women, investors and concerned neighbors were some of the people in attendance tonight. City councilman Harold Stokes, Dr. Kelvin McDonald an attending physician of Internal Medicine and Human Resources Director Ross Thomas are the executive partners in this project and are close acquaintances of Gabrielle. Gabrielle sat with a group of supports and generously took advantage of the free buffet. Ross was currently speaking at the podium as Gabrielle watched Professor Aaron James, an unexpected guest to her knowledge, arrive fashionably late. Aaron makes eye contact with Ross before taking a seat.

"I want to thank all of you for coming out this evening to help support Project Hope. A little later, those of you with questions and concerns will have the opportunity to address them. This is what we do know. The problems with other state developers and contractors out of New York have backed off their efforts and interest on the sites property to further a shopping center. Equal votes from local supporters and the manpower of our lawyers out weighted their strategies for success. As you all know, the proposed plan of Project Hope is a Health Clinic for low income individuals and families. With the high rate of HIV infected cases, low screenings for breast cancer and silent killers such as heart disease and high blood pressure, health care providers are in great demand for the provision of black Americans. Affordable healthcare far exceeds the overwhelming demand of shopping centers. Our biggest obstacle for Project Hope has been funds. Generous donations were helpful, but not sufficient enough, while corporate developers and contractors of New York sit back and smile, hoping that our financial negligence would cause failure and allow us to pull out of our project. A few days ago my partners Harold Stokes and Kelvin McDonald and myself stressfully discussed placing Project Hope on hold, but miraculously what I like to think through the grace of God, a financial savior was sent to us. Thanks to the overwhelming financial support of this worthy and honorable man, Project Hope starts construction development next month."

A grand applause broke out among the guest in attendance.

"It is my pleasure to present to you the man responsible for making Project Hope possible. This man is a positive African-American role model, a respectful business man, a professor at Chicago State University and the president of the New Generation Black Panther Party Organization. Please welcome, Dr. Aaron James."

Another healthy round of applause was given as Aaron James makes his way to the podium. Ross Thomas shakes Aaron's hand and pats his back before turning the stage over to him.

"Thank you. I would like to thank Ross Thomas, Harold Stokes and Kelvin McDonald for allowing me to climb aboard this project. It does my heart glad to share my wealth with such good people. I'll make sure my loan sharking interest rate are suitable."

A sense of humor touched the audiences.

"But seriously, I'm not going to turn this speech into a long lecture, because this is not my show. I will say this much however, if we do not help our people, then who will? What is the catch, what do I plan to get out of this in return, some of you may ask. My answer is, only a name. With my hearty donation to this project, all I ask, is that I have the privilege in naming the health clinic. For those of you who do not know who Percy James is, he is my brother. Percy could not be here with us tonight, but sends his approval from heaven above."

Aaron speech went on for a few more minutes followed by heavy mingling with guest after the meeting. Gabrielle was speaking with her acquaintances, congratulating the partners for their accomplishment and eventually makes her way over to her wealthy generous friend. Aaron was alone long enough to receive a drink from the open bar.

"I waited for your call last night."

"Gabrielle what a pleasant surprise. I apologize, hopefully not too long."

"No, I must say I am surprised, didn't think I would see you here tonight, as a major contributor nonetheless."

"Oh really, why not?"

"I mean, I know you give back to the community, just wasn't aware of your ties to this particular project."

"When you do the common things in life in an uncommon way, you will command the attention of the world. George Washington Carver."

"Well at this time, the attention of the world is on the death of JFK Jr. among other things like, the murder of a defense attorney."

"I personally, do not acquire the attention of the world, just the attention of my good deeds."

"What are good deeds going for these days Aaron?"

"Oh, I'll say more than a few Grover Cleveland currencies." "Trying to buy your way into heaven?"

"There is no such offering and no, it's better to give than receive my darling." Aaron casually leans over to whisper in Gabrielle's ear.

"Meet me at my car in ten minutes."

Aaron then walks away to speak with the Mayor who was headed his way. Gabrielle used her ten-minute window to go to the ladies room. Her mind elsewhere, Gabrielle wasn't aware of the heavy stare of hateful eyes that were following behind her. Overly anxious to speak with Aaron, Gabrielle makes her way outside the Hyatt Regency Hotel. She searched for Aarons Jaguar XK8, the one he prefers to drive most. After passing a few parked cars, Gabrielle was snatched between a couple of parked SUV's.

"Jesus Christ Aaron! I was about to baptize you with mace." "Quiet!"

With their undivided attention of silent's, they were able to hear a few guest go by. Then they both gradually heard the footsteps of one individual slowly walking. Aaron waited a few moments for that presence to appear. The eyes of that particular individual approaching, searched the parking lot for a second then proceeded back inside to the conference meeting. Aaron looks from behind one of the SUV's, but didn't see anyone.

"What's with the secrecy?" she asked.

"I wanted to make sure we were alone."

"Well you picked a wrong time and place, guest are coming and going." "Detectives paid a visit to my home yesterday."

"I doubt if you were surprised, if that's what you meant by being detained yesterday?"

"Yes, and I'm sure police has a detail on me. Anyway, as you know, Stuart Elliott's death was ruled a homicide."

"Did you honestly think they wasn't going to come question you?" "I have nothing to hide."

"Aaron, you threatened Elliott along with officers Harris and Peterson back then and you see where they ended up."

"I will state it again, like I did then. I did not murder officers Harris or Peterson and the same fact applies for Stuart Elliott. Although, I would consider throwing the person responsible a party."

"That isn't funny Aaron."

"I wasn't trying to be funny; I'm just stating the obvious." "Well, dead men don't feel the need to hang themselves."

"Same thing can be said about dead men and the tales they don't speak of." "Death sure has a strange way in expressing its self."

"Death, has many shapes and forms of variables that can be expressed Gabrielle. Murder, usually make specific point."

"Are you happy he's dead Aaron?" "Well I'm not sad."

"You did a good thing tonight. Percy would be proud."

"It's never enough. It could never be enough to honor his memory, not the scholarships program, donations to the Boys & Girls club, not even naming a clinic after him. Nothing I do feels worthy to ever be enough."

Gabrielle observes Aaron closely. His voice still seems to express emotional hurt after all this time.

"His life was worth so much more; much more important than any donation I could ever give."

"Aaron, what you have done for Percy in his memory does matter and like you said, I'm sure he sends his approval from heaven."

Aaron's eyes began to compose themselves from the past. They shift slightly to refocus, returning to his sharp and witty image.

"So Gabrielle, what about you?" "What about me?"

"Do you believe Percy would be proud of your life?"

The question seemed to catch Gabrielle off guard, as she gives Aaron a prudently strange stare of uncertainty.

"I haven't giving it much thought, but yes. I believe so."

Gabrielle then looks at her watch. "8:15, I best be getting home." "Of course, allow me to walk you to your car."

Gabrielle thoughts on the way home were distracted, filled with concerned opinionated approval of, in which she honestly believe is the love of her life. She truly deeply feels that Percy would be proud of her life, but there was this reoccurring dream of disapproval that continues to visit her. For reasons unsurely known, every so often Gabrielle would experience the same hurtful dream. Her and Bryce are walking in a park, in a distances

Percy appears. Gabrielle smiles and waves at Percy, but he doesn't return the loving gesture. Percy would eventually go on to turn his back on them. He disappears before Gabrielle can run over and make contact with him.

The dream first appeared six months ago and would reoccur a least once a month. Gabrielle sometimes feels Percy is expressing jealousy or painful resentment. She's certain Percy is proud of her life. What she isn't certain of is, Percy's disapproval, he may disapprove of her and Bryce relationship and this sometimes draws a despondent form of sadness for Gabrielle. How can she ever truly be happy with Bryce, if Percy doesn't approves. When Gabrielle did finally make it to bed, the picture of Percy accompanied her. She talked briefly on the phone with Bryce before closing her eyes for the night. Having his picture next to her doesn't always guarantee a visit from him, but she likes to feel he is watching over her.

The next day downtown at the Black Panthers Urban Headquarters, Aaron was going over future events for his organization. He wasn't schedule for a class until later that afternoon. His time is limited, always well used and wise enough to arrange his life accordingly, which allows him to use his power and freedom to come and go as he chooses. There was a knock on Aaron's office door and his assistant gave word that his eleven o'clock appointment was here. Now aware of his visit, Aaron waited for his cousin to enter his office. On his way inside the office, Demarco looks over Aaron's assistant as she walks pass him and he likes what he sees.

"Shawty got an onion butt, that body is banging." "Demarco come in and close the door."

"Hey, yo Aaron, I know you gotta be hitting that?"

Aaron ignores his cousin remarks as Demarco makes his way over to his desk. He gladly takes a seat across from Aaron.

"What's up cuz?"

"You tell me, you asked for this appointment."

"Why you started tripping when I came out on campus yesterday?" "As far as I'm concerned, you are not welcome there."

"Damn, that's cold."

"Demarco, what is the purpose of this visit?"

"Jesse has been asking for you. Why don't you go see the man? You know he's on death row."

Aaron sits back comfortably in his chair before responding.

"Jesse has money on the books; his son and daughter are taken care of. What could he possibly want with me?"

"How about brotherly love."

"Stay out of this Demarco. If you are still involved with his line of work, then you too may very well someday share a cell with him, if you don't end up dead first." Demarco quietly ignores Aaron's advice while helping himself to a cigar off Aaron's desk. He runs the cigar underneath his nose and breathes in deeply.

"Cubans, only the best for you, huh Aaron?" "That's right."

"Well don't go speaking too proudly my brother, because a man is known by the company he keeps and I remember only too well, the corrupt operations the Black Panthers were involved in, illegal practices that would find you guilty in any court of law, not to mention the work on the side I've done for you when I first moved to Chi-town."

"There you go, throwing the past in my face again. I never claimed to be a saint."

"No, you continue to front, allowing the people of Chicago to think that you are." "You know, Jesse brought you here to this city and now I am left responsible for you."

"Man, you ain't my damn daddy! I'm handling my own, never once asked for your help since Jesse been inside."

"That's right, you've manage to ruin your life all by yourself."

Demarco calms down and relaxes back in his chair, allowing the moment to breathe. "You know Aaron, although I still managed to get by on my own and you disown me as family from time to time, my door is always open for equal share holders."

"Demarco, when you are ready to turn your life around and get into some real business, come see me."

Aaron's statement produced a swift surprised reaction as Demarco looked at Aaron very hard. "When I turn my life around, come see you? N e g r o Please!" Demarco stands from his chair. "The very wolf in sheep clothing."

"I've paid for my sins and prayed for forgiveness."

"If your way of doing legit business is anything like the past, then that old saying is true. The grass is really greener on the other side. You must have forgotten where you come from son?"

Aaron rises slowly from his chair. "I have not. I am proud to say I come from Cabrini Green projects."

Demarco laughs. "Yeah right, you be cool cousin, you be cool. I'm out."

Demarco makes his way out of Aaron's office. In the process of leaving, he stops to flirt with Aaron's assistant. After not much luck, he continues to make his way out of the building. As soon as Demarco walked out of the building and turned the corner, a man appears before him.

"Damn man, where you come from?" "Did he accept your proposal?"

"Man your boss is a trip. He's full-"

"Did he accept the proposal, yes or no?"

"No, lighten up man. Did you really think he would get tied up in this business?" "Just continue with our little arrangement until I figure something out."

"I wonder what Aaron would think if he knew you were moonlighting?" The man grabs a hold of Demarco and pushes him against the building. "He won't, because if he does, you'll lose four liters of blood."

"Don't threaten me motherfucker!" "Shut up!"

Demarco pushes the man off him.

"Just stick to the plan and report to me when needed. Hopefully I won't see you again anytime soon."

"Yeah ok, but if I were you, I would be careful, because Aaron knows just about every illegal trade or business dealing that go on in this city."

"I'll handle Aaron; you just make my day by disappearing from my sight." Demarco walks off then throws up a clenched fist in the Black Power Salute. "Cynical bastard."

CHAPTER NINE

In Vino Veritas

In the Heart of Dixie on the 2000 block of 8th Avenue North, you will find Birmingham's Museum of Art in Birmingham, Alabama. Known as the Pittsburgh of the South for its steel and iron production, Birmingham, Alabama was the landmark for racial violence during the civil rights era and on the third floor of the Birmingham's Museum of Art, you will find the Dwight and Lucille Beeson Wedgwood collection, the finest collection of Wedgwood outside of England. Any worthy art collector's paradise, these limited, eclectic antiques and modern collections contains yellow, lilac, black and blue as well as many other sought after pieces. These valuable objects illustrate the entire production of Wedgwood factory from its early years through the early 19th century.

Jasper or Jasperware rather, refers to a precious stone found in Greece similar to green quartz. Wedgwood defined Jasper in the sixth and final edition of the 1787 catalogue. Jasper: a white porcelain bisque of exquisite beauty and delicacy. In the city of Chicago, Illinois, you will find another Jasperware. Jasper Lamar Ware, a twenty- eight year old full-time Black Panther activist. When it comes to the Black Panthers Organization, Aaron James has three important main men. Tyrone Hampton, Robert Lee and Jasper Ware are those three important men. Tyrone Hampton is the Vice President of Chicago's New Generation Black Panthers Party Organization. Tyrone knows everything that goes on with the Black Panthers Organization. He runs the place if Aaron is away. He's Aaron's number one go to man and if Tyrone doesn't know, then it probably isn't so. Robert Lee is the Black Panthers Party personal attorney. He is also a well know civil right attorney.

Jasper Ware is Chief of Security of Defense for the Black Panthers. Jasper is head of security for a reason, he thrives in leadership. When it comes to Black Panthers demonstrations, events and protests, Jasper Ware excels in his field to provide the utmost security protection. He withstands and instills a courageous defiance in authority, sometime asserting aggressive affirmative power for defense. Jasper's men are the African-American version of Secret Service men. Jasper cover's Aaron's ass at all cost. Stare into his deep dark skin, his distinctive facial features that included large lips and wide nostrils, eyes so dark they can be mistaken as black. As you imagine his fleshly characteristic, you would have never guessed that Jasper Ware has unjust ripples, a family connection of unspoken civil rights ties.

Many Americans may know about the tragic Sixteenth Street Baptist Church bombing that claimed the lives of four little girls in Birmingham, Alabama, but another innocent soul was involuntarily taken on that day as well. Virgil Ware, Jasper Ware's late uncle was gunned down at the age of thirteen while riding home on a bicycle with his brother. Virgil Ware was slain by a sixteen-year-old white boy who was also riding home with a friend after leaving a segregationist rally. His death failed to receive the attention due to the heart wrenching headlining exposure of the Four Little Girls deaths. The boys responsible for Jasper uncle's death, only received two years probation and Virgil Ware's murder was a foreseen memory lost in a black hole. Jasper's father one of four siblings alive, moved his family to Chicago shortly after burying his brother with no headstone.

Jasper Ware was thirteen years old when he was told riveting details about the murder of his uncle. It drew a strong dislike toward whites for Jasper. It angered him to know that not so long ago, justice took a back seat for many black Americans and that whites were most likely to get by with only probation for killing blacks. Now today, all a black person has to do is draw a gun and get locked up for life. Family say, it was events of his family's past that changed Jasper's outlook on life. Then again, psychologist states that sociopaths are just not born with a conscious. Jasper had somewhat of a dark side to him, but that didn't stop him from believing in equal rights for his race. He didn't appreciate the harassment and racial profiling African-Americans received from white cops. He also didn't get a kick out of racism and the strong influence it carried over the black race. Jasper didn't know at the time that after attending a not so peaceful Black Panthers Party protest for police brutality, would change his life. In fact, it was that particular protest that saved the man responsible for Jasper's uncle's death, life.

When Jasper turned eighteen years old, he bought a Greyhound bus ticket to Birmingham, Alabama. Jasper wanted revenge for his uncle's murder and was about to take justice into his own hands. Just so happen after purchasing that ticket, Jasper walked into a protest by the Black Panthers Party. Aaron's powerful speech was ringing not so distance dreams of hope for the black man. After listening to Aaron's powerful words, Jasper cashed in his bus ticket and immediately joined the Black Panthers Organization with hopes of making a difference. Now a proud member of an organization he looked up to, Jasper diligently strived to promote equal rights and to stop police brutality, even if it meant that justice would be served through a barrel of a gun.

Jasper's loyalty and aggressive willingness to protect Aaron caught Aaron's attention. As Aaron's New Generation Black Panthers Party Organization grew, so did Jaspers advancement, which led him to the prestigious position he gratefully holds. With Jasper's more than dedicated help, any problems Aaron was plagued by would silently disappear. Jasper had proven to be trustworthy to Aaron, which produced a tight bond and friendship between them. He looked up to Aaron and as far as he was concern, Aaron James was the future first black President of the Untied States of America and if anyone stood in Aaron's way of that happening, then they probably would be staring down the barrel of his loaded gun.

Two weeks after a private memorial for the deaths of JFK Jr. and his wife, the world seem to resume steady life again and construction of the Percy R. James Health Center had begun. This health clinic will be a world-class facility with a wide range of health care practices from internal medicine to dentistry, along with free HIV testing. The purpose of this clinic is ideal for the poor and economically challenged people with no health insurance, which can keep hospital emergency rooms for just that purpose, emergencies.

The completion date of this new health center is scheduled for spring of 2001. Although the site would have been a prefect location for new expansions of shopping centers, issues with the location of the new clinic kept rising. Local developers wanted an area that reached everyone, leaving no one behind to seek and benefit from affordable healthcare. Gabrielle was more than glad to be apart of this project. Her expertise in her field of medicine will help provide a better access to mammograms and cancer screenings.

Gabrielle was all smiles the next morning as she step off the elevators on to the floor of Lynn Sage Breast Cancer Center. She was definitely in a refreshed good mood after arriving home late last night. The cause of such sensational vibes was from the rewarding perks of a weekend away with Bryce. Little did she know her day was about to change.

"Excuse me, Dr. Michaels?"

"Yes." His presence caught her off guard.

"My name is Detective John Mackey with Chicago police. I was wondering if I

could ask you a few questions about Ross Thomas?"

"Oh-ok, I hope he isn't in any trouble?" she glared a smile.

Detective John Mackey is a white male that stood 5'10, 200 lbs, light brown hair, a shadow of a beard with a visible bulging gut. He smelled of Marlboro lights cigarettes, a smoker, an on again off again habit he swears he's done with, at least that's what his wife thinks.

"Dr. Michaels, I'm with homicide division, we are investigating the death of Ross Thomas." A heavy wave of grief rushed over Gabrielle that left her speechless. "Dr. Michaels." Tears began to form in her eyes.

"Dr. Michaels." Gabrielle walks off to a window near by and detective Mackey follows her. Gabrielle reaches in her purse for a Kleenex.

"Dr. Michaels are you alright?" "This can't be true."

"I'm afraid so, weren't you informed?"

"No, I've been out of town for the weekend." "My apologies."

A few tears rolled down Gabrielle's face as she raised her head. She quietly wiped the tears away with a Kleenex.

"What relation is Ross Thomas to you?" "He, he was my friend."

"How long have you known Ross Thomas?" "Four years."

"When was the last time you spoke with him?" "Last Thursday, may I ask what happen to him?"

"Mr. Thomas was found hanging dead in his apartment by his fiancée." Gabrielle was embraced with shock.

"My God, suicide?"

"I'm not at liberty to say, but it doesn't appear so." Fear emerged across Gabrielle's face.

"We have spoke with administration and gone through his office. After looking over his planner, I noticed a scheduled lunch with you today. Is that true?" Gabrielle turns away from detective Mackey, realizing her and Ross's monthly Subway lunches together.

"Yes."

"Was there anything special about today's lunch?"

"No, not really. Ross and I have lunch together all the time."

"Is there any information you could give me that will help us in this investigation?"

Gabrielle shakes her head no.

"Anyone that you know that would want to harm Mr. Thomas, a threat possibly?" Gabrielle shakes her head no.

"Well I'm sorry for your loss. If you think of anything, please contact me." Detective Mackey hands Gabrielle his card before leaving.

Gabrielle didn't feel well anymore. She felt that this was all a bad dream, that the death of a close acquaintance was not real. Gabrielle was too upset to work and left work early after stopping by the ER. No after work ritual could help her mental status. At home, Gabrielle was on and off the phone most of the morning. It wasn't long before she began to realize it would have been best to have stayed at work. Every moment between calls, the silently dull and distressful somber of grief would over come her and she would breakdown and cry.

A little later in the day, Gabrielle managed to dose off to sleep and was awakened around three to a ringing phone. Jack was cuddled up next to her in bed. Somewhat dazed and confuse of her surroundings, she answers her home phone. It was Amber checking in on her. A second call beeped in and Gabrielle clicked over to answer it, then clicks back over to Amber.

"Amber, I'll call you back." Gabrielle clicks the phone line back over to Aaron. "Aaron, where have you been? I've been trying to reach you most of the day."

"In meetings most of the day. I'm just getting a chance to check my messages." "He's dead Aaron. Ross is dead. He was murdered!"

"I know. The story is just now making headlines. Have you eaten, would you like to meet me somewhere?"

"No I haven't and really don't feel like getting out." "I could come over and bring some takeout." "Could you?"

"What would you like?"

"Some Chinese would be great." "I'm on my way."

"Thanks Aaron."

Gabrielle sobbed in Aaron arms like a baby. After letting her go through two Kleenex tissues, he did managed to finally get her to eat something. They sat at her dining room table rummaging through the bags of takeout. Gabrielle pour's Aaron a glass of wine and refilled her glass while feeling obligated to discuss Ross's death.

"I mean I just spoke with him last Thursday at work before Bryce and I went away for the weekend."

"I spoke with him Sunday afternoon." "What!"

"We were going to meet sometime this week to discuss Project Hope."

"Do the cops know, is that why he was murdered? Could this somehow be connected to Stuart Elliott's murder?"

"No, I can't say for certain, but I am sure detectives will be looking to speak with me again."

"Have you spoken with Kelvin and Harold?" "No, but I plan to."

While the two were talking, they heard Gabrielle's front door open. Gabrielle gets up from the dining room table to find out just who her guest may be.

"Oh honey you came." Gabrielle wraps her arms around Bryce. He kisses her on the cheek. "How you doing baby?"

"Better, I asked Aaron to come over."

"Smells good in here, what are you guys eating?" "Aaron brought over some Chinese."

They both walk over into her dining room. "What up Aaron, what's going on brother?"

Aaron places his glass of wine on the table and the two men shake hands. "Nothing much Bryce, just trying to make an honest dollar like everyone else." "Yeah right, you know you don't need to work."

"I can say the same for you Mr. Whitney."

Bryce helps himself to the takeout and joins them at the table.

"Man I can't believe this. I knew Ross from the hospital. He was a great guy. I can't believe he's dead."

"It was murder." Gabrielle adamantly stated. "Let's not hope in vain." Aaron added.

Gabrielle walks over and turns on the TV, hoping to catch any information from the news. The three of them stayed at the dining table for hours discussing their mutual friend. As they drink heavily under the influence of alcohol, honest words of what they really feel were expressed through In Vino Veritas. There is truth in wine and relatively not far from a glass of wine, lies the truth. Meanwhile, outside of Gabrielle's apartment in a parked car was a pair of prying eyes.

The next day, Gabrielle went in to work with not many answers to the gruesome death of her friend. It was Tuesday and she usually meets with her sister for their weekly lunches. Gabrielle's mood wasn't as enthused. It was Gabrielle time to pick the restaurant and Ivy's time to buy. Ivy was shocked, fully sympathetic to hear the news about Gabrielle's friend. Ivy wanted to know more about the big corporate heads that may have been disgruntle about losing out on that sites property.

All Gabrielle could inform her sister was that New York developers bid for the property had expired for whatever reason on their part and city leaders and neighbors opposed their plan to expand a new shopping center. The local voters were more acceptable to Ross and his partners' new clinic proposal. When Project Hope proposed plan was granted and they succeeded in obtaining the rest of the financial assistances needed without raising taxes, the developers began construction on the new health clinic. Ivy believes that Gabrielle's friend may have been murdered because of this. At least that was one thing both sisters' agreed on during their lunch together. Ivy also told her sister that she is going to check into those New York corporate developers to see what she could find out.

Friday's happy hour or girl's night out was canceled. It wasn't a weekend to celebrate when Gabrielle was burying a friend the next day. The funeral services were held at Mount Pilgrim Baptist Church that Saturday afternoon. There were many in attendance of Ross William Thomas funeral service. He was well known and like and it was hard for many to say goodbye, especially his mother. When services concluded, Gabrielle and Bryce spoke with other guest before heading to the cemetery. Gabrielle spoke briefly with the two remaining partners of Project Hope, but not like how she would have like to. She looked for Aaron, but did not witness his presence.

"Gabrielle, Bryce, hi, are you guys going to the burial?"

"Dr. Lyndon, I didn't know you knew Ross." stated Gabrielle.

"Yes, Ross and I got acquainted when I transferred from my last hospital."

"Well Ross made it his job to try and get to know every staff member aboard Northwestern."

"I'm sorry for your loss; I hear you and Ross were close." "Oh, how did you hear that?"

"From Bryce of course."

"Gabrielle we best be going." Bryce interrupts.

"My shift begins in an hour, so I can't attend the burial. See you guys around." Family and friends closest to Ross said their final goodbye when they laid him to rest at Graceland Cemetery. There, Gabrielle gave her condolences to his parents. When Gabrielle and Bryce were about to leave, she innocently looks off in a distance and smiles. Gabrielle was pleased to know another friend of her's is there to show his respects. Aaron waves at them both.

The following Friday, girls night out was held at Webster's Wine and Bar on Webster Ave. With still no leads in Ross Thomas case, Gabrielle and her friends tried to get back to normal. Webster's Wine and Bar is a casually cozy, classy place for real wine lovers, a place where friends can sit and enjoy a relaxing moderate laid-back conversation. On the girl's first visit to Webster's, there was one small incident. I guess Webster's Wine and Bar wasn't use to seeing many African-Americans there. Their new server had bit of a prejudice attitude. Obviously, she hadn't met Amber Ella Carr Hudson. The server seemed reluctant to serve them. Of course, Amber stepped right up and rose to the occasion with her overly assertive attitude. Amber asked the server very loudly and very boldly, and I quote. "What! Ya'll don't serve Colored here?" After a brief talk with the manager and round of drinks on the house, problem solved.

Despite one bad encounter of racial depreciation, Webster's Wine and Bar turned out to be the girl's second hangout spot. The more they became well aware regulars, all was well. Sometimes you just have to get people told straight from the start. Not all African-Americans are poor. Blacks are entitled to fair and good services like everyone else, regardless of your annual income. What, black folks suppose to hang in the streets and on corners all night shooting dice, playing dominos or Spades for entertainment and only eat at greasy spoon restaurants. Hey I love fried chicken, collard greens, macaroni-cheese and cornbread, but not everyday. I mean, why does the other race and the well off get to live the good life and have fun. Any race with the means to do so, should have the right to splurge.

Gabrielle and her two friends were on their first round of drinks when acquaintances of their heritage were seen headed their way.

"Don't look now Amber, Fletcher and Reese are here."

Amber pretends not to notice two fashionably dressed young black men walking their way. Adding a little more color to the scenery, as Fletcher likes to put it. Their intellectual hip-hop personality had enough flavor to spread around for others to absorb. Please be advised, there is history between Amber and Fletcher. They were high school sweethearts up until they graduated. Their relationship ended when Fletcher was accepted into Georgia Tech. His father was an electrical engineer, his father's father was a mechanical engineer, and Fletcher is a computer engineer. Fletcher is employed with the Yahoo Inc. on North Michigan Ave.

Amber didn't believe in long-distance relationships and ended their relationship. Amber loves Chicago, and has no desire to leave. Trying to get Amber to leave Chicago was like trying to take diamonds out of her pocket. Now, the breakup didn't bother Fletcher too much because as soon as he graduate he planned to come back and marry his woman, but a guy by the name of Trey Hudson, a newly signed member of the Chicago Bulls rained on Fletcher's parade. Fletcher would come home to visit and was aware that Amber was dating a pro basketball player, but he still didn't seem to mind.

It didn't seem to bother Amber who Fletcher may have been seeing down at Georgia Tech. She knew most black fraternity brothers are usually buck wild anyway. A year before Fletcher was to graduate, he stop coming home to visit and the first day he does come back for a visit, Amber was walking down the aisle. I bet that bothered him some, hell a whole lot. Fletcher didn't stop the wedding and went back to finish college. After graduation he stayed in Georgia another year, since he didn't have anyone to run back to. Ever since Fletcher has moved back to Chicago, he has been living a carefree life as a bachelor. His best friend Reese, well he's nothing but a player with a degree in communications, a pretty boy who DJ's on one of the local radio stations. Rumor has it, Fletcher still have deep feelings for Amber.

"Good evening ladies, you too Amber."

"Cute Fletcher, have you been practicing that little joke all day?" Fletcher nudges his lips to reply with a kiss.

"What is your poison tonight friends?"

"Why Reese, are you offering to buy around?" asked Gabrielle. "Maybe."

"Gabrielle, now you know if Reese bought a round of drinks, he wouldn't have enough money to pay his cab-fare."

"Ah-ha, well Amber, I rather be short on cab-fare than on Welfare."

The waiter comes over and asks the men would they care for something to drink. Fletcher slides into the ladies booth next to Amber and lifts up her drink. "Yes, I think I'll have some of this here."

Amber politely confiscates her drink back.

"One vodka martini and for you sir?" asked the waiter.

"I'll have some Mad Dog 20/20; ya'll have that don't you?" "He's joking." Jillian replied.

"Of course." said the waiter. "I'll take a Michelob."

"Certainly, I'll be right back with your drinks."

Reese takes a sit in the booth next to Jillian; of course you know Amber wasn't going to let Reese get away with that last comment.

"Oh by the way Reese, I read your momma's book."

"What book? Girl you crazy, my momma didn't write no book." "Sure she did, How to Raise an Ugly Child."

Amber smiles before taking a sip of her drink and continuing with more words. "I must say, she did a marvelous job with you, but she might wanna stop dressing you though."

Everyone laughed as the waiter returned with their drinks. "Oh you got jokes, little Miss Diva on recall."

Another round of laughs were heard before Jillian and Fletcher stepped in to stop the madness, before it gets out of control.

"Now now children, let's play nice or I will have to take away your drinking privileges."

"Ladies I hope Reese and I are not intruding?" "Always." replied Amber.

"And will your better halves be joining you ladies tonight? Jillian, have you found a better half yet?"

"No, and I'm not looking."

"Fletcher, when do the fellas ever join us on girl's night out?" asked Gabrielle. "Just checking, didn't want to get my clothes dirty tonight."

"Too late." replied Amber.

"So fella's, what are you guys getting into tonight?" "Hopefully some draws."

"Reese, please!" Jillian disapproved. "You asked."

"We are just making a pet stop before the clubs." advised Fletcher. "What's wrong Fletcher, haven't found Miss Right yet?"

"I'm not looking Amber, unless you and Trey are getting a divorce." "Dream on."

"Gabrielle, guess who's coming into town?" "Who Fletcher?"

"Your boy Tru."

A mildly attentive expression elated across Gabrielle's face. She seemed calmly surprised, as did Amber and Jillian.

"Oh really I haven't heard."

"Just some free info I thought you would appreciate." "When was the last time you heard from Tru?" asked Jillian. "A year ago when he got signed to Damon Dash label."

"Yeah boy! Now that's what I'm talking bout and who said Chicago don't have worthy rappers?"

"Looks like your boy, forgot about you Reese." bragged Amber.

"Nonsense, he has been busy that's all. You'll see me and Fetcher in the next music video."

"Sounds like Tru is coming back to claim his woman." "Fletcher, I'm with Bryce. Tru and I were never a couple."

"No, everyone in high school just thought you were." stated Jillian.

"But we weren't. Tru and I became really close after Percy died. He is a really good friend."

"Your home girls were your friend. What Tru was offering, we couldn't provided, and where is Bryce tonight?" asked Amber.

"I think he's hanging out with Brian."

"You mean fine Brian Gassaway. Mr. Ultimate Fighter?" "Yeah, him and Bryce workout together."

"Now you see, that's a brother that would make me rethink my wedding vows and read over the clause in my prenup."

"Well that's our cue to bounce Reese. Sounds like some girls gossip is about to begin."

After finishing their drinks, Reese gets up from the booth and lays two twenty dollar bills on the table. "This round is on me and Amber, you can keep the change. I'm sure you will need some lunch money next week."

"Gee thanks Reese, I will be sure to also thank your mother for giving you extra allowance money this week?"

A round of laughs was heard before Fletcher and Reese departs company from the ladies. Gabrielle and her friends continue to enjoy their version of happy hour. Without giving much awareness, Gabrielle gave her participation in tonight's gathering, but sat with two particular interests in mind, the death of one friend and the past friendship of another.

CHAPTER TEN

First Comes Love

Truman Porter the third, aka Tru is an up and coming rapper straight out of Chi Town. His distinctively unique and fresh style is taking Hip Hop to a whole new level. The reason Tru's dazzlingly elaborated and flamboyant style of rap was so acoustically acceptable, was due to his appreciation of all various forms and categories of music, which is the reason why him and Gabrielle got along so very well. Tru is a real music lover, open to all art forms of music. His particular interest in music other than Hip Hop and R&B, were contemporary Jazz, Alternative Rock, Classical, even Country, something the average young black rapper probably wouldn't stand for.

Tru did however, have his limit to what his acceptable vibe of sounds would appreciate. He was not especially fond of Bluegrass. He respected Bluegrass, but it just was not mentally consuming. Ten seconds was the maximum amount of time he would allow and could stand for, otherwise Bluegrass was a form of music Tru could never get use to on any day of the week, including holidays. There were other generations of music worth sampling. Tru didn't believe in limiting your mind to only one culture.

Truman Porter the Second, was never acceptable to the idea that his first-born career path was headed to the entertainment business, especially one that has been proven to be as violent as rap. So far, the rap nation has loss two great extraordinary and phenomenal rap artist of their time. Tupac Shakur and Notorious B.I.G. are legends, conquerors of the rap music industry, who lives are now loss over squash-able circumstantial beef and for what? In the end, can anyone possibly say, including the artists themselves, believe it was worth it, now two black powerful voices of Hip-hop are gone forever.

Tru's father didn't have anything positive to say about the career his son chose. He himself came from the era of the Temptations and Gap Band. Truman the Second, desperately wanted Truman the Third to follow in his business minded footsteps. All Tru could do was respect his father's opinionated beliefs and keep faith in his destiny. Some parents don't realize that their children decisions in life and careers are their children's choice, their life and not their parents. Children's hopes and dreams are for them to live out hopefully, not live out their parent's dreams.

That's why it's important to keep striving for your goals and dreams. No matter how many people say you can't or if racism blocks your climb up the ladder. No matter how many times you fail or if failure has knocked you down, get back up and keep getting up until you accomplish your goals. Let your voice be your own motivated coach. Don't ever allow someone to take away your beliefs and dreams. If your dreams are right in God's eyes, then you will be blessed in achievements and wealth will soon follow.

Gabrielle opens the door to her apartment and automatically embraces a warm hug full of smiles. She welcomed a guest of an old high school friend she hasn't seen in a while.

"Tru, I can't believe it's really you." "The one and only."

"Come in and have a seat."

Tru follows Gabrielle inside her lovely apartment into the living room as she makes her way over to the bar. He was impressed. Gabrielle prepares them a drink before they embark on getting reacquainted.

"So what's up Gabrielle, how you *feeling*?"

"Right now I'm feeling the sounds of Tru and a Long Island Ice Tea."

"You look amazing. Your place is amazing. The practice of medicine serves you well. No need to ask how you been making out."

"Thanks, you're looking handsomely successful yourself."

"Right right. I guess we both succeeded in our dreams."

"That's true, how are things in the Hip Hop industry?"

"Gabrielle, it's nothing like I expected. It's explosive. I am still comprehending the business aspects of it, but with the guidance of my boy Damon Dash influence with the biz, my future looks promising."

"That's great Tru. Now, I'm going to need an autograph picture for my niece." He laughs. "No problem." Gabrielle joins her friend in the living room and hands Tru his drink. "Did you ever think about giving up because of the time it took to finally get signed?"

"No, never that. No matter how many doors were slammed in my face, I kept writing and rapping. It was worth it and paid off in the end."

"How's the family Tru?"

"Good, good. Dad though, he's not feeling me."

Tru eyes indicated a little disappointment. Gabrielle reaches over and lays a hand on his shoulder. "Give him time, he'll come around."

"Enough about me, what about your family. Ivy still reck-n things in the courtrooms of justice?" Gabrielle gave a brief laugh.

"She still gives them hell as always, but yeah. Everything is everything. You are aware of my precious little one?"

Tru wasn't quite sure at first, but quickly realized whom Gabrielle was referring to as her precious little one. "Oh you mean your cat."

"Yes, my baby Jack."

"Where is he? I've never met him."

Gabrielle points behind Tru before taking a sip of her drink. Tru turned around slightly and looked on the floor. His eyes expanded just a bit. "Hey buddy, damn, he's kinda big and looks a little angry. He's not going to come jump on a brother is he?"

Gabrielle laughs before telling him no. Tru turns back around and zooms in on Gabrielle's hands, her left hand particularly.

"So Gabrielle, I see this guy of yours isn't too bright after all." "What do you mean?" she asked.

"The fool still hasn't married you yet." Gabrielle laughs again briefly.

"When ready, in due time. I'm not rushing it."

"Man if you were my lady, we would be celebrating our second wedding anniversary all ready."

"Well I'm sure you will be walking down the aisle soon, because I know there's someone special in your life."

Tru smiles before denying it. "No, not really."

"Tru come on now. There is someone worth mentioning, right?" Tru tried to playfully deny it once more.

"Well, there is this one girl."

"You see, I knew it. So what's her name?" "Teyana, nothing serious."

Tru then turns to Gabrielle and places his drink down. He then takes her by the hand. "I have attracted a lot of money hungry groupies in which I have no desire for and then there's Teyana, but she can easily be turned away, if you gave me a reason to believe there could be a chance for us."

Feeling graciously flattered, Gabrielle's heart was tenderly humble, somehow an offer of that nature was expected.

"Tru, I'm flattered, but do you remember a quote I said to you in high school our senior year?" True didn't appear quite sure.

"Not exactly."

"Well, lets see. I hope I can remember it correctly. Don't walk in front of me, I may not follow, don't walk behind me, I may not lead, just walk beside me and be my friend."

Tru slowly nods his head. "Not a chance in hell huh?"

"I wouldn't say that, but the point is, I think of you as a friend. That's all I have to offer now. Plus and most importantly, I'm with Bryce. I do love him, just as you will grow to love Teyana, when you fully allow yourself the chance to."

"Gabrielle thanks, it's understood. I knew my chances with you were a million to one, but it was necessary for me to ask and know for sure."

Tru appeared a little disappointed. "Are we still friends?" she asked.

"Tru that, always." He willingly smiled, as did she.

"You will always be my number one choice Gabrielle. Now let's get out of here, I've made dinner reservations."

"Great, I'm starving. Where are the reservations?" "TRU, on North Saint Clair, where else?"

"Wow, it must be nice to have a restaurant named after you?" "Yeah, too bad I don't own the joint."

Love is all things, it never fails. In the bible, First Corinthians thirteen, four-eight of the New World Translation of Holy Scriptures, it states and I quote.

"Love is long-suffering and kind. Love is not jealous, it does not brag, does not get puffed up, does not behave indecently, does not look for its own interests, does not become provoked. It does not keep account of the injury. It does not rejoice over unrighteousness, but rejoices with the truth.

It bears all things, believes all things, hopes for all things, endures all things. Love never fails."

It's mind boggling, Love that is, the misconceptions humans have about it. What qualifies as such and in what degree does love honestly exist. Truelove, is there really such a thing and if so, why does many people search their entire lives for it only to be disappointed in the end. Does the sometime infatuated state of being in love, level in scales the personification of actual love and how long it desires to exist?

Most healthy relationships develops or start out with an A for effort, the longing need to make one's life complete. In time however and not much quality time, the relationship somehow down spirals to an F and fails. Then again, no couple starts out hoping for the worst. This inaccurate prediction holds true to most marriages, but don't take my word for it, love, truelove, the act of being in love, in whatever degree is solemnly necessary for a well balance life. Now that, you can take my word for and if you don't believe me, then just ask your therapist.

Yes, love is all things and actual love never fails. Oh the inevitable punishment we put ourselves through to endure, accept and acknowledge such emotions, deep rooted feelings, young or old, new or been around the block a few times, questionable feelings that may ask yourself in the end, was it really worth it? For those who agree and find these truths to be self-evidence, may I say this. Before the instant attraction, the curious adventure of infatuation, the breaking of silence, the moment of contact and the well deserved vacation that sends your heart on an emotional roller coaster, swim, sink or sail, before going through all of that which for the most may lead to heartache, we blindly go through steps of a puzzling order of arrangements without fully realizing it and before we subconsciously willing to agree to all of this, somehow, first comes love.

As far as Tru's love for Gabrielle is concerned. Well, who knows, maybe Tru and Gabrielle will become more than friends someday, if its destiny, then just maybe, but it doesn't mean to hold out for it. Even though disappointingly sometimes, love itself should encourages you to try, try again, but don't take my word for it. Love isn't all what it's cracked up to be. Love is however, the ultimate epitome of pure affection, which makes us human.

CHAPTER ELEVEN

Then Comes The Rain

The Cloud

*D*id you witness the melancholy mist of vapors that set forth over my life yesterday, it arrived without notice or warning, carrying forth with it, heartache and sadness. Dwell for a moment if you will, ponder the past, for memories are all you will spare to cherish, preserve them for safekeeping. Once, not long ago, eternity smiled upon me and begun to circle our future together, then gradually, yet quietly flew away. Now I am alone.

Did you witness the melancholy mist of vapors that set forth over my life yesterday, uninvited vapors, bringing forth a pre-existence occurrence undetermined without love. It formed overbearingly into a thick gray visible mass and tenderly relieved the downing pressures of life on to me. The cloud, reality of truth, has begun its course of sorrow and will somehow linger. Lord, when it rains it pours.

At home the swift strident churning sounds of a blender is heard, as Gabrielle blends herself a thick chocolate shake, cheesy nachos were also included in her late night snack. Late night treats usually mean she would skip breakfast in the morning, with the exception of a big healthy glass of OJ. She enjoys her comfort snack curled up on the couch watching a late night movie with Jack by her side. Like most people, not often, but every once in a while, Gabrielle gets into these can't sleep moods. It usually occurs when she has much on her mind. Much on her mind indeed, this weekend Sunday September 26 particularly, Gabrielle looked forward to turning a year older and celebrating her twenty-six birthday.

It was Bryce weekend to work, but he made plans to be off on that day. They will most likely spend the day together, but Gabrielle is not expecting something out of the ordinary, something simple, a quiet dinner at her favorite restaurant. Geja's Café on W Armitage Ave, is the perfect romantic hideaway. They haven't had the pleasure in visiting their favorite dwelling place in a while. Flowers would be nice, but then again a diamond tennis bracelet would be better. Going to see a play at a theater was considerable, or maybe a relaxing sail on the lake, whatever she wanted or found delight in that would satisfy her day. Birthdays doesn't necessarily always mean hitting the clubs and partying, although, a tasteful party given is also a joy. One thing for sure, no one should spend their birthday alone.

The day before her birthday, Gabrielle and Amber hit the stores to go shopping. Gabrielle wanted to buy a new outfit for her birthday. They had the whole day planned to get their hair and nails done along with facials, a day at the spa, a treat from Amber to Gabrielle. This treatable girly tradition has been going on for years. It was around noon when Gabrielle and Amber were seen leaving 900 North department store on Michigan Ave. Their shopping splurge hadn't quite topped their ability to do some real damage, and the way Amber lives to shop, there was always room to buy more. They phoned Jillian and told her to meet them at a restaurant near by for lunch before the three of them head to the spa.

The two friends were walking the sidewalks on Michigan Ave headed to a restaurant near by, then without warning, an unexpected life altering form of event occurred. Gabrielle was window shopping, minding her own business, just enjoying her Saturday afternoon, when she heard Amber holler. The same dreadfully explosive holler Gabrielle remembered so distinctively a little over a year ago. Somehow unawarely, it was almost like dejavu all over again.

"Oh Hell No!"

Gabrielle quickly turned to Amber frighteningly concerned. "Amber what's wrong?"

"Girl, I don't believe this shit!" "What!"

Amber points straight ahead and Gabrielle's head slowly followed. Surprisingly there it was, the bomb dropping, life altering, unexpected occurrence happening right before her eyes. A short distance further down the sidewalk was Bryce, embraced in a romantic kiss with another woman and not just any woman, but a White woman. Immediately a particular song jumped inside Gabrielle's head, that particular song, "Chain of Fools" by Aretha Franklin. Gabrielle looked hurtfully shocked. Infidelity, this coming from a man she thought she knew so well, a man who didn't like showing public displays of affection. Well he sure didn't seem to have a problem with wrapping his lips around this broad.

"I knew he was a two-timing dog! Girl, what are you still standing here for? We need to get down to the bottom of this!"

Amber snatches Gabrielle by the arm and pulls her along. Shortly after grabbing her, Gabrielle pulls loose from Amber and walked diligently along beside her. Bryce and the woman seemed happy together and were playing around like teenage lovebirds. At first, Bryce was all smiles until he turned around to see Gabrielle and Amber walking their way. He discreetly pushes the woman away. She then looks around for the reason of Bryce's discomfort and see's Dr. Michaels and a friend approaching.

"I knew you were a two-timing dog! I should have kept my surveillance cameras on you."

"Amber please." Gabrielle interjected. "Gabrielle I can explain."

Gabrielle stared at Bryce pitifully and slowly shook her head.

"Please do Bryce. What could you possibly say to rectify this situation?" "Gabrielle, its not-"

"Dr. Lyndon, your comments are not needed." "Yeah trick, step off!" advised Amber.

"Gabrielle I was going to tell you. I mean, I was suppose to tell you the weekend we were away."

"So it was better for me to find out this way, a day before my birthday?"

Gabrielle walks off and Bryce immediately follows her trying to express his apologies. "It figures, said Amber. Bryce would go for some white lily hoe." Amber rolled her eyes at the woman before walking off to catch up with Gabrielle. Bryce was steady walking beside Gabrielle trying to explain, but soon made a bad mistake by grabbing Gabrielle by the arm to get her attention. A fierce roar of a mountain lion could be heard as Gabrielle quickly turned around in anger and slaps Bryce in the face. The slap was so harsh and so fast that Bryce himself was amazingly shaken. It also stopped Amber in her tracks.

"Damn! I know that hurt."

"Don't touch me! You have nothing else to say to me, ever!"

Gabrielle walked off again and Bryce did not follow. Amber walked up to Bryce as he just stood there expressionless on the sidewalk.

"She bobcat slapped your ass!"

Bryce looked at Amber furiously before she laughs and walks off. Amber called after Gabrielle twice before making her stop and turn around. "Girl I know you're angry and upset, but where are you going?"

"Call Jillian, I wanna go home. Tell her its been a change of plans."

There goes their trip to the spa. Amber took her friend home and Jillian soon came over. Jillian was speechless. She couldn't believe Bryce would cheat on Gabrielle. At least it wasn't a man, Jillian expressed. Gabrielle dear friends stayed with her most of the evening trying to comfort what was left of her dignity, but at the moment, there was no real cure for her pain. Before it got too late, Gabrielle sent her friends home.

Always fully stocked, Gabrielle grabbed the first thing from the bar to forget the pain. Wine was not on the menu tonight. She needed the good stuff, the hard stuff, she needed Jack. After dropping a few ice cubs into a rock glass, Gabrielle opened a new pint of Jack Daniels and poured herself a full dose. She sipped the liquor slow to savor the potent taste while waiting for the antidote to numb the pain. Gabrielle walked into her bedroom and removed the picture of Percy from its safe haven and admits, she now know the reason for Percy's reoccurring and disapproving dream. She then cries herself to sleep. Observantly outside in a parked car sit's an unwelcome guest with rejoicing eyes. Misery loves company.

When Gabrielle woke Sunday morning on her birthday, she woke to light rain and a heavy hangover. She also awoke with the picture of Percy in her arms. So far she has had six missed calls. Gabrielle did remember calling her sister before turning the ringer off to her phones before lying down. Two of the calls were from Bryce. Gabrielle screened her calls as they came in. Amber and Jillian both called to wish her a happy birthday despite the circumstances and tried to get her to get out and do something, but Gabrielle refused. She wanted to stay at home, didn't want any company and like Greta Garbo, she wanted to be alone.

Gabrielle stayed in bed most of the day totally ignoring Bryce calls and messages. He didn't dare come over. If Gabrielle was angry enough to slap him, there was no telling what else she could be capable of committing.

Around three thirty that afternoon there was a knock on her front door. She didn't remember buzzing anyone inside the building, but kinda knew who it was. Gabrielle opens her front door for her sister, who was bearing balloons, flowers and gifts. Gabrielle was not pleased to see her.

"Happy happy birthday baby girl." Ivy enters Gabrielle's apartment. "Ivy thanks, but I'm not in the mood for company."

"Gee, I'm glad I didn't bring the girls over with me. They send their birthday wishes. You look like crap doll."

"I care."

"How are you *feeling*?"

"Like the sounds of Macy Gray and a glass of Wild Irish Rose." "That bad huh?"

Gabrielle returned back to her bedroom in order to climb back into bed, while her sister put her flowers in water. Jack appears in the kitchen begging for food and Ivy pours him some. Also while in the kitchen, Ivy began fixing a light meal and brought it to Gabrielle on a tray in her bedroom. Gabrielle had her bedroom dark with the blinds drawn down and the curtains closed with bed sheets over her head.

"A, R, A, E, Awake, Rise, And Eat. I've made food."

Gabrielle grunts and groans under the covers. Ivy places the tray down and opens up the curtains and blinds to bring more light into the room. "Gabrielle, my dear baby sister. Just because your life is going through and experiencing a melancholy episode, doesn't mean you have to give up on life and stay in bed all day."

Ivy notices the empty rock glass and the half bottle of Jack Daniels on the nightstand. She sits down on the bed and lifts backs the covers off of Gabrielle. Wearing pajama bottoms and a Cornell University t-shirt, Gabrielle's body was restlessly facing the opposite direction. Ivy taps her a few times on the shoulder. "Come on now, let's get up." Gabrielle says no. Ivy slowly and gently pulls her up and places her arms around Gabrielle. Gabrielle innocently lays her head on her sister's shoulder and within seconds embraced her hug. Gabrielle began to weep.

"There there, like Aaron Nevels song would say, every one plays the fool sometime, and I know it hurts."

"I loved him Ivy. I really loved him." "I know, I know."

Still embraced in a hug, Ivy looks down at the picture of Percy beside Gabrielle. Sisterly love, the only thing better than sisterly love is motherly love and since Gabrielle no longer have her mother's shoulder to cry on, Ivy's comfort was absolutely by all means needed. After a good long cry, Ivy tried to get Gabrielle to eat something, which wasn't much. Gabrielle home phone rings abruptly. Ivy ignored Gabrielle calls while trying to console her sister through a rough time.

"Are you going to work tomorrow?" asked Ivy. "Yes."

"Good, because it won't do you any good to lay around feeling sorry for yourself."

"I'm not the kinda person that feels sorry for my self, but I am human and I hurt. This hurts."

"Yes, and hopefully you wont suffer long. Like they say, first comes love, then comes the rain. This is just the bad rain finding its way over your life."

"Well I definitely did not see that cloud forming."

Ivy eyes made contact again with the half bottle of Jack Daniels on her nightstand. "Gabrielle, I see you have been drinking."

"Don't start Ivy. I am an adult."

"Your father is stable now, but did suffer from alcoholism. You know that's why he couldn't take care of you after mom died."

"I'm fine. I don't have a drinking problem; I have a problem with my personal life."

"Gabrielle?"

"What, did you think I was going to sit around here drinking Sunny Delight at a time like this?"

"No, I expect you to take the time needed to grieve, but get over it and climb back on that horse again. Redefine yourself if you have to, but don't allow this to keep you down. Happiness may not be right around the corner, but when this gloomy period does pass, be happy, live happy, but most of all, Breathe. If you can accomplish all of that without constantly drowning your soul in a bottle of alcohol, then it may speed up your recovery process and make you stronger." The phone began to ring again and Gabrielle just stares at it. Ivy stands up and walks over to Gabrielle's bedroom door. "I've gotta go, but know this. All curves have to end sooner or later. I'll call you later."

The first day back to work is always the hardest after a relationship ends, especially when you're subject to run into that person on the job. After experiencing the kind of weekend Gabrielle had, it's a miracle she even got out of bed. Gabrielle however, found the strength needed to compose her true feelings of her well-being. Bryce stopped calling in an effort to give Gabrielle time to absorb the situation. Strangely, somehow the day went by fast and before Gabrielle knew it, she was in her car performing her after work ritual. Sadly, pleasant thoughts did not do her any justice.

Gabrielle drove the long way home trying to soak up the remaining rays of the sun and breathe in as much fresh air as possible. She stopped and picked up some takeout before finally heading home. Jack greeted her at the door and for once today, Gabrielle gave an honest smile. Her and Jack sat in the kitchen enjoying their meal together. She had one glass of wine and began to ponder broodingly how she was ever going to get use to the way things will be. The telephone rang and after screening the call, she answers it.

"Gabrielle, I called you twice yesterday, once on your home phone, the other on your cell phone to wish you a happy birthday. Surely you couldn't have been indisposed both times."

"Hello Aaron, I'm sorry you weren't able to reach me, but I was having one of the worst weekends of my life."

"Not on your birthday I hope not?" "I'm afraid so."

"Well I'm sorry Gabrielle; you want to talk about it?" "Thanks, not really, but you should know?"

"Know what?"

"Bryce and I are no longer together."

There was a moment of silence on the phone.

"A break up on your birthday?"

"Not exactly on my birthday, the day before, but the lingering extinct of it followed on through my birthday. You know how it goes."

"I am sorry Gabrielle, may I ask why, after two years of dating?" "I caught him cheating with someone he works with."

"You are someone he works with, just not directly."

"Yeah well, my name isn't Jennifer Lyndon and I'm sure as hell not White." "Goodness Gabrielle, are you alright?"

"Not really, but it's expected." "Do you want some company?"

"No, not really. I'm eating on some takeout and plus I need this time alone." "Well when you're ready, I'm sure your home girls will take good care of you." "I know."

"I apologize again Gabrielle for the awful birthday; I do have something for you when I run into you again. If you need me, you know how to reach me."

"Thanks Aaron." "You take care." "I will, bye."

Aaron was right; Gabrielle managed to attend Friday's happy hour and hung out with her girls all weekend long. In fact, for three weekends straight, they did nothing but hang out, sometimes even during the weeknights. Jillian was happy to have another single on board with her. Gabrielle did admit to Jillian that she now knows on a first hand level, the life draining pain she went through with Dennis. They both shared the burning pain of betrayal by someone they loved.

After three weekends straight of dancing to the rhythm of Cindy Lauper's song, "Girls Just Wanna Have Fun" reality was slowly creeping back into Gabrielle's life. She took a break from her home girls and took the next weekend to herself. She rented movies, ordered pizza and ate a lot of ice cream. She just relaxed at home and chilled with the one friend she knew that honestly loved her, her cat Jack. Sadly for her girlfriends, Gabrielle wasn't in a hanging out mood for the next two weekends. Gabrielle seem to have developed a boring routine, go to work, come home, eat, watch TV, go to bed. Her girls couldn't seem to get her back in the scene of hanging out again. Gabrielle was also dreaming more and more about Percy lately. There in her dreams with him, she could always find happiness.

6:00 am on a Tuesday morning, Dr. Bryce Whitney woke up to go running, as he ran he could see flyers on trees, on street post and stop signs, but didn't pay it much attention. After running his three miles, he stops at an intersection. Taking a rest to catch his breath, he finally had chance to read one of those flyers on a wall by a newsstand. It was a picture of Bryce on the flyer and the flyer reads, Beware of Cheating Dog. Ticked off at the childish prank, Bryce went back to every spot he saw a flyer and removed them. 2:30 pm that same day on duty at the ER, Bryce was in conversation with one of the nurses on staff. A white female dressed up in some type of showbiz attire, wearing a black Top hat, suite, stockings and had a cane, was looking for a particular person. She was eventually pointed in the right direction.

"Excuse me, Hi are you Dr. Bryce Whitney?"

Finding her costume amusing, Bryce acknowledged that he is Dr. Whitney. "Singing telegram Sir!"

She blows on a small harmonica to warm up before proceeding with a fantastic smile on her face.

"You're a dog and you know it, so why not let everyone know it. You're a dog and you know it, may you develop heartworms and die!"

Bryce rolls his eyes before handing the nurse a clipboard and walking away. Bryce didn't find the amusing woman so amusing anymore.

"Dr. Whitney, I'm not finished." she yells out and then runs up behind Bryce with a new tune. "Why must you be like that, why must you chase the cat, nothing but the dog in you."

After kindly getting rid of the singing telegram with a nice tip, Bryce pays a visit over to Lynn Sage Breast Cancer Center.

Gabrielle was walking with another doctor when she see's Bryce approaching. She knew eventually they would run into each other, but just wasn't expecting it today. "Hi, excuse me, Dr. Michaels may I speak with you for a moment?" Her colleague continued on without Gabrielle.

"Ok Gabrielle, point taken. So would you please stop putting hell on me?" Looking completely obfuscated, Gabrielle had no earthly idea what Bryce was speaking of, on the verge of anger. "Bryce, what are you talking about?" "You know damn well what I am speaking about." he whispered.

"No Bryce, I don't."

"The flyers in my neighborhood this morning, portraying me as a cheating dog and just now, a singing telegram at work referring to me as a dog."

A small smile gently emerged across Gabrielle's face. She then quickly resumed a straight face. "Bryce, I had nothing to do with that, honestly, but I think I might know who may have."

Bryce thought for a second and immediately knew who the culprit was. "You tell Amber to stop bothering me with these childish pranks."

"Yes, I will speak to her about that. Is that all?"

"No, Gabrielle, its been weeks. I would like to talk about-" "That won't be necessary."

Gabrielle tried to walk off, but Bryce stepped in her way. "Please, may I call you tonight? We need to discuss this."

Gabrielle thought for a second. It was time to put all this behind her and move on with her life.

"Ok fine, you may call me tonight at nine. If that's a problem, then that's not my problem."

"Thank you, and please speak with your friend." "I will."

When Bryce was out of view, another gratifying smile slowly emerged across Gabrielle's face. Five minutes later, Gabrielle was on her cell phone with her friend.

"Really Gabrielle, I have no idea what you are speaking of."

"Thanks for trying to get back at Bryce, Amber, but I do not desire to get even with him."

There was a few seconds of silents over the phone.

"Are you sure Girl? Because I can make him pay as long as you hurt." Gabrielle laughs.

"No, just leave him be Amber." "Are you sure Girl?"

"Yes." "Ok." "Ok."

There was another moment of silence on the phone. "Singing telegram huh?"

A burst of laughter erupts from both ends of the phone.

5:15 pm Gabrielle was in her car and just completed her after work ritual. In thought, she asked curiously, *So how are you feeling?* After the kind of day Bryce was having, she replied in thought, "I'm feeling the sounds of the theme song from the Partridge Family, Come on, Get Happy, with a Coke and a smile." Meanwhile, back in the exciting world of the ER, Bryce had just walked into the doctor's lounge after discharging a patient.

"There you are Dr. Whitney; I've been looking for you. This came special delivery from Frances Bakery. I had to keep them from the nurses."

"Thanks Isabella."

"You be sure to save some for the staff, after you have picked out your favorites."

The other doctor leaves the lounge and Bryce walks over to pink box on the table. After the kind of day he was having, he no doubt had a bad feeling about it. He opens the box anyway. Relieved, there was a variety of baked donuts. Although relieved it wasn't another prank, Bryce did not dare partake of the goodies, he laughs the gesture off and walks to his locker. As soon as Bryce opens his locker, he quickly turned away before slamming the locker door shut. Inside his locker was one pound of dog shit.

"Amber!!!"

Working quietly in her office, Amber turns away from her desk and leans back in her chair. She views Chicago lovely city up high from her window. An evil smile slowly expands across her face, followed by a sneaky giggle.

Nine o'clock that night Gabrielle received her phone call. "You have five minutes."

"Five minutes."

"Yes, that should be enough time to explain your cheating heart." "How have you been Gabrielle?"

"Good, considering."

"Gabrielle I was hoping I could come over to-" "That is out of the question."

"Ok, I expected that, but I need more than five minutes." "Four minutes now, what is she to you Bryce?"

"Dr. Lyndon and I, use to date a long time ago." "When, where?"

"At Stanford, during my residency."

Gabrielle thought for a second as she put the connection together.

"Jennifer Lyndon is the bad breakup that sent you home?" "Yes, it was complicated, her parents and all."

"How long?"

"How long what?"

"How long was I a fool, while the two of you were falling back in love?" "Gabrielle."

"Don't lie."

"I'm not in love with her, but I guess four months."

"Four months, she transferred here six months ago. I've heard enough." "Gabrielle please don't hang up, it meant nothing."

There was a moment of silence on the phone before Gabrielle replied.

"It meant nothing, but serious enough to cheat and end our relationship." "You say it's over, I haven't accepted that yet."

"Well you need to."

"All I need is one night Gabrielle. Let me take you to dinner." "No, why should I do that?"

"Because I love you and I know you still love me." There was another moment of silence on the phone. "I don't know Bryce, I don't think it's a good idea."

"Please, one dinner and if you still have negative feelings, I won't bother you anymore."

More silence settles over the phone conversation as Gabrielle seriously considers whether to have dinner with her former boyfriend.

"Alright Bryce, we can get together tomorrow night for dinner." "Thank you, I'll pick you up tomorrow night at seven."

"That will be fine, goodbye."

6:51 pm the next evening, Bryce was knocking on Gabrielle's apartment door. The door opens and Bryce stood handsomely dressed with all smiles and flowers. His smile soon faded.

"What do you want Fido?"

Bryce enters Gabrielle apartment with a heavy eye on Gabrielle's friend.

"I'm here to take Gabrielle out to dinner. You know you have a lot of nerve doing what you did."

"I can say the same for you. Care for a dog biscuit?" "I should call the police."

"There's a phone by the bar, a cordless phone in the kitchen and a one in her bedroom, take your pick, here, use my cell phone if you like."

"You know what-"

"Uh excuse me, I'll take those flowers." "Gabrielle, you look lovely. Why is Amber here?" "I could be here to neuter your ass."

"Ella!"

"Shouldn't your crazy behind be at home watching Lifetime Television or something?" "Not when there's a Lifetime Original Movie playing live and in living color before me." "Gabrielle?"

"Ok, Amber I will talk to you tomorrow. Bryce I'm ready to go, let me get my purse and put these flowers in water."

"Don't take no shit from him Girl." Amber whispered. "Goodbye Amber."

When Bryce and Gabrielle walked outside of her apartment, Gabrielle noticed Bryce was driving his Bentley.

"What's the occasion? You hardly ever drive your Bentley."

'Spur of the moment decision. I had it washed, waxed and detailed today and felt like showing it off."

Bryce opens the passenger door for her, as Gabrielle elegantly slips herself inside. Gabrielle could sense something excitingly strange about Bryce's mood tonight. He was eagerly happy, confident. The ride to the restaurant was quietly somber as if they were riding to a funeral. After ten minutes of empty thoughts, Bryce finally broke the silents.

"I can't believe fall is already here."

"I'm not; the abrupt change in my life helped me to appreciate the seasons." "You really do look lovely tonight Gabrielle."

"Thank you."

"Is that a new fragrance?"

"Why yes it is, just a little new inspiration when I've made altering changes in my life."

"So you have already made a decision about the future of our relationship." Gabrielle easily brushed off that question by turning up the radio some. They soon pulled up to the restaurant valet.

"Geja's, my favorite restaurant. We haven't been here in sometime, I guess that should have been an indication you were cheating."

"Gabrielle, is this attitude the program on TV tonight, because if so, you need to switch channels."

"You asked for this dinner, was I suppose to forget you cheated on me?" "Gabrielle, I know I asked for this dinner. I don't want to argue, so please be nice, okay?" The valet attendant walks up to the car and opens the door for Gabrielle.

Making reservation in advance, Bryce and Gabrielle walked into the crowed restaurant together and were seated immediately. Gabrielle missed the charming settings of her favorite restaurant. She missed the fluttering candles and the soothing live music of a guitar. Ted Richine has been serenading the customers for years. The dark warmth of this intimate café possesses a lingering romantic atmosphere for all couples to relax and absorb. Gabrielle looked forward to the lobster tail fondue.

Bryce and Gabrielle's dinner together was going exceptionally well, except for Amber's interruption calls. Amber's first call came in while Gabrielle was in the ladies room. You could hear rigorous out bursts over

Gabrielle's cell phone of emotional support. Don't listen to him Girl and don't get sucked into his bullshit, were some of the outbursts heard from the two calls. Gabrielle had to eventually hang up on Amber and turn her cell phone off. Toward the end of dinner, Gabrielle ordered her favorite Belgian Chocolate Fondue dessert. She waited anxiously to indulge herself in such an almost sinful pleasurable delight. The waiter comes over with the dessert under a tray. "Your dessert ma'am." The waiter happily lifts the top off the tray. Surprisingly, there sat a four-carat diamond engagement ring from Harry Winston Jewelers on the tray, sparkling brighter than any star. It somehow amazingly brought more light into the dark low-lit room.

Gabrielle was utterly shocked. Bryce gets up from his seat and takes the ring off the tray as the waiter leaves. An expression of, you got to be kidding me, rushed across Gabrielle face. "I know damn well he's not trying to pull this off here and now." she thought with a straight nervous smile.

"Bryce we need to talk." she said.

Bryce got down on one knee and some people in the restaurant took notice of the surprise-wedding proposal.

"Oh hell, this can't be happening now." she thought.

"Well, this is what you've been waiting for. Gabrielle Delniece Michaels, will you marry me?"

She was speechless and stared at Bryce with a blank face. Gabrielle wasn't mentally ready for this.

"Bryce, I think we need to talk."

Feeling a little nervously embarrassed, Bryce continue to wait on his knee for an answer.

"Bryce we need to talk."

"We are talking, this is what this dinner is about." he said through a smile.

"No, this dinner is about the adventures of your lies, cheating heart and rekindled relationship with Dr. Lyndon."

"Look woman, you want me, you got me. Now will you marry me or what?" "Bryce I highly suggest you adjust your tone."

The next thing Gabrielle knew, she heard screeching tires drive away from her apartment complex. "Man, I missed out on my chocolate fondue."

CHAPTER TWELVE

Time To Think

That same night on the phone with her girlfriends, Gabrielle went over details of her and Bryce's dinner. She couldn't resist telling her friends about Bryce's quick fix wedding proposal to resolve his cheating indiscretions. Why do men do that? Why is it when a woman catches a longtime boyfriend cheating, the best solution the man thinks can accommodate for his mistakes, is to ask the longtime girlfriend hand in marriage? That's like getting caught test-driving another car only to remain with the one you already have. Keep the old car, buy a new set of tires, maybe a brand-new paint job, yeah, that will do the trick and if that woman's mind is unstable enough at that time, to go on and marry him, well that's just agreeing to allow him to cheat again.

Gabrielle's three way conversation with her girlfriends carried over to 1:00 am the next morning. Jillian was the first to pull out of their on going gossip. With the ever-demanding condition of teaching third graders, Jillian needed all her energy to suffice their needs. Plus, she had to be at work an hour before her friends did. They did however; finish their conversation Friday night at happy hour. Gabrielle hadn't heard from Bryce since his grand gesture of a marriage proposal, but received a phone call from him late Friday night after she got home from girls night out.

"Hello."

"Did you enjoy that little stunt you pulled Wednesday night?" "I don't recall pulling any stunts."

"You wanted to embarrass me, didn't you?"

"No Bryce, I wasn't expecting a wedding proposal given the situation."
"Where were you tonight?"

"Where do you think? It's Friday, or was Friday."

"I'm sure you gladly told Amber and Jillian what happened?"

"Of course, but what I re-laid to my friends isn't the reason you called."
"No, I need to know what are you going to do about us?"

A moment of silence joined their conversation.

"I'm not sure Bryce."

"Surely you have some idea."

"What I have is a failed relationship on your part. Now you're asking me to fix your mistakes."

"I know I was wrong in every way, but I'm sure you can relate to old feelings from a past love?"

His comment made Gabrielle think of only one past love, which was Percy and that comment brought about a reaction with a touch of anger.

"Don't even go there with that. My past love is dead and if he was alive, I doubt if I would be going through this hell. I would be a lot happier."

"So you're not happy?"

"Would anyone be after what has happen to me?"

Bryce didn't answer that question, just replied with another question.

"So are you ready to end our two year relationship?" "Bryce I can't answer that now."

"What is it that you need Gabrielle?" "I need time to think."

"You've had time to think. Hell, you have been given a wedding proposal. That should indicate where my heart still lies."

"Look, maybe we need some time apart, a break. I guess I need more time to myself, see where my heart lies."

"Maybe you're right. Let me know when you are ready to take this relationship seriously. Just don't make me wait too long Gabrielle. As you know, I'm not the type of person who has to wait by a phone. Goodnight."

Gabrielle appeared a little sad before hanging up the phone. Bryce was right; he wasn't the type of person that has to wait for a call. He's a handsome man and could attract any woman he desired. Gabrielle just wasn't sure if it was her, he really wanted or Dr. Lyndon. Two more weeks passed as the cold weather season calmly settled into their lives. In those two weeks, Gabrielle received a gift from Bryce. He sent her a CD of a song that expressed his true feelings. That particular song of meaning was, "Don't want to loose your love" by Freddie Jackson. When Gabrielle played the certain song he suggested at home one night, all she could do was weep.

A family that prays together, stays together. Luckily for Gabrielle, this particular family lived in the same Hoffman Estates neighborhood as her sister. Thanksgiving Day Gabrielle was seen passing by Bryce's parent's house on her way to Ivy's place. She saw Bryce's blue Porsche parked outside to confirm that all of the siblings were home for the holidays. Gabrielle did have more time to think and the outlook wasn't looking good.

Before bringing a pecan pie over to her sister's, Gabrielle took a drive through the city of Chicago. It's was sort of the best time to have the city to yourself. She parked her car in a parking deck and walked the city alone from Lakeshore to where ever her heart leads her. She dressed warmly for her walk in fashionable boots, coat, scarf, gloves and hat, allowing the cold air to breathe across her face. Gabrielle was able to fulfill her best thinking while walking the streets alone. Throughout her journey there were some people out and about, people traveling to get to relatives. Gabrielle even took the L train. All the while upon this walk and journey, a certain song played in her head and all around her. Her mood, the song, "Why should I Care" by Diana Krall.

Gabrielle waited two days after Thanksgiving Day to contact Bryce and discuss their future together. They agreed to meet at the same coffee house where they first got acquainted. There, Gabrielle told Bryce with a heavy heart that she believes it would be best if they went their separate ways. She honestly didn't think she could ever trust him again. It would be different if they were already married, something worth considering saving. Gabrielle was the one for Bryce, but unfortunately their monogamous relationship was challenged and most of the time all it takes is an ex and unsettled feelings to divert another person away from their current relationship, but don't feel bad for Bryce. When the opportunity to stay true to his monogamous relationship or cheat, presented its self, he chose to cheat. He had a choice, but like most men, he was thinking with the wrong head.

Do you blame Gabrielle for her decision? She has the right to decide painfully or not, what's best for her life. Given the situation, Gabrielle just didn't want to have to compete for his love. Why should anyone have to? To deeply love someone, you must love them with your whole heart, mind and soul. To continue or go through a long-term relationship any other way, is a waste of time, a waste of your time and a waste of their time. Bryce was naturally disappointed, but Gabrielle believed she made the right decision. It just hurt more to let him go which threw her back into a very mild case of depression.

Three weeks before Christmas, Gabrielle's life was recycled back into her boring routine, go to work, come home, eat, watch TV and go to bed. She had only been out once with her girlfriends since the official breakup. Gabrielle seems to have found comfort in her dreams. She dreamed of Percy more and more. Sadly, her devotion to her nightly dreams was an acclimation, an adjustment she was securely becoming accustomed to, a little too well. One Thursday afternoon, Gabrielle took off work a couple of hours early. On that sunny and cold Thursday afternoon, she stopped by a market. Gabrielle likes when she can beat rush hour traffic. Too bad getting over a breakup was something she couldn't beat so easily. Even her short workday was mildly irritating. Celine Dion song "Where does my heart beat now" seems to catch Gabrielle on her drive home for the third day straight.

Taking a break from takeout, she decided to prepare dinner for herself. Cooking is however, relaxing. Gabrielle has never admitted to anyone that she's capable of arranging chef worthy meals, but she can dibble dabble eatable creations. Although the healing process was lazily inclined, Gabrielle was somehow getting use to not having Bryce in her life. She sometime wondered how he was handling the breakup. There was a magazine article in Ebony about getting over a failed relationship, but Gabrielle remembered she left the magazine in her car. She immediately grabbed her keys and before she could walk out the kitchen, her cell phone rings.

Gabrielle walks over to the kitchen counter and answers it. There didn't appear to be anyone on the line as the call failed. She searches the cell phone for the caller, but didn't find one. They'll call back, she thought heading out the door. As soon as Gabrielle closed her apartment door, the cell phone rings again. "Hello." she expressed.

"Good afternoon Gabrielle."

"Aaron hi, was that you trying to call a minute ago?" "Yes, bad connection."

"Hey it's been a while, where ya been?"

"I've been in the same city; routinely doing the same thing over and over that happily justifies my life."

Gabrielle took the stairs down to the first floor.

"How have you been?" asked Aaron.

"Ok I guess, Aaron, this really isn't a good time."

"Nonsense Gabrielle, I was thinking, how about you and I go for a drive?"

"Gee Aaron, I don't know. I mean, I just started preparing a meal. Today is not much of a good day."

"Gabrielle, this is Aaron you are speaking to. Carpe diem, that's Latin for, Seize the Day, in other words, live in the present. You don't need any more sympathy, just someone who cares. So just let go."

"You're breaking up, what?" "Just let go Gabrielle!"

Gabrielle had just walked out of her apartment building after Aaron's last statement, and there sat Aaron in his brand new Aston Martin automobile on his cell phone smiling. Gabrielle shook her head with a look of, I should have known expression on her face. She couldn't help but smile back.

Aaron was always there at the right time. He really knew Gabrielle like none of her girlfriends do. A good friend is like each breath you take, although it may seem insignificant, but each one is vital for dear life, so preserve them for safekeeping.

Aaron is Gabrielle's good friend. He is like a big brother lending his support. If reality meant a table for one, today didn't have to be that day. Gabrielle happily returned back up stairs to cancel her cooking plans then took off into a leisurely filled remaining afternoon.

They drove for miles talking and laughing, innocently passing time. The sun was casually melting into set as Aaron and Gabrielle cruised down the coast of Lakeshore. In the background, you could hear sounds of the radio, as a certain song played, that particular song, "Golden Time of Day" by Maze featuring Frankie Beverly. Naturally, as the two continued to enjoy each other's company, Gabrielle and Aaron ended up having dinner together. Sophisticatedly chilling at Rushmore restaurant on W Lake Street, they were perceived as old friends who have known each other all their lives. As they would have it, music was the current conversation of choice.

"So Gabrielle, tell me. What song would you say describes me? What song comes to mind?" Gabrielle hesitated uncertainly before a song and artist seem to jump into her head."

"I would have to say, "Peculiar Situations" by Earl Klugh." "Really, I can see that, I can see that."

"And how about me? What song and artist describes me?"

"Well Gabrielle, there are many I'm afraid, but the one that stands out the most, I would have to say, "Mermaid" by Sade."

"Oh I love Sade. That song is off her Love Deluxe CD right?" "You're absolutely right. So you know the song?"

"Of course, very mellow, very soothing. I can see that about me."

Aaron had just taken a swallow of wine before inquiring her first answer further. "Then what's so peculiar about me?" Gabrielle laughs at his question.

"Well you know Aaron; you're distinctive, different from the usual." "What's usual?"

"Hummm, uh if people were breakfast and the usual is eggs and ham, then you would be Green Eggs and Ham." Aaron laughs.

"Point justly taken."

Gabrielle takes a well deserving swallow of her wine before letting the moment settle tastefully into a dark subject.

"So have there been any leads in Ross's murder investigation?"

"I haven't heard anything. I did speak with detective Mackey, I believe." "Yes, that's his name. He is leading the investigation."

"I told him I spoke with Ross the same day he died."

"I still can't believe he's gone. Who would do something like that to him?"

"Well Gabrielle, it's hard to say. I believe the police next step was to investigate those New York based company and contractors."

"Ivy has done some investigating on them. Those New York corporate heads have very deep pockets and can be viciously lupine, but weren't desperately seeking that particular property. The Norwood Group has land development and shopping centers all over the country. Ivy doubts one failed shopping center expansion proposal is worth killing over."

"Well his untimely murder doesn't make sense. Why lynch him?"

"Maybe it was a copycat attempt stimulating from Stuart Elliott's murder, unless they are somehow connected."

"I don't see how Gabrielle, Ross was smart enough not to consult with such a schmuck." Gabrielle settles comfortably into a slightly vague and logical question.

"You wanna know what's surprisingly frightening?" "Is it what I think it is?"

"More than likely, you are in some way shape or form, were connectedly involved in both Stuart and Ross's lives and now both men are dead, murdered."

"I was waiting for you to connect the two, but allow me to say this. Ross Thomas was a good business acquaintance. Stuart Elliott I despised, but would never be stupid enough to stoop as low as to commit such an act."

"I know Aaron, but do you feel that someone is possibly trying to set you up." "Maybe I would, if I was charged with their murders, but why would anyone want to do that? I'm aware of my enemies."

"Aaron, you don't believe that. Everyone has enemies whether they are aware of them or not. Don't even get me started on Haters."

"Let them hate, but they should know it doesn't do them any good, only makes them look bad not to mention jealous."

"Actually Aaron, it's the aggressive and overly determined Haters that wish to do you harm physically or mentally."

"You sure do know plenty about enemies and haters." A small streak of anger quickly ran across Gabrielle's face.

"Aaron look at me, my skin complexion particularly. I've had my share of dark skin sista's hatred. Hey, I'm African-American too, just with a lighter shade of origin. They don't have to know me, just see my lightly colored face and immediately are drawn to dislike as if I had some special privilege in the choice."

"Gabrielle, you are not experiencing anything new that many African-Americans don't already go through with Caucasian perceptions of blacks."

"I am aware of that, but blacks shouldn't have to experience prejudice behavior from our own race. Fortunately, I've learned from my mother to over look people's jealous nature and smile."

"That's good advice to give."

"I guess my complexion wasn't light enough for Bryce."

"Alright Gabrielle, that will be quite enough. On to a happier subject. So are you looking forward to a nice Christmas?"

Gabrielle formed a somewhat sad expression.

"Well, two months ago I was, but since Bryce and I are no longer together, no not really."

"Don't let it get you down. It's just another day of the week; people are just inclined to exchange gifts."

"Yeah it sounds that simplistic, but it's something much more."

"If you set aside the traditional meaning, the birth of Christ and the festival of Kwanzaa, what's left is family, caring, sharing and giving." "Yes, something I'm slowly losing sight of."

"Are you finished eating Gabrielle?" "Yes."

"Good, let's get out of here before I put you back in the mood as I found you."

Aaron and Gabrielle rode out in search of a new mood altering change of scenery. They drove carefree cruising the open road just a little while longer before ending up at the movies. It's always nice to go for a long drive, it's especially pleasing for the passenger, you see much more of life. It also gives you the opportunity to let your mind find a secluded road of relaxing serenity. Toni Braxton song "Let It Flow" was playing on the radio on her ride home and as she listens to the words of the song, it was naturally making sense to Gabrielle. She looks over at Aaron and smiles, in which he gladly welcomed. It was at that very moment Gabrielle knew every little thing would be all right. As Aaron pulled into Gabrielle's apartment parking lot, a pair of envious eyes waiting in a parked car scoots down from the risk of being seen. He curiously observes the nature of Gabrielle and her guest association, drawing a close eye to Gabrielle especially.

"Well Aaron thank you for a lovely evening. You saved me from a possible disaster in the kitchen." Aaron laughs.

"I thought you said you can cook well enough to survive?"

"I did and can. Cooking is relaxing. I however, wasn't in a terrific mood earlier and sometimes meals can turn out accordingly."

"Well I'm glad you enjoyed yourself. We must do this again real soon." "Sure, as long as you drive, particularly this extravagant machine."

"So you're really feeling my new ride?" "Absolutely, in every luxurious way."

"Gabrielle, if you don't mind, would you tell me another song that comes to mind when you think of me?"

"Sure, may I ask why?"

"Just something gratifyingly nice to know."

Gabrielle thought for a few second with a warm smile on her face then replied her answer. "Well it just so happens that the song "Stand by Me" by Ben E. King comes to mind." Aaron breathes a hearty smile.

"I like that, I like that very much."

"And may I have another song from you please?"

"Of course, and given your situation, I gladly say, "Lean On Me" by Bill Withers." Gabrielle smiles approvingly.

"That's sweet, thanks Aaron, you're the best. Call you soon." "You're quite welcome. Goodnight Gabrielle."

"Goodnight."

As Aaron watched Gabrielle safely enter her apartment building and leaves, those envious eyes staring from the parking lot slowly evolves to anger. I doubt if Gabrielle knew that those angry eyes belonged to Bryce and that he was spying on her. Sometime later that night, both Gabrielle and Aaron thought of the songs expressed earlier that night. Gabrielle enjoyed her evening so much that her and Aaron hung out the next two weeks. They hung out so often, that Amber actually had to call Aaron and ask him to return their friend.

Christmas Eve night, while some families huddled close to a fire and other families just gathered together warmly to embrace the holiday spirit and share quality time as a family, Gabrielle sat at home alone with her cat Jack. Her sister begged her to come over and spent the evening with them, but Gabrielle just wanted to be alone to reflect, hoping the evening would pass posthaste. She did look forward to visiting her family later on Christmas day. It would be the first Christmas Eve ever, Gabrielle would spend alone. Last Christmas Eve, her and Bryce were in Aspen eating on Hickory House succulent ribs and sipping on pink champagne. Now she's faced with the reality of loneliness.

At first, she didn't want to be bothered with a Christmas tree, but soon found her change of heart worth the comforting effort. On that lonely Christmas Eve night, Gabrielle stared out her balcony window focusing heavily somewhere far far away. Her thoughts were eclectically unique like each snowflake that harmlessly fell to the earth, a gift of nature from God to purify acts of kindness. The city always seems so peaceful this time of the year, too bad statistics will prove otherwise.

As she sipped on spiked eggnog desperately trying to blend into the holiday season, Gabrielle realized that she now know the answer to an aged old blues question. Gabrielle can honestly say she now knows what the lonely do for Christmas. Regrettably, it's a depressing common reality that people one way or another may experience someday in their lives. Gabrielle is grateful for so much this holiday season, her health and each day above ground most importantly. She knows that there are other people and families going through worst situations than her problem of loneliness and when you think of others and give unconditionally from the heart, God rewardingly approves.

New Year's Eve 1999, the last evening before the new millennium, the thousandth anniversary, all month long the song 1999 by Prince played repeatedly over many radios stations to announce future turn of events. Many people were afraid of the Y2K bug, that computers would crash and wouldn't carry over to the new millennium. They say the Y2K virus was subject to ruin any and all electronic forms that would utilize human's contemporary way of life. People stocked up on everything from water to toilet paper, go figure. It was an exciting yet fearful time, but whatever happens, you didn't want to let this New Year's Eve pass you by because as life would have it, you were less likely to live and witness another end of a thousand year period.

Dateless, Gabrielle and Jillian, Amber and her husband Trey all spent New Years Eve on the New Year's Odyssey Cruise in Chicago. It didn't bother Jillian nor Gabrielle that they were dateless. It was a good time to be had by all. They just wanted to be apart of life's historical journey of events. These good friends sipped champagne and mingled appreciatively in a not too intoxicated friendly mood. When the ball did finally drop again and the clock struck twelve their time, they celebrated the new era stupendously. The new millennium was a time of diachronic change, resolutions, hope and new beginnings for all. Gabrielle optimistically looked forward to new beginnings, leaving all past heartaches, problems and worries behind. She faced the New Year head on, sincerely with a clear and genuine conscious. Hopefully, God willing, this will be a better year for Gabrielle. Once again, little did she know, Gabrielle was building castles in the sky.

CHAPTER THIRTEEN

New Millennium, New Face, New Friend

Comes a time every New Year that people will start anew, a fresh new beginning to be fulfilled by all. Humans make New Year's resolutions, which are nothing more than promises very few keep. Are people perceptive to determinative discipline? Well, that depends on their overwhelming will to acknowledge and obey ones own rule. Determinative discipline is however, what will be needed to accomplish any new years resolution goal. If you're not willing to devote one hundred and ten percent of your time, than don't take it too seriously. It's better to go through a new year happy with the idea of change, then to go through a new year grumpy from failed attempts.

Aaron James is a man that never felt the need to obligate himself to New Year's resolutions. Basically, he believed people will do whatever they want, whenever they want, when they see fit. His point, New Year's resolutions doesn't have to be designated at the birth of a new year to be beneficial to ones positive outlook. Aaron did consequently; believe in Hinduism and Buddhism, Hinduism particularly. Due to a curse placed on his family's life, he was perceptive to determinative discipline in Hinduism, the dominant religion of India.

On the first day of every New Year, Aaron visits a man of Hindu priesthood and have him re-bless his soul. This yearly ritual act is to preserve his life the entire year from karma, negative forces, or misfortune that may linger from the past year. Aaron isn't even one hundred percent sure of this potential curse, but has lost most of his family in death, enough haunting sorrow to seek out Hinduism powerful form of religion. Aaron is however, sure of voodoo or black magic. Voodoo positively exist as sure as the devil, in someway shape or form. Its dark omen is not to be taken lightly and to avoid at all cost.

9:45 am Saturday morning New Year's Day, Aaron was seen leaving the home of a Hindu priest. He meets with him the same time 9:00 am every New Year's Day. With his soul now safe, he is ready to go forth with the brand new millennium. Aaron was never the type to go out the night before to a New Year's Eve party or gatherings. He was aware of a hidden occurrence very few people know of. October 31 Halloween night, an evening observed for ghost and goblins to rise up and walk the earth. Believe it or not, New Year's Eve just so happens to portray the same image. Forget ghost and goblins or trick or treating and concentrate on the most evil form of spirits, deadly spirits walking the streets with an agenda to bring back as many souls with them as they can and they do. You usually read or hear about their victims the next day in the news. No, Aaron wasn't the New Year's Eve partying type. He rather stay at home and watch the ball drop with Dick Clark.

8:45 pm the first evening of a new year, Aaron receives an urgent call at home. "Hello."

"Brother James?"

"Yes Brother Hampton?" "We have a situation."

"What seems to be the problem?"

"A black man has been arrested, fallen victim to police brutality." "A Black Panther Member?"

"No, a local Chicago citizen, Charles Avery." "Where is he now Tyrone?"

"He's at the First District Police Station on State Street. They say he was severely beaten."

"Call Robert, have him meet us there."

Aaron hangs up and immediately makes a call. "Brother Ware?"

"Yes Brother James?"

"Get your men; have them meet me at the First Precinct on State Street as soon as possible. They are to bear arms along with their permits."

"Yes Brother James, we are on our way."

9:25 pm downtown at State Street First Precinct, Aaron enters the police station accompanied by Tyrone Hampton, the vice president of the Black Panther Party and Robert Lee, their attorney. Aaron spoke with the officer at the night desk. "May I help you gentlemen?"

"We are here to post bail for Charles Avery."

"Sorry, we have a hold on Mr. Avery. He is charged with driving under the influence, try back sometime tomorrow."

"Officer, what is your name?" asked Aaron. "Officer Randall."

"Officer Randall, this is Robert Lee, Mr. Avery's attorney. He will need to speak with his client at once."

Officer Randall asks another officer to escort Robert Lee to the holding cell and Robert Lee follows the officer, as Aaron continued to speak with Officer Randall concerning Charles Avery.

"We have reason to believe that Charles Avery sustained intensive injuries during his arrest and may need medical help."

"If he's in a holding cell, then he's fine." The officer replied uncooperatively. Just then, a night supervisor just transferring to this precinct from another state enters the lobby and asked can he be of assistances. "Yes Lieutenant Lewis, I am Aaron James and this is Tyrone Hampton and we are trying to post bail for Charles Avery, but there seems to be a problem."

"He has a hold sir, for driving under the influence." stated Officer Randall. "Then I'm afraid Mr. Avery will remain in our custody for a little while."

"Aaron!" their attorney shouted. "Yes Robert?"

"Mr. Avery is hurt bad. He needs a doctor."

"Now just a minute." stated the supervisor. "If he is in a holding cell he's-" "Lieutenant Lewis!" Officer Randall interrupts.

"What is it Randall?" "What year is it?"

"What do you mean what year is it?"

"I think you need to look outside sir."

Lieutenant Lewis turns around and stares out the entrance glass doors. Three hundred black men dressed in all black, from black coats to black boots standing in the streets and on the sidewalks, front and center of the police station. The Lieutenant looks back over at the two men before him.

"Now just who did you say you are again?"

"I am Aaron James, president of the New Generation Black Panther Party Organization; this is Tyrone Hampton, vice president and our attorney Robert Lee. Mr. Avery needs medical assistances immediately and my men won't move one step until he is taken to a hospital."

"Now wait just a damn minute, you don't have any authority here. You can't do this?" "I can and will, and if Mr. Avery isn't taken to a hospital right away, I will personally see to it that Internal Affairs and the FBI thoroughly investigate my written complaint that will be on the captain's desk in the morning and did I for get to mention my respectful friendship with the Mayor."

Lieutenant Lewis drew a very mean streak to Aaron demands. "Is that a threat Mr. James?"

"Don't take it as such; take it as a vow that may cost you your career."

"And I will tie this precinct up with so many liable lawsuits that they will carry over into the next millennium." stated Robert.

Lieutenant Lewis stares at Aaron and his attorney carefully then at the vice president. "Randall, call an ambulance for the prisoner and Mr. James you clear your men from outside this building right this minute."

"Of course, as soon as the ambulance arrives." Lieutenant Lewis walks off in anger.

10:15 pm at Cook County Hospital

"Which of you is Aaron James?" "That would be me doctor."

"I'm doctor Dupree. Mr. Avery is on his way to surgery. Good thing they brought him in when they did. He has a damaged spleen and internal bleeding. He wouldn't have lasted through the night."

"Thank you doctor, my attorney will need a written statement and medical report from you, when convenient."

"Sure thing, I can have a medical report ready on Monday. Your attorney can contact me then."

As the doctor walked away, Aaron turned to face his Black Panther members. "Tyron and Jasper, I want to meet sometime tomorrow to discuss plans for a police brutality protest. Robert, we need you to get the ball rolling and collect as much information you can regarding this incident."

Sunday January 2, 2000, 2:30 pm Black Panthers Urban Headquarters

"Tyrone what do we know so far?" asked Aaron.

"Mr. Avery was pulled over for a traffic violation. After he was pulled over, police had reason to believe Mr. Avery had been drinking which led to the arrest."

"Were there any witnesses to the arrest?"

"Yes, Mr. Avery's son was in the car with him and said cops got behind them and followed them for two blocks before they were pulled over."

"So racial profiling possibly?" asked Aaron.

"That may be the case, but Mr. Avery's son said that when his father refuse to take a breathalyzer test, that's when the incident occurred."

"How old is Mr. Avery's son Tyrone?" "Fifteen I believe."

"Good, he can stand as a witness."

"Aaron, I'm going to check with the hospital for Mr. Avery's blood alcohol level."

stated Robert.

"Robert, it seems as if Mr. Avery may have resisted arrest." replied Aaron.

"Yes, but anyway you look at it, its excessive force police brutality which could have cost this man his life. We will get more details when Mr. Avery regain conscience and is stable."

"Good, Jasper you get your men prepared for the up coming protest and Tyrone, you handle the necessary paper work needed for our records. I plan to speak to the Mayor tomorrow."

"You know Aaron, it's sad that the millennium has to start out this way."

"Yes Robert, but what's even sadder, is that decades, centuries, even millenniums may pass, but the ignorance of racism will always remain apart of this slowly evolving world."

Monday January 3, 2000, 10:17 am

Law Offices of Lambert, McGhee and Hewitt

Every office has one, you know, that certain employee that everyone seems to agree on undeniably. This individual may be one of Satan's little helper's that willingly spreads negative charisma among the work place with a sole purpose to try and promote him or herself to a securely legit position at the top. An older male associate with the firm casually strolls pass Ivy's office, but was commendably uplifted to stop and step back for small talk. Ivy did see the colleague go by and as he makes the few steps back to the opened door to her office, she tries to keep her opinions of him to herself.

"Knock knock." "Yes Blake?"

"Well it looks as if you've done it, you got what you wanted. I hear on good word that you landed the high-profile Walsh case."

"Yes that's correct. It was a surprise; I wasn't looking to represent him." "They say he asked for you personally. How does that make you feel?" "It actually makes me feel proud of my reputation."

The associate eagerly smiles before walking further inside Ivy's office. "I say he did it, he killed his wife."

"Mr. Walsh is entitled to the best defense his money can provide Blake." "If you pull this case off, you're sure to make partner."

Ivy gives an abrupt expression.

"Excuse me Blake, but I've never had to pull off any case. I represent the innocent and only the innocent."

"Of course, but can your friend Mr. Johnnie Cochran say the same for his client OJ Simpson?"

"What exactly is your problem Blake? Is it that I was chosen to represent this case or that I will most likely make partner before you will, or maybe it's all black people."

Blake gives a brief candid smile.

"I wasn't aware I had one, of many."

"I know you have acquired more years here with this firm, but I've allowed my experience and hard work to carry me to my status. My lips are allergic to kissing ass."

"So now all of a sudden I kiss ass?"

"That's just one of your admiring qualities."

"By all means, please tell me more, off the record of course."

Ivy gladly accepts the invitation.

"Well Blake, in case you haven't fully had the chance to adjust the inevitable fact, with your almost white passable complexion and all, you're African-American too and just because you spend your time sucking up to the partners with leisurely lunches than actually pulling some weight around here, doesn't exactly makes you a shoe in for partner."

"I made my mark here while you were still in high school. I help build this firm to their remarkable status."

"That's right, but you got comfortable too soon. Your good will toward others became discriminatory and your eyes would descend to green from envy."

"Is that so?"

"Yes Blake, you thought your creditable past history with the firm and backstabbing, brown nosing attempts to bring other associates down was the key to unlocking the door to partnership. Everyone is aware of your treacherous; wanna be white, uppity ass."

"Now just wait just a minute!" Ivy stands from her seat.

"No, you just hold on. I admit, you do your share around here regardless what others say, but out of the twenty-six members of this firm, only three members are African-American. Blacks are always quick to say that whites try to keep us down, when actually, it's our own race that keeps us down."

"I am proud of my race and I can not speak for every black person of this nation." "You know Blake, I hope when I get to be fifty years old, that I have made a real difference in this firm and yes, it's more than likely I will make partner, but what you have to ask yourself is, will you be willing to work with me or against me, because I'm not going anywhere anytime soon."

The colleague associate calmly draws a counterfeit smile with an everything is everything composure.

"Hey, we're all friends here Ivy. You are always in my best interest. No harm no foul."

"Well I'm glad to hear that Blake."

"You say you represent the innocent and only the innocent." "That's correct."

"Well their all innocent until proven guilty and the district attorney is guaranteeing a conviction. He's willing to bet his next term in office and that's on the record." Ivy stares at Blake suspiciously.

"Is that right?"

"Yes, so good luck with that. I'm sure Lambert, McGhee and Hewitt has no worries and all faith in their star, but you let me know Ivy if I can be of any assistance."

The associate slowly dissolves his smile before leaving, as employees outside her office resume the act of pretending to work. Ivy sits back down in her seat and cautiously absorbes the free information.

"Yeah, I'm sure his version of being of any assistances, is a machete waiting in the wind."

Tuesday January 4, 2000, 11:50 am Downtown Chicago

Pumping vigorously strong from the heart of the civil right movement, with a steady flow within the arteries of the black power movement, to the fist of the black power salute from the Black Panther Party for Self Defense, this non-violent police brutality protest march takes place. Bravely disregarding Chicago's deep freeze and non-compassionate frigid weather, hundreds of barricaded spectators and voluntary participants would witness this event, while others took part of the New Generation Black Panthers Party protest march. Supporters and non-supporters, common visitors from around the way, the homeless to the junkies, thugs, pimps, hoes and winos were also present, along with ordinary citizens and hundreds of Chicago finest to keep the protest peaceful.

It was a news media frenzy for the best story, interviews and live coverage of the event. Justifiably leading this protest march were Aaron James, his vice president, Tyrone Hampton, their attorney, Robert Lee and Charles Avery's family. Marching faithfully behind them were four hundred New Generation Black Panther Party associates. Leading his strong group of men out front with a sharp alacrity is chief of security, Jasper Ware. The Black Panthers protest march started from the First Precinct on State street to City Hall on N. LaSalle street where the march was concluding after Aarons powerful speech. A news reporter from WBBM TV was the first from the mob of reporters to question Aaron after his speech.

"Dr. James, what is the purpose of today's march?"

"Our views are expressed accordingly. This is a statement to advise minority citizens of the misconduct and violent acts of hostility generated from predominately white police officers that still carries forth from the past, but most importantly to put an end to racial profiling and police brutality, that their excessive force practices are unacceptable."

A burst of questions erupts from the reporters.

"Professor James, does the New Generation Black Panthers Party Organization express anti-police behavior tactics from the past?"

"The New Generation Black Panther Party Organization is not against law enforcement officers. We are anti-police brutality and racial injustices if anything. Gun battles with the police from the past are not what we represent, although we reserve our right to bear arms legally. We are still sincere in wanting to help the black community."

Another burst of questions erupts from the crowd of reporters.

"Dr. James, was this protest march influenced by past incidents of this nature, particularly the death of your brother Percy James?"

"Charles Avery was fortunate, my brother was not, but the heart of this police brutality protest stimulates from all past injustices of law enforcement."

The crowd of reporters expedited another round of questions, but Aaron humbly stated he was not accepting any more questions. The chief of police who was standing beside Aaron steps up to the podium and the crowd of reporters flooded him with questions. The chief of police kindly ignored their questions and made a brief statement.

"All law enforcement officials are working diligently under fair cooperation polices to get this matter resolved. The two officers involved are on paid leave pending a thorough investigation. If a crime has been committed, justice will be served swiftly. Thank you."

The chief of police walked away as the crowd of reporters continues to voice more questions concerning the incident and protest.

Somewhere in Peoria Illinois, a phone call is taking place. "Hey Mitch, is Mark there?"

"Yeah Patrick hold on." "What is it Patrick?"

"Mark are you watching TV right now?" "Yes I'm aware of the protest march."

"Do you believe this nigger, who the fuck is this spook?"

"Don't worry yourself over that boy. He's a parvenu nigger, one that wishes to make a historical mark in the world by means of establishing a powerful black presence among his race. His agenda or so-called purpose is to revolutionize a replica of strong influential voices of the past, through men such as Malcolm X, Huey Newton and Martin Luther King Junior. He's nothing, left over's if anything."

"I thought those Black Panther niggers ended in the seventies?"

"They pretty much did. This nigger and a growing number of other states represent the New Generation Black Panther Party Organization. Aaron James is what Malcolm X, Huey Newton, and Martin Luther King Jr. all have in common."

"They're all niggers?" "They're all dead niggers."

The cousin laughs.

"So are you giving me permission to whack this fool?"

"No, Aaron James is already dead in my eyes. Be patient, these types of trouble makers tend to take themselves out."

"Well I don't like him and I want him dead."

"I've had my eye on this boy for a while. I too am becoming a bit restless of his kind, but willing to remain patient a little longer. If his weak agenda escalates into our priorities, I will personally give you a call."

"Well, my patience is about as secure as quicksand." "Patrick!"

"What?"

"Just remember, I call the shots around here, okay."

"Hey lighten up cousin, I wouldn't dream of having it any other way."

That night, Gabrielle caught bits of Aaron protest march on the ten o'clock news. She was pleased to know that Aaron was successfully administrating human rights, fighting the good fight, something he enjoyed expressing any day of the week, including holidays. The first week of the new millennium went by in a hurry. It was Friday before anyone could finish washing their face for Wednesday. The first happy hour girl's night out of the New Year was held at the House of Blues with musical guess Rodney Jones, a soul-jazz guitarist. It was a refreshing change from the norm and it kept the girls out later than usual. Gabrielle was awaken around 8:30 the next morning by a phone call. A sleepy voice answers the call.

"Hello."

"Good morning Gabrielle."

"Hi dad, when did you get back to Chicago?"

"Last night, Happy New Year Millennium my dear." "Thanks, same to you." She clears her throat.

"It's early, did I wake you?"

"No, I needed to get up anyway."

"Did you receive my Christmas present?"

"Yes, thank you, I love it. I love 18th century black impressionism work." "Well good, I'm glad, I was wondering what you were doing a little later?" "Around what time?"

"Oh around 2:30 or 3:00 pm." "Nothing until later on, why?"

"I wanted to know if you could stop by the studio?" "Sure, I can do that. I'll see you then."

"Good, see you then."

Since Gabrielle no longer had a date on Saturday nights and Amber husband was out of town, Gabrielle and her two best friends planned to go out again tonight. They planned on having dinner first at the Cheesecake Factory restaurant. Gabrielle arrived at her fathers studios around 2:45 that afternoon. She hasn't seen him in about six months due to concert dates. Every time Gabrielle sees her father, that along with looking in the mirror, she is reminded of his Creole descent, a major contributor to her light skin complexion. She doesn't blame him though, we are what we are.

"There's my girl."

"Hi dad." A tender hug is given. "How's the medical world?"

"Good, proud sponsor of my occupation." "Wonderful, you look great."

"Thanks, so do you."

"Good for a fifty-four year old I guess. Come on in here, there's some guest I

would like for you to meet."

Gabrielle walked with her father further inside the studio and couldn't believe her happily ecstatic eyes. "Oh my goodness, no way."

Phillip Michaels proudly put his arm around his daughter and introduces her to a couple of well-known jazz musicians.

"Fella's I would like you to meet my daughter Gabrielle."

Herbie Hancock and Herb Alpert both spoke and shook Gabrielle's hand. "I can't believe this, I'm a big fan of you both."

"So you are the legendary GABRIELLE that put your father on the map?" asked Herbie Hancock.

"Well my dad only borrowed my name. The real masterpiece is in the music." Her father was pleasantly surprised at Gabrielle's response.

"Listen to her; did I mention Gabrielle's is a doctor?"

"Yes, along with what university she attended and what hospital she currently practices medicine." said Herb Alpert with a smile. Gabrielle was flattered.

"So what's the special occasion?" asked Gabrielle?

"Well these talented men just so happen to be working in collaboration on my seventh album."

"That's great dad, any titles in mind?"

"You didn't hear this from me, said Herbie Hancock jokingly, but GABRIELLE part II seems to settling over the cover." Gabrielle was breathlessly surprised again. "Is this true dad?"

"Maybe, with your blessing of course." "Absolutely, I'm honored."

Phillip Michaels pulls Gabrielle close to his side and kisses her forehead. "No, I'm honored."

After genuinely socializing with her fathers guest, Gabrielle left his studio with signed copies of his guest CD's. Gabrielle still had some time before meeting her friends and thought she would stop by a record store to up date her collection.

As Gabrielle browsed through the Hip-Hop section of CD's, she wasn't aware of it at first, but she had an alluring admirer. The would be admirer, didn't anticipate encountering such a kind spirit. He was for the most, having a cloudy day. In fact, the song "Another Saturday Night" by Sam Cook was playing repeatedly inside his head just before Gabrielle walked in the record store, but when his eyes were drawn to her, a different tune came to mind. "Summertime Madness" by Kool N the Gang, seemed to wash ashore on to his thoughts.

When Gabrielle did finally look up from the CD's and caught the gentleman's gaze, she dismissed it. It was a hiccup, an uncontrollable reaction to a brief moment, but as she moved over to reach for the Outkast CD and glanced his way again, she caught the gentleman staring once more. She ignored him at first and picked up the CD anyway. Gabrielle immediately went into thinking mode. She began to question herself in thought. "Is he staring at me?" She looks his way again and the guy looks up from the Alternative music section and smiles. Gabrielle smiles then looks back down at her selection of CD's and resumed her thinking mode in thought. "He was staring at me. He's cute. I wonder, Na, never mind. Oh shoot! He's making his way over here. Maybe I should take the CD's and run. No, he'll think I'm nuts. Oh God, two seconds before approximation!"

"Hi there." Gabrielle turns to face her admirer.

"Hello." she said softly. "Gracious, he has lovely eyes." she thought.

"I hope you don't mind me coming over to speak. I watched you enter the store and found you defining." Gabrielle laughs quietly in moderation.

The gentleman looks around with a curious smile. "What?" he asked.

"I'm sorry, that's original." "What's original?"

"Was that your best pick up line?" she asked. He finally gets the humorous moment.

"Oh I see, you believe this is a pick up line." "So are you saying that wasn't one?"

"No, not really. When I observe someone strangely fascinating as yourself, I inquire, like one would be drawn to a painting. Hi, I'm Malcolm, Malcolm Reid." He offers his hand.

Gabrielle slowly reaches over and shakes his hand gently. "I'm Gabrielle."

"Hello Gabrielle, actually I watched you enter the store and head straight over to the Jazz section. That's something unusual for someone so young."

"Well I am a lover of all music especially contemporary Jazz." "Really, do you mind?" He looks over at her choices.

"Jonathan Butler, Chris Botti good choices, Rick Braun and oh I see you also have Outkast, great Jazz duet."

Gabrielle laughs innocently.

"What, isn't Outkast legendary Jazz artists?"

"No actually, not unless they have crossed over without the Hip-Hop nation knowing about it."

"You have a lovely smile." "Thank you, Malcolm is it?" "Yes, that's right."

"And your choices?" Gabrielle peeks over at his CD's choices.

"David Sanborn, Pearl Jam. I'm familiar with them both." "Really?"

"Yes, and I doubt Pearl Jam would be considered contemporary Jazz. Now if you will excuse me, I must be going."

"How old are you? If you don't mind me asking?" "Twenty-six and you?"

"Oh, I'm old, thirty-two."

"Only if you believe you are, you don't look like you're in your thirties." "Why thank you."

"Now that you know I'm old enough to buy this parental advisory Outkast CD, I think I will check out now."

"I'm sorry; I didn't mean to crowd you."

"No problem." Gabrielle turns to walk away. "Maybe we could have lunch sometime?"

Gabrielle stops and gives an unlikely expression before turning around.

"You're joking right?" she asked.

"Why do you ask that?" He appears a little confused.

"Because you're wearing a wedding band." He looks at his left hand. "Oh, forgive me. I'm not married, I'm-"

"Sure you're not."

"I'm a widower actually, breast cancer, haven't had the heart to remove it." Gabrielle felt a little bad. A sense of sympathy fell over her.

"I'm sorry. The ring, I assumed-"

"It's ok; maybe we can discuss it over dinner?" "Sorry, I actually have plans."

"How about lunch tomorrow then?"

"Look, I don't think this is a good idea. I just got out of a relationship, plus you and I aren't exactly compatible."

"Does my race offend you?"

"No, I've dated outside my race before."

"So do I have permission to contact you?"

For reasons unknown, Gabrielle stared at the gentleman inquisitively, compelled with a strangely unaccustomed attraction of cognition. She gives a clever smile. "Sure, I will gladly take your number, if you can tell me the names of the two artist of Outkast?" A few minutes later Gabrielle was checking out and Malcolm was writing his number down. Gabrielle agreed to call him later and both went their separate ways. He went one way and she another, but both had particular songs on their minds. They were complementing songs with meaning, for Malcolm, it was "Wrapped Around Your Finger" by The Police and for Gabrielle; it was "Beautiful Stranger" by Madonna.

It was around 7:30 that evening when Gabrielle met Amber at the Cheesecake Factory restaurant. Jillian was running late as usual. Gabrielle and Amber were seated in a booth and were making small talk. Bragging helplessly, Gabrielle was eagerly inclined to inform Amber about her VIP guest pass to meet Herbie Hancock and Herb Alpert. After getting sociably comfortable with their drinks, Gabrielle was about to share with Amber her strange encounter with a new face, when in walks the end to a lovely evening. Amber looks up and gives a distasteful stare.

"Don't look now, but guess who's coming to dinner?"

Gabrielle placed her drink down and turns around. She watched the hostess seat a couple two booths over from them. Bryce and Dr. Lyndon just so happens to be that couple. Naturally, unhappiness draped across Gabrielle face before turning back around to face Amber.

"Of all places, I can't believe he would be here with her." said Gabrielle.

"Well it was bound to happen sooner or later and now at least you know he was never yours in the first place."

Amber, one to never hold her tongue or allow her best friend to suffer more humiliation, stands up and walks over to the couple. Gabrielle quickly tried to stop her, but Amber kindly ignored her.

"Hello Fido, aren't you going to introduce me to your new lady?

My bad, she couldn't possibly be new since you've been sleeping with her all along." Hiding behind a menu, that was Gabrielle cue to get up and stop her friend from charges of disorderly conduct.

Bryce rolls his eyes before placing his menu on the table.

"Amber, we are not in the mood for this mess. This is a public place, if you didn't know." Jennifer agreed.

"That's right; we would like to be left alone." Amber looks over at his date.

"Girl, didn't your mother teach you manners, speak when spoken to."

Bryce steps out from the booth as Gabrielle comes over and grabs Amber by the arm. "Amber let's just go." Gabrielle whispered.

"Hell no, we were here first, let them leave." Dr. Lyndon shakes her head pitifully.

"I see why most black men run to white women."

Amber turned around so fast, that her soul joined her two seconds later. Bryce steps in front of Dr. Lyndon. He knows a sista well.

"Let's get something straight, I am not as nice as Gabrielle and I will whoop your bony ass all over this restaurant!"

Amber began taking off her earrings. "Amber please." whispered Gabrielle. "Would you just leave." stated Bryce.

"I have plenty of bail money saved up for myself to use on my husband, but I don't mind using some of it to beat your ass."

The manager comes over and asks if there's a problem.

"No, replied Bryce. We were just leaving." "That's right, you do that." Amber suggested.

Jennifer gets up and grabs her purse, but Amber wasn't going to allow her to leave that easily. "Oh by the way Jennifer, as far as black men running to white women, well all men have their own preferences and I can understand why Bryce took a interest in you. You're half sheep, half Shih Tzu right?"

Bryce grabs Jennifer's hand and continued to walk away. "Nice Amber, real classy." voiced Bryce shamefully.

"I bet you wish you were one of those black sheep's huh Jennifer? Baa baa black sheep, have you any wool? Yes sir, yes sir three bags full."

Gabrielle apologizes to the manger before walking away. "See ya Fido, baa baa bitch."

"Excuse me ma'am?" said the manager. Amber turns around.

"What, we cool, just needed to clear up some bad weather that's all."

The manager walks away to apologize to a few guest and makes small talk. Amber looks around at the people staring at her. "What ya'll looking at? Come back tomorrow, same time for part two of when the shit hit's the fan." Gabrielle hurries back over and grabs Amber by the arm, and pulls her along with her back to their booth. "What? I was using my indoor alley voice." vowed Amber.

Luckily the restaurant wasn't as crowded and only one couple got up to leave. Ten minutes later Jillian arrived and sees the stressful look on Gabrielle face. "Amber, what you do now?" she asked. Despite the drama appetizer, Gabrielle and her two friends stayed and tried to salvage what was left of a swell evening. The three friend's next stop was at the House of Blues once again with special musical guest, Patti Austin. When Gabrielle did arrive home, it was twenty minutes after midnight. After running into the ex tonight, Gabrielle was touched with a small form of depression vapors, but those sad vapors would soon clear up. When Gabrielle walked over by her bar, ready to pour herself a drink, she found Malcolm's number. It was now twenty minutes until one and she wondered was it too late to call him. After three attempts, she finally allowed the call to go through. "Hello." said a not so sleepy voice on the other end.

Eleven o'clock the next day Gabrielle and Malcolm met for brunch at Jane's, a cozy little house on W. Cortland Street. Gabrielle was speaking with the hostess when she looked over out into the restaurant. She spots him and Malcolm waves. Gabrielle waves back as she follows the hostess to his table. Malcolm stands when his guest arrives.

"Hi there."

"Hi Malcolm." He pulls her chair out and they both take their seats. "How do you do that?" he asked.

"Do what?" she asked curiously.

"Control the sun." Gabrielle smiles briefly.

"Ok, I agreed to meet you and eat some form of a meal with you. You can stop the flattery."

"No, seriously. If you remember, yesterday it was mostly cloudy and while browsing in the record store, I just so happen to notice the suns favoritism to finally show its face, moments before you walked into the store."

"Come on now Malcolm." she blushingly insist.

"Really, you walked in with this aureole, heavenly rays of the sun shimmering upon you. My eyes followed you over to the Jazz section, one of my favorite loves, art and wine are my other loves. Right then, I was compelled to know you."

Gabrielle sat there with a half-drawn smile thinking, man what have you been smoking this morning?

"Ok Gabrielle, I admit it sounds a little far-fetched, but seriously once again, I was waiting for you to arrive. It was cloudy this morning right?" "Yes, I believe so."

"Ok, while sitting here, I noticed the sun was raising one eye open and I looked up front and there you stood with a beautiful smile."

Gabrielle looked over and out the closest window near by. Sure enough, the sun was on the verge of jutting out to warmly express itself. A server comes over to take their beverage order.

"I will have a cappuccino and a glass of ice water please." "And you sir?"

"That sounds good, make that two."

"You look nice and warm. Tell me Gabrielle, have you been here before?" "Thank you, no, not for brunch actually."

Gabrielle stares into his stumbling blue eyes then observes his facial features. Malcolm is clean cut with light brown hair and smooth shaved skin. He has a dimpled chin, perfect teeth, nice smile, an average size nose and thin lips, distinctively handsome for a white man.

"I didn't mean to call you so late, but I did promise to call you later." "I'm glad you called. I thought I would never see you again."

"This actually, is a great little place for dates." Gabrielle gladly shared. "Really, I haven't heard."

"Are you from Chicago?"

"Springfield, Illinois originally, born and raised. For the last ten years Orange County California has been my home."

"Oh really, what brought you back to Illinois?"

"Well, I've been in Chicago for a week now because of a temporary job opening. My wife died a year ago and I guess I needed a change of scenery."

"What is your occupation?" "Would you like to Guess?"

Gabrielle gave a nervous smile.

"Let me see, I'll say you are an architect."

He smiles. "Honestly, I look like an architect?" "Maybe, I know, are you a doctor?"

"No, maybe if I were, I could have somehow helped my wife." He appeared a little grief-stricken.

"I'm sorry."

"Don't be, guess again." He resumed his smile. "Gee, I don't know."

"Here's a hint, one of my favorite loves."

Gabrielle thought for a second before giving her answer. "You teach Art."

"No, but close. I am the Director of the Art Institute of Chicago, on S. Michigan Ave."

"Really, I wouldn't have guessed it. That's great."

The server returns with their coffee and takes their light food order before leaving.

"And you Gabrielle, what's your profession?" "Would you like to guess?"

"Sure, I would say you are an investment banker." "Really?" she said with a smile.

"Yes." he said confidently. "No."

"Then my final guess would be that you are a nurse. I believe you like helping others."

"Close, I'm a doctor of oncology."

Malcolm sits his cappuccino down and stares at Gabrielle impressionably inspired with admiration.

"Are you really?"

"Yes, going on my fifth year residency."

"That's amazing, very unexpectedly refreshing to know."

"Thanks, I'm dedicated in every way possible, not only that, we share something in common."

Malcolm looked curiously intrigued. "What's that?"

"We both have lost someone close to us to breast cancer." Malcolm eyes once again appeared amazingly surprised. "Really, who have you lost, if you don't mind me asking?" "No, not at all. My mother. I was thirteen when she died." "Gabrielle I'm sorry, were you close?"

"For the limited years gratefully cherished, yes." "Good memories I hope?"

"Well, it doesn't bring much comfort to dwell on the moments of suffering." "Yes, I soon found out."

Gabrielle takes a sip of her coffee before continuing.

"My sister told me the moment our mother died that, it's always the ones with the weakest yet most precious hearts that are taken away. Their hearts were so weak because they fought so hard to give all their love and strength to their love ones so that they may carry on."

Malcolm's face expression softens. He looked at Gabrielle tenderly as if she was an angel sent from the heavens.

"Thank you Gabrielle. I needed that." They both smiled to uplift the moment.

"This is amazing Gabrielle, maybe our encounter wasn't a coincidence." "I don't know about that, but everything seems to happen for a reason."

"Well Gabrielle Michaels, I believe this is the beginning of a beautiful friendship in progress and I would be honored to know more of you."

"Friendship in progress, I can see that. I would like that."

The server had returned with their food order. As Malcolm and Gabrielle talked soul to soul whole-heartedly, they found themselves charmed, enchanted and captivated by one another. He made her smile and she appreciated that a lot. All the while they were getting acquainted, Gabrielle felt tremendously grateful to have found a new friend.

CHAPTER FOURTEEN

Margarita Night

Margarita night was originally a book club, but so many race issues kept popping up that it pushed the book right off the coffee table and out the door.

Before you assume, it's not what you think. It isn't as if they get together just to talk about white people. There are some important issues involved in these discussions. To speak of the other race was something virtually no way around it. It's like getting out for the day and not running into or seeing one entire person. It's possible, and if you can, please tell me which side of the moon do you live on?

Besides, it's not like white folks don't sit around and have the same type of discussions about black folks. Hell, they probably host dinner parties for their discussions. Honestly, there's no real truth to the matter, but who's to say I'm wrong. Actually, the only group of white people that are known to sit around and speak ill of blacks and other so-called minority's, are the Ku Klux Klan and skinheads. The difference between margarita night and prejudice types of organizations, is that margarita night doesn't involve Hate. For the most part, it's just talk, another small function that meets every couple of months or so, on Thursday nights.

The book of the month still manages to pop up through out the evening, for those who got a chance to read it, that is until the card games begins. Tonight's margarita night is held at Amber's place over in Batavia off Martin Lane and although Amber tends to take some of the topics personally, she manages to keep a cool head. Margarita night is just a small group of young professional black woman voicing their opinions on certain issues, sipping on margaritas with a whole lot of stereotyping going on.

"And when I saw that story on the news, I knew it had to be a white person because no black person ever felt the need to climb a damn mountain."

That remark was from Carman, one of Amber's associates who works at her office. At this time, a card game is going on. Jillian is always the only one who manages to bring her copy of the novel just in case a real discussion came up. "Oh I'll climb one alright, put a million dollars at the top of that mountain and I will go buy the right boots." That would be Jasmine; she's on paid administrative leave from the University of Chicago. She's having race relations problems with her coworkers. Apparently some of her white colleagues don't like to see a sista doing well for herself. Would you believe one of her white colleagues took it upon themselves to call her a nigger to her face at work? Now why she wanna go and do that, huh? Jasmine was about to get fists of fury wild up in that place. Jasmine did manage to remain professional, but when it was all said and done, Jasmine was the one sent home on paid administrative leave. There is a racial discrimination lawsuit pending.

"Jasmine girl, you will climb any mountain if you thought a good black man was waiting at the top." Amber replied.

"You damn right, because a Good Black Man is hard to find."

"Well it wouldn't matter anyway because once you make it to the top, there will be some white heifer sitting there who has already snatched him up."

Tationna made that comment. She's an RN at the same hospital emergency room where Bryce works. Tationna's brother is married to a white woman.

"Well all I want to know is, how she got up there so fast?" asked Gabrielle. Amber was more than happy to answer that.

"Girl you know a sista always has to struggle to climb to the top and by the time we make it there, some white hoe has flew up there in a damn private jet and their ass are up there eating lobster and sipping on champagne."

Everyone laughed at Amber's statement, which sparked a response from Jillian. "If that's the case, then don't limit your odds. Give yourself the same opportunities the other race would have. If she takes a private jet then you take a helicopter." The ladies all agreed except Amber.

"Well we would Jillian, but we would have to apply for a bank loan for that helicopter purchase and you already know the odds of blacks obtaining a bank loan. You have a better chance in winning the lottery."

"Amen to that!" said Jasmine. "You ain't lying." stated Carman.

"Do we even have black pilots?" asked Tationna.

"Like Oscars, very few, replied Amber, but at least we get a free toaster for coming in and applying."

Gabrielle kindly shook her head with a smile. She had very little to say tonight. Maybe her limited conversation involvement was due to the fact that she has been socializing heavily with a member of the opposite race. Would it offend her friends that she have been communicating with the other race? Does it matter that her and Malcolm have an intense bond that ties them together? Would it matter that her and Malcolm could possibly become involved in a relationship? The answers to these questions is yes. Gabrielle and Malcolm could be sister and brother from a different mother, but the main issue of conflict would be that, one person is black and the other is white.

That Sunday after Gabrielle and Malcolm enjoyed brunch at Jane's, they went on to have lunch together Monday, Wednesday, and today. This was more than convenient for them both because they worked in the same geographical region. They also plan on having lunch together Friday. The two got along well, a little too well. They talked every night sometimes very late. Gabrielle did advise Malcolm that Friday nights are reserved for girl's night out, but he looked forward to their first official evening engagement Saturday night. It wasn't for certain, if it would be an actual date. One thing for certain, Gabrielle has been happier than she have been in a while. What bothers Gabrielle the most, is that she haven't shared her newfound friend with Amber or Jillian, but feels that Jillian would be more understanding.

Yes, Gabrielle contributes her share of participation to margarita night as often as needed, but didn't dare speak of Malcolm. In fact, she thought about Malcolm so often that she allowed her daydreams to remove her from the social setting. "Gabrielle hello, it's your play" said Jasmine.

"What? Oh ok."

"Girl I hope you haven't had too much to drink because I'm not taking your behind home." stated Amber.

"I'll take you home, if you need me to Gabrielle." offered Jillian. "Guys I'm not tipsy." Gabrielle replied.

"Ahh there goes Trey calling. Let me get that." Amber gets up from the table to go answer her home phone.

"Hello sweetheart." There was silence on the other end of the phone.

"Hello, hello!" she demanded. The person on the other end finally spoke up. Amber turns her back to the ladies and walks to another part of her home.

"This is not a good time, what? I don't know. I will have to call you back."

Amber thoughtfully brings in another pitcher of margarita. "Trey ready to come home Amber?" asked Gabrielle.

"Oh uh, wrong number. Margarita refills anyone?" "Over here waitress." said Carman.

"Who would like to be the first to share their latest racial bias encounters?' asked Tationna.

"I would." volunteered Jasmine.

"Would anyone like to discuss the novel? I have my copy with me."

"Maybe a little later Jillian. Girls would you believe Walgreens had someone following me around in the store like some secondary precaution as if I was going to steal something."

"You too Jasmine, the same thing happened to me." stated Tationna.

"Hell, as if all the security cameras zoomed in on every black person in the store wasn't good enough." Jasmine added.

Gabrielle receives a call on her cell phone and answers it immediately.

"Hello. Oh hi, yes kinda, I'm attending a book club meeting tonight remember? No problem, so I will call you a little later, ok bye."

It was Malcolm.

"Who was that?" asked Amber being nosy. "Oh just my dad."

Gabrielle hated to lie, but now was not the time to let the home girls know about her dear white friend. She know she will eventually tell her friends about Malcolm, just not anytime tonight.

Meanwhile 8:45 pm at a police station downtown Chicago, Detective John Mackey along with three other detectives were discussing unsolved murder cases, two were main cases that were day by day turning colder. Loosen ties, unbutton collars and pulled up sleeves were the results of a ten hour shift already put in today. They dined on Pepto-Bismol worthy takeout and sipped on potentially stale, indigestible, pancreas dissolving coffee for the most part of the evening. The non-dairy coffee creamer is complimentary perks of the job and if used correctly, it could enhance the coffees cruddy taste.

Up on a board in a privately confined room to themselves was a picture of Stuart Elliot with very little information pertaining to the case and on the right side of that board is a picture of Ross Thomas, also with very little information pertaining to his case. Between both pictures is a picture of Aaron James with plenty of information. Detective Mackey is the lead detective in Ross Thomas murder investigation and seem to be catching the most heat about it, yet all the detectives in the room appeared a little burned out over stress related cases. The black people of Chicago hasn't been in much harmony over Ross Thomas unsolved death which keeps humanity divided and on the edge of potential riot disaster.

It isn't much help to them when the media and newspapers speculate and try to do their jobs for them. Some of the news latest predictions linked the two unsolved murders together while portraying a potential serial killer. Race related and bad blood between the two cases were also a factor of motive. A major tumor of a headache is what detective Mackey has had since the investigation has begun and he knows no over the counter medication, prescription drug, or surgery will make the headaches subside. He needs to close this case and so far, they still have no tangible leads.

"Alright men, I know we've been working other cases, but let's refresh our memory on a couple of high priority cases. First subject, Stuart Elliott is a forty-three year old Caucasian male defense attorney. He was found hanging dead in his home by his housekeeper. Due to his lovely Condo location, he is pretty much out of our jurisdiction. Subject two, Ross Thomas, a 29-year-old African-American Human Resources Manager at Northwestern University Hospital and business man, he was also found dead hanging in his apartment over in Mount Greenwood. So what makes these two different murders relevant?"

"Both men were found hung. Same death sentence, different variables?"
"What are the variables separating the two?"

"Thomas was found hanging with his hands tied behind his back. Elliott was not. Elliott was hung with some type of cable wire and Thomas was hung with a thick fiber rope."

"And that's pretty much all the information given on Elliott. So what do we know for certain Pearson?"

"Different M O, different killers." "Possible, what are your thoughts Carter?"

"That Elliott and Thomas may have known each other, possibly did business together and when Elliot ended up dead, Thomas's death may have been payback."

"Likely, and we can't rule out any theories."

"John, we seem to be going in circles with Ross Thomas case. Twenty-First Precinct leads Elliott's investigation and don't see the two cases as one. Aaron James, this Black Panther Activist was the last person to speak with Thomas the day he was murdered. Aaron James did contribute money to Project Hope. Maybe he needed the money back and Thomas refused."

"What was the actual amount of the donation Watts?"

"1.2 million and I hear through an informer that James is the prime suspect in Elliott's murder case."

"1.2 million, w h e w! Maybe I should start my organization and beg for donations. Both are very good points, but James has a solid alibi during the time of Ross Thomas death. All we can do is work our case and let Twenty-First Precinct work theirs. They do however; have a few tangible suspects for Elliott's case. We on the other hand have possibly one. Carter, what's the word on the streets?"

"Nothing! Not a goddamn word. We also checked our leads on those New York developers and didn't find a high or creditable worthy motive."

"The whole city has spoken and is in an up roar about Thomas's death claiming hate crime, stirring up mix views." replied detective Pearson.

"And that's what we don't need." stated detective Mackey. "The captain has been chewing my ass out about this case, more now due to this police brutality investigation."

"Cops didn't kill Thomas." stated Carter.

"That we do know, but racism, police brutality and hate crimes are all related to the past and ties in together. It just gives the media something to report. Yet, both cases seem to have hit a dead end wall."

"Well, we have covered all our leads John and still came up cold."

"Until we find better leads and get people talking, we will treat Thomas and Elliot cases as two different murder investigations. We may have to sit, wait and pray that another body doesn't turn up in the same circumstances."

Friday night's happy hour was held at Webster's Wine and Bar and Fletcher and Reese have made their pit stop joining the ladies for one drink. Everyone was in a pleasant get right mood for the weekend. Reese had just finished bragging about him and Fletcher wild New Year's Eve party. Once again, Gabrielle thoughts were elsewhere. She was anticipating her and Malcolm's dinner tomorrow night. "Earth to Gabrielle, come in Gabrielle."

"I'm sorry Fletcher, what were you saying?"

"How about welcome to the moment." said Amber.

"I said, I'm sorry to hear about you and Bryce, but I guess Tru will have his chance now huh?"

"Actually, Tru is seeing someone and I'm not ready to start dating again." "That's what all women say, but are desperately searching for a man to come and save them." stated Reese. Amber disagreed with Reese's statement.

"Reese, women and men are not the same. We all don't always have to have sex nor do we just have to be involved in a relationship."

"No, but women do need a good lay every once in a while during their transition period." Reese then slides over closer to Gabrielle.

"Can I be your transition man Gabrielle?"

"I'm not even looking for one of them." Gabrielle replied. "That's what vibrators are for bonehead." said Amber.

"Yes and I'm sure that's a device you own since Trey is always out of town, but what I want to know, do you own one Gabrielle?"

"Why would I need a vibrator when Trey keeps me well satisfied?" "Silence woman, my question was for Gabrielle."

Keeping a cool and calm face, Gabrielle lifts up her wine spritzer before taking a sip and replying. "I'm sorry I don't recall sending out personal invitations to discuss my sex life."

"You heard the woman, in other words, her sex life is none of your business."

stated Amber.

"Hey did you all hear that those two police officer got fired?" said Jillian. "No I haven't." said Gabrielle.

"Yeah, the boys downtown know they have another lawsuit headed their way." Fletcher added.

"Just another case of racial profiling, if you ask me." stated Reese.

"Do you honestly believe just because it's a new millennium that racism has ceased to exist?" asked Amber.

"Now you know you can't stop racism, that's like trying to stop the sun from rising." Jillian replied.

Changing the subject, Fletcher thought he would try to get the ladies to come hang out with them tonight. "You ladies wanna come hang with me and Reese at the clubs tonight?"

"Thanks, but not this weekend Fletcher. We don't want to be out late tonight and I believe Amber is meeting Trey in New York sometime tomorrow." said Gabrielle. Fletcher and Reese eyes both focused on Amber as she innocently takes a sip of her vodka martini.

"Don't look surprised. Like I said, Trey keeps me very satisfied."

That was information Fletcher didn't desire to hear, but his best friend came to his aid to reply to Amber's statement.

"Well maybe if his performance on the court was as half as good as you claim to be in the bedroom, then maybe he wouldn't have been cut from the Bulls."

"Don't hate Reese, Trey still plays pro-ball with the Pacers."

"Well ladies, it's about that time for us to dip. So this round is on me."

Jillian and Gabrielle both thanked Fletcher.

"Yeah Fletcher, that's very thoughtful of you." said Amber. "You have a safe trip. Ladies, have a good evening."

As Fletcher and Reese make their way out of Webster's Wine and Bar, a pair of loathing eyes watches them from across the room. Those hateful eyes then returned to join Gabrielle and her friends. The ladies know they can't begin to get into their real gossip talk until after the guys leave. The pair of jealous eyes observing them watches as Gabrielle laughs at whatever Amber was sharing, someone too envious of Gabrielle's once again happiness.

Analyzing the layout of her place, the rich unique artifacts of fine art and furniture that makes Gabrielle apartment a home, Malcolm's attention was deeply occupied. He was walking through her living room when he spots a picture of Gabrielle and her father.

"You know Phillip Michaels?"

Gabrielle smiles peacefully before responding. "Yes I do."

"Are you?" Malcolm was putting two and two together.

"Wait a minute; don't tell me Phillip Michaels is your father?"

"Yes, Phillip Michaels is my father."

"As much as we discussed music, contemporary Jazz mainly, not once did you ever mention that Phillip Michaels is your dad."

Gabrielle smiles helplessly. "I know and I apologize, but I thought I would bring that to your attention when the time was right, didn't want to brag."

"I'm so glad I met you." Malcolm takes a seat on Gabrielle's lavish couch. "So Gabrielle, how are you feeling this evening?"

"Oh, I'm *feeling* the sounds of Sade with a glass of chardonnay." Malcolm gives an uncertain stare with a smile.

"You're feeling who with what?" Gabrielle smiles.

"I'm feeling the musical sounds of Sade with a glass of chardonnay. That's just my personal little habit that describes my mood and the moment."

"Ah, I see. You have a lovely place. This is a condo right?"

"Almost, but no. I've always said the owner should have named the place, Almost Condominium Luxury Apartments." "I can certainly see why."

Gabrielle walks over to her bar and asks Malcolm would he care for something to drink. "Water, if it's not too much trouble."

Gabrielle opens the door to a small refrigerator and grabs one bottled water. "Would you like a glass?"

"Yes please."

"So what's on the agenda this evening?" She hands Malcolm the glass and bottled water before taking a seat beside him.

"Thank you, well I thought we would have dinner at Café La Cave, have you been there?" She nods her head yes with a smile.

"Yes, once for a wedding reception, charming place."

"Great, then I would like to give you a tour of my temporary job at the Art Institute of Chicago, but I see you have your own little fashionable art museum right here." Gabrielle gives a gracious smile.

"Yes somewhat, but I do not own masterpieces of art work by Picasso, Van Gogh, or Monet."

"Ahh, but what you do have makes me curious enough to have them appraised." Gabrielle thought happily for a second.

"Well I wouldn't go that far. I just like nice things. Nothing wrong with appreciating the finer things in life."

"No, you're absolutely right." "It helps to have good taste." "Also true."

Jack walks into the room right up to Malcolm.

"Well hello there Jack. It's good to finally meet you. I hear a lot of your cat talk in the back ground on the phone." Jack meows in response.

"Jack likes to meet everyone that comes over." "Friendly fellow."

"Well he usually keeps his distances, but seem to have taken an interest in you, all of a sudden."

"I love pets. I miss my dog."

"You didn't tell me you have a dog."

"Well my folks are babysitting him. I'm thinking about bringing him here." "What kind of dog do you have?"

"A spoiled Scottish Terrier that goes by the name Ralph, a name my wife chose. I didn't argue. She said he looked like a Ralph."

"Jack was already named when I received him. I can't really say if he looks like a Jack or not."

Malcolm takes another sip of his water and stands up.

"Well if you are ready to get this evening started, I know I am." "Yes I am, let me grab my coat."

Café La Cave is an exceptionably charming dining experience with a great atmosphere. Live music brings out the scenery in which Friday and Saturday nights are reserved for a live pianist. Marble fireplace and beautiful French windows adds to the touch of elegance. All are welcome, but just don't come cheap. The meals are a bit pricy, as is all upscale classy dining restaurants. Malcolm let his 1998 Audi take advantage of Café La Cave valet parking and checked both his and Gabrielle coats in the cloakroom. After being seated, Malcolm excused himself to visit the restroom. Gabrielle sat with all smiles absorbing the delightful atmosphere. While doing so, she receives a call on her cell phone from Jillian.

"Hello."

"What's up girl, whatcha doing?" "Oh nothing much."

"I rented a couple of movies if you want to come over and watch them with me." "Uh Jillian, actually I'm out with someone right now."

"Out on a date with someone?"

"No, not a date, but out with someone." "Who girl?"

"Girl, just Aaron."

"Well excuse me then, call me later." "Ok Jillian."

As soon as Gabrielle ended her call, she turned off her cell phone. Malcolm returned momentarily.

"So Gabrielle, was there a particular drink you wanted to order or are you in the mood for some wine?"

"Wine is fine."

"Do you mind if I choose?"

"Not at all, you're the expert." she expressed.

Malcolm smiles. "I wouldn't say that, but it's always helpful to know good wine and great wine."

"True." The waiter comes over for their drink order.

"We will have a bottle of Chateau Ste. Michelle Artist Series Meritage." "Yes sir, very good sir." said the waiter before leaving.

"So is that a good or great bottle of wine?" Gabrielle asked. "I would say very good."

"What would be considered a great bottle of wine?"

"Napa Valley's Constant Diamond Mountain Cabernet Sauvignon." "And Chateau Ste. Michelle Artist Series Meritage is Columbia Valley."

Malcolm was briefly surprised. "Correct, you know your wine."

Gabrielle smiles. "A little, so what makes Constant Diamond Mountain Cabernet Sauvignon better?"

"Oh, about a hundred and seventy dollars more better." "I see."

"I attend cheese and wine tasting party's all the time, especially at the museum. Maybe you would like to come sometime."

"I would like that." she happily agreed.

Malcolm looks over at Gabrielle and exhale with a smile, aesthetically absorbing her beauty.

"You know, I just can't get over that Phillip Michaels is your father." "Well don't make a big deal over it, I don't."

"But you are GABRIELLE."

"Yes, that is my name and my name just so happens to be on the cover of my father's first album."

"Amazing, but I won't continue to put you on a pedestal about it." "Thank you, and if you're really good, I might allow you to meet him." "Would you really?"

"Sure, what's your favorite track off the GABRIELLE album?" "I would have to say Gabrielle."

She smiled. "It's also my favorite."

The waiter returns and pours Malcolm and Gabrielle a glass of their wine in a round deep glass two thirds full. Malcolm then raises the glass, swirls the wine to release the aromas. He holds the glass up to his nose and inhale. After doing so, he takes a small sip of the wine. He agrees with the taste. The waiter asked to pour more and Malcolm gladly accepted. The waiter pours Malcolm more of the wine before taking their food order and leaving.

"Malcolm I'm impressed with your wine expertise." "Don't be, it's just one of my three favorite loves in life." Gabrielle takes a sip of her wine.

"How is it?" he asked.

"Well, I know I can't describe the mood nor the ripeness of the grapes or the hands it was picked from, but good. My wine is good."

Malcolm gives a brief laugh, as Gabrielle smiles along with him.

After taking another sip of his wine, Malcolm began to question Gabrielle about her personal life. "Gabrielle, we rarely touch on the subject, but why in the world are you single? You are single, right?"

"Yes, rarely touch the subject, as were you with your late wife."

"True, but my wife is deceased. I'm sure your ex is still around somewhere." "Yes he is." Gabrielle takes a sip of her wine before continuing.

"I guess you can say love has been a little bit hard on me, but to make a long story short. He cheated with his ex girlfriend and I chose to end the relationship."

"Sorry to hear that, how long were you both involved?" "Two years."

"That's a longtime Gabrielle." "Tell me about."

"We men can be so stupid sometimes, but we are not all the same. He must have been out of his mind to jeopardize you all's relationship with such a beautiful, extraordinary and phenomenal young lady as yourself."

Gabrielle gives a heartfelt smile.

"Well thank you, and I'm sure he realizes that now." "Do you miss him?"

"Sometimes, but not half as much as he misses me." "There you go. Allow him to sleep in his own misery."

"That I'm sure of, but I'm also sure he's probably still sleeping with the woman he cheated on me with."

Malcolm takes a generous sip of his wine before responding.

"I don't know, if you truly love someone deeply, it hurts just to look at someone else for a longtime, let alone sleeping with another."

"Well I guess he didn't love me deeply then."

"This is after the fact he got caught cheating that he realized that he truly loved you, and I'm sure it's eating him up inside."

"Maybe, I don't know."

Gabrielle could understand what Malcolm was trying to clearly and mentally justify the different variations and levels of love and its affects, but she wasn't ready to forgive or excuse Bryce and his cheating practices. What Gabrielle wasn't ready to realize is, that forgiveness is a major healing process in life.

Halfway through dinner, Gabrielle listened compassionately and sympathetically as Malcolm opened up and spoke about his wife and losing her to breast cancer. Love can be expressed through many ways and forms. Malcolm spoke tenderly how his wife carried so much loving feeling just in her hands, that her touch alone sometimes felt magical, almost powerful even. "And the only time she lost that loving feeling and tenderness in her hands, is when her life slipped away as I held her hand for the last time."

Gabrielle was touched by his remembrance of his wife and their love. She hated that the *beast* took his wife away, but knows breast cancer doesn't discriminate.

"You know Gabrielle I was glad you came along and said what you said about how cancer patients fought so hard to pass all their strength and love onto love ones so they may carry on. For a longtime I felt she gave up too soon, but when doctors and medical treatment was no longer a factor, fighting to pass all they had left on was the only possible option."

"It was the same for my mother. Cancer, the *beast* I like to call it, just came back with revenge and succeeded with its plan."

"How old was your mother when she died?" "She was forty."

"And you said your wife was three years older than you."

"Yes, her mother and great grandmother also carried the breast cancer gene." "But still, she was so young."

"We were married only four years, no children."

Gabrielle gave a heartfelt unfortunate expression.

"Interesting and somewhat uncommon, but there are more than one form of breast cancer. Researchers are seeing a pattern of mutation in a more aggressive form that is faster growing, common in premenopausal woman of African ancestry and in postmenopausal white women."

"Well my wife knew her family history, but somehow believed it was something to be concerned about later in life because her mother and great grandmother were in there fifty's when cancer struck them, but I guess she was wrong."

"I am really sorry to hear that Malcolm."

"It helps more than you know to talk about it."

"Yes, I know, in more ways than one."

It was a little after 9:00 pm when Malcolm and Gabrielle set foot on the property of the Art Institute of Chicago. The only staff available was security, monitoring the property inside and out. So Malcolm and Gabrielle pretty much had the entire place to themselves. He showed her his office first before giving her a personal guide and tour. Gabrielle had to admit, it's been almost two years since her last visit to this particular museum. They had just finished exploring architectural drawings and were headed to African sculptures, when Gabrielle gave Malcolm a pop quiz question.

"Malcolm, do you know who the first African descent to have a solo exhibition at the Museum of Modern Art in New York?"

"Hummmm, lets see. I believe that would be William Edmonson." "You're absolutely right. I see you know your history of art."

"But of course."

"You still haven't told me what you do in California, and no more guesses please." Malcolm smiles.

"Ok, I am in real estate, a real estate broker."

"Really, I saw you more as a teacher or professor, but that's great and quite lucrative I might add."

"Yes, the commission can be." "What agency are you with?" "Ameriquest Mortgage Company."

"Have you sold homes to any Hollywood stars out there?" "Yes, I have actually."

Gabrielle was curious to know more.

"Who was the last Hollywood star you sold a home to?" "Well, Will Smith was looking at a home in Malibu." "Get out of here, no way!"

"Really, but Jason Presley bought some property in Palm Springs."

"Wow, I still can't get over the fact you met Will Smith. Now I would marry him any day of the week, including holidays."

Malcolm gives a brief laugh.

"Do you meet a lot of movie stars?"

"Not really, but my wife worked at a Sacramento Magazine and hosted many charity events and social functions with a few stars that are household names."

"That must have been exciting."

"She loved it. Now, what are your thoughts on one of my favorite legendary artist, Elizabeth Catlett?" asked Malcolm.

"Really, she's one of my favorite too."

Malcolm and Gabrielle covered every inch of the museum talking art and life. They enjoyed each other's company. The most important aspect of their relationship of a friendship, is that neither one of them spoke through the stereotypical nature of one's race. They saw pass the color of their skin and spoke respectably, one human to another as people should do. It was twenty minutes after eleven when Malcolm pulled into Gabrielle's almost condo worthy apartment parking lot. He opens the car door for her and walked her to the front entrance of the apartment building.

When Malcolm did leave, a particular song was on his mind. The song "Satellite" by The Dave Mathews Band was circling his thoughts. Gabrielle also had a particular song on her mind as well. The song "I Could Fall in Love" by Selena breezed around her. She was happy in more ways than one and tried not make their relationship out of something more than it really is, which is nothing more than pure friendship. Gabrielle and Malcolm were actually suppose to be as they say, two ships that pass in the night, but their intense moment had a lingering affect too powerful to ever allow them to just pass by in a distance. After Gabrielle returned Jillian's call and spoke with Malcolm once more over the phone, she went to bed with pleasant thoughts and yes, parked outside of Gabrielle's almost condo worthy apartment, were dark and angry eyes hovering and watching with a particular song on his mind as well. The song that seemed to be playing all around him was, "Every Breath You Take." by the Police.

Never far away, Percy's picture was close by, but she hasn't had the pleasure of his company in her dreams lately. After a restful and sound sleep, Gabrielle woke the next morning cheerful and in a blissful mood. It was Sunday and she was feeling the sounds of some gospel music. She joined her sister and family at Mount Pilgrim Baptist Church. After receiving a healthy dose of righteous medicine, another dear friend of Gabrielle was on holy ground and was delighted to see her. Aaron walks over to her after service had ended. He waved at Ivy and Family as they were leaving. "I missed you at the library on Thursday."

Gabrielle turns around with a warm smile. "Hi Aaron, I had lunch out with a friend." "And I thought I was your only friend."

"Well if it's any comfort to you, you are one of my closest and dearest friends." "Well thank you, it does bring much feelings of relief. Tomorrow is Martin Luther King Jr. day, as usual the pastor represent his day well." "Always."

"Will you be attending the annually Martin Luther King Jr. unity prayer breakfast tomorrow Gabrielle."

"I can't say for certain, but I will try."

"What will you do to acknowledge one of our most important forefathers of the struggle?"

"Tomorrow is a holiday, a day full of marches, recognition and remembrance. For one, I attended church service today. To not honor him in some way shape or form is like turning your back on the past."

Aaron agrees.

"Well said and welcome home. It's been a while since your last visit here at Mount Pilgrim."

"Yes it has, I see you have been stirring up trouble with the police again." "No trouble, but civil rights for justice."

"I heard those police officers were fired."

"And that's only the beginning. They will be brought up on attempted murder charges."

"That's sad you know."

"Would you like to go somewhere for lunch Gabrielle?" "No thanks, I'm good."

"Well how about another round of chess. It's been a while and I believe I'm ahead, let's see, how many games to your one?"

"Any-way, it's on."

Aaron and Gabrielle ended back at her place sipping on General Foods International Coffee and playing an intense game of chess. Both are big fans of poetry and in the mist of Gabrielle concentrating her next move, Aaron spoke poetry to her.

"There are no beaten paths to glory's height, There are no rules to compass greatness known, Each for himself must cleave a path alone, and press his own way forward in the fight.

The Path, **Paul Laurence Dunbar.**"

After a few moments, Gabrielle responds.

"O Thou bright jewel in aim I strive to comprehend thee. Thine own words declare wisdom is higher than a fool can reach. **On Virtue, Phillis Wheatley.**"

Gabrielle finally makes her chess move and presses the timer button.

"Thou art fool, said my head to my heart, Indeed, the greatest of fools thou art,

To be led a stray by the trick of tress, By a smiling face or ribbon smart, **Retort,** by my same poet."

Aaron casually makes a chess move and presses the timer button. Gabrielle stares at his move carefully and she sees a window of opportunity.

"How did those prospects give my soul delight, a new creation rushing on my sight? Still, wond'rous youth! Each noble path pursue, on deathless glories fix thine ardent view: **To S.M., A Young African Painter, On Seeing His Works**, my same poet."

Gabrielle makes her move and pushes the timer. Already calculating her move, Aaron smiles with confidence and seemed to relax before making his strong move.

"Tried to ketch me up last night, but you bet I wouldn't bite.

I jest kep' the smoothes face, But I led him sich a chase, Couldn't corner me, you bet- I skipped all the traps he set.

A Confidence, my same poet; along with Check and Mate."

Gabrielle stares closely at the board bringing her head closer as well. "Aaron, you know I love ya, but I really hate you sometimes."

Aaron gives a hardy laugh, as Gabrielle shakes her head with a smile.

"And if its wisdom you seek, may I offer the first half of this verse. He that is walking with wise persons will become wise. Proverbs 13:20." suggested Aaron.

Interrupting their quality time together, Gabrielle receives a rang on her intercom box from a visitor. Gabrielle gets up and gladly walks over to answer it.

"Yes, hello."

"Hello Gabrielle, its Malcolm."

Aaron gives an abrupt look and Gabrielle immediately looks at her watch. "Oh hey Malcolm, come on up."

"Malcolm, who the hell is Malcolm?" he thought. "That better be Malcolm X." She clearly lost track of time. Gabrielle unlocked her front door.

"Aaron I apologize. I lost track of time. I have other plans." Aaron stands up from his chair. "It's quite alright Gabrielle."

By the time Aaron returned from taking their cups of coffee to the kitchen and grabbing his coat, Gabrielle's guest was now present. Aaron was a bit surprised to see the gentleman standing before him.

"Aaron James, I would like you to meet Malcolm Reid. Malcolm, this is my good friend Aaron James."

Aaron smiles briefly before offering his hand to shake. Being run out of her place was bad enough, but to be over chosen by a white man seem painfully worst. "Now just who is this pretty boy cracker, jive turkey?" he thought.

"Pleasure to meet you." said Aaron.

"Same here, hope I'm not interrupting anything important?"

"No, just finish beating Gabrielle in a game of chess again that's all." Malcolm looks over at Gabrielle. "I didn't know you played chess?" "Obviously not that well as you heard."

"Well, I better be going. It was good to meet you Malcolm." "Likewise Aaron."

"Call me when you get a chance Gabrielle." "I will, bye Aaron."

As soon as Aaron closed Gabrielle front door, a gloomy feeling came over him and a certain song came to mind. He walked to the elevator and pushed the button to go down. The song that seemed to plague his mind once again was, "Ain't No Sunshine When She's Gone" by Bill Withers. The same song came to Aaron's mind the day he met Bryce and after meeting him, Aaron and Gabrielle's encounters were brief for the next two years. Malcolm and Gabrielle had plans for dinner and a movie. Aaron didn't stick around long enough to find out that Malcolm and Gabrielle are really just friends or are they. Sadly, Aaron has seen all he needed to see and was for the most, disappointed in Gabrielle's choice.

CHAPTER FIFTEEN

Proverbs 15:3

The pair of observant eyes that watched Aaron leave Gabrielle's place, followed him back to the Black Panthers Party Urban Headquarters. Those private eyes waited patiently thirty minutes for Aaron to return back to his car and resumed the act of following him once again. Aaron picked up some take out before cruising the final destination home. Those pair of surveillance filled eyes that tailed him, parked his unmarked car inconspicuously. He watched Aaron enter his home then made a phone call from his cell phone. Detective Stephen Peterson with the Twenty-First Precinct Police Department answers the call. "The subject is now home, looks like for the evening."

"Good, you know the routine, sit on him until your shift is done and your relief has arrived. No Naps! And keep me posted."

"Alright."

Detective Peterson along with his partner detective Dan Cross sits at their desk discussing their main cases. Unlike First Precinct police, Peterson hasn't willingly committed himself to any other murder cases. Detective Stephen Peterson is the lead detective in the Stuart Elliott murder investigation and seem to have a healthy appetite of mad obsession to go along with it. Disappointingly, his inherent craving is a possible appetite for destruction. Peterson's won't let up obsession with this case is personal. It goes back a little over five years to what was believed as a murder set up of two police officers, Kenneth Harris and Rodney Peterson. Rodney Peterson was the nephew of Stephen Peterson and he no doubt, always fingered Aaron for those officers death, but couldn't prove any day of the week, including holidays.

So when Elliott ended up dead, it was somewhat of a blessing for detective Peterson to reopen the cold case investigation of his nephew's death. This however, wasn't easy for his captain to grant Peterson clearance because of severe past circumstances. After the death of his nephew and out of the prejudice of his own heart, detective Peterson, a regular police officer at the time, harassed Aaron constantly, so often that a restraining order was placed on him by the courts. Aaron filed more formal complaints on Officer Peterson than any other police officer in their precinct and state, which grounded Peterson to desk duty for a while and nearly cost him his career.

Officer Stephen Peterson over aggressive obsession with Aaron grew hostile and led to a change in precincts. Even after his change in precincts, Petersons driven determination to bring Aaron down was relentless and he was not only ordered, but forced to back off and receive counseling for anger management. Now with his authority and career on the line, Peterson had to sit back and digest the bullshit that was handed to him on a paper plate, that the system was being used against him. Not only did he have to come to his senses, but Peterson was advised to let it all go, everything for the time being. For the far most part of his calming down period, Peterson did what he was told and kept a low profile, but still tried to keep a close eye on Aaron from a distance. A close eye was something he need not keep. If detective Peterson were a religious man, Proverbs 15:3 would serve him well.

Standing 5'9 and weighing one hundred and seventy pounds with black and gray hair, beard and mustache, Detective Stephen Peterson remembers the past clearly, as if it happened yesterday. He was there that day when Stuart Elliott, his nephew and officer Harris all walked out of the police station together after the two police officers were placed on paid leave. He also remembers distinctively, the words Aaron uttered in form of a threat. Those words and I quote, "Those who represent the guilty are as guilty as their clients and will be punished one way or another along with them." Peterson regrets not taking those words seriously.

Years passed by and detective Peterson still carried animosity. The bitter resentment he carried was occasionally expressed in his blood pressure. Peterson hated Aaron with a vile passion, so deep that he felt it in his bones. As the years passed so did detective Peterson's undercover surveillance. His watchful eye became less persistent and unaware. Peterson cursed himself ten times over when Elliott's death dropped from the cable cord he was hung from. After begging, pleading and kissing his captain's ass six ways from Sunday and a promise not to go near Aaron, his captain granted Peterson permission to work Elliott's murder case.

With permission to work the case, Peterson would be thorough, leaving no stone unturned, taking creditable sworn statements from legit witnesses and seizing all evidence. He couldn't afford to screw up his second chance investigation and allow his main suspect to get away with murder again. Unfortunately, detective Peterson like detective Mackey investigation have come up cold and has nothing to really go on. Just like the death of his nephew, Officer Rodney Peterson and his partner Kenneth Harris, detective Peterson honestly believe Aaron was involved with Elliott's murder. He was willing to bet his gold shield on it. He wanted Aaron James rotting in a prison cell. He preferred an eye for an eye, but would settle for by the book justice and will not be satisfied until he can place those shiny handcuffs around Aaron's wrists and hear those prison cell doors slam, where a future needle in the arm will await.

Another Tuesday afternoon lunch with her sister, Gabrielle sits chatting in good spirits with Ivy in the restaurant her sister chose. Gabrielle knew it was her time to treat, but also knew it was her time to share her and Malcolm's intriguing friendship with Ivy. The two sisters were in the middle of enjoying their lunch while Gabrielle calmly supplied Ivy with the current information concerning her personal life.

"And we've been socializing everyday since meeting in the record store."

Ivy sat across the table from Gabrielle and appeared cautiously surprised with the information just received.

"Is he nice?" Ivy asked.

"Do I ever waste my time with less pleasant people?"

"Well it's about time. How long have it been, three months?" "Ivy, Malcolm and I are not dating. We are just friends."

"White, black, yellow, or Martian green, who cares, long as you are happy." "You're not listening to me."

"Hey I get it, not dating, just friends. Hell, he could be an imaginary friend as far as I'm concern. What I do see, is that sad puppy dog expression given from Bryce lifted from your face. I haven't even met the guy and I like him already." Gabrielle approves with a gesture of a smile.

"Malcolm just seems to bring my life a website full of enchanted possibilities. Our connection and interaction is quite appeasing, intriguingly dreamy." Gabrielle takes a sip of her beverage while Ivy places hers down.

"Do I dare ask how you *feeling*?"

"More mellow than MelloYellow." Gabrielle replied.

Ivy smiled briefly before asking a straightforward question. "So I take it you're over Bryce?"

Gabrielle's smile diminished a half inch before answering her sister's question. "I'm getting there."

"Well keep consuming Malcolm's positive and radiant rays. He seems to be worth the tan. Have you seen your ex lately?"

"Not since that embarrassing incident at the Cheesecake Factory."

"That reminds me, tell Amber to back off of Bryce and his woman before she ends up with a restraining order against her, not that I would be surprise if she didn't already have many from other people."

"She doesn't and I will. Like I said before, Amber is really a sweet person. You know that." Ivy rolls her eyes briefly.

"Well, she should wear a T-shirt stating that. I know how dramatic her attitude can become. It's a time and place for everything."

"You're right." Gabrielle agreed.

"So what do your girlfriends think of Malcolm? Oh, and Meredith's piano recital is tomorrow night. I told you a million times already so please be there and you can bring Malcolm if you like."

"Yes, I know, and I haven't discussed him with them just yet."

"Well good luck with that, especially with Amber. I have attended you all's so called book club meetings."

"Just as with you, when the time is right and convenient I will share with my friends, my new friend. As far as Meredith's piano recital is concern, you know I will be there, Malcolm I don't know. I don't want to pressure him."

"I understand, don't want to rush things with my future brother in-law."

"Ivy." said Gabrielle with a blossomed smile.

"I know, I know, you're just friends."

Gabrielle and her sister finished enjoying their lunch together. Their weekly lunches keep them in contact and close as they should be. Ivy was one person off her list of people to inform about "da white man" now associated in her life. Gabrielle still haven't found the nerve to tell her girlfriends. She was willing to wait just a little while longer before springing it on them. It will no doubt, be a no holds bar wave of reactions. Hopefully Amber won't be too upset and more accepting.

The next day Gabrielle and Malcolm had lunch together. She didn't ask Malcolm if he would like to attend her niece's piano recital, but did mention that's where she would be tonight. Malcolm gladly shared with her that the last time he attended a piano recital, was the recital of his own niece, six years ago. So while on the topic of discussion, Gabrielle insinuated a welcome invite and he gladly accepted. After having lunch together, Gabrielle and Malcolm were seen leaving a restaurant and walking the sidewalk together. Whatever he was sharing with her at that time made Gabrielle laugh, he then cracked a huge grin himself. Not only did they appear to be a couple, they seem very happy together.

Coincidently, Bryce just so happen to be walking out of another restaurant with takeout and sees Gabrielle and Malcolm across the street walking cheerfully together. At first, he couldn't believe his eyes. He just stared at them with a somewhat less joyful face. Gabrielle did not see Bryce nor was she aware of his stare. A particular song came to mind when Bryce saw Gabrielle with another man. The song that seem to immediately jump inside his head was, "Not unusual" by Tom Jones. Bryce seem to be in shock or frozen by the weather because before he knew it, a customer coming out of the restaurant bumps him by mistake and knocked Bryce's takeout to the sidewalk; looks like the rest of Bryce's day isn't looking so good, pretty much cloudy with a good chance of rain.

Later that evening, Gabrielle and Malcolm did attend her niece's piano recital. Gabrielle was a little reluctant to introduce Malcolm to her family, but Ivy didn't judge and was on her best behavior. When little Meredith's piano recital was over, Ivy shook Malcolm's hand again and gladly informed him that it was a pleasure to meet him. That was right before taking Gabrielle to the side and whispering in her ear. "He's handsome, friends my ass. Call me later." Gabrielle tried to keep from blushing as she smiled innocently.

It was Thursday when Gabrielle got around to calling Aaron. She informed him after getting his voicemail that she would be at the library for lunch if he wanted to meet her there. Since Aaron and Gabrielle encounters seem to have been brief lately, this was an opportunity he happily looked forward to gladly. Gabrielle arrived at the library around noon to find Aaron already there reading. "What's this, you're reading. Someone who has probably read every book in this library." Aaron gives a warm smile.

"Not quite, but almost and hello to you too Gabrielle."

"Hey Aaron what's up?" She takes a seat at the table with him.

"You tell me, I hoped you would have called me sooner since Sunday, but I guess you have been too busy with your new man."

"Ok, maybe I deserved that, but to quickly clear something up right away, Malcolm and I are just friends."

Aaron closes the book he was reading to give Gabrielle his undivided attention. "Really, define friends between you and Malcolm."

"Acquaintances, one attached to another by affection or esteem, a favored companion."

"Ahh, there it is. So tell me Gabrielle, this attachment you have with Malcolm, is it great affection or esteem? If you both are dating then I'm sure he is a favored companion."

Gabrielle slowly takes a deep breath before responding.

"Aaron my dear dear friend. Why must one assume such wrong theories?" "Am I wrong, please forgive me. You and I are friends are we not?" Gabrielle nods her head yes. "Yes, yes we are."

"So what's so special about you and Malcolm's friendship than ours?" "Only one distinct difference."

"And that would be?"

"That you are one of my dearest and closest friends and Malcolm is an acquaintance I'm getting to know. A friendship in progress."

"A romance in progress." replied Aaron. "Aaron don't, please."

"Ok, so how are you *feeling* Gabrielle?"

"Oh I'm feeling the sounds of Kenny G with a Tom Collins." "In good spirits I see."

"Yes, how are you Aaron?" "Good, always good."

Since Aaron did bring the topic of Malcolm up, she was curious to know what he thought of her new friend.

"So what were your thoughts when you first met Malcolm?" "Gabrielle, I'm not one of your girlfriends."

"Oh come on, you did have some thoughts." "Of course I did."

"Were they negative, they were negative weren't they?" "Not really."

"Oh you had some negative racial remarks. What were they?" "Gabrielle."

"Aaron this is Gabrielle you are speaking to, so let me have it."

"Alright, I wanted to know who this pretty boy, white saltine cracker was you were going out with?" Aaron whispered.

Gabrielle stares at Aaron with a partial smile.

"And this coming from a man who teaches Ethics & Society in Philosophy."

"I teach Economics as well, and my social science concerns to achieve maximum satisfaction of economic wants may also have bias preliminaries perspectives opinions."

"Spare me your lecture of an excuse Aaron."

"Oh Gabrielle I didn't mean it. Everyone has their moments of racist thoughts, including yourself. You can think about robbing a convince store twenty-four seven, but it isn't breaking the law until you actually do so."

"Well like all attempted robberies, they can be dangerous and proven to be deadly."

"You are offended from me calling your friend a cracker?" Aaron whispers. "No, but I know you Aaron and suspected a little more human kindness."

Aaron leans forward closer to Gabrielle.

"Oh and this coming from someone that take part in stereo-typing criticism of the other race in their margarita night book club meetings."

"Point taken, so we are even, but I will say this, I do more listening than contributing negative remarks."

"I know Gabrielle and thank you."

"For what?"

"For establishing your real feelings about Malcolm."

"Alright Aaron, you obviously feel that Malcolm and I are really dating, but what if that were the case. What if it were true?"

Aaron sits back in his seat before responding.

"Honestly?" he asked. "Yes."

"You can do better."

Gabrielle rolls her eyes at Aarons remark.

"You know Aaron, don't trip about this. You don't even know Malcolm. Yes, you and I are close and even though we go, one—two—two w a y back, doesn't give you the right to judge me or who I choose to associate with. Furthermore, as far as race and nationality is concern, people are people until proven otherwise."

"You forgot something." said Aaron with a straight face.

"And that would be?" she asked with a serious face on the verge of anger. "Checkmate."

Gabrielle face released her serious mindedness and burst out with a smile of laughter. They both laughed quietly.

"Gabrielle, you are right. I apologize."

"Gee Aaron; are you trying to ruin my day?"

"No, not intentionally. Let me make this up to you, allow me to take you to dinner this evening. Miles Jazz club is having spoken word tonight."

"Aaron I would love to, but I already have plans." "With Malcolm I take?"

"Yes, is that a problem?"

"No, couldn't stand another minute of your blaring rays the sun on my back." Gabrielle smiles.

"But seriously, Malcolm and I are just friends, okay?"

"Ok, so where are you guys going, if you don't mind me asking?" "We are attending a wine tasting event."

Aaron was mildly surprised. "Really, if I knew you were interested in wine tasting, we could have been attending events a longtime ago."

"I didn't know you were into wine Aaron?"

"Yes I am, but you know I'm fond of my Hennessy." "Yes, so can I take a rain check?"

"Absolutely Gabrielle."

Gabrielle stands from her seat. "Well I better be heading back. I'll call you this weekend, maybe we can go do something then."

"Gabrielle don't make promises you can't keep."

"I don't, we'll do something this weekend. See ya Aaron." "Gabrielle?" Gabrielle sits back down in her seat.

"Yes Aaron?"

"Be careful." said Aaron with seriousness as if he was worried. Gabrielle smiled briefly. "I will, talk to you again soon."

Gabrielle stepped off the elevator to the penthouse at the Sterling Private Residences off N. LaSalle Street. Malcolm was waiting with an open door in the hallway. "I see you had no problem finding the place?"

"You didn't tell me you lived in the penthouse."

"Like you, I don't like to brag. I'm just leasing by the month until I know for sure if my stay in Chicago will be longer than expected."

Gabrielle walks inside the penthouse and fell in love with the large dwelling. The penthouse was magnificently gorgeous, richly sophisticated with contemporary fine furniture.

"This place is huge, I love it. Is all the furniture yours?" "No, I could never design my own place."

"Oh, and you have a bar."

"Why yes I do, would you care for something to drink?"

"No thank you, I'm good for now. I just can't get over this penthouse. It's amazing with a great view of the city."

"I kinda like yours better."

"No way, I would take your penthouse over my almost condo worthy apartment any day of the week, including holidays. I would however, bring my artwork."

"Well I'm glad you approve Gabrielle."

Gabrielle takes a set on Malcolm's lavish couch.

"So you're still not sure if you will accept the permanent position as the Director of the Art Institute?"

"Well that depends, I'm temporarily filling the position until the position is filled. If they haven't found a candidate before timed allotted then they will offer the position to me. So I'm weighing my options."

"Are you looking to change careers?"

"I do have a life back in California with two homes. I like to think it's helpful in life to have a couple of degrees to fall back on just incase you want to change careers, but change can sometime be beneficial."

"That's so true. I enjoy cooking and could see myself as a chef on a cruise ship or one of those fancy restaurants."

"Maybe you should look into a culinary institute."

"Well, I still have two more years' residency in my field, but maybe a little later in life. Who knows."

"It's always best to practice or work in a career field you have passion for, something you feel comfortable performing long term."

"Well I definitely have my hands full with my profession." "Most importantly, you are helping make a difference."

The wine tasting gathering was held at Webster's Wine and Bar, a place Gabrielle knew all too well, but not once attempted to attend their wine tasting events. A few of the employees at Webster's Wine and Bar that were somewhat acquainted with Gabrielle presence from girls night out, spoke to her candidly with warm smiles, that only prompted Malcolm's curiosity to know the connection. Gabrielle gladly told him that Webster's Wine and Bar is one of the frequent hangout spots for girl's night out. Malcolm mentioned he might have to swing by there one Friday night. Gabrielle just smiled and turned her head, bucking her eyes briefly with an expression of, that's all I need. She's sure Amber would have a field day, that along with kicking her under the table most of the night.

Wine tasting was a new adventure for Gabrielle that she sincerely enjoyed. Malcolm was her professor and guide, teaching her the basic wine tasting criteria's. There were two things Gabrielle wasn't aware of concerning wine, one was the degree of astringency, how much a wine makes your mouth pucker, red wine mainly; and two, residual sugar, indicates how sweet or dry a wine is. Gabrielle had harvest plenty in her first wine tasting gathering and tasted a host of great wines. It was an experience she will soon never forget and also a new love she appreciatively welcomed into her life.

Friday is a day Aaron is free from teaching at Chicago State University. He sits no doubt dressed for success in his office at the Black Panthers Party Urban Headquarters along with vice president Tyrone Hampton. They are going over an application of a potential new member. A new member was something Chicago's New Generation Black Panther Party hasn't had in over five years. Jasper Ware, chief of security brought this new prospect to Aaron's attention. This particular applicant has been trying to join the New Generation Black Panther's also for over five years now.

Aaron is very strict and prefers all members to have a disciplined type attitude, loyal and able to assist their organization at a moment notice. This individual has to be trustworthy and believe one hundred percent in the private organization he or she may join, fear no one but God and be dedicated and willing to die for what the Black Panther Nation stands for.

Aaron receives a call from his female assistance that Jasper Ware and his guest has arrived. He asked his assistance to send them in please. A few moments later, Jasper and his guest enters Aaron's office. Aaron stands from his desk and Tyrone also stands from his chair. They both shake the prospect hand.

"I'm Aaron James, president of the New Generation Black Panther Party and this is Tyrone Hampton, vice president."

"It's a pleasure to meet you both." "Have a sit." offered the vice president. "Brother Ware." said Aaron.

"Brother James, Brother Hampton." Jasper replied. "Brother Ware." said Brother Hampton.

Jasper Ware remained standing.

"So, Mr. Kelsey Alexander Rice. I hear you have been longing to join the New Generation Black Panthers for sometime now?" asked Aaron.

"I go by Alex, but yes sir, that's correct. I believe you all stop accepting applications around the time I wanted to join."

Aaron glances at Mr. Rice application before continuing.

"I see you own your own cell phone and pager business?" "That's correct, for two years now."

"And before that you worked for the telephone company?" "For ten years Mr. James."

"Mr. Rice, why do you wish to join the New Generation Black Panther Origination?"

asked Aaron with concern.

""This is an organization I've always wanted to be apart of, but my job and other responsibilities prevented that. I believe I can make a difference in what the Black Panthers Nation stands for."

"And what is that?" asked the vice president.

"The Black Panther Party represent Black Power, self defense, equal justice for all African-Americans and most importantly, to end corrupt wrong doing of police and police brutality."

Tyrone Hampton nods his head in agreement with Mr. Rice words.

"Mr. Rice, are you aware of freedom of association?" asked Aaron. "The right to form your own societies and groups."

"You have the right idea. Freedom of association is the right to form societies, clubs and other groups without interference by the government.

This which, Huey Newton and Bobby Seale exercised their right to do so, now in which, I and Tyrone Hampton along with other states still carry on proudly today." Aaron sits back in his comfortable chair before continuing his interview process.

"Are you married?" "Yes I am."

"Have Children?"

"Two boys, twelve and sixteen."

"A family man." Aaron said with a smile.

"True."

"How does your wife feel about your interest in the Black Panthers Organization?" "My wife acknowledges my role as the man of the house. She is submissive, reasonable, an understanding woman, that is aware of and accepts any decision and interest that I may have."

"So if Brother Ware phones your home at 3 am for assistances in an emergency regarding our organization, you or your wife wouldn't have a problem with that?"

"Absolutely not."

"All Black Panther members are on call twenty-four seven." advised the vice president to the applicant.

"Mr. Rice are you aware of civil disobediences?" asked Aaron. "The refusal to obey the law?" Mr. Rice suggested.

"Once again, a close general idea. Civil disobedience is the refusal to obey a law out of a belief that the law is morally wrong. Would you have a problem with that Mr. Rice?"

"No I would not."

"Is that a fact, you would have no problem challenging the police authority?" "No, I would not." said the prospect calmly.

Aaron draws a worthy smile.

"Mr. Rice as you know, these are basic routine questions and of course you will answer any question in your best interest. When it comes down to it, we like to know if you can hold your own ground, possess leadership without supervision." Mr. Rice nods his head in agreement.

"That I can do sir."

Aaron stands from his seat and stares Mr. Rice directly in the eyes. "Are you afraid to die Mr. Rice?"

"No I'm not."

"If you succeeded in becoming a loyal member of the New Generation Black Panther Party, would you die for the organization you stand for?"

"If that's what it takes for justices to be served. I would be loyal and dedicated in every way." Aaron seemed to approve of his responses.

"Do you own a gun?" "Yes, a 9mm."

"So you can obtain a permit if needed?" "That, I already have sir."

Aaron gives another worthy, but light smile before taking a seat in his chair.

"Mr. Rice, although my questions may appear mediocre to you. I can assure you the New Generation Black Panther Party is not. We are political and social activist, one of many things, but more a family above all things. We represent a non-violent, drug-free atmosphere. We are for civil rights, fair justice, voting rights, against all forms of discrimination and demand the stop of racial profiling and police brutality, but we are also an organization that gives back to our community. We sponsor charity events, set up programs for inner city children, support free health clinics and meal programs, yes we are political and social activist that help our race. Our people have come a long way only to continue to endure persecution for our God giving right."

"This is true." stated the vice president before allowing Aaron to continue.

"Due to the Black Panthers Party history, the police are not our biggest fans, but knowing our rights as a human being keeps them in line and we no doubt are willing to stand up for those rights any day of the week, including holidays. Now I could go on, but I won't, because all I have said I truly believe in and have much respect for. You, must now take time and consider this organization carefully and ask yourself are you worthy, ready and willing to devote your life to the New Generation Black Panther Party Organization." Aaron stands from his chair.

"After a thorough background check, we will make our decision in a week. Thank you for coming in today Mr. Rice, you are free to leave."

"Thank you both for your time."

Mr. Rice stands from his chair and proceeds to shake Aarons and the vice president hand once again before leaving."

As soon as the elevator doors shut with Mr. Rice inside, talk of his chances begins. "Brother Ware, is this the man you recommended that is so eager to join our organization?" asked Aaron.

Jasper steps forward closer to his members.

"Yes sir, he's a good guy. His family back home has had some legal battles with the police that didn't work out in their advantage."

Aaron appeared concerned.

"Back home, is Mr. Rice from Alabama?" "Yes sir."

"Are you both related?" "No sir."

"Do you trust him Brother Ware?" asked the vice president. "Yes Brother Hampton, I do."

"What do you think about Mr. Rice, Tyrone?" asked Aaron.

"Any fool can answer questions, but he seems as if he has the ability to lead and the drive to establish power. He also seems to have a discipline attitude, possible military experience. We will know more after a sociological test."

"And those are always interesting." said Aaron.

"Well Aaron, I need to call Robert back about the Avery case. If you need me, I'll be in my office. Brother Ware."

"Brother Hampton."

Aaron waited for Tyrone to close his office door and asked Jasper to have a seat. "Brother Ware, you have been persistent about this possible candidate for almost two years now. You know him better than I do. Can we trust him with our family?"

"Absolutely Aaron."

"Because we need strong members to help our organization, not be against us. If you understand where I'm coming from?"

"I do."

"Personally, I'm not impressed. I've interviewed better candidates and I get a bad vibe about him."

"Yes sir."

"But since you recommended him, I may consider allowing Mr. Rice to join our organization, but only from a positive background check, more thorough than the CIA would give."

"Absolutely, I'll take care of it."

Aaron picks up Mr. Rice application and study's it briefly before laying it back on his desk. "Now Brother Ware, there is no doubt I trust you, but if this guy isn't who he claim to be, then there will be problems. As you know, Stuart Elliott's murder investigation is not closed. It may be cold, but not closed and I'm sure Officer Peterson is working double overtime to try and pin this murder on me. What I am emphasizing is, I don't need a stool pigeon in our organization."

"Aaron I promise you, Mr. Rice is legit. I will do everything in my power to see to that sir." Aaron takes a seat in his chair as Jasper stands from his.

"We must always keep our members four hundred or more strong and since Marcus Cameron is moving to another state, we will need to fill his spot. From this day forth, you are Mr. Rice keeper and find out all you can. Now I know you are handling other special assignments for me, but will that pose a problem?"

"Not at all Aaron."

"Good, like I said find out all you can on Mr. Rice and do this before our decision to accept him as a member, because I will hold you personally responsible for an unlawfully entry."

"Yes sir, I understand." Jasper turns around to leave. "Brother Ware?"

Jasper turns back around to face Aaron. "Yes Aaron."

Aaron sat with a very firm and serious expression on his face that would make death its self, feel uncomfortable.

"Don't disappoint me. Disappointments are failures I do not favor, nor do they set well with me. If, you know what I mean?"

Jasper nods his head. "I believe I do sir."

CHAPTER SIXTEEN

Red Twenty

Tuesday January 25, 2000 10:45 am
Cook County Court
People VS. Tyler Walsh

After District Attorney Richard Devine worthy award winning opening that clearly convicts the defendant without further necessary means of a trial, that along with going through his reliable list of witnesses, Judge Paul Biebel asked Mrs. Jackson to call their first witness.

"Your Honor the defense calls Glen Fisher." stated Ivy Jackson.

A middle age man with salt and pepper hair stands from his seat and makes his way forward to the stand. The clerk swears him in. Ivy stands from her seat and walks toward her witness before proceeding.

"Mr. Fisher, would you state your name for the court?" "Glen Alan Fisher."

"And what do you for a living Mr. Fisher?"

"I'm in insurance, an Asset Protection Consultant." "Do you know the defendant Tyler Walsh?"

"Yes I do."

"How do you know the defendant?"

"Tyler and I have been friends since high school. We attended the same university and I stood as best man at his wedding."

"So you know the defendant well?" "Yes."

"You could stand as a fiduciary representative of Mr. Walsh true character?" "Absolutely."

"Mr. Fisher, what kind of person is Mr. Walsh?"

"Good natured, wholehearted person, honest, a true friend, good father and husband, and a man that couldn't dunk a basketball if his life depended on it."

The defendant smiled as some of the people of the court shared a moment of humor in the witness last remark.

"Is Mr. Walsh the type of individual that would be considered violent or could pose harm to another human being?"

"Not the Tyler I know. He's a man with a gentle soul, wouldn't harm a hair on anyone's head."

"Would you say Tyler Walsh is a law abiding citizen?" "Yes, I don't think he have ever received a traffic ticket." "Mr. Fisher, did you know the defendants wife, Gail Walsh?" "Yes, I knew Gail."

"Would you say you know the Walsh family well in general?" "Yes."

Mrs. Jackson walks back over to her seat before continuing her questioning. "How would you say Tyler's and Gail's relationship were prior to Gail's death?" "Tyler and Gail had a wonderful marriage, one right out of a fairy-tale from what I've perceived; their relationship was loving, happy. If there was problems, I wasn't aware of it."

"So they appeared happy?" "They were happy."

"Objection, speculation." voiced the district attorney.

"Your Honor, my witness is just giving his honest opinion about the defendant and his wife marriage. I can assure you this is not a trick question that will automatically solve this murder case."

"Overruled, carry on Mrs. Jackson." ordered Judge Biebel.

"Mr. Fisher, where were you on December 30, 1999 between the hours of 7:30 and 8:00 pm?"

"Tyler and I were playing a game of racket ball at the recreation center downtown Chicago."

"And what time did you and Mr. Walsh leave?"

"We left the center around 8:30 pm. I remember needing to stop by my office that night. I also told Tyler that one of his tires looked a little low before checking my watch."

"So you and Mr. Walsh were playing racket ball at the recreation center between the hours of 7:30 and 8:00 and parted company around 8:30 pm."

"Yes, that's correct."

"Your Honor, let the record show accurate reports from crime scene investigators and the crime lab, that the time of death of Gail Walsh was between the hours of 7:30 and 8:00 pm."

Mrs. Jackson hands a copy of that report to the D.A. before asking permission to approach and presenting a copy to the judge. "One final question Mr. Fisher. Do you believe that after twenty-five years of marriage, that Mr. Walsh would take a knife and stab his loving wife repeatedly five times to death?"

"No, absolutely not."

"Thank you Mr. Fisher. I have no more questions."

Mrs. Jackson takes her seat before the D.A. begins his cross examination from his chair.

"Racket ball player are you Mr. Fisher?" "Yes I am."

"Great sport, I'm sure your heart thanks you. How many games of racket ball did you and Mr. Walsh play?"

"Two."

"Do you recall the actual time that first game began?" "I would say around 7:30-7:40 pm."

The D.A. stands from his chair and walks toward the witness.

"Mr. Fisher, isn't it true that you and Mr. Walsh first set of racket ball began at 8:15 pm because during the time of 7:30 and 8:00 pm you were playing a game of racket ball with a colleague by the name of Bill Morrison and that Mr. Walsh arrived late?"

"I did start a game with William, Tyler and I game started promptly after that game."

"You say you stopped by your office after leaving the recreation center, is that correct Mr. Fisher?"

"Yes I did."

The D.A. walks back over to his table and grabs some papers. He hands one to Mrs. Jackson before continuing.

"The log in and out sheet with security at the Prudential building put your time in at 8:35 and out at 9:15 pm. Now, either your watch was a little off or you're lying." The D.A. hands his second copy of the sheet to the judge. The witness appeared confusingly uncomfortable.

"You didn't play racket ball with Tyler Walsh on the night his wife was murdered, did you Mr. Fisher?"

"We did, Tyler arrived a little late, but we did play a game."

"A game, a few minutes ago you said two, which is it? Are you lying for your best friend Mr. Fisher? How much is he paying you?"

"Objection! Badgering the witness." cried Mrs. Jackson.

Judge Biebel strikes his gavel a few times to bring order to the court.

"Sustain, D.A. Devine will direct one question at a time to the witness and the witness will answer." ordered the Judge.

"Mr. Fisher, how many games did you and Mr. Walsh play on the night of questioning."

"We played two quick games after he arrived."

"And what is the correct time of Mr. Walsh's arrival?"

"I don't know how to explain it. I was sure my watch carried the correct time." The D.A. smiles at the witness before continuing.

"So your times given for Mr. Walsh's arrival to the time of departure are inaccurate?" asked the D.A.

The witness clears his throat before answering yes. "No further questions."

"Do you care to re-direct your witness Mrs. Jackson?" asked the judge. "No Your Honor." replied Mrs. Jackson disappointingly.

"Very well, you may step down Mr. Fisher. We will break for lunch and resume proceeding at 3:00 pm sharp. So everyone please be sure your watch has the correct time. Courts adjourn until 3:00 pm."

Judge Biebel strikes his gavel. "All rise!"

Ivy turns to her client. "We need to have a little talk." Ten minutes later, Ivy opens the door to a small private room of the courthouse where Mr. Walsh was waiting inside. Once inside, she slams the door. Mr. Walsh body jumps from the harsh closing.

"Did you or did you not ask for me personally to represent you?" "I did."

"In case you're not aware of my reputation, I represent the innocent and only the innocent Mr. Walsh."

"I am innocent."

"No, that's not what the jury will be discussing over their tuna sandwiches. They and I most importantly, will want to know why your best friend lied about the time you arrived at the recreational center and why you arrived late. You told me you were playing racket ball with Glen Fisher between the hours of 7:30 and 8:00pm. Now, I want to know just where the hell you were between that time until 8:15 pm on December 30, 1999, and don't even think about fabricating your answer."

It was around 11:50 am that same afternoon when Gabrielle received a call from her sister to cancel their lunch today. Gabrielle understood and was sort of glad because she was in the mood for some down home cooking. Gabrielle is a healthy eater, but every once in a while she needs to indulge in her roots. She needs the taste of some good and righteous soul food down at Mama Pearls Place. Gabrielle was walking to her car when she received a call from Malcolm on her cell phone.

"Hello."

"How are you Gabrielle?" "Good and you?"

"Great, have you had lunch already?" "No, I was just headed to get a bite." "With your sister?"

"No, something came up and she had to cancel."

"So you're free for lunch, do you mind if I join you?"

There was a brief moment of silents. "Damn, there goes my taste of heaven." she thought.

"Uh, sure."

"Did I catch you at a bad time, you want to be alone?"

"No, I was actually headed on the other side of town for some good home cooking."

"Yeah ok, I can do that, if you don't mind me joining you?" "Not at all, I'm already headed to my car, so I will pick you up."

The area of town Gabrielle drove to wasn't familiar to Malcolm, but he would occasionally hear about on the evening news. This particular area of town wasn't always crime prone, just only after dark. Every black person that lives in Chicago knows where to go for the best soul food in town, and that's at Mama Pearl's Place. The other race even makes frequent lunch visits and takeouts, but wouldn't dare drive by the place after sundown. Mama Pearl's Place has a 100% health rating and the food is out of this world, our world, soul food heaven. When Gabrielle and Malcolm walked into Mama Pearl's

Place, all eyes seem to focus on them. This would be a moment when not another white person was insight for a visit at the time.

"Good afternoon, welcome to Mama Pearl's. Hey Gabrielle, dining in?"
"Hey Stephanie, yes for two please."

"Great, right this way."

After being seated, they were given paper menus. "Someone will be right with ya'll."

"Thanks Stephanie."

Malcolm also thanks the hostess before looking over his menu. "This is different, do you eat here often?" he asked Gabrielle. "Once maybe twice a month."

"This is what they consider soul food delicacy huh?" "Absolutely." said Gabrielle with a smile.

One of the daughters of the restaurant owner, who right then after seeing her two guests, didn't approve of the view and naturally walked up with an attitude.

"Welcome to Mama Pearl's place, our special today is fried pork chops, collar greens and neck bones."

"Hey Samaria, how you doing girl?" asked Gabrielle.

The employee cuts her eyes over at Malcolm before answering. "Fine and I'm sure you are doing even better."

Gabrielle kinda brushed off her insensitive remark and smiled. "Malcolm do you have an idea what you may like to order?" "Mm-, that's already obvious." muttered the employee.

Gabrielle was surprisingly embarrassed by the employee rudeness in which she drew a slight frown.

"Excuse me Samaria, is something wrong?" asked Gabrielle?"

"Yeah, you got some nerve bringing him up in here. I guess you put the brother down for someone that better meets your criteria."

"Samaria, I don't see how my personal life is your business?"

"All I'm saying is, just because some brother's stray to the other side, doesn't mean sista's have to."

"Maybe we should go somewhere else Gabrielle?" Malcolm suggested.

"No, Samaria this is not going to turn into a scene from one of Spike Lee movies. Walk away if you don't want to serve us."

"Girl, you ain't said nothing but a word."

The moderately rude employee turned her head and ass around so fast, tossing her long weave ponytail with her in motion before switching off.

"Malcolm I apologize."

"It's ok, you don't have to."

The hostess hurries over to Gabrielle and her guest. "Gabrielle I apologize Girl."

"Stephanie I would say it's ok, but it's not. Samaria knows she isn't right." "You're right, what can I get for you and your guest?"

"I would like the special with macaroni and cheese, cornbread and lemon iced tea to drink. Oh, and some of you all's peach cobbler." said Gabrielle.

"Sounds good, I'll have the same." "Coming right up."

"Thanks Stephanie." "No problem."

Gabrielle shakes her head after the hostess leaves. "Malcolm, I apologize again."

"Forget about it. I do have one question though?" "Oh yeah, what's that?" asked Gabrielle.

"Why isn't there any pictures of white people on the wall?" said Malcolm with a smile.

Gabrielle couldn't help but smile before releasing laughter. "Now don't you start too." she replied.

Close to the end of their meal, a large well dress black woman was seen walking over to Gabrielle and Malcolm's table as the disapproving employee walked slowly behind her.

"Good afternoon folks. Dr. Michaels good to see you again." "Hey Mama Pearl, how you doing?"

"Ooooo child, you don't wanna know. I hear my youngest child was causing trouble for you and your guest?"

"Well Mama Pearl, you know I love your cooking and me and my guest just came down for a good meal when Samaria released her problems with my guest on to us."

"That's what I heard and I believe my daughter owe you both an apology."

Still trying to hide behind her mother, Samaria finally steps forward with her arms folded. She was still trying to hold on to that funky attitude.

"Girl, what are you waiting on? Don't make me knock you down and step on you in front of these guest!"

"I apologize for disrespecting you and your guest Gabrielle."

"Thank you Samaria, apology accepted." said Gabrielle with a smile. "You and your guest meals will be on Mama Pearl today."

"Thanks Mama Pearl." said Gabrielle. "Very kind of you." expressed Malcolm. "You both come back real soon, ya hear."

"We will." stated Gabrielle and Malcolm both.

Mama Pearl lifts her arm, points her hand toward the kitchen and Sarmaria turns around and heads in that direction.

"Go on, head to the back because you will be washing dishes until Martha Stewart stops in for dinner!"

That Thursday evening at the Black Panther's Party Urban Headquarters, there was a special ceremony held in the auditorium for the newest member joining their organization. Not all members of the militant group were in attendance, just the VIP executives and one hundred officers of their security unit. Alex Rice would be apart of the Black Panther Party security unit with room for advancement. He will be introduced to the entire security squad when they meet for their monthly meetings where training and educational sessions takes place. After Mr. Rice was sworn in, there was a small reception where heavy socializing was going on. Aaron was speaking to one of their members when he see's Jasper Ware making his way over to him. The other member excused himself from Aaron after Jasper had arrived.

"Brother Ware."

"Brother James."

"Looks as if you may have chosen a creditable candidate after all."

"I stand by him one hundred percent and know he will live up to his status." "Oh he'll do fine. He's a little over anxious, but he'll do fine."

Jasper approves with a rare smile before taking a sip of his drink. "Jasper, there was something I wanted to speak to you about." "Yes Aaron."

"Brother Eddie Franklin mentioned he saw you down at the local lounge shooting pool. That my cousin Demarco may have been your company?"

"Yes, last week I did run into your cousin there." "Do you hang at that particular pool hall often?" "No, not really. Just in the area at the time."

With no reason to be worried, Brother Ware takes another sip of his drink.

"I certainly hope you and my cousin brief encounter was a coincidence?"
"It was, we didn't speak long."

"You know Jasper, Demarco is my cousin, family and even I limit my association with him, given the fact he is a well-known drug dealer."

"Yes, I am aware of that sir."

"And I'm sure I don't have to remind you about the company you keep?"
"Not at all sir."

"What I am saying Jasper, is don't give the police a reason to investigate us." Jasper turns to face Aaron directly and looks him straight in the eyes.

"You have nothing to be concerned about sir."

"Good, let's keep it that way. Now if you will excuse me, there are other members I need to speak with."

Jasper watches Aaron makes his way across the auditorium to speak with another Black Panther member. He observes their conversation quietly, Jasper then sees Brother Eddie Franklin walk by headed toward the exist doors. Jasper places his drink down on a near by table and begins walking that way.

Later that same Thursday evening, Gabrielle was enjoying a drink up at Malcolm's penthouse. After that incident at Mama Pearl's Place, she knew the time has come to reveal her new male acquaintance to her girlfriends. She just hopes Amber or Jillian doesn't stop by Mama Pearl's Place before she can get to tell them herself.

"Gabrielle, did you know alcohol beverages were outlawed in the 1920's and 1930's, enforced by the Volstead Act?"

"Yes, I believe I remember reading about the prohibition that outlawed the production and sale of alcohol."

"Good thing the amendment was repealed."

"Malcolm could you imagine the world without alcohol, the pleasure and exquisite taste of wine or other alcohol beverages?"

"No, but everything has a purpose in life. If the Volstead Act continued to be enforced today, sadly the consequences would be the same as the selling and distribution of illegal drugs."

Looking out a large window with an amazing view of the city, Gabrielle seemed a million miles away. "What's wrong Gabrielle? You look a little upset." Gabrielle unattached herself from the view at the window.

"Oh, I'm sorry, that incident at Mama Pearl's Place is still on my mind."

"Don't bother your thoughts over that. People have a right to form their own opinion."

"But she made it seem as if we were a couple when we are not." "Regardless of color, people are entitled to respect and good service." "Malcolm, I know we haven't really touched on the subject, but what do you think about dating outside your race?"

"There was a time not long ago when some group of individuals thought that people should date within their own race."

"They still do." Gabrielle added.

"Yes, some people, but like I said, people have the right to form their own opinion. Honestly, you can't control who you become attracted to, but to answer your question. I am not sure if God intended for us to marry off to others than our own race. I'm sure God didn't intend for there to be only one race on earth or one race that was suppose to be superior. No one is superior than God."

"You are so right Malcolm."

"Attraction can be a powerful thing, that desire, curious inspiration to know someone. Regardless of race, you can't control who you fall in love with."

Gabrielle was drawn into every word coming out of Malcolm's beautiful mouth. She imagined what his mouth felt like on hers and wondered was he thinking the same. Actually, both Gabrielle and Malcolm had a particular song that lingered in the back of their minds, which was, "No one is to blame" by Howard Jones.

"Malcolm you said you dated outside your race before?"

"Yes I have. This was before I met my wife. I dated a lovely and educated Asian woman for three months."

"Really, may I ask what happened?"

"A promotion moved her to New York. What about you, you dated outside your race right?" A bit of a frown came across Gabrielle's face.

"Yes I have. A Caucasian as yourself." "Oh really, may I ask what happened?" "Definitely the wrong guy."

Malcolm smiles before asking to refill her glass of wine. "No thank you."

"You know Gabrielle I would love to take you away one weekend to visit a wine vineyard."

"Oh that would be wonderful."

"So does that mean I can plan to book us a trip one weekend?" "Just tell me when."

"Great, I'll check into that."

It was a cold brittle Friday morning and the wind chill didn't help the situation with its brisk greeting. This kind of cold-hearted greeting slaps you in the face with a wet towel. Gabrielle stopped at Starbucks for a cappuccino. The place was crowded as expected. Everyone was getting started for the last workday of the week. Gabrielle paid for her coffee with cash, a twenty-dollar bill to be exact. After receiving her change, she thanked the cashier and went on her way looking forward to this evening gathering of girl's night out.

Two customers later, that same twenty-dollar bill of Gabrielle's was given as change back to Jim Richmond, a businessman who bought two cups of coffee and broke a fifty-dollar bill. He placed that twenty-dollar bill in his wallet and went on his way. Later that afternoon Jim Richmond treated a small group of associates out to lunch. He paid for their meals with a Visa credit card and gave that same twenty-dollar bill from Starbucks to the server for a generous tip. Jessica Thronhill gladly accepts the tip and went on her way. Around 9:30 pm that night, Jessica got off work and took a taxi home. The taxi drops Jessica off at 2274 Parkview Lane. She paid the driver with that same twenty-dollar bill she received as a tip and told the diver to keep the change.

Joseph Trefil accepted the fare and the five-dollar tip and went on his way. He drove seven miles to his destination in downtown Chicago and stopped at a local convenience store and to buy cigarettes. He paid for the cigarettes with that same twenty-dollar bill that was giving to him as fare. His last fare, the tip from the server was paying for those cigarettes. As Joseph Trefil placed that same twenty dollar bill into the cashiers hand, another customer place a gun in the cashiers face. The gunman snatched that twenty-dollar bill from the taxi driver and demanded more from the cashier. The taxi driver throws both hands in the air and the cashier slowly grabs a brown paper bag and began filling it with money. The gunman kindly thanked the cashier and ran out the store. The cashier pushes the silent alarm and immediately gets on the phone.

James Moore, a comma street punk easily robbed that convince store and went on his way in a hurry. A few minutes later, cops were given a description of the robber. Police officers Beckman and LaFontaine with the

Chicago police heard the call come in and were two blocks from the robbery. Driving to the location, they spot the suspect fitting his description. They turn the spotlight on James Moore and ordered him to stop. Naturally, the suspect fled and the officers pursued him on foot calling for back up. After running a few blocks the police officers splits up as the suspect was seen running through snake alley. A few moments later shots rang out that echoed through the alley. Officer LaFontaine quick foot pace eased to a slow cautious walk. His short walk further into the alley finds Officer Beckman standing over the suspect with his gun drawn. As Officer LaFontaine looked down at Moore, he observed the suspect with two gun shot wounds to the chest. With the same gun he used to rob that convince store not far from his side and money scattered all around him, James Moore laid dead in snake alley on which seem to be the coldest night of the year. That same twenty-dollar bill that Moore took from the taxi driver lay beside him in a pool of blood, now a red twenty.

It's amazing, the aspects and turn of events in life, the way you come in and the way you leave out, that is. Your soul surely doesn't have a say so about it. Who says you get to go peacefully or with your eyes closed, James Moore eyes wasn't. One thing for sure, there's nothing worst than to see your own blood slowly seep from your body before your life slips away. Slip away, that's too kind, a word for the elderly accepting the inevitable. For others that are murdered, their lives are snatched away, and right now at this very moment, somewhere in the world someone is plotting, conspiring death, murder.

CHAPTER SEVENTEEN

Beyond The Pale

After a night of chilling at Miles Jazz Club and going to a popular dance club, happy hour ended very late into the next the morning and the girls decided to have breakfast at Orange restaurant off N Clark Street. Gabrielle knew she had plans with Malcolm tonight and it was no time like the present for Gabrielle to spill the beans, explain to her closest friends just who she has been spending her leisure time with these days. The server had just served their beverages that included two hot chocolates and a cappuccino.

"And that's who I've been communicating with." said Gabrielle calmly.

The booth the three friends occupied became quite as Gabrielle reached for her cappuccino and takes a sip. "Communicating with?" asked Jillian.

"Yes, just communicating." replied Gabrielle.

"Well I'm happy for you. You're back out there again." expressed Jillian. "No, I wouldn't go that far." stated Gabrielle.

Amber, who had been quiet and in somewhat dismay since Gabrielle broke the news, just stared at Gabrielle disappointingly before allowing her displeasure to be known. "Communicating with, oh is that what they are calling dating these days?" asked Amber candidly.

"Here we go." replied Jillian.

"No, it's fine Jillian. Amber has a right to her opinion. Please, by all means, share your feelings Amber?"

Amber takes a deep breath before turning to face Gabrielle directly. Jillian takes a sip of her hot chocolate before giving a nonchalant expression, as Gabrielle waited patiently for the rude awakening. Amber looked over at

Jillian then back at Gabrielle, then for some odd reason, adjusted her mood accordingly. Amber smiled before fixing her attire. She spoke calmly and quite elegantly. "You know, sweet dreams are made of this, and as the song goes, who am I to disagree?"

"Really?" said Jillian shockingly.

"And you're alright with that, not that Malcolm and I are exactly dating?" asked Gabrielle with a strange eye.

"No, no problem. It's you're thang, do what you wanna do." "Praise the lord and pass the syrup!" said Jillian in an outburst.

The server had just brought them their food order and asked did they need anything else.

"Yes, replied Jillian. Do you have anything for amnesia, because my friend isn't feeling well?"

Gabrielle smiled, but knew her best friend only too well. Something was definitely up.

Still morning, Gabrielle was home only ten minutes when her telephone rang. She didn't have to guess, but had a feeling it was Amber. Gabrielle screened the call before answering and as figured, she was right.

"Yes Amber, I was about to lay down for the rest of the morning?"

"You know Gabrielle, I'm not going to yell, scream, or shout. You are an adult and can make your own decisions."

"Why now Amber, why couldn't this be said when it was on the table for discussion?" "Oh you know why?"

"What's wrong with dating another race Amber, not that Malcolm and I are even dating?"

"Nothing, nothing at all, but one, you haven't had much luck with white men and two, the past was something you didn't quite discuss with Jillian did you?"

"Amber not all white men are like that, and I wasn't ready to explain those events to Jillian at the time and felt who knew was all that needed to know."

"Gabrielle you know how we have our discussions about the other race on margarita night, but I'm not racist or prejudice."

"Oh really." said Gabrielle amazingly. "Girl, don't play."

"I know, but you haven't even met the guy. So please don't judge." "I'm not, all I'm saying, think about what you are considering?"

"I have, you're jumping to conclusion and Malcolm and I are not even dating." "Just be careful Gabrielle."

"I will, I'll call you later."

"Yeah, you do that Ms. Thang."

When Gabrielle finally did crawl into bed with Jack at the foot, she began to think which delayed her sleep time even more. One particular question on her mind, if they are not dating, then what exactly is happening between her and Malcolm.

The morning passed swiftly as well as part of the day like most weekends, in which Gabrielle spent most of that sleeping. When she did get up it was a little after 2pm. Gabrielle looked forward to seeing Malcolm tonight. Her cell phone that had been charging up front had three missed calls all from Amber. She wasn't in any hurry to argue with Amber and decided to call her later. Gabrielle wanted some alone time to herself. Popping in one of her exercises videos, Gabrielle decided to give her body a healthy workout. She kinda missed the other workout she received from Bryce, but since that form of exercises was no longer apart of her new life at the moment, she had to settle for Denise Austin Pilates. Either way, both are good for you.

After her workout, Gabrielle turned off all phones and TV's then began to meditate for an hour. After that, she took a long hot bubble bath. Before she knew it, her and Malcolm were having dinner at Narcisse on 710 N Clark Street. Narcisse is a highly recommended downtown trendy hot spot with exceedingly attractive eats, drinks and clientele. Malcolm had just received an important call on his cell phone and excused himself from the table. Gabrielle was admiring the scene, its remarkable atmosphere, wasn't long before her cell phone rang, Amber of course.

"Hello Amber."

"Why didn't you return my calls?" "I was busy, what's up?"

"Where are you?" Amber asked nosily. "I'm out right now, why?"

"Out with who?"

"Out with Malcolm, is that a problem?" "Oh really, didn't we have plans tonight?"

"No, when do we ever really have plans on a Saturday night?" "Ever since you caught your ex boyfriend cheating?"

"Well, we haven't been out many Saturday nights lately." "Where are you?"

"I'm out trying to have dinner." "Yes, but where?"

"At Narcisse."

"Ooooo Narcisse, the playground for the beautiful. How the hell did you all get reservations?" Gabrielle laughs briefly.

"Look I gotta go, I'll call you later." "Gabrielle don't you dare hang up on-"

Gabrielle turned off her cell phone and Malcolm returned back to their table. "Hope everything is alright down at the museum Malcolm?"

"Yes it is, some artwork arriving from London, two exhibitions which will be on display for three months."

"Oh yeah, what artwork?"

"The Old Masters & Impressionists, two exhibitions of glorious French painting."

"Really, I think I may have to return back there for another visit."

"Certainly, I will be more than delighted to give you a personal tour. Have you looked over the menu?"

"Not quite, I was waiting for you and your suggestions."

They both smiled before going over their menu. Malcolm began to explain some of the rich tasting food he would recommend, but only if her taste buds were in the mood. Gabrielle and Malcolm carried on like a couple, laughing, talking, and communicating well. They seem to fit right in the scene, just a couple of beautiful people sharing some leisure time together. Although it was deep in Gabrielle's mind, the extent of their friendship, possible relationship, she wasn't going to bring it up. Gabrielle didn't want to push or put a damper on her and Malcolm's good friendship. However, she still wondered is he even attracted to her that way.

Malcolm and Gabrielle were in the process of leaving Narcisse and receiving their coats from the coatroom when. "Let me help you with your coat." said Malcolm. As Gabrielle turned around to slip her arms inside, that's when she got the answer to her question. Not only did Malcolm breathe in a dose of her sweet alluring perfume, but when Gabrielle turned around to face him, it was then she finally saw it for the first time, the look. That particular look, was the look in his eyes of attraction. The look Gabrielle so often received from strange men wanting to know her. Gabrielle just smiled as did he and they walked out together. After viewing a play at a theater, Malcolm was now taking Gabrielle home.

She invited him up for coffee and he gladly accepted. After pouring him a cup of Swiss Mocha's Generals Foods International coffee, Gabrielle sit's a small tray with cream and sugar down in front of him. She tells Malcolm to help himself and he does. While Malcolm stirs his coffee to his perfection, he asks Gabrielle to come sit by him and she did. She also stirs her coffee with ingredients for pleasing satisfaction. They spoke about the evening, the play, still enjoying each other's company while listening to some of Gabrielle's contemporary Jazz selection. They seem so comfortable around each other. Their conversation was generally well, that is until the subject of his deceased wife came up, in which he brought up.

Gabrielle is not the least bit insensitive to the pain he may still carry for his wife, but when he began to speak about her, that look in his eyes was now starting to fade. "You have lovely hands Gabrielle."

"Thank you."

"My wife had thin lovely hands just like yours and also kept her nails done." "Just one of the pleasures of being a lady." she expressed with a smile.

"Indeed, may I borrow one of your hands for a moment?" "Sure."

The question caught Gabrielle off guard as they both place their cup of coffee down on the coffee table. She smiled before slowly offering her right hand to him. He slowly takes the end of her arm feeling the unique and graphic nature of her hand, which makes each of us distinctively different. Handling her hand ever so gently, Malcolm viewed Gabrielle's hand like a piece of artwork being appraised.

"You have soft hands."

"Thank you, I try to take care of them."

For the first time, Gabrielle felt a little uncomfortable, but she liked it. He gave her hand back. Feeling a little awkward at the moment, Gabrielle thoughts were in search of a new topic when Malcolm sighted something in her hair. Before Gabrielle could respond or react to his attentiveness, Malcolm reached over and got the tiny object out of her hair. When he came close to her, she could smell his handsome cologne. That only made her desire him more. Malcolm picks up her saucer and hands Gabrielle her coffee. She thanked him as he collects his coffee. They would conversant a little while longer before Malcolm looked at his watch and decided it was time to go.

Gabrielle walked him to the door and thanked him with a friendly hug for dinner and a lovely evening. In that embrace, he actually felt a strong connection to Gabrielle. Malcolm eyes closed with that embrace. When he turned her loose, he looked into her eyes and there, she saw the attraction again. Malcolm slowly leans in for a kiss, but was interrupted when Jack walked up to the door and let out a rather loud unusual meow as if he had something on his mind, which ruined the attempt. Malcolm smiled briefly after losing his nerve.

"I better go." he said.

"Ok, call me when you get home." "I will, good night Gabrielle." "Good night."

Gabrielle watched Malcolm get on the elevator then closed her door. She placed her head back against the door and thought about Malcolm. Jack walks back up to the door begging for attention. "Thanks a lot Jack!"

Gabrielle telephone rings and she goes to answer it, but when she said hello, there didn't appear to be anyone on the line. She hangs up the phone. A pair of jealous and hateful eyes sits in Gabrielle's parking lot. He pushes a button to end the call from his cell phone.

Malcolm called Gabrielle just as he said he would. They spoke briefly and called it a night. It was five minutes until midnight and Gabrielle was preparing herself for a goodnight's rest. Meanwhile, other people's night were just beginning. About twenty miles south of Chicago, the underworld that's below the levels of ordinary life was in the mist of corrupting activities. An illegal sport was currently taking place, the what seem to be unstoppable and growing sport of dog fighting. Dog fighting is big business, an illegal multi-million dollar a year business if you know the right people and have the right dog.

In a wooded area on fighting grounds where security to keep Task Forces and State Police out were tight, frequent sport participants had certain codes along with special invitations for admittance. Let's just say, just because you walk in off the streets with a top champion breed dog, doesn't mean you will be allowed inside. There are rules and specific guidelines to this type of illegal sport business. You have to have connections, most likely know someone already in the trade. Oh yeah, you must have plenty of money to circulate, these types of events isn't like your typical horse races.

A fight was currently taking place on the fighting grounds, two dogs practically mutilating each other. It's a fight to the death and believe me; one of the dogs usually dies, most of the times by his opponent or his owner. Two black male spectators observing the fight communicates among themselves.

"You see, didn't I tell you Cujo is a champion dog?"

"Well you best been right this time. The last dog cost me five grand." "Hey it ain't no thang, you win some, you lose some, right?"

"Did you get rid of its litter that weak bitch had bred?" "Oh no doubt, we can't have weak ass prospects."

"Have you talked to your cousin anymore about my proposal?"

"Man I'm telling you, Aaron is not going to be interested in your plan." "I believe he can be persuaded, if you stay on him."

"You should have known Aaron when he was first starting out as a Black Panther organizer. You know, when his hands were crooked like handicap."

"Never mind that Demarco, just present this matter to him fully and be persistent until he at least considers it."

"You're not listening to me Jasper. We might need to keep this deal proposal between us. You are doing fine yourself. Trust me, Aaron don't need the money."

"Then he can make even more, whether you realize it or not, dog fighting is big business and will continue to grow. Do you know how many sports athletes and rappers are involved in this business?"

"Yeah you right, plenty of brothers." "And don't they have plenty of money?"

"You know, you're right, but you have to have plenty of dough to be apart of this circle."

"As I said before, stay on him until he at least considers the idea, then I can take it from there. Now, go collect my money so I can get the hell out of here."

Also that same night over in the area of Elmwood Park, Illinois, right outside of Chicago where that shady commercial building is located, a particular file without the special poker card game was pull from a second draw of a black steel cabinet. Not all the members were there this late night. In fact, only two members were burning the midnight oil.

"You needed to see me Sam?"

"Yeah Mitch called and said for you to go over this file. He may need you to make contact with this client."

"Yeah ok, who is it?" "It's all in the file."

The supervisor tosses the file on the desk. The member opens up the folder on the desk and looks over it. The member then closes the folder and lifts it up off the desk.

"I will call you if it's a green light in contacting this client, until then stay on red and out of trouble and Patrick?"

"What?"

"Don't fuck this up. Fuck up's are beyond the pale, if you even know what that means."

"Oh don't worry, I believe fuck up's are for retards."

It was a beautiful yet cold Sunday afternoon and Gabrielle had just come home from attending church services. Spiritual words, along with a dose of good gospel music can always put your life back into positive perspective. Gabrielle had received a call from Amber on her drive home and unfortunately, Amber was on her way over, most likely part II to their unfinished discussion. Gabrielle was in search of food in the fridge when she heard the buzzer to her call box go off. She makes her way toward the front to buzz her guest in, also letting Amber know her door is unlocked.

Waiting patiently by the bar, Gabrielle began to fix herself a drink. A minute later, there was a knock on her front door as Amber opens the door letting herself inside. "I'm at the bar Amber!" yelled Gabrielle.

Amber makes her way around into the living room. Dressed very warmly in Baby Phat jeans, boots with the fur, a stylish coat and a very cool laid-back hat, even Amber's chilled out casual clothes represent her well.

"Well I see you made it home safely after your date with da white man."

"I was just making myself a drink, would you care for one?"

"Don't even try to liquor me up, we need to talk."

"Are you sure, I have a brand new bottle of Absolut. I can make you a vodka martini if you like?"

"No, thank you. Now tell me all about the new love in your life?"

"First of all, he's not the new love in my life. Second, we are just friends."

Gabrielle thoughts went straight back to last night to recap when Malcolm was leaning in for a kiss. "Hello! I said how did you both meet?"

Amber removes her coat before taking a seat. Gabrielle places her drink down without once taking a swallow and makes her way over to Amber by the couch.

"Amber it's not what you think. We met at a record store ok." "And how long have you both been so called communicating?" "Gee, I don't know, three or four weeks maybe."

"Three or four weeks! And you just now telling us?" "It's no big deal, we are just friends."

"Mm-hmmm, and you also said the same thing about another lily white fellow at Cornell University."

"Amber please don't bring that up." "Why not, you-"

"Amber it's the past. I can't judge every white man based on one bad experience. That would be wrong." Amber stands up from the couch.

"Bad experience, bad experience, don't you mean nightmare. It left you terrified for months and you vowed to stay with your own race remember?"

"I know, I know. Amber I don't want to discuss that, not that, not now. My own sister isn't giving me as much heat as you are and she's a defense attorney."

Amber sits back down beside Gabrielle.

"Well it wasn't your sister that flew back and forth there for several weekends to calm your nerves and get you through that bad experience."

"Yes I know. If she thought I couldn't handle it, she would have made me come back home. You know that."

"Ok listen, look me in the eyes and tell me you're not seriously thinking about getting involved with this guy."

Gabrielle stands up and began to walk away. Amber gets up and follows her over to the bar. When Gabrielle did turn around, Amber was right there in her face. "I said look me in the eyes and tell me are you seriously considering getting involved with this guy."

Gabrielle goes to grab her drink and Amber stops her. "I would like your thoughts clear."

"They are clear."

"Well?"

"No Amber I'm not."

"No?" asked Amber still searching for the truth.

"Maybe, I don't know?"

"You don't k n o w?"

"No, I don't, but what if I did get involved with Malcolm?"

"Then I would have to say, this is beyond the pale, totally unacceptable."
"Oh Amber all white men to you are beyond the pale."

"Is not. Hey I went out on dates with my share of white men way before Trey came along and they just weren't my cup of tea."

"That's right, for you. So to each their own."

"So you are going to get involved with this guy?"

"Amber, as of right now, Malcolm and I are just friends. So you might as well deal with it okay?"

Gabrielle grabs for her drink and Amber moves her hand away as Gabrielle takes a small swallow of Bacardi rum.

"You feel better now?"

"I don't need a drink to feel better Amber."

"Don't you, because as I recall, that bottle of Jack Daniels had never been open before until you broke up with Bryce. Now there's less than half left and a new bottle. So who's fooling who?"

"Oh Amber please, what, you're my therapist now?"

"Maybe I should be."

"I don't think so." said Gabrielle with a not so approving expression.

"That's right, because I'm your friend. So don't you forget that!"

Amber walks back over to the couch and grabs her coat.

"Amber wait, don't leave this way. We've been friends too long to have another fallout over a guy."

Amber turns back around with elementary school days on her mind.

"The only other one was Jonathan Mitchell."

Gabrielle smiles and Amber returns the gesture.

"Look Amber, please just be open minded about this. Be my friend and don't judge who I may or may not decided to get involved with in a relationship. You were acting as if I decided to marry the guy."

Amber gives a slightly wary expression.

"Let's pray it doesn't come to that." Amber suggested.

The two friends laughs before walking a short distances to embrace with a hug. "You hungry?" asked Gabrielle.

"Girl, I'm starving. I was about to pick up some takeout when I called you." "Let's go out for a bite, my treat."

"Well it's the least I can let you do, since you have been withholding information from me."

"Well everyone knows now, thank you very much."

"Speaking of food, may I say one thing about dating the other race?" "What the hell, you might as well."

"You've heard of the saying, oil and water don't mix right?"

"Yeah."

"Same thing applies to Caviar and Collar Greens." Gabrielle shakes her head with a smile.

"Only you can come up with some out of the ordinary combination like that."

"Which also reminds me, there's this great guy in my office I think would be great for you." "Amber."

"Yes Gabrielle?"

"Be my friend, not my matchmaker."

CHAPTER EIGHTEEN

Taste Like Leukemia

"Well it's about time my sister became available to meet me for lunch again. What has it been, a month?"

"No, two weeks and this Walsh murder case is kicking my behind."

"Not going well huh?"

"Don't ask. Local reporters are sometime worst than the paparazzi."

"So did he do it?"

"Would I be defending him if he did?"

"Hey, you never know."

"Ain't that the truth? Just need to reform a few errors, but it would help if people would tell the truth."

"There's two sides to every story Ivy and when it comes to trials, courts and prison, there's no telling what lies beneath the truth."

"Lies and more lies, I just need to find out which lie is the truth. Enough about my life, how's things with my future brother in-law?"

"Nice inquisitive subject change. Malcolm is not your future brother in-law. Like I told Amber, Malcolm and I are just friends."

Ivy takes a sip of her tea before responding.

"Amber, if you told her I know she tried to perform an exorcism on you."

Gabrielle smiles. "Well she did have a small fit, but she's adjusting, but seriously, Malcolm and I are good friends. I'm helping him cope with the loss of his wife to breast cancer."

"Yeah I'm sure you would like to help the hell out of him with your body."

Gabrielle laughs as the waiter walks up to their table with information.

"Pardon me ladies, looks like this is your lucky day at Chicago's Chop House. Someone had paid for you all's check."

Ivy and Gabrielle look at each other oddly astonished.

"You got lucky Gabrielle, just who is this kind guest?" asked Ivy.

"It's the gentleman right over there, oh, I guess he left already. He did give me a generous tip though."

"Well we would have liked to thank him, but thank you, it's greatly appreciated." Gabrielle expressed.

"Let me know if I can get you ladies anything else?"

"How did this gentlemen pay if you don't mind me asking?" Ivy inquired.

"With cash, a hundred dollar bill to be exact."

"Thank you."

"Yes Ma'am."

As the waiter leaves, Gabrielle and Ivy both leans forward toward each other to speak about the unexpected consideration of a stranger.

"Ok who you got following you around with generous pockets?"

"Me, maybe it's one of those reporters trying to buy information."

"I don't like it, he could have introduced himself."

"Be thankful Ivy. This doesn't come along often. I mean drinks maybe, but entire meals. I wonder if Tru is in town."

"Who?"

"Truman Porter, we went to high school together."

"Oh, the rapper."

"Right, but Tru would come over to speak."

"Listen Gabrielle I've gotta get back to the office, but call me later."

"Ok, your treat next time."

"Yeah I know, let's just hope that mysterious guy comes around again."

As Gabrielle drives back to her profession, she couldn't help but wonder, just who was the kind stranger. Much to her surprise, the compliments of kindness hadn't stop. When Gabrielle did return back to work, she found flowers waiting for her. A lovely arrangement of Tulips awaited her. Tulips, just so happens to represent a declaration of love. Flowers are always a lovely surprise to receive, but there was no card attached. That seem odd and Gabrielle couldn't get much information from the medical assistant, only what florist delivered them. Now Gabrielle's mind was really wondering, curious to know if lunch and the flowers are associated with the same guy. She immediately makes a couple of calls.

"Hey Malcolm, how are you?" "Good Gabrielle, how are you?" "Good."

"Had lunch with your sister I take it?"

"Yes, and would you believe a strange man bought our lunch today." "That was nice and lucky for you."

"Yes, but he left before we got to see who it was and when I got back to work, I received some flowers, tulips. You wouldn't know anything about that, would you Malcolm?" she said with a lovely smile.

"Gabrielle, I feel embarrass to say so, but no, not me."

Gabrielle appeared somewhat disappointed.

"Oh, well I asked because the flowers had no card and I was just checking to be sure."

"Maybe it was your ex boyfriend, you know next week is Valentine's Day."

"Gee I don't know, I think he's still with that same female."

"Gabrielle I have a meeting in ten minutes, can I call you later?"

"Ok, talk to you then."

Gabrielle makes another call. She believes she has an idea just who the kind stranger is. "Hello Gabrielle, how are you these days?"

"Well Aaron and yourself?"

"Oh couldn't be better, now that I know you haven't lost my number."

"Hey Aaron were you at Chicago's Chop House an hour ago for lunch?"

"No, I had classes to instruct. In fact, just leaving campus."

"Oh that's right. So you wouldn't know anything about some Tulips sent to my job?"

"Come now Gabrielle, if I intend to send anyone flowers, they will know it came from me."

"You're right, but I was just checking."

"You mean there is another man besides Malcolm in your life?"

"No Aaron, not that I'm aware of."

"Tulips, that's the declaration of love."

"Yes Aaron, I've heard."

"Gabrielle I'm sure you have many admires, but love, well that's a bit deeper than fondness."

"Aaron, I hate to cut you off, but I have to get back to work. Can we finish this conversation another time?"

"Of course and Gabrielle?"

"Yes Aaron?"

"Don't be a stranger."

Bow down to me and believe me when I say, one way or another you will, for the dominating withdrawal effects of my treatment will have you on your hand and knees, trusting out the very specialized contents of bodily fluids in which I desire. What taste does it bring forth? What overwhelming feeling does it brings, unsettling in every way. I own your body, mind and very well possibly your soul. One could never question this corrupt healing of abuse, for without it, you will positively die. There there now, let the ride calm itself, transpiring the depths of my effects and leaving you with only an adequate amount of existences and sense of realistic control. That is, until we meet again.

As Mrs. Bayer finishes throwing up the remaining unidentifiable contents in her stomach, she slowly wipes her mouth. Eyes tearful, skin pale and somewhat cold, she is too weak to rise to her feet, so the private nurse helps her. Looking in the mirror, she has a hard time identifying with the person she sees with less hair. The baldness doesn't bother her as much. Growing her hair back little by little was something easy to adjust to, trying to grow your life back, well that's not so easy. Mrs. Bayer's surgery to remove the *beast* was successful. Her progress through the aftermath of breast cancer is still touch and go. The only thing left to endure at this point is chemo and radiotherapy, which leaves you feeling unlike your normal self.

Breast cancer can go either way, mostly its way, if you let it. Mrs. Bayer has thrown up so much, along with what seem to be all of her blood cells, that she truly believes she has tasted cancer itself. If cancer has a taste, what would it taste like? Honestly, I doubt if anyone really knows. It is a possibility that cancer could taste like leukemia, and what does leukemia taste like? My guess to that question is an odorless mixture of cod-liver oil and turpentine, something to surely leave a bad taste in your mouth. Despite the courses of treatment, Mrs. Bayer will do what's necessary. Although chemo leaves her weak from these down spiraling episodes, her willfulness to live is strong.

Gabrielle was home for the evening relaxing and enjoying the beautiful view of her flowers. She was watching TV, something she hardly had time for lately when her telephone rang. Gabrielle was anxiously expecting a call from Malcolm, but unfortunately this was not the call.

"Hello?"

"Hey girl, it's your cousin Je'brace."

"Je'brace, what a pleasant surprise. How are you?"

"Beautiful, always beautiful and you?"

"Lovely, just lovely. What's up?"

"Well, a friend and I will be in town this weekend and I was just checking to see if you and Ivy will be around?"

"Of course. It's been a while, how's my favorite and only Uncle Gary and your mom?

"Mom and dad are fine. He said you could call him more often."

"I know, we all have busy lives-"

"Mm-hmm, tell it to him. So be prepared to take me out on the town. See you then, au revoir."

"Bye girl."

Gabrielle shakes her head after ending the call. She knew with her cousin coming into town, that it will be quite interesting. Amber and Je'brace get along as well as a migraine and appendicitis, either way, both are a pain. Malcolm did call Gabrielle to inform her he will be out of town for the rest of the week due to obligations back in California. So it looked like Gabrielle's weekend was free to hang with the girls.

Friday night's happy hour, girl's night out was in preparation. Gabrielle was at home getting ready and waiting for Amber to come over. Gabrielle had just buzzed Amber up when she received an anonymous hang up on her telephone. She dismissed it and continued to get ready.

"Knock knock, it is I, Amber, more beautiful than paradise has arrived."

"Hmm, well if you are the vision of paradise, then I need to flush that sight away and wait for fresh water." said a voice in Gabrielle's living room.

Amber appeared a little surprised to that response.

"Gabrielle?" she said. Amber makes her way around into the living room and lay eyes on her adversary.

"Oh, it's you." said Amber in an unwelcome way.

"That's right, the true essences of beauty." stated Je'brace.

"Didn't know fair-weather friends could come around during the winter?"

"You should, you live here year round."

"Let me tell you something, little Ms. America reject."

A whistle was heard from the kitchen entrance. Gabrielle walks into her living room playing her part as the referee.

"Ok ladies, have we gotten the negative talk all out, because I don't want to hear anymore arguing or insults from neither one of you for the rest of the night. Amber this is Je'brace friend, Emerald. Emerald this is Amber, one of my friends that will be joining us tonight." The two women speak.

"So do I make myself clear ladies? I want Modus Vivendi, a compromise between you both." Gabrielle demanded.

The room became quiet. Amber pulls Gabrielle into her kitchen.

"Why didn't you tell me your guest would be your cousin?"

"It doesn't matter, you both are too grown to be carrying on the way you do."

"Hey, I don't have any history of mental illness in my family."

"Cute Amber."

"I heard that!" said Je'brace.

"Good, that means you finally cleaned all that wax out of your ears!"

Happy hour started out at Webster's Wine and Bar, you know, a couple of relaxing drinks before the rest of the evening. Now Webster's Wine and Bar is an atmosphere of acquired taste and let's just say, it wasn't the appeasing taste for Gabrielle's cousin Je'brace.

"Girl the place is depressing me, feels like we are at somebody's wake vigil." Amber gives an expression of, it figures.

"It would, probably not use to socializing with good people."

Gabrielle speaks before her cousin could respond.

"Well Je'brace, we are just chilling with a drink or two. As you know we are waiting on, speak of the devil."

In walk Fletcher and Reese. "Ladies, how are we doing this evening?" asked Fletcher with a rather large smile.

Je'brace rises up from her seat with a big smile and gives Fletcher a hug.

"I keep forgetting they already know each other." said Amber.

However, there was something else Amber didn't know and that would be that Je'brace's friend Emerald and Fletcher knew each other as well. Emerald elegantly gets up from her seat and walks over to Fletcher, giving him a warm hug followed with a kiss on the lips. That certainly caught

Amber's eye. "Gabrielle, Jillian, and Amber I know you have just met Emerald, but I would like for her to get to know ya'll little entourage because since Emerald and I are back dating again, she might decide to move up here to Chi Town."

The group seemed wonderfully surprised. Gabrielle did look over at Amber briefly, but Fletcher's news didn't seem to bother Amber. If it did ruffle Amber's feathers, her carapace was holding her composure well. Gabrielle was now checking out the interaction between her cousin and Reese. Amazingly, they have never met before.

"Je'brace, I thought you were so ready to leave this place?"

"Oh uh, ok. Where are we headed?" Je'brace eyes were still on Reese.

"Any where your pretty little self like." answered Reese.

Seem like Je'brace and Reese were making a love connection and Webster's Wine and Bar just so happen to be the right place after all.

This episode of ladies night out wasn't exactly just for ladies. The group went out to eat at Gaslight Bar and Grille on N. Racine Avenue then all attended a concert at the Opera House with special guest, Chaka Khan. Friday night's outing ended a little after 2am. Jillian was always the first one to leave. Fletcher's lady Emerald, left with him and they dropped Reese off at home. Je'brace talked to Reese on her cell phone all the way back to Gabrielle's place. Amber was the last one to head home for the night from Gabrielle's apartment, staying awake wouldn't be a problem because there was only one person on her mind, Fletcher.

Monday February 14, 2000

Gabrielle had only spoke with Malcolm twice since he has been out of town. She tried not to think about the special day, but that was impossible because every aspect of it is always in your face. Last year, she received roses, diamond earrings and had a romantic dinner at Geja's with Bryce. This year, of the new millennium, she's single and has no one to share this day with. It really sucks to be alone on Valentine's Day.

Looks like Gabrielle will get to experiences what Jillian has become accustom to on a daily bases.

Gabrielle got home a little after 5 pm and was about to get ready for a quiet evening alone when her intercom box rang. It caught her off guard with a scare because she wasn't expecting company. Gabrielle walked over to answer the call. "Hello?"

"Flowers delivery, for Dr. Michaels." "Oh ok, come on up."

Gabrielle presses the button to buzz the delivery guy in and began to think. She wondered who sent her flowers. Are they from the anonymous person that sent her Tulips? Gabrielle signed for one dozen red roses and thanked the florist delivery guy. She no doubt was surprised; it brought a pleasant change in her downing mood. Gabrielle took the roses into the kitchen and began to read the card, it read.

> *Just wanted you to know I am thinking of you. A red rose represents love, however, the love expressed, is brotherly. Happy Valentine's Day.*
>
> *Your friend, Aaron*

Aaron's kind thoughtfulness almost brought tears to Gabrielle's eyes. Her telephone rings and she goes to answer it.

"Hello."

"Hello Gabrielle, how are you doing?" "Aaron, thank you so much for the roses."

"Don't mention it. I take it; you and Malcolm are going out this evening?"

"Actually he's out of town."

"It may be my lucky day, can I interest you in dinner then?"

"Aaron I would, but I know it's just going to be a bunch of couples out professing their love for one another."

"You still have to eat."

"I know, just not ready."

"Ok then, how about takeout and a game of chess?"

"Now you're talking, it's so on."

Chinese was the takeout that Aaron brought over for them to devour. Gabrielle was grateful for the company. They were in the middle of their intense chess game and Aaron seemed to be on the verge of winning. He was studying his next move when some unexpected words out of Gabrielle's mouth caught him by surprise.

"Hey Aaron, would you like a kiss?"

Aaron eyes slowly rose from the chessboard to look up at Gabrielle. "I'm sorry?"

"Would you like a kiss?"

"A kiss?" Aaron asked surprisingly.

"Yes Aaron, a kiss."

"Uh, well Gabrielle. You know I have always respected you as a friend, more like a sister if anything."

For the first time Gabrielle seen Aaron uncomfortable, not the cool collective in control. "Relax Aaron." she said.

Gabrielle leans over and grabs Aaron's left hand then places a Hershey Kiss in his hand. Aaron smiled. "You got me." Gabrielle replied with a smile.

There was an unexpected ring from Gabrielle's intercom box and Gabrielle appeared oddly surprised. "Are you expecting company?" asked Aaron.

"No, not that I know of."

Gabrielle gets up and walks over to answer the call.

"Yes, may I help you?"

"Florist ma'am, delivery."

"Oh ok, come on up."

Gabrielle wasn't sure who these flowers were from, but Aaron had an idea. When Gabrielle opened her door, the delivery guy had with him a lovely dozen of pink roses. Gabrielle signed for the flowers and thanked the delivery guy. Great, Aaron thought. Even out of town, this guy manages to ruin another evening with Gabrielle. Gabrielle was smiling from ear to ear as she began to read the card. It read.

Wish I were there. Happy Valentine's Day Gabrielle.

Sincerely, Malcolm

"Well, I certainly wasn't expecting flowers from Malcolm, that was sweet of him to think of me." Gabrielle telephone then rings.

"Excuse me Aaron." "Of course."

"Hello."

"Have you received your delivery yet?" asked Malcolm.

"Yes, and thank you. That was sweet of you Malcolm."

Gabrielle got to talking to Malcolm as if Aaron wasn't in the room. After five minutes, Aaron gets up and grabs his coat. Gabrielle places a hand over the receiver. "Don't go, I won't be long." she said.

"I think I better go."

"You don't have to Aaron."

"I know, I know, you're winning anyway, but keep the pieces where they are. We will definitely finish this game another time."

"Are you sure Aaron?"

"Yes, I have papers to grade. Enjoy the rest of your evening Gabrielle."

"Ok Aaron, thanks for everything." "Just don't forget about me."

"I won't, take care Aaron."

Aaron waves at her as he let himself out and Gabrielle carried on her conversation with Malcolm. Looks like her Valentine's Day as a single woman wasn't so bad after all. However, as a pair of jealous and hateful eyes watches Aaron drive away from Gabrielle's place, he on the other hand would have enjoyed and liked nothing better than to see Gabrielle's heart suffer.

Malcolm was expected back in Chicago either Thursday or Friday, depending on when he could finish taking care of business back home. Amber's Valentine's Day was romantically divine of course and Jillian actually had a date that night. She wouldn't really go into details or information about the guy, only that it's not serious. Gabrielle had a good workweek, she only diagnosed two women with breast cancer, but she alone doesn't make up for the other doctors or patients that have been seen this week and didn't survive good news.

Friday night Jillian and Gabrielle met over to Amber's place. No happy hour lounging this Friday, it was Reese's birthday and he was throwing a party in which they were all invited. Gabrielle and Amber both rode with Jillian in her Lexus to the party. The ladies were all in a get right partying mood and the song Jillian put in her CD player confirmed it. The song that was playing as they drove to the party was, "Dance Tonight" by Lucy Pearl and Raphael Saadiq. Reese had rented a place for his party and there were plenty of people there, the ladies noticed that as they pulled up to park.

"Well my friends, the time has come, raise the roof and have some fun." Suggested Amber. Gabrielle and Jillian both agreed.

"Reese wasn't lying about the guest." said Jillian. "Look at all these cars here."

"At least the drinks are free." Gabrielle added.

"Unfortunately, I am driving so, Mock-tails, alcohol-free cocktails for me?"

"I hope he got good caterers."

"Gabrielle if it was left up to Reese, we would be feasting on chicken wings and drinking forty's." stated Amber.

The birthday boy and Fletcher were greeting people at the door and were more than delighted that some of their real friends could make it.

"Happy Birthday Reese!" said the three friends in unison. Reese thanked them for the birthday wish and stood with his hand out.

"Gifts?" he asked.

Amber slaps her hand down on to his hand giving him five.

"How you doing, where's the food and alcohol?" she asked.

"You know that's real cold Amber." advised Reese.

"So is the weather, but I'm not complaining, and you know I only buy my man gifts."

Gabrielle and Jillian both had gifts for Reese.

"Thank you ladies."

The ladies all stepped aside to allow more guests to enter the party.

"Who are the white people?" asked Amber.

"They are here for decoration." replied Reese.

Fletcher speaks to Amber and she just looks him up and down before walking away. "She's just hungry." explains Gabrielle.

Gabrielle and Jillian follows Amber to the bar.

"Be nice Amber, Reese didn't have to invite you." said Jillian.

"Do you think I'm worried about Reese and his parties?"

"Of course you're not." said Gabrielle. "But why are you being rude to Fletcher?"

"I'm hungry, you know that. My mood will improve once I eat and it looks like Reese actually has worthy carters. I'll be over there fixing a plate."

It had only been an hour into the party and Gabrielle and her friends were now just standing around with their drinks taking in the atmosphere. Neither of the women has yet to dance to the proper music bumping that kept the dance floor packed.

"Hey Jill, there's Benjamin, looks like he might be headed this way to ask someone for a dance." Gabrielle warned.

"Girl, I hope not. He dances like he has mad cow disease.

"Stop the press, who is that joining the party?" asked Amber.

Jillian and Gabrielle turned around to see who was coming through the door. A warm and proud smile appears across Gabrielle's face.

"Ladies you know I'm not into the other race, but I wouldn't mind being his urologist for a day." stated Amber.

"My dear friends, that handsome white face just so happens to be Malcolm."

"No way! You invited him here Gabrielle?" asked Amber.

"Well, he just got back into town and wanted to know where I was going to be this evening."

"Does he have a brother?" asked Jillian.

Gabrielle throws her arm up and waves to get his attention. Malcolm sees her and smile before heading their way.

"He favors that Jazz artist, Chris Booty." said Amber.

"I'm sure you mean Chris Botti." replied Gabrielle with a brief laugh.

"Yeah, that's what I said."

Jillian also agrees with his resemblances.

"I'm glad you both think so because I thought I was the only one."

"So, fuck him yet?"

"Ella! We are just friends."

"So you're not sexing him?"

"No."

"No, well allow me."

Amber began to walk forward and Gabrielle grabs her by the arm.

"Ok Ms. Coquette, your flirtatious ways becomes you. Behave, here he is." "Amber Hudson, Jillian Asbury I would like you to meet my friend Malcolm Reid." Malcolm shakes both their hands as he spoke.

"Well, Amber and myself are going to refreshen our drinks and leave you two alone."

"Are we, my drink is just fine." "Nice meeting you." said Jillian. "Likewise." Malcolm said with a smile.

Jillian slightly pulls Amber along with her to leave as Amber also replied that it was nice to meet him, and Malcolm said the same. They leave

Gabrielle and Malcolm alone and walk over to the bar. Jillian and Amber wasn't there five minutes when a male friend of Jillian's comes over and asked her to dance. Thankfully it wasn't Benjamin, so she gladly accepted.

Just about everyone at the party took to the dance floor to begin a popular Chi Town dance. Gabrielle and Malcolm were now seated on a couch sectional catching up on time apart.

"What type of dance is that?" asked Malcolm.

"Oh that's the bop or stepping, very popular in Chi Town."

"Can you do that?"

"Of course."

"I would ask you to dance, but I would only embarrass you if I tried."

"It's ok, I'm just glad you are here."

"So am I." he replied.

A few songs later, Amber was back over at the table of food looking for second helpings when Fletcher walked over to her.

"Have you eaten yet?" asked Fletcher. "Maybe, why?"

"Just checking to see if you were still in a foul mood." "Where's Emerald, is she not coming up this weekend?" "She's running late, but she'll be here."

"Then why are you bothering me?"

"Just holding conversation Amber."

"Don't waste your time."

"Is that all we were, wasted time?" "Obviously so."

"I called and called, you didn't return my calls. I'm a man. I get lonely too."

"Well you're certainly not lonely anymore."

"Emerald is sweet and can be good for me. She's in Business and Marketing."

"Seem like the only thing she's marketing is her breast."

"Don't hate on the girl because she was blessed and yours didn't reach full maturity."

"My average breast size satisfy's Trey just fine, as did they you at one time or another."

He didn't reply in reference to her breast, but did have more words for her. "Well you already know what you can say to change things."

Amber looks at Fletcher with bold confidence. "Don't hold your breath darling."

Amber tried to walk away, but Fletcher steps in front of her. "You're in my way."

"Amber it's me; you can drop the too proud act."

"If this is an act then I deserve an Oscar."

"Amber please."

"What Fletcher?"

"Be nice."

"Why should I?"

"Because at one time you did love me, now, I'm not so sure."

"This is getting old."

"Dance with me."

"No, why should I?"

"Because you want to."

"That's it, I'm gone." Amber tries to leave, but Fletcher steps in front of her again.

"Now what?" she cried.

"I'm sorry, because I want you to."

A slow song had just came on, "Let Me Know" by Aaliyah.

"Amber please, what will it hurt?"

Talk about your high maintenance, spoiled and too proud ways, Amber just so happens to possess all three. She did however, give in and agreed to slow dance with Fletcher. Back over where Gabrielle and Malcolm were sitting, two females, white females had out of the blue joined them. One was trying to hit on Malcolm of course. Gabrielle didn't want to be rude, but she wishes the heifers would disappear. The two mood spoilers tried to talk around Gabrielle, you know, act as if she wasn't there. Malcolm could tell Gabrielle was getting restless of the situation. One of the females, the one that was really persistent in getting to know Malcolm, said out loud how she loved that song playing. That was Malcolm cue to make a move and he did. Malcolm stood up and politely asked Gabrielle would she like to dance. A smile came across Gabrielle face as she stood up and happily accepted the invitation.

As Malcolm and Gabrielle walked away, the two females felt disappointedly hurt, but that didn't stop them from hating. You could hear one female say, oh no he didn't, while the other expressed the word, whatever! Malcolm and Gabrielle took a spot on the dance floor and slowly evolved into one as they began to slow dance. This was their first time being very close to one another, which wasn't a brief hug. It was the kind of up close and personal face-to-face interaction that have your mind wondering is your breath fresh enough. Gabrielle wasn't the least bit worried about fresh breath. She knew her breath was minty fresh. Gabrielle didn't appear to be nervous while dancing with her friend Malcolm, in fact she felt very comfortable. Naturally, they were getting some odd stares from some of the other guests, but that's their problem.

"Who sings this song?" asked Malcolm.

"Aaliyah."

"Yes, that's what I thought. she's very talented."

"The girl is one in a million. I love her music."

"Hey do you think you can teach me how to step?"

Gabrielle began to smile.

"What? You laughing at the thought of me trying to learn that dance?"

"Not really, just didn't think you would be interested that's all."

"I think it's neat, unique."

"Well in that case, I will be more than happy to teach you."

"Great, but just not here tonight, deal?"

"Deal."

Malcolm held Gabrielle closer to him and Gabrielle took a deep breath and slow exhaled. She couldn't believe how wonderful he made her feel. Despite the race difference, she wondered could she allow herself to possibly love him.

Still dancing to Aaliyah's song, Amber's mood had seemed to calm down. Actually, she was sort of ticked off that the one man she believed she had a hold on, has moved on with his life.

"Amber I don't see how you put up with yourself."

"Maybe because I love myself. You have to love who you are, the good and the bad. You can't always count on someone else's love."

"Why not?"

"Because other people's love, isn't strong enough or unconditional."

"How do you know that?"

"Don't be naive Fletcher."

"I'm not, but who's to say we won't end up back together?"

Amber suddenly stop dancing. "What?" asked Fletcher.

"The person behind you is that person to say." replied Amber.

Fletcher turned around to find Emerald standing there. Amber then walked away.

The night ended sort of early for the ladies. They parted way around eleven thirty. Malcolm took Gabrielle home, Jillian took Amber home, and Fletcher and Emerald argued all the way back to his home. I don't think Emerald stayed the rest of the weekend. Gabrielle and Malcolm's weekend went pretty well. They attended a Dave Mathews Band concert Saturday night and after the concert, Malcolm ended up back over to Gabrielle's place where she began teaching him how to Step. Malcolm actually caught on pretty fast and before she knew it, they both were stepping to the sounds of Herb Alpert song, "Rise".

CHAPTER NINETEEN

Why Not?

March 16, 2000

Thursday evening at the Black Panther's Party Urban Headquarters, Aaron and Vice President Tyrone Hampton waited patiently in Aaron's office for the arrival of Jasper Ware, the Chief of their Security of Defense. Aaron secretary was gone for the day, so when the elevators to the top floor opened, Mr. Ware stepped off the elevator and proceeded to walk down to Aaron's office. He knocked before entering and his members welcomed him.

"Brother Ware, so glad you could make it." said Aaron.

"Brother James, Brother Hampton."

"Brother Ware." replied the Vice President.

"Have a seat." insisted Aaron.

Jasper unbuttons his coat and took a seat. The Vice President continued to stand and Aaron remained in his seat as he began to speak.

"Brother Ware as you know, Brother Hampton and I are both pleased with your work, very pleased with the assistances at this years Martin Luther King's Jr. Let Freedom Ring March."

"Thank you sir."

"This is just a yearly evaluation with members and this won't take long."

"How are things going in your life Brother Ware?" asked Brother Hampton.

"Well, very well I might add."

"No personal problems we could assist with?"

"No Brother Hampton, everything seems to be good."

"How is your mother?" asked Aaron.

"Better, thanks for asking."

"Having any problems with other Black Panthers members?"

"No sir, Carl Sims is back on night shift at his regular job, but says it won't be a problem with his on call status."

Aaron smiles briefly before continuing. "Good, glad to know things are going well."

"Yes sir, thank you sir."

"However, we still have no leads on who jumped Brother Eddie Franklin the night Alex Rice was sworn in as a new member." said Aaron in concern.

"Yeah, real shame. I hear his broken jaw is healing nicely." replied Jasper.

"How is our new member doing?" asked Brother Hampton.

"He's a natural, born for our group."

"Really, how so?" asked Aaron."

"He kinda reminds me of you sir."

Aaron appeared intriguingly surprised.

"Continue Brother Ware." he asked.

"Well sir, Alex Rice has strong leadership skills. I would like to promote him to Sergeant someday, behind Brother Burton of course." "He's doing that well?" asked Aaron.

"Yes sir, I never doubted him for a second."

Aaron expressed a notion of being pleased before continuing his evaluation. "As you know becoming a Black Panther member is strictly voluntary. That's why many of our member's are successful with employment and or have their own business. However, that doesn't mean we don't help our own in financial crises. So what I am asking you Brother Ware, are there any financial problems you may need help in?"

"Not at all sir." Jasper quickly replied.

His quick response made the Vice President want to question him further. "So as a manager at a top security firm, things are going well financially." "Absolutely Brother Hampton."

"Well that's what we like to hear Brother Ware." replied Aaron. "We are done here. We will see you at our weekly meetings to discuss up coming events."

"Yes sir Brother James."

Jasper stands from his chair and proceeds to leave Aarons office. "Brother Hampton." said Jasper.

"Brother Ware." replied the Vice President.

Jasper closed the office door as Brother Hampton continues to write information down and Aaron answers his ringing phone. Brother Hampton walks over to the window and after a few minutes, observes Brother Ware crossing the street. He watches Jasper get into his car and drive away. Aaron then hangs up his phone.

"So Brother Hampton, what do you think?"

"I think he's lying, he's lying about his employment situation."

"He still manages that security firm right?"

"Yes, but they have lost three of their main contracts. The firm may fold before the year is out."

"Well a man is not going to admit he needs help financially. Just keep me posted if and when his firm goes under. We will be there for him."

Meanwhile back at Gabrielle's apartment, margarita night was taking place. Margarita night, which supposed to be a book club however, due to heavy topics on racism, card playing, generous amounts of margarita's consumed; margarita night was formed with a talk show atmosphere where the discussions is always about gossip and the other race. The book this month is Blind Ambitions by Lolita Files. All the woman generally read each novel however, discussions of the book lasts about a hot five minutes if that and that's before the card games begins. Make no bones about it; margarita night is full of gossip with a substantial amount of straight talk on the other race.

"And I told Kelvin, I'm your sister not your marriage counselor. Don't come to me with your problems, because no one made him marry that white girl." said Tationna.

Tationna is the RN that works at Northwestern University Hospital.

"Well let me be the first to say, told you so, because the grass is not always greener on the other side." replied Jasmine.

Jasmine was on paid administrative leave from the University of Chicago where a colleague called her a nigger to her face. Her lawsuit is still pending, but in great favor on her part as far as the University settling out of court.

"I'll see your ten dollars and raise you twenty." said Amber.

"Anyone needs a refill on their margarita?" asked Gabrielle.

Everyone's margarita was straight at the moment, as Gabrielle returned to the kitchen for snacks.

"Amber you have been somewhat quiet, no thoughts on the subject of Tationna's brother?" asked Carman.

Carman works with Amber at Ariel Capital Management.

"Not really, all couples have their share of problems. I don't think it has anything to do with her race. He did marry her, so he obviously loves her."

All talking ceased and with just music playing in the background, all eyes zoomed in on the queen of talk, Amber.

"Girl, what's got into you, are you feeling alright?" asked Tationna. "I guess the same thing that got into Gabrielle." replied Carman. "Shhh, I thought we agreed not to bring that up." whispered Amber.

"Agreed not to bring what up, what ya'll talking about?" asked Gabrielle.

Gabrielle had just walked back into the room with some Rotel dip and tortilla chips. The women became quiet.

"Let me help you with that dip." Jillian insisted.

"Agreed not to bring what up?" Gabrielle asks again.

She takes a seat and grabs the cards dealt to her.

"Well, don't get quiet on me now, because I assume the subject was about me. Am I right?"

"Gabrielle, I was at Reese's Birthday party." said Jasmine.

"Yeah so." replied Gabrielle.

"What Jasmine is saying Gabrielle; she walked into the party and saw you slow dancing with a white man. You know, the other race." stated Carman.

"And so what?"

"Well, we would just like to know have you crossed over, is that white man your new man?" asked Tationna.

With just the music playing, Gabrielle looks at each guest in her home then looks over the cards that were dealt to her.

"And what business is that of you all's?" replied Gabrielle calmly.

"Hey, no one's, but the many discussions we have had on the other race, I didn't think da white man was your cup of tea." said Carman.

"I'll see your twenty and raise you fifty." replied Gabrielle.

"Damn." said Amber.

Jillian looks at her hand and tosses them in.

"I'm out."

So was everyone except Carman.

"Oh, so it's like that Gabrielle? You gonna raise the stakes?" asked Carman.

"Yes dear, it's like that?" she replied.

"Well I'll see your fifty and throw in two more fifty's because the hand I have, is what I'm trying to get Gabrielle to do about withholding information. Flush, that's right. Now what you got Ms. Thang?"

Carman lays her cards down, waiting for Gabrielle to respond.

"Well ladies, as you know I'm a lover of wine, but enjoy tea just fine, Long Island ice tea preferably. However, my choice to sample other alcohol beverages doesn't mean I've given up on my love for fine wine. Furthermore, I'm in control in every way, especially when it comes down to what's best for me. Control is something you definitely have when you have a Full house." Gabrielle smiles as she lays her cards down and Carman's jaw drops.

"Oh snap!" said Amber. "Well said." stated Jillian.

Gabrielle reaches over to collect her winning pot.

"And my new Monolo shoes thank you all." said Gabrielle.

"So it's true, you're dating a white man?" asked Tationna. "Because I did hear what happened down at Mama Pearl's place, but thought you may have been with a co-worker."

"That's not the only place, because I heard about it at Chardonnay's Salon where we get our hair done." Carman also added.

"Listen ladies, da white man and I are just friends and if it develops into something more, then that's my decision. I don't see anything wrong with dating another race."

"Another race, we are talking about da white man Gabrielle." said Jasmine.

"Yes and why not? Why not date the other race? There's no harm in dating outside your sector."

"Why not?" asked disgruntled Carman.

"Yes Carman, why not?"

"Gabrielle we have had too many discussions on the white man. First of all, they only see us as sex objects, wishing it was back in the day when they could visit the slave quarters and take what they want."

"I can't believe you are going there Carman."

"Yes, and second, it's not uncommon to see a black man with a white woman, but rare to see a white man with a black woman."

"Carman is right Gabrielle, the only time you really see a white man with a black woman is because she is famous, rich or both." said Jasmine.

"You mean they have time out of their racist lives to date a black woman?" "Come on now Carman, you can't stop racism" said Jillian. "That's like getting a racists person to register as one. Sex offenders required by law to register, so why not racist people; you know, race offenders"

"Good point Jillian, but I don't think it's uncommon to see a black woman and white man together."

"Of course not Gabrielle, when you are that couple." stated Tationna.

"Actually it is uncommon Gabrielle" said Amber. "There are more than a few beautiful black sisters out there doing well for themselves. However, a white man would feel disgraceful, inferior, or of poor quality to date or even considering marrying a black woman."

This was the blown out of proportion discussion Gabrielle was dreading, but stood her ground with her incisive opinions.

"Amber you know our discussions are mainly based on stereo-typing, stereo-typing that characterizes black men as angry, white men as serial killers, black women with attitudes and white woman as stuck-up."

"Let me answer that Amber." said Carman. "Yes, mostly stereotyping, but what about incidents that do make headlines, sistas ending up dead so their white husband can collect the insurance money. I don't recall America Most Wanted ever being fictional."

"Ladies, ladies, listen to yourselves. You guys are over reacting and incidents like that can apply to any marriage Carman."

"Well I couldn't do it." stated Carman. "Who I am as a successful black woman wouldn't allow myself to date a white man."

"Well thank you for that comment Carman, but to each their own, plus like I said, da white man and I are just friends."

"Just friends huh?" replied Carman.

"Yes, just friends. Can we start the card game back up now?" "Would anyone like to finish discussing the novel?" asked Jillian. "NO!!!" everyone replied.

Just friends, Gabrielle vowed. I wonder did her friends know that Malcolm is taking her away this weekend to visit a wine vineyard. Malcolm's and Gabrielle's sweet escape get away of wine tasting will be on the estates of Beringer Vineyard in Helena California. This time honored tradition with enticing flavor is always entertaining with food or wine events. Berninger Vineyards is the eldest ongoing operating winery in Napa Valley and the first to offer public tours.

Malcolm and Gabrielle took a flight from Chicago to his second home in Sacramento, California. Talk about a change in atmosphere, the two left the windy city gray skies with highs in the upper thirty's, to arrive in sun bursting smiling skies, with highs in the lower seventies in Sacramento, California. Gabrielle would stay at Malcolm's second home since he did after all live in California and has plenty of room at his place. Upon arriving at Malcolm's property, Gabrielle couldn't help but complement Malcolm's beautiful home. It was a nice three bedroom, two and a half bath vacation home on the countryside not far from the beach, a home full of many pictures of his deceased wife.

That Friday evening after getting situated, they would dine at Chanterella's, a popular and attractive restaurant in Sacramento. Later on that Friday night after Gabrielle got settled in which seem to be a very large and lovely guestroom, her thoughts kept her up most of the night. Gabrielle wasn't sure if it was due to sleeping in a strange place, or the daydreams that Malcolm would come knock on her door. She could accept friendship, but curious to know would Malcolm make a play for her here a thousand miles away from Chicago. Gabrielle got cozy under the covers and turned on her side. There, on the nightstand was a picture of Malcolm's deceased wife. She was pretty, thin, with true blond hair, definitely a keeper. Gabrielle politely turned over to the other side, facing away from the picture. She closed her eyes to sleep, but knew her chances for romance were bleak and would try to enjoy her weekend sweet escape, a private getaway in which she told Amber and Jillian it was a medical conference.

A whole new world, just marvelous, glorious, couldn't even begin to describe the next day. It was as if Malcolm and Gabrielle left his home and drove right onto a panting by Vincent Van Gogh. This unique oil painting on canvas would describe a lovely scene and background fill with a mist of soft light colors that illuminates beauty; an amazingly wonderful scene of trees, exquisite gardens, a tunnel, aging caves, and a gravity flow winery. With a variety of tours to choose from, it's hard to imagine where to begin, thankfully Malcolm did. Him and Gabrielle began with the Historic District and Vintage Legacy tour. Next, they would tour the tasting room, also included was tasting in the cellar. They even attended a wine and cheese-pairing seminar. It was a picture perfect Saturday afternoon as Malcolm and Gabrielle explored the grounds of Napa Valley, an afternoon of learning, tasting and sipping on the finest crème del la crème of wines that Beringer Vineyards had to offer.

Malcolm and Gabrielle were enjoying lunch outside at one of Beringer's elegant dining areas where the employees lionize their guest.

"Are you enjoying yourself Gabrielle?"

"Oh I am. California is wonderful. I could live here. I just feel at peace."

"Really, but this isn't your first trip to California?"

"No, I took a trip with my sister and her family to Disney Land. I think I was nineteen years old then."

"Well I'm glad you are enjoying yourself. California suits you well."

"Thanks."

"And you look lovely. You always seem to know just what to wear, turquoise looks nice on you."

"Why thank you Malcolm. You really think so?"

"Absolutely."

The waiter comes over and asks did they need anything and they both agreed they were fine. "So Gabrielle, do I dare ask how do you *feel*?"

"Oh I'm pleasantly feeling the sounds of Mozart with a glass of Napa Valley, Opus One."

"That's great, terrific actually. However Gabrielle, in a day if enough people ask how do you *feel*, you should be highly intoxicated?"

Gabrielle gives a brief smile at Malcolm's questions.

"Well, not exactly. I don't always feel the mellow affects of alcohol. I could be feeling the sounds of Hip Hop with a Coke and a smile. It just depends on the day, moment, circumstances and mood."

"You're right Gabrielle."

Malcolm takes a sip of his wine. He then gives Gabrielle a captivated stare with a handsome smile, but looks away as if he is shy.

"What? What are you thinking?" asked Gabrielle with a healthy smile.

"Nothing really, just thinking of a poem."

"Oh really, by who?"

"Maya Angelou."

"I love Maya Angelou, which poem?"

"Passing Time." he said.

Gabrielle humbles herself in thought with serenity as she thinks of that poem and began to recite it.

"Your skin like dawn, mine like dusk, one paints the beginning of a certain end." Malcolm peacefully joins her to finish the poem.

"The other, the end of a sure beginning."

Gabrielle and Malcolm both smile before lifting up their wine glasses and tipping them toward each other before taking a sip. They sat with a peaceful aureole, a luminous radiance surrounding them as Malcolm aesthetically observes his view of her.

Passing time indeed, after touring Beringer Vineyards, Gabrielle and Malcolm went sightseeing the rest of their Saturday afternoon. They ended their day walking the beach, laughing and absorbing each other's company with not a care in the world. That evening Malcolm had a private chef come over to his home and cook dinner for them. This was something out of the ordinary for Gabrielle, a new dining experience. However, it was an acclimation she could accede. They were in the middle of their masterpiece meal when Gabrielle questioned Malcolm's music.

"Isn't that Jim Brickman's song "Angel Eyes" playing?"

"Why yes, I keep forgetting you listen to a variety of music."

"When you said we would be having dinner at your place, I kinda thought you would be cooking. So how long have you had your own personal chef?"

"My wife was a major health nut. So I'll say, about three years now."

"Must be nice?"

"I promised my wife I would try to eat right."

"That's a healthy state of mind."

"Well I'm not much good in the kitchen. So it helps. Question Gabrielle?"

"Yes."

"I guess I should have asked when we were walking the beach, but I couldn't get the words to the song right."

"And that would be?" asked Gabrielle curiously.

"Do you like pina colada's, getting caught in the rain, the feel of the ocean and the taste of champagne?" he asked with an attractive smile.

Gabrielle laughs quietly before answering him.

"Yes, yes I do. However, in my own words, I like Mai Tai's, getting lost in a sunset after the rain, the feel of a Jacuzzi and the taste of Rosé."

Malcolm gives a hearty smile of astonishment.

"Now that's what I mean. You are exceptional. Aaliyah has nothing on you. You're one in a million, one in a million."

Gabrielle and Malcolm talked late into the night, mostly about his deceased wife. Gabrielle didn't complain, but was sincerely grateful to be there. As Gabrielle prepared herself for sleep in the guestroom, she was glad to know friendship would be the destination of her and Malcolm's relationship. Who said men and women can't be friends? However, a sudden knock at the guest bedroom door may bring a different outcome after all.

"Gabrielle, have you gone to bed yet?"

"No, just a second."

Gabrielle fixes her hair some before walking over and opening the door.

"Ah, you haven't laid down yet."

"No, just turning down the bed."

"Well, I was just checking to see if you needed anything, another blanket or pillow perhaps?"

"Oh, I'm good, but thanks for asking."

"I've really enjoyed your company. You're a breath of fresh air, bringing life back into this home again."

"Thanks for having me."

"My pleasure, and if you need anything, I'll be right down stairs."

"Ok, thanks Malcolm."

"Goodnight Gabrielle."

"Good night."

Gabrielle slowly closed the door and stood with her back against it. After a few moments wondering if he would knock again, Gabrielle runs and leaps onto the bed and throws the covers over her head. Malcolm was walking down the steps when a song slowly came to mind. When he reached the last step, the song was now playing heavy on his thoughts. Malcolm calmly turns around and began walking back up the stairs. Gabrielle laid in bed a few minutes with the covers still over her head when a song began to play in her mind. Gabrielle slowly pulled the covers off her head. That song was now heavy on her mind. She quietly got out of bed and carefully tiptoed back to the bedroom door, she gently laid her head and right hand against the door. Little did she know, Malcolm was standing on the other side of the door, head down and right hand up against the door. Both had a particular song on their mind, for Malcolm, "I'm on Fire" by Bruce Springsteen and for Gabrielle, "Love to Love You Baby" by Donna Summers. Malcolm's right hand across that bedroom door was becoming a soft fist, ready to knock, a knock that could change Gabrielle and Malcolm's status of friendship into something more.

CHAPTER TWENTY

Last Call

Sunday evening Gabrielle arrived back home from her trip to California with Malcolm. I wish I could tell you that after Malcolm knocked on his guest room door that he rushed in and made passionate love to Gabrielle. What actually happened was, Malcolm gently knocked on his guest room door, which made Gabrielle's heart jump. She opened the door and there stood Malcolm with a charismatic smile. "Would you like to talk?" he asked.

"Sure." she replied. Gabrielle stepped back as Malcolm opened the door wider to enter the bedroom. He quickly walked up on her and they began to kiss. Their first kiss after all this time together was beyond passionate. Their first kiss was soft with a touch of aggressive hunger. If you can imagine the both of them trying to kiss a sweet juicy strawberry at the same time, while craving small bites of their pleasure to vitalize and savor each sensual taste, well; that's how Malcolm's and Gabrielle's first kiss was.

They make it over to the bed, still kissing as if their life depended on it. As they lay across the bed, still kissing each other strongly, Malcolm hands began to caress Gabrielle's body. He began to kiss her neck and as soon as he lifts up to remove his shirt, he glances over and sees the picture of his wife on the nightstand smiling at him and that pretty much put the fire out. Malcolm began to apologize while saying he can't. Gabrielle knew why and was somewhat disappointed, but understood. They did talk. He told her how much he liked and respected her and she felt the same way. They both agreed they needed someone in their life, but didn't want to take a chance on ruining a wonderful friendship.

No doubt, Malcolm wanted Gabrielle in every way, but just the same, didn't want to jeopardize what they built up in a respectable friendship. Before Malcolm left the room, he gave Gabrielle a long true hug. Talk about leaving someone hot and bothered, Gabrielle had to take a cold shower. When she did turn in for the night, of course what could have happened was on her mind. For some reason their first kiss kept playing over and over in her head. She turns over on her side to try to get some sleep, but sees the picture of Malcolm's wife smiling at her. Gabrielle reaches over and lays the picture face down before closing her eyes to sleep.

When Gabrielle did arrive home that Sunday evening from her trip, it was dark outside and bitter cold, goodbye sunny blue skies, hello arctic air. She pulled into a parking space at her apartment building and began to observe her surroundings. There didn't appear to be anything out of ordinary or some stranger lurking around outside of the apartment building. No matter how safe and secure you feel around the place you reside, there's always a reason to be cautious, especially at night. This applies to all females, young and old. It's just better to be safe than sorry. Regardless of who you are or what status you hold, death knows no color. However, red just may be the last color you see if your life ends violently. There's nothing sadder than to see your own blood seep from your soul before closing your eyes in death. If you had a choice in how you should die, how would you go? For some, they would say make it quick, faster than the next heartbeat. Then again, when it comes to death, who said you have a choice.

As Gabrielle got out of her car and grabbed some overnight bags from the trunk, she thought she heard footsteps approaching. She looks around observing her surroundings again, but didn't see anyone. Gabrielle doesn't believe in guns, but carried a powerful can of mace. She grabbed her overnight bags and began to walk toward the building. As soon as she reached the door entrance and unlocked the door to go inside, someone walked up behind her in a hurry.

"Gabby!"

Gabrielle spun around frighten with her can of mace drawn.

"Jesus Christ Bryce! Are you crazy, walking up on me like that? I was about to mace you."

"Calm down, I'm sorry okay."

"What are you doing here Bryce?"

"I've been trying to call you all day."

"I'm just getting home from being out of town."

"What, some medical conference?"

"No, I was in California with a friend."

"Who is the friend?"

"That isn't your business Bryce, now if you will excuse me."

"So I guess it's true then Gabrielle?"

"Is what true?"

"That you are seeing someone, someone of another race."

"What does that have to do with you Bryce?"

"Is it true?"

"Yes, I have a new friend in my life."

A tenant of the building walked up to gain access inside and Gabrielle stepped aside. Once the man was inside, Bryce continued to question Gabrielle.

"Do you love him?"

"Bryce, I'm tired and don't have time for this."

"Just answer the question, please."

"Yes, I have feelings for him."

"That's not what I asked."

"Look Bryce, you and I are done, why are you here?"

"Because I still love you and was hoping-"

"Bryce it's over! I'm over you. I'm moving forward with my life, not back into the past."

"So you no longer have love for me?"

Gabrielle throws the strap to one of her bags back over her shoulder, then makes direct eye contact with her ex.

"No Bryce, not in any degree. The love is gone."

Bryce takes a few steps back with words.

"Yeah ok, that's cool. I hear your new man is white?"

"What is it to you if he is?"

"They say, a black woman with a white man is like a slave being with their own master."

"You can believe what you want Bryce."

"I just want to know, how does it feel to be with your Master?"

"I can ask you the same!"

Gabrielle quickly opens the entrances door to the apartment building as Bryce continued to talk loudly.

"Hey I still have love for you baby! I'm the best thing that ever happened to you!" When Gabrielle was out of sight, Bryce finally shut his mouth. He rolled his eyes and walked off angry from the property to his car.

On her way up stairs to her apartment, Gabrielle thought how she was so glad she changed the locks to her apartment a month ago. Gabrielle just wanted to come home, take a hot bath and relax, but as soon as she opens her apartment door, Jack began fussing at her through the sounds of meow. He was a little upset because Gabrielle left him alone a couple of days. Her home phone rang and she went to answer it. As soon as she said hello the person on the other end hung up. She checked her caller ID, it read unknown caller. That made Gabrielle think to call Malcolm to let him know she made it home ok.

Gabrielle and Malcolm talked briefly before ending her call. Doing what she had in mind, she ran a hot bath and so she wouldn't be disturbed, she turned off all phones. Ten minutes later, Gabrielle was relaxing in a hot bubble bath with candles burning all around in the bathroom as she sipped on a glass of chardonnay, Napa Valley of course. To help calm her mood, she had the sounds of smooth jazz playing. Despite not getting laid, Gabrielle had a marvelous weekend and looked forward to another workweek.

"Damn him! Damn that son of a Bitch!"

"I knew if she continued to stay with that bastard, he would kill her!"

"Somebody needs to fuck his ass up!"

"It makes no sense, now her two kids will grow up without their mother."

"Well if he is in jail, they need to keep him there, because if he dare come to the funeral, they might be having services for him as well!"

These were some hostile comments coming from a group of angry women, friends of Rachel Payne. The late Rachel Payne was the fourth wheel to Gabrielle's and Amber's little entourage. Rachel knew Amber first when they were in kindergarten, but became closest to Gabrielle after they met later on in teen years. Rachel was a victim of domestic violence. She was not just a victim of physical abuse, but of verbal, psychological and emotional abuse as well. Did you know a woman is physically abused every nine seconds in the United States, and the statistics surrounding domestic abuse is alarming?

As stated earlier, Rachel Payne was a part of Gabrielle's and Amber's entourage. Rachel was an educated black female doing well for herself. She was an Optometrist and with a career dealing with the human eye, you would think she could see the wrong guy a mile away, but who am I to judge, especially when they say love is blind. All of Rachel friends saw the signs in the beginning, not just the sign of a jealous man, but of an abusive one. Everyone seems to see the signs of potential domestic abuse expect the one directly involved. Who knows what blinds them, the love or the loving, but before they know it, they are in too deep emotionally to walk away.

Not all men start out as abusive right away. I mean, they don't see a female they like, walk up to them and punch them directly in the face and say, "Hey bitch, wanna go out sometimes?" No, it's not that obvious. He's in his nice to you, getting to know you and your weaknesses stage. Sometime this misunderstanding of real men and who they really are, can quickly be cleared up for those women trying to identify and steer clear of the generic ones, by simply obtaining a background check, sad to say.

Rachel's husband Brandon, wouldn't acknowledge her success. Brandon was just an hourly worker at one of Kraft's Foods Processing plants. The problem in their marriage got worst when Brandon didn't get the opening position as a supervisor, despite the seven years already put in at his job. Some white kid right out of college got the position instead. Rachel had graduated in her field and was doing well. Brandon was jealous of the fact that Rachel made more money than he did. Rachel and Brandon were blessed with two children, Ryan is six and Brianna is four. Each child was born at a high point in Rachel's career, and even though Rachel didn't want to believe that her husband was deliberately trying to get her knocked up to slow down her success and dreams, sadly it was true.

Despite the sometime physical and emotional abuse from her husband, Rachel believed it was for the best that they stayed together for the children sake. Gabrielle and Amber saw less of Rachel after she got married, even less of her after she popped out two kids. Selfishly to say on Brandon's part however, if Rachel was able to get his temper under control and boost his self-esteem; then maybe it was possible for Rachel to get out of the house for a few hours on ladies night out. The last time Rachel hung out with her friends for more than a few hours, was two weekends after Jillian found out her husband was gay and on the down low. Gabrielle was the one Rachel confined in the most about her marital problems. Gabrielle, being the good friend she is, tried to support Rachel emotionally as much a she could, even offering her a place to stay if and when Rachel was truly ready to leave him. Support them is all anyone can do, especially when they keep going back.

Gabrielle, Amber and Jillian all sat over Rachel's place, along with other friends and family members giving their deepest sympathy to her mother. Gabrielle stared at Brianna, Rachel's daughter as she sits close to her grandmother. Brianna looks so much like Rachel. Out of all the guest there, Gabrielle felt the worst. Last night before Rachel got her head bashed in, she attempted to make a call. Rachel last call was to Gabrielle when she realized that Brandon's arguments was about to become extremely physical. Unfortunately, Gabrielle had turned the ringer off to her home phone and was soaking peacefully in a bubble bath.

Gabrielle tried to call Rachel back after she got out the tub, but the line was busy. Rachel's call to Gabrielle was the only other call Gabrielle received that night. Gabrielle thought that Rachel would just call her back later. Later the next day as Gabrielle was walking out the door from work, she received a call from Amber that Rachel died this morning from a subdural hematoma. Rachel died from a fractured skull and intensive bleeding on the brain. Gabrielle felt awful and could not hold back the tears. Her after work ritual couldn't possibly be much comfort to her nor would it bring Rachel back. Gabrielle couldn't help but blame herself. Maybe if she wouldn't have been selfish and turned off her home phone, maybe Rachel would still be alive. Now Gabrielle has to deal with the fact of Rachel's attempt to reach out for help and her last call, for the rest of her life.

That Friday's girls night out was canceled. Amber and Jillian was over to Gabrielle's place reminiscing over old times with Rachel and trying to cheer Gabrielle up, but despite the effort, there was enough sadness to go around.

"Don't feel bad Gabrielle." said Amber. "Do you think Rachel would want you to sit around being depressed over this?"

"I just can't help but think, what if I didn't turn off the ringer to my phone. She could be here with us right now."

"Don't beat yourself up Gabrielle." said Jillian. "It was just her time to go."

Amber rolls her eyes at Jillian statement.

"I don't believe that." Amber Replied.

"Hey, none of us like it, but when it's your time, it's your time."

"Yeah well, I never heard of anyone calling for help when it's their time." Said Gabrielle angrily.

"Gabrielle, I know Rachel was closest to you, but she is in a better place now." Said Jillian sympathetically.

"Well I think Rachel's place is here, not there." said Amber logically.

Amber stands from her seat, walks over to the bar and makes herself another drink. "You might wanna slow down Amber." said Jillian. "This will be your fourth Vodka Martini."

"Who's counting, besides the second one was for Edgar Allen Poe anyway and another thing, we should have done something about Brandon years ago."

"Like what?' asked Gabrielle.

"Getting her out of there would have been a start. Rachel could have come stayed with Trey and me. I would have dared Brandon to try and bother her while Trey is there." Jillian cracked a smile at Amber's last statement before commenting.

"And just what would have Trey done, buy him a diamond?"

"And what exactly would have your ex husband Dennis would have done, ask to suck his dick!"

"Ella! cried Gabrielle.

"Oh, you just hold it right there Amber Hudson! You wrong for that! You didn't have to go there." expressed Jillian.

"Well, don't start nothing, won't be nothing."

"Ladies, please!" said Gabrielle.

Jillian stands up from her seat.

"It's getting late Gabrielle; I'm going home before this really gets ugly."

"Ok Jillian, call me when you get home."

"Okay, try to get some rest."

Jillian grabs her coat and began to put it on. Gabrielle gets Amber's attention silently while Jillian's back was turned, suggesting that she shouldn't let Jillian leave this way. However, all Amber said before Jillian left out Gabrielle's door was, bye.

Saturday afternoon the three remaining friends attended Rachel's funeral services to say goodbye to a dear friend. Fortunately for Brandon, he was still in jail on second-degree murder and manslaughter charges.

After the three friends witnessed the burial of their dear friend, most in attendances accompanied the family back to her mother's house. Gabrielle gave an honest smile when she saw Bryce there. After all, he was Rachel's friend just as much as Gabrielle was. He walked over to Gabrielle to speak and to apologize for his behavior that night. Speaking of apologizing, Amber excuses herself from Trey to offer an olive branch to Jillian. Amber also apologized for her unbecoming behavior. Jillian accepted her apology and they were good friends again, as they should be. Anger, disagreements and misunderstandings shouldn't be taken lightly, especially when it comes to friends and family. You never know what last words expressed will be your last to them or that of theirs to you. As the saying goes, never let the sun go down on an argument. Furthermore, who knows, that very well may be someone's last sunset.

If losing one dear friend wasn't enough for Gabrielle to handle, how about a little more bad news to come to terms with. That evening when the three remaining friends parted company, Gabrielle called Malcolm and he invited her over for coffee. There, while Gabrielle was enjoying her cup of coffee, Malcolm informed her that this week coming up would be his last week in Chicago. Dealing with the death of one friend and the announcement of departure of another, was a little too much for Gabrielle and he could tell as tears began to fill her eyes.

"I'm sorry Malcolm, all this bad news can be over whelming."

"It's quite alright. I was just getting use to you in my life and Illinois again." Malcolm stands up and walks over to hand Gabrielle a Kleenex.

"Thank you. I can't believe they filled the position at the museum. I thought it would be yours for the taken."

Malcolm takes a seat beside her on the couch.

"Well, I knew the position would be filled eventually. It was only a matter of time. She's an educated and qualified woman that studied over in London."

"Did you not want the position?"

"Yes and no. Our agreement was to secure the position until they were ready to hire someone qualified to meet their requirements, but after ninety days if the available position was not filled, they would consider offering it to me."

"Would you have accepted it?"

Malcolm takes a deep breath before answering.

"Now that's the hard part. Like I said, I was just getting use to you apart of my life. However, my life is back home in Orange County, California. It would have been a tough decision."

"Do you have to go? I miss you already." Gabrielle smiled and Malcolm returned the favor.

"Yes, I'm afraid so and I feel the same."

Still sitting beside Gabrielle on the couch, Malcolm leans over and bumps shoulders with her. He gives her a hopeful smile with a wink of the eye. Her heart blushes from the friendly gesture.

"Hey, we have all week. Let's not waste it crying over spilled milk. Let's take advantage of this week and enjoy this time together. These couple of months of knowing each other has been precious and carefree time that will build cheerful memories to last a life time."

Gabrielle was touched by his words.

"Yeah, you're right."

"And you know you are always welcome to come visit me anytime in California."

"As are you, always welcome to visit me in the windy city."

Gabrielle lays her head on Malcolm's shoulder and he turns around to embrace her with a hug. Gabrielle and Malcolm did just that, they took advantage of their last week together. They spent every lunch and evening for dinner together. Thursday was officially Malcolm's last day at the museum, so Gabrielle took a half day at work on Friday and they spent the afternoon and evening on the town. 10:01 pm Friday evening, Gabrielle and Malcolm could be seen sitting at Café Deluca off N. Damen Ave, talking and laughing over coffee. It was a scene that seemed to be right out of Vincent Van Gogh 1888 oil on canvas painting, The Night Café.

CHAPTER TWENTY-ONE

In Search Again

Life was never quite what it was suppose to be, for me rather, just dreams blowing in the wind. Happiness, which was always finger tips away, but never seem to be in strive to reach its final destination, lingers with patients. I could cry, but why waste tears; I would only dehydrate my well-being. The cost of better to have love than to have never loved at all, has bankrupted my heart, though my life was never rich, just pieces of coined memories rolling around in search of a real home, a home not so far insight, but still far far away. Away, washes the seconds, minutes and hours, bringing forth a bud to a flower, yet still I lay, wonder and sigh, my, does time fly.

Time does fly indeed, one month after Malcolm's departure, Gabrielle was in strive to pick up the pieces of her life and regroup. With her two remaining closest friends, Gabrielle went on with her life as normal as possible, but was still longing for that special one to call her own. Malcolm and Gabrielle has deep feelings for each other, but the kind found in most close friendships. However, Gabrielle had no problem nor did she see anything wrong with dating outside her race. Let's just say, she could definitely see herself romantically involved with Malcolm if the situation presented itself again; but as of right now, one song could describe Gabrielle's current situation and that would be, Gilbert O'sullivan's song, "Alone Again, Naturally".

Yes, life went on as usual for Gabrielle, as far as getting back into the habit and swing of things. Of course girls night out went on, though it will always be an empty void among them, knowing Rachel will never accompany their presences again. Spring had arrived in the windy city, but the people of Chicago already know that they never actually witness spring there like most southern states. If the sun happens to shine upon them from its vacation, you can best to believe that the shadow of winter's air is still breathing down their necks.

Relaxing at home one Sunday afternoon, Gabrielle thought she would take a trip to the roof of her mid-rise apartment building for some fresh air. She had just spoken with Aaron on the phone and was expecting him over for company. Gabrielle was already on the roof and saw Aaron pull into the parking lot. She calls him on his cell phone and tells him she would be on the roof, and that she left a book between the entrance doors of the building. Gabrielle took a deep breath with a smile and looked out toward the sky. She then noticed some plants and flowers out on the roof. Walking over to view them closely, she picks up an empty old pot filled with rainwater and attempts to water the flowers. Aaron had just walked outside on the roof; he sees Gabrielle and smiles graciously. He makes his presents know by uttering some words of a poem, "The Seedlings" by Paul Dunbar.

"The sunshine poured upon it, and the clouds they gave a shower; and the little plant kept growing till it found itself a flower."

Gabrielle smiled peacefully; she answered Aaron's poem lyrics with another poem by the same author, "Ode to Ethiopia."

"Sad days were those-ah, sad indeed! But through the land the fruitful seed of better times was growing."

Aaron walks over to Gabrielle and gives her a hug.

"How are you Gabrielle?"

"Good, good and yourself?"

"Better, now that I see you."

"I saw you at Rachel's funeral."

"Yes, I hadn't seen much of her in a couple of years, and can't believe she's gone."

"We all can't Aaron."

"And now you have to deal with the departure of another friend."

"Yes, but I still hear from Malcolm from time to time. I will never hear from Rachel again."

"True, but she's in a better place and you will see her again, someday."

"Do you think she will forgive me?"

"Gabrielle, that's not a question for you, her husband maybe. However, all is forgiving in death."

"I hope so."

Gabrielle looks out over the city and Aaron views the earth below them. "You enjoy coming out here, don't you Gabrielle?"

"Yes, I like to catch some fresh air, breath in new possibilities and perspectives in my life. I recap past episodes of my life, ponder and dwell on the future."

"How does your future look Gabrielle?"

"It's coming together slowly but surely."

"Good, don't rush it. Life is short enough."

"You can say that again."

"So how are you really *feeling* Gabrielle?"

Gabrielle braces herself with an honest smile.

"I'm feeling the sounds of Kim Waters with a wine spritzer."

"Sounds inviting."

"Well my mellow pieces of thoughts are in constant search of peace and is usually pleasurable, not all the time, but most of the time."

"Gabrielle, you are a rare gem, one in a million."

That last remark from Aaron made Gabrielle think of Malcolm. Malcolm was the last person to say that to her.

"How is Project Hope coming along?"

"Very well, the clinic should be ready sometime the first of next year. Harold has been keeping me up to speed on potential problems."

"That's good; I know Ross would be pleased."

"Yes, I just wish we had some closure to his death."

"I'm glad they ruled out suicide. He was murdered Aaron."

"So was Elliott, but no real leads on his case as well."

"Sooner or later it will come to pass."

"Will your search for true love come to pass Gabrielle?"

Gabrielle turns to face Aaron with secure and positive eyes. "I hope so. I certainly hope so." Aaron stares at her tenderly.

"Still searching for the secret to happiness, are we Gabrielle?"

"Yes I am, waiting on your theory of this mystery."

"Well Gabrielle, here's the thing." Aaron cell phone rings.

"Excuse me Gabrielle."

"Certainly."

A few minutes later, Aaron announces to Gabrielle that he have to go. "Yes, always at a time when your valuable opinions are needed most."

"We will finish this discussion another time. Maybe you could stop by my office one day this week?"

"I'll try."

"Oh and Gabrielle?"

"Yes?"

"A hint to your question, breathe."

"Breathe?"

"Yes, ponder that and I hope to see you again real soon."

"Bye Aaron."

"Call me."

Still occupying the rooftop, Gabrielle watched Aaron exit the building and drive away. She immediately thought of Aaron's hint to the secret of happiness. Gabrielle takes a deep breath and looks out across the bright filled sky. She kinda had an idea of what Aaron was trying to exercise in her mind. To dwell on it would only obfuscate her rational thoughts to the point of any real meaning being unclear. Gabrielle however, believed she knew where to find some realm of happiness. Her most satisfying experience of felicity came at night when she closed her eyes to sleep. There, and only there, Gabrielle found all the happiness in the world with Percy, but even then, in their brief magical encounters, Gabrielle realizes she must awake and go on with her life, a life that has left her in search again.

Located at 1028 N. Rush Street, Gibson's Steak House is known for its long waits despite reservation. Luckily however, Tuesday around lunch time Ivy and Gabrielle had no problem in being seated on the far side of the dining room. It was Ivy's turn to treat and Gabrielle is always thrilled about that.

"Now let me see, what I have the taste for today."

"Knowing you, everything since it's my turn to treat."

"Hey, Mr. Walsh is paying you big bucks to represent him. So save the guilt trip about putting two kids through college speech. This trial alone will put your kids and mine through college."

"Yeah, well the trial may carry on until then."

"Don't be ridiculous Ivy."

"Being ridiculous is easy, obtaining a reliable witness, now that's hard. Have you heard from Malcolm lately?"

"I talk with him last night."

"So Casanova wasn't Mr. Dream come true. You cherish the moments and move on."

"Yeah, I suppose you're right."

Ivy stares at her sister closely.

"You have moved on right?"

"Well I'm trying."

"Try harder."

"I have my career to think about."

"Have you tried those online internet dating services?"

"No way, I mean I'm sure they have their benefits for some people, but I'm just not one of those people."

"Doesn't hurt to try."

"I just would like to meet someone, get a feeling about them and take it from there."

"Well good luck, but don't wait too long little sister, before you know it, your youthful days have passed you by and all you have to look forward to is another cold winter in Chicago."

"Excuse me ladies, are we ready to order?" "Yes we are." replied Ivy.

While Ivy began her elaborate order, Gabrielle continued to look over her menu. Sadly however, what she wanted was not on the menu. If it were, Gabrielle's order would consist of a tall, dark and handsome, heterosexual man with a career, a man that is stable and financially secure. Her entree would include that man to be honest, charming, loving with a sense of humor on the side, also included with her order, an appetizer always full of romance with seductive four play. Her tall drink of water, also included with her meal, would fully contain respect for her, appreciates her and always has her best interest at heart.

"And you're order ma'am?" asked the waiter.

"Gabrielle, you've been staring at that menu like it's an x-ray picture. Do you even know what you want?"

"Yes, I'll have the roasted chicken and potatoes."

After work Gabrielle found herself in Aaron's office staring at some of his tasteful yet peculiar artwork. He has a painting of Ganesha, a popular

Hindu deity, God of wealth and well-being. The particular painting Gabrielle was now studying was Aaron's version of Mount Rushmore. Instead of the four traditional president's heads, which included Washington, Jefferson, Lincoln, and Roosevelt, Aaron's own version of Mount Rushmore National Memorial included, Freddrick Douglas, Martin Luther King Jr., Malcolm X and Huey Newton. After all, Mount Rushmore is in the Black Hills of South Dakota. Moments later, Aaron enters his office with a child.

"Sorry to keep you waiting Gabrielle, I'm glad you have made yourself comfortable." Gabrielle turns around and sees the boy with Aaron.

"Oh my goodness, is that Percy?"

"My one and only indeed."

Gabrielle walks over to the boy and squats down to him with a smile.

"Percy you remember me speaking of my dear friend. You may not remember her, but this is Dr. Gabrielle Michaels."

The boy extends his hand for Gabrielle to shake as he spoke. "Hello Dr. Michaels."

"Hello Percy, the last time I saw you, you were four years old. How old are you now? asked Gabrielle.

"I'm six in a half. Are you the lady who was supposed to be my auntie?"

Gabrielle smiles humbly. "Yes, why yes I am."

Gabrielle couldn't help but give him a hug. She stares at him lovingly before standing upright. The boy favored his father and deceased uncle with the same name. "Boy, you're getting big." Just looking at Aaron's son made Gabrielle think of what his uncle and her children may have looked like. Little Percy hurry's over to the other side of Aaron's office where a game of chess was ready to be played. He takes a seat at the table and began to play with the pieces.

"I had to pick Percy up from his grandmother's."

"How is your mother?"

"Well, thank you for asking. You know, he's quite good at chess, would give you a run for your money."

"Oh, I don't doubt it for a second. I stopped by to see if you were up for company and possibly dinner, but I didn't know Percy was in town."

"He arrived Sunday, spring break. I'm willing, if you don't mind my youngling tagging along."

"I don't, but I know you don't see much of him and this is you all's time."

"Nonsense, I see much of him in D.C. actually. It will be fun."

"No, I'm gonna go, but call me for lunch when you think you're free."

"Gabrielle are you sure?"

"Yes, I'll just call Jillian and see what she's up to."

"Well you are welcome to join us if you change your mind."

"Thanks Aaron, so long Percy, hope to see you again soon."

Little Percy would wave bye to Gabrielle with a blessed smile.

Gabrielle left Aaron's office and walked a short way to the elevators. Aaron's receptionist wished Gabrielle a good evening as the elevators doors opened. On her ride down, Gabrielle couldn't help but think of little Percy. He was a joy to see and reminder of what if, possibilities of the past. Even though little Percy's mother and Aaron are not together, Percy is a very lucky and blessed child. Back in Aaron's office, Aaron was looking over some papers when little Percy walks over to him with a question.

"Is that her daddy? Is that the lady you wish was my mother?"

Aaron lays those papers he was reading down and stares at his child. "Yes Percy, that she is, but always remember, that's between us, okay?" Little Percy nods his head to his father that he understands.

As Gabrielle gets into her car to leave, she did not notice the pair of hovering eyes watching. It was a pair of deceitful and hateful eyes that didn't care too much for her presences. Gabrielle picked up some takeout and went home. She called Jillian and Amber for a quick chat before calling it a night. When she did climb into bed, her 8x10 black and white picture of Percy accompanied her, which wasn't necessary because not even amnesia could possibly keep Gabrielle from remembering what tomorrow was. April 19th is the anniversary death of Percy James.

On her lunch break, Gabrielle could be seen at Graceland Cemetery. This was another ritual she preformed every year. She would visit Graceland Cemetery twice a year, once on mother's day and on Percy's anniversary death. As she makes her way over to Percy's grave, Gabrielle had with her one white rose, a declaration of her love that she still holds deep with in her soul. She tries not to weep, but one or two tears always make their presences noticeable. Gabrielle wipes her eyes with a Kleenex. Another presence Gabrielle wasn't aware of was that of Aaron's. He knows her routine well and sits quietly in his car and observers her from a distance. Aaron always respects her privacy and never disturbs her.

The next evening while little Percy was at his Grandmother's house, Vice President Tyrone Hampton of the New Generation Black Panther Party presents some information and pictures to Aaron in his office. They were pictures of a Black Panther member engaging in unauthorized and confidential situations that violates the status of a true Black Panther member. We are talking creditable and substantial documentations that if left unresolved, could potentially cause extensive problems for the New Generation Black Panther Party. Aaron was not pleased as he looks over the pictures and information. He then picks up his telephone and makes a call.

"Brother Ware, I need to speak with you immediately. Meet me at the spot in twenty minutes."

Twenty minutes later, Aaron enters an old factory warehouse over near Clarke Junction. The building is off limit to trespassers with signs clearly displaying those very words. Nevertheless, it was a place Aaron and only a few others know about where they could speak in secrecy. Aaron makes his way inside the building and before he could switch on some form of electricity, Jasper Ware lights up a cigarette.

"Jasper were you followed?"

"No."

"Did you circle the block before entering the building?"

"Of course I did man, what's up?"

Aaron switches on the front lights and walks closer over to Jasper. "How long have you've known me Jasper?"

"Eight, maybe nine years, why?"

"Do you take me for a fool Jasper?"

"No, what's this all about?"

Aaron holds both hands out.

"Do my hands look handicap to you?"

"No."

"That's right, because I've been straight for many years now, but you already know how crooked my hands were before my son was born, shady connections that can be linked to Larry Hoover and Jeff Fort, among other crimes committed."

"This I already know."

Aaron walks up on Jasper and slaps the cigarette from his lips. "Aaron what the hell?"

"I wanna know everything. I wanna know who else is involved, are you directly involved and how long have you been corrupt?"

"Hold on! Just hold on man!"

Jasper tries to collect his thoughts, but knew his moonlighting scheme was up. Aaron knows about his involvement with his cousin Demarco.

"I trusted you like a brother. Tell me you're not what I believe you are?"

"Aaron?"

"Tell me!" shouted Aaron.

"Man keep your voice down, calm down! Tell me what you are talking about?"

Aaron pulls a folder from his coat and holds it up.

"I have evidences that your B o y Alex Rice, is a police informant."

Jasper eyes fell upon Aaron surprised as if he just snatched the life out from him. "What did you just say?" asked Jasper.

"I said, the man that you vowed as good as gold, is a snitch, a fucking stool pigeon!" Said Aaron harshly.

"That's impossible!"

Jasper reaches for the folder and Aaron pushes him back then grabs his gun from his waist. "You gonna point that gun at me Aaron?"

"I wanna know are you involved with this set up?"

"What set up? Aaron, this is new information to me!"

"Are you wearing a wire?"

"A wire, what the fuck?"

"Shut up!"

Aaron quickly walks up on Jasper and points the gun at his head and Jasper raises his hands into the air. Aaron places the folder back into his coat.

"What! You gonna frisk me now?"

"You damn right!"

"There, you see! No goddamn wire. I'm not a cop Aaron."

"That don't mean shit."

"Aaron you gotta believe me, I didn't know, I didn't know."

"Are you an informant?" Aaron demanded.

"Aaron please."

"Answer me, are you some fucking informant!"

"NO! I swear on my mother, I'm not."

"How can I trust you? How do I know if you're not lying?"

"Because I have much respect for you and the Black Panther Organization and would die before I betray that trust."

Aaron points the gun between Jasper's eyes.

"Is that right, you would die before you would betray me?"

"Yes, and if your Brother Percy could come down and speak for me now, he would tell you-"

Aaron throws a hard left punch, knocking Jasper to the floor. Aaron points the gun down at Jasper on the floor.

"Don't you dare speak my brother's name."

Jasper looks up at Aaron with a bloody lip.

"It's the truth Aaron. I'm not an informant. I love you like a brother man!"

"Shut up!"

Aaron returns the gun back to his waist. "Get up."

Jasper staggers to position himself on his feet.

"I wanna know what Alex Rice knows about me and any wrong doing with our organization."

"Nothing!"

"Don't, lie to me Jasper!"

"Nothing! Nothing that the rest of the members don't already know."

"You better be telling the truth Jasper."

"I am."

"You're going to fix this mess. We cannot disbar Alex Rice from the organization; the police will know we are on to them. You will however, limit his association with us. That is, until you can find away to dispose of this matter."

"Aaron I'm sorry!"

"You should be, there has been a breach in our custom relations. You have allowed the enemy to infiltrate our organization."

Aaron reaches back into his coat for the folder with information. He tosses it to Jasper and the folder hits Jasper's chest before falling to the floor.

"You will fix this, and fix it appropriately where the police will not show reason for probable cause, or give us any heat to shut us down. Are we clear Jasper?"

"Yes sir."

"Good, because any ripples, even one, and you will live up to your words. You know, the part how you would die before you would betray my trust."

Aaron fixes his attire before leaving the warehouse. Jasper bends down and began picking up the information and pictures from the folder. He had only himself to blame for this. Jasper was however, relieved to find out the heat was really on Alex Rice and not his shady dealings with his cousin. If Aaron would have know anything, he would have brought it up with this information; and if Aaron really doubted him for a second, then Jasper would have already laid dead with a bullet in his head.

Jasper was telling the truth; Alex Rice didn't know anything about Aaron and their organization that other members didn't already know. Unfortunately, Jasper cannot say the same for himself. Jasper and Alex had become tight. Jasper trusted him enough to bring him along on some of his dog fighting trips. Alex knows Jasper's association with Aaron's cousin Demarco and that he's a well-known drug dealer. If anyone is looking at any prison time, it would be Jasper. I guess you can say the future wasn't looking too great for Alex Rice, because Jasper will do anything and I do mean anything, to have things between him and Aaron right again.

CHAPTER TWENTY-TWO

The People VS. Tyler Walsh

Monday April 24, 2000
2:00 pm Cook County Court

Ivy Jackson certainly got what she wanted, what she has been longing for, another high profile murder case. What she wasn't counting on, was the fact that this case has drained every bit of the well-privileged life as a successful defense attorney right out of her. Don't get her wrong; Ivy Jackson is still sharp as a tack, keeping a wise edge that is poised with a straight poker face against district attorney Richard Devine prosecuting team. Her marvel and ability to do just about anything include; multitasking every bit of her career, motherhood and a devoted loving wife, all in a one woman show juggling act. Her family life still managed to suffer tremendously. Date setbacks of the trial, not having reliable witnesses and removing of two jurors has all played its part to calculate stress, the kind of stress that has ulcer forming potential, if this trial isn't put to bed soon.

In light of new evidence brought to Mrs. Jackson's attention two days ago, just might be enough to improve her reputation as the exceptionable, hard ass defense attorney she is. The prosecuting attorney was informed about Mrs. Jackson's new witness that is to come forth to testify, giving the D.A. considerable time to establish this fact. It didn't seem to bother him none because as far as the district attorney is concerned, he has this conviction in the bag. Tyler Walsh would plead the fifth to his where a bouts at the time of his wife's murder and not only that, the murder weapon was found in a empty locker next to Tyler Walsh's locker at the recreation center.

Given these circumstances and very little help from her own client, Mrs. Jackson was forced to consider other alternative options, possibly throwing in the towel and make a deal. However, the truth was something Mrs. Jackson always trusted and believed in. Ivy believed that not everybody's lies all the time and that someone with good intentions who wasn't selfish or trying to save their own ass, but someone or evidence with true integrity of what's right, would prevail. That's the victorious history with most of Ivy Jackson cases. She fought with the righteousness of true integrity in justice, for all.

"Mrs. Jackson please call your next witness?" ordered Judge Biebel. "Your Honor, the defense calls Lilly Rush to the stand."

Mr. Walsh looks at his attorney fearfully surprised. "I didn't approve this." he uttered.

"I know, I went around you." said Ivy cleverly before standing. "You can't do this. You can't do this!" he yells.

"Order, order in the court! Mrs. Jackson, please contain your client from anymore out burst."

"Yes Your Honor." Ivy sits back down beside her client.

"Mr. Walsh, please keep quiet. You had your chances to explain your where a bouts during the time of the murder. It's time for the truth to speak."

Lilly Rush walks pass the people of the court and is sworn in. "I didn't want to involve her, not this way."

"It's too late." whispered Ivy. She stands back up to question her witness.

"Will the witness please give her name for the court?" "Lilly Ann Rush."

"How old are you Mrs. Rush?" "I'm twenty-five."

"Are you married Mrs. Rush?" "Yes I am, to Daniel Rush."

"Mrs. Rush, are you related to Mr. Glen Fisher, the best friend of Tyler Walsh?" "Yes I am."

"How are you and Mr. Fisher related?" "Mr. Fisher is my father."

"Objection, relevance." stated the D.A.

"Your Honor, relevance is something I'm trying to establish. My line of questioning is on proper course to relay those facts."

"Overruled, continue Mrs. Jackson posthaste."

Tyler Walsh looks back at Mr. Fisher sitting among the group of people then turns back around and holds his head down.

"Mrs. Rush, do you know the defendant, Tyler Walsh?" "I do."

"How do you know the defendant?"

"Well for one, Tyler Walsh and my father are best friends. Tyler is a friend of the family. Tyler and I were also involved romantically, we were having an affair." Chatter began to escalate in the courtroom.

"Quiet, quiet in the courtroom." demanded Judge Biebel.

Mr. Fisher looks over at Mr. Walsh sadly surprised as Mr. Walsh continues to face forward.

"Now Mrs. Rush, you say you were involved in romantic relationship with Mr. Walsh, is the affair still going on?"

"No it's not."

"How long has this affair been going on Mrs. Rush?" "For a year."

"And when did the affair end?" "December 30, 1999."

"Are you sure of the date Mrs. Rush?" "Yes I am."

"Where and what time did this farewell take place?"

"At my apartment, between the hours of 7:00 and 7:30 pm."

"What time did Mr. Walsh leave your apartment?"

"Around 7:30-7:40 pm, I tried to convince him to stay, but he refused, said he was running late and was meeting my father at the recreation center."

"Let me make this clear for the court. Tyler Walsh was at your apartment December 30, 1999 between the hours of 7:00 and 7:30 pm, ending a year long affair? "Yes, that's correct."

"No further questions. Your witness Counselor."

District Attorney Devine stand from his seat and walks a few steps in front of the witness before questioning her.

"Mrs. Rush, and why on earth would these good people of the court find favor in you or believe your statement of Mr. Walsh's where a bouts at the time of the murder?"

"Don't take my word for it, let the surveillance cameras at my apartment building and the cameras on E. 8th Street be my factual words."

"So the apartment building you and your husband live in has surveillance cameras Mrs. Rush?"

"Yes, cameras recording twenty-four hours a day, seven days a week. The cameras are located outside, up by the entrance doors of the high-rise building, but like I said, don't take my word for it. Check it out for yourself."

"That we will do Mrs. Rush. No further questions."

"You may step down Mrs. Rush. Mrs. Jackson, call your next witness." The judge ordered.

"The defense recalls Mr. Fisher Your Honor."

Mr. Fisher stands and proceeds to make his way back to the witness stand, but not before giving Tyler Walsh a hard stare along the way. Mr. Walsh just drops his head with guilt. Judge Biebel reminds Mr. Fisher that he is still under oath before Mrs. Jackson began her questioning from her seat.

"Mr. Fisher, did you know about your daughter and best friend affair?"

Mr. Fisher repositioned himself in the witness chair and cleared his throat before answering Mrs. Jackson first question.

"Yes I did?"

Mr. Walsh raised his head up and looked at Mr. Fisher honestly surprised.

"How long have you known that your best friend was sleeping with your daughter Mr. Fisher?"

"I saw Tyler leaving out my daughter's apartment building eight month's ago and put two and two together."

"Were you angry after learning of the affair?"

"No, hurt, disappointed in Tyler if anything."

"So what did you do about this information learned Mr. Fisher?"

"Nothing, just prayed it would end."

Ivy stands from her seat and began to walk toward her witness.

"Isn't it true Mr. Fisher, that you and your wife after twenty-five years of marriage, are going through a divorce?"

"That is correct."

"Where is Mrs. Fisher, Mr. Fisher?"

"At home, she uh, She's not well."

"Not well, please explain?"

"My wife has been depressed about the matter of divorce."

"Isn't it true Mr. Fisher, that your wife suffered a nervous breakdown six months ago and has been seeking treatment as an outpatient from a state institution?"

"Objection!" voiced the D.A.

"Just where are you getting this information?" asked Mr. Fisher.

"Please answer the question Mr. Fisher." suggested Mrs. Jackson.

"Your Honor please! I don't see how any of this benefit's the defendant case?" advised District Attorney Devin.

"Your Honor, it will make perfect sense and will benefit my client if allowed to further question my witness."

"Lets see where this is going, overruled. The witness will answer Mrs. Jackson last question."

"Yes, my wife did suffer a nervous breakdown and has been seeking treatment." "Mr. Fisher, why after twenty-five years of marriage are you asking for a divorce?

You are the one asking for the divorce, right?"

"Yes, I asked for the divorce."

"Why Mr. Fisher?"

Mr. Fisher appeared a little sad, sympathetic to the reason. "We fell out of love."

"Isn't it true that you fell out of love with Mrs. Fisher and fell in love with the defendant's wife, Gail Walsh?"

Tyler Walsh's eyes rushed upon Mr. Fisher with shocking amazement, as chatter spreads among the courtroom.

"Quiet, quiet I say!" Judge Biebel strikes the gavel down a few times and tells Mr. Fisher to answer the question. Mr. Fisher looks over at his best friend Tyler Walsh with sorrow in his eyes.

"Yes, I loved Gail Walsh. We were having an affair."

"How long have you and Gail Walsh been having an affair?"

"For three years."

"Gail Walsh was supposed to meet you the night of December 30, 1999 at your office to end the affair, but didn't show, is that correct?"

"That's correct."

"Mr. and Mrs. Walsh were going to work out their differences and remain together. Isn't that correct Mr. Fisher?"

"Yes, that's what she told me. I begged her to meet me that night so I could talk her out of it."

"Mr. Fisher, who is Mathew Fisher?" "Mathew is my son."

Ivy walks from the jury back over to the witness stand.

"And what role does nineteen year old Mathew Fisher play in all this sin?"

"Nothing! You leave him out of this!"

"I'm sorry Mr. Fisher, I can't and may I remind you, you are still under oath."

"Mathew is just a kid; he was having a hard time dealing with the divorce." "Having a hard time dealing with the divorce indeed, isn't it true Mr. Fisher that Mathew found out about your affair six months ago?"

"He must have followed me one night and confronted me when I got home."

"Isn't it true, Mathew Fisher blamed Gail Walsh for ruining you all's happy home, causing his mother to suffer a nervous breakdown and in fact, threaten Mrs. Walsh at her place of employment?"

"I was told of the incident."

"Isn't it true Mr. Fisher that the reason why Gail Walsh didn't meet you that night is because your son Mathew Fisher went to the defendant's home and brutality murdered Gail Walsh by stabbing her five times?"

"Objection! Circumstantial." voiced the D.A.

"Overruled, the witness will answer the question." ordered the Judge.

Mr. Fisher was now sobbing uncontrollably on the witness stand. "He's just a kid; he didn't know what he was doing?"

"Did your son Mathew Fisher murder Gail Walsh Mr. Fisher?"

"I have reason to believe my son is responsible for Gail Walsh's death. I had just come home that night and Mathew met me outside. His hands and clothes were all bloody. He told me what happened and that he still had the murder weapon on him. I made him give the weapon to me and told him I would take care of it. I returned back to the recreation center and placed the weapon inside the locker next to Tyler's locker. You have to believe me, my son is not well?"

"Thank you Mr. Fisher, no further questions."

Mr. Walsh now sat with hatred in his eyes staring at his best friend with resentment. "Mathew killed my wife? You are responsible for all of this, you bastard!" Mr. Walsh charges from the table toward the witness stand as the sheriff deputy and prison guards stops him. The courtroom was now a ruckus of mixed emotions as the judge tries to bring order to the courtroom. Ten minutes later, Mr. Fisher was being taken into custody and being read his rights. His son Mathew Fisher was being booked as his father was testifying on the stand. All charges against Tyler Walsh were dropped and the case was dismissed. District Attorney Devin didn't like it one bit, but had to give proper credit where credit was due. No doubt, Mrs. Jackson is the truth. Later that afternoon, Champagne corks were being popped as the top executives attorneys and managing partners of Lambert, McGhee and Hewitt, celebrate Mrs. Jackson's victory. That's not all what they were celebrating, Ivy Jackson has now made partner to the prestigious law firm she hope to devote the rest of her career.

The next day, Ivy was having lunch with her sister. Not only was Ivy on cloud nine that the trial was over and that she won, but it was Gabrielle's turn to treat and that made it even better.

"Well now, let's see what my expensive taste in good food is in the mood for?"

said Ivy.

"I have to give you your props, your reputation precedes you Mrs. Jackson. You did your thang. I would say go easy on the order, but you deserve it."

"Amen to that."

"How are you and Wade going to celebrate?"

"Well that reminds me, are you busy this weekend?

"No, not really."

"Good, I was hoping you could come over and baby-sit the girls Saturday night while Wade and I go out."

"Done, no problem."

"Great, Wade and I need this time alone."

"Any other plans I should know about?"

"Like what?"

"Oh like, the possibility of still wanting to give Wade a son."

"Girl please, what did I tell you. Wade is happy with his girls and I'm not trying to produce anymore. Plus, I put a restraining order on my ovaries anyway." Gabrielle laughs willingly as she agrees with Ivy's statement.

"I heard that."

"Ladies are we ready to order?" asked the waiter.

After Gabrielle and Ivy gave their food order, Ivy questioned Gabrielle's somewhat distraction. Something seemed to be on Gabrielle's mind.

"Gabrielle, is everything alright with you? You seem a little distracted."

"Yeah well, now that you mentioned it, do you sometimes ever get the feeling someone is watching you?"

"Of course, but because of the publicity of the Walsh trial, I knew it was the media. What's up?"

Gabrielle appeared a little embarrassed, but smiled briefly before answering. "It's just that I've been receiving anonymous hung up's on my home phone and I sometimes gets the feeling someone is watching me, like before I came inside the restaurant. It felt like I was being followed."

"You think you might have a stalker?" "I hope not."

"Well when did the hang ups first start?" "Off and on maybe six month's ago."

Ivy appeared concerned.

"That long, do you have an idea who this person could be? You think you might need to get the police involved?"

"At first I thought it was Bryce, but the hang ups were going on right before we broke up. He frighten the hell out of me one night by showing up at my place just when I was about to enter the building."

"What did he want?"

"Nothing, things must not be going well with him and Jennifer and probably looking for some kind of balance with me. I did ask him after Rachel's funeral was he calling me and hanging up?"

"What lie did he give?"

"He said it wasn't him and I honestly believe him. Maybe it's nothing and hopefully I won't have to get the police involved."

"Well you be careful little sister, because I don't have to tell you how many weirdo's, sickos and murder's are out there ready to make an example out of their next victim."

"Yeah, I'm always careful. I just hate that feeling."

"We all get bad vibes from time to time. However, some negative feelings can be grounds for potential harm."

The waiter returned with their beverages as Gabrielle silently consumed her sister's advice. She didn't want to ruin Ivy's victory celebration lunch, so Gabrielle quickly changed subjects in light of a better mood. Hauntingly however, parked outside a block away from the restaurant was a pair of potentially dangerous eyes, watching and waiting for Gabrielle's presences to return.

Somewhere at home in East Peoria, Illinois, a commercial van sits less than a block away from the home of Mark Hale. The FBI has twenty-four hours detail surveillances on the white supremacist after being linked to a followers deadly shooting rampage in July 1999. Hale receives a call from his cousin on an unidentified cell phone that cops are not aware of at the moment. Even though Hale is assured that this particular phone is safe, he don't doubt the police willfulness and power to continually target him and acts accordingly.

"Patrick didn't I tell you not to ever call me here?"

"Hello to you too cousin."

"What is it Patrick?"

"Sam got me sitting on jobs. What's the hold up?"

Hale smiles. "Feeling a little useless are we?"

"More than a little, what gives?"

"Time, it's all about timing. Patrick you already know about the heat I'm receiving from our good friends the FBI on Smith's shootings."

"Smith had a weak mind and no leadership skills."

"And now this fucking U.S. District Judge, Linda McPherson, is going to order me to stop using the name World Church of Masters Creator Society because it had been trademarked by some Utah based religious group with no ties to us."

"Yeah I heard, can that nigger bitch do that?"

"Well you know me; I'm always going to fight within the legislation. It's my given right."

"So, are you gonna exterminate the rodent?"

Hale walks over to a window and looks outside.

"That special information has already been provided, if you interested, you have the license to do so. Just keep our contacts that are directly involved out of this." The cousin smiles.

"Consider it taken care of and what about our other potential clients?"

"They're not going any where, but their time is limited. One customer is pressing us, but you know what I say?"

"What?"

"Fuck him! If he doesn't have the balls to do it himself, but financially invest in us to do the job, then it will be on our terms."

"I'm moved by your words."

"Hey wise ass, don't humor me on this and another thing, I don't want to know any detail of this event. The next time you feel the need to call me, don't. In other words, don't call me, I'll call you." Hale pushes the end button to disconnect the call.

May 8, 2000

Two weeks later, Chicago police were investigating the gruesome murders of U.S. District Judge Linda McPherson, her husband and mother. Judge McPherson and her family members were found shot dead execution style in her home on Chicago's NW side. Mark Hale was arrested and brought in for questioning. However, the feds didn't have crucial evidence or any proof to connect Hale at this time for these crimes. Hale walked out of custody with a big smile on his face as a free man. Hale went home and got directly on the tapped phone line of his East Peoria home. The FBI recorded a conversation in which they over heard Hale laughing about the fatal shootings of U.S. District Judge Linda McPherson and family members.

The FBI turned up the heat on their investigation on Hale. They invaded his home with search warrants twice in one week. The police even served a warrant on Hale's group members at that shady commercial building over in Elmwood Park, right outside of Chicago. The law had the same luck they had at Hale's home, which was nothing. Important files and information are removed from that building on a daily bases. Plus the building had a furnace for easy disposal. All authentic copies of files, documents and information was always keep hundreds of miles away from the World Church Creator Society Organization in a highly safe and secure place. Honestly, the only way the police could find that vital information, is if God himself came down and showed them the exact location.

Hale's cousin, Patrick Reddick wasn't catching any of Hale's heat. In fact, cops didn't see Reddick as any real threat, just some country redneck, with no real criminal record that was free to walk the streets of Chicago. Then again, when you're walking the streets of any city, you're bound to run into someone you just don't particularly care for. That particular someone might not set well in your eyes to suit just what you may acknowledge yourself to be. That negative prejudice approach can sometimes pose a problem with future repercussions.

It was a sunny afternoon in the ongoing month of May, one week shortly after the murders of U.S. District Judge Linda McPherson and some of her family members. Patrick Reddick and another group member were walking the sidewalks of Michigan Avenue, also walking the same sidewalk from the opposite direction, were Jasper Ware and another Black Panther member. Reddick sees the two Black Panther members approaching and gives a distasteful stare. When the four men did meet up in passing, Reddick bumps Jasper Ware with a hard right shoulder that almost stumbles Ware.

"Excuse you." said Jasper aloud as he stopped and turned around.

"You're excused boy." said Reddick as they continued to walk.

"What did you say punk?" asked Jasper.

Reddick and the other member stops and turns around. "I said you are excused boy."

Feeling insulted, Jasper makes his move toward Reddick, but the other Black Panther member stops him.

"Don't even waste your energy Brother Ware."

"What's wrong boy, not tough enough to fight a real man?"

The people of Chicago continued to walk pass and around them.

Jasper smiles at Reddick. "You're ignorant and I don't fight the handicap."

"Come get some boy!" demanded Reddick.

Jasper and the other Black Panther member turn around to leave, but then Jasper stops and turns back around with words.

"I got your Boy, and your number."

"I have your's too boy!" replied Reddick with a wink and a smile.

Both parties turned around to part way and continue to walk in the opposite direction.

"Patrick, are you trying to get arrested? Mitch said not to draw attention to yourself."

"Man forget Mitch and fuck those niggers."

"Brother Ware, you already know we are a non-violent organization."

"Yes, but sometimes you have to put your foot down, fucking country crackers."

At home later that same evening, Aaron and Gabrielle were having a casual conversation over the phone. The topic of U.S. District Judge Linda McPherson came up in discussion. In fact, it was the number one current affair headliner of Illinois. "My heart goes out to her family, but I'm just relieved that the police are not knocking on my door, trying to bring me in for questioning." "Not yet anyway." replied Gabrielle with a smile.

"Gabrielle I tell ya, I believe you put more hell on me than cops. Please take your harsh sun rays off my back."

"Come on Aaron, I'm not that bad."

"Maybe you should have become a lawyer too. You will have no problem learning from the best. Your sister is a role model in African-American heritage."

"Now that I will agree with you."

"I think Mark Hale was arrested and questioned about those murders."

"That's what I heard."

"Do you think your sister would defend him if needed?"

"Only if he's innocent, but judging from his background as a white supremacist leader, I doubt if her services would be needed."

Aaron breathes out a heavy smile. "So are you ready Gabrielle?" "Ready for what?"

"My moderate chemical equation to the secret of happiness." "Am I ever."

"Ok, what is happiness? Happiness is to be fortunate, felicity, to be content with your overall well-being. People's search for happiness or delay on satisfying fulfillments of life, never cease to amaze me. Just because something is not complete or on schedule with your life, doesn't mean you postpone truly living life to your best."

"Well, I wouldn't say something is not on schedule with my life."

"In a word, breathe. Life begins with one breath and as you continue to do what is natural, as your life grows, the happiness that you produce inside yourself flows, as you live and evolve. No one has to tell you to breathe, do they?

"No."

"Of course not, it's a natural reflex. So why do people have to be told when they should be happy, pleased, or in contentment from a level of status, piece of paper, or success in achievements in life."

"Maybe because that's what life is hyped up to be for true happiness." "Gabrielle, when you deny your body, mind and soul, your very life, which isn't very long, the right, the pleasures of the simple acts and fulfillment of breathing, then you are your own worst enemy."

"Yes, but it's different for others with depression."

"Yes of course, people who are depressed are depriving their brain from oxygen, the act of breathing healthy thoughts. People who are depressed have sad repressed thoughts. They should seek medical help if possible and try to rebuild their life and connect to some form of happiness from there. Are you depressed Gabrielle?"

"No, I'm not."

Aaron smiles willingly.

"No, I didn't think so. Happiness is not what you can accomplish, or succeed, for other's its vital, so more power to them. Happiness is what truly makes you smile with a carefree spirit that I'm going to make the best of this day. When you got up this morning and went to work, you did all the things that make your life your very own, right?"

"Yes."

"Still, you had no idea if you would actually return home. Sure, we think about what we need to do when we get home, but who's to say that you'll reach your destination. You can lay down tonight and not awake in the morning, before you closed your eyes to rest, were you happy?"

"Well it depends on the kind of day you had."

"True, but did you spend that day searching, wishing and waiting for the right time to expose happiness or did you give every moment possible a breath of blessings, evolving an atmosphere of potential happiness only you can make possible."

"All possibilities have levels and cautions."

"Are there levels of happiness? Yes of course, and no, I don't mean the kind of levels you would receive from a buzz or high, after taking a puff or two of marijuana. Levels of happiness depends on your inner being of circumstances."

"Yeah, circumstances that can shape you or break you."

"Gabrielle, if you are a good person, I mean a genuinely good person filled with love, especially love to give and help others, then you should be one of the happiest people on God's green earth. Happiness is not a secret to find. Happiness is a breath of fresh air, a blissful, grateful way of life that you share with others. Don't search for it Gabrielle, breathe it."

In Gabrielle's moment of being speechless, Aaron gets another call. "Excuse me Gabrielle."

"Certainly."

A few minutes later, Aaron clicks back over to Gabrielle.

"I'm sorry Gabrielle; I must speak to this person further. Can I catch you at the library on Thursday?"

"Of course."

"Good, until then, take my words to heart and have a good night."

"You too Aaron, maybe then you can answer my other question, the meaning of life."

"We will see Gabrielle, good night."

"Good night."

Gabrielle spent the rest of the evening watching TV. Later when she did prepare herself for bed, the picture of Percy accompanied her. After twenty minutes of lying comfortably in bed with Percy's picture on the pillow next to her, she found it difficult to sleep. What Aaron said was on her mind. Gabrielle thought, what if today was her last day on earth and she went home to be with the lord. Would she be satisfied with her accomplishments, has her life been filled with much reward and happiness, did she receive all the possible love that could be given to one person, was she suppose to experience the true meaning of love only once and live out the rest of her days alone, but most of all, is she really happy? You can find out this and much more as soon as you go on to the next chapter, until then, Gabrielle tossed and turned with her thoughts for an hour before drifting off to sleep. Unfortunately, she never did come up with the answers to her questions before dosing off.

CHAPTER TWENTY-THREE

The Re-incarnation of Love

Drifting Reverie

The thump of my heart is quieter than sand, it flows like water on clouds that flutters. The charisma of my hands is gentler than lotion, but lay like leaves, they change my thoughts repeatedly, like the wind that blows beneath trees. My eyes are distance, but are in close view, they watch life in a slow and beautiful sequence harmony of blue. The craving wavelength activity of my mind is steady with clues, it jumps at the sight of images forming too soon. My soul is well and at ease, it praises holiness of higher good, it rest like love and is at peace.

Peace, was something that didn't accompany Gabrielle to sleep last night. Her cat Jack awaits on the end of her bed staring at his owner, waiting patiently for her to awake and join him. Only some rest, was received with the not so sufficient six and a half hours given. Why, Percy didn't even honor her dreams with his presences, but that didn't stop Gabrielle from waking up with a wonderful smile on her face. Just to wake with his picture on the other side of her was however, sufficient enough to get the day started. "Good morning Jack." she said enlighten.

"Meow." Jack replied.

After saying her prayers for the day, Gabrielle began her routine to prepare for work. No need to place Percy's picture inside the armoire, the threat of anyone being jealous was long gone. So Gabrielle now keeps Percy's 8x10 black and white picture on the nightstand right beside her bed. After kissing a finger, that finger slowly comes across Percy's lips of his picture before leaving her bedroom ready for work, as Jack follows her. She pours Jack some dry cat food and gives him some fresh water, then pours herself a glass of OJ. The sun was alluring bright and seemed like a hopeful day. Gabrielle opens her balcony window and steps outside. It was the month of May of the year 2000 and Gabrielle looked forward to warmer weather. With not one negative thought on her mind, she smiles and takes an honest deep breath. She was doing what Aaron told her to do, breathe.

Taking his advice, she would start the morning out by giving herself a gift, a gift of a breath of happiness. She would have liked to take that first breath of fresh air and quality of happiness on the roof of her apartment building, but there was no time, if God would allow her, maybe some other day. Gabrielle went through her day in high spirits productively. When her workday was over, she performed her after work ritual. Her after work ritual had been on the right course as far a good healthy state of mind. Aaron's perspective on happiness made Gabrielle's after work ritual a little more imaginative and refreshing. He opened her eyes to rewarding possibilities. Any day without the diagnosis or announcement of the *beast* of cancer, is always a good day, but as long as Gabrielle feels and strives to make a difference, every workday in her profession is always worth it.

It was a good day in every way in which Gabrielle was proud to be thankful for and truly blessed. Sadly however, the happiness breathing freely in her mind came to a discomforting end as soon as she turns the key to open her apartment door. Once Gabrielle opened the door, she decoded the alarm and Jack waddles up to her with a lonely meow of hello, and that's when it hit her. No matter all the happiness she breathes or all the good she tries to will, it still left Gabrielle without someone to truly love. That's one thing Aaron forgot to mention about this dose of contrive form of blissful happiness, the side effects was reality and easy letdowns.

Two nights later at the United Center, Gabrielle and her two closest friends attended a Chicago Bulls basketball game. Amber's husband Trey, was somehow traded back to the Bulls from the Pacers, but was still one of those guys you hardly ever sees until another player is about to foul out. With his trade back to the Bulls, Trey is a free agent at the moment while still making millions, not bad for someone who gets paid to practice than actually having playing time. The girls had great courtside seats and seemed to be enjoying the game. Jillian had just told the girls that she has met someone with high potentials, which is good because after what she's been through, Jillian deserves a real man.

"And we've been dating for a month now."

"That's great Jillian." said Gabrielle. "I'm happy for you."

"Well it's about time girl." replied Amber. "What's his name again?"

"Caziah Martin."

"You said he's somewhat in the medical field. What's his profession?"

"Yeah, what does somewhat in the medical field mean?" asked Amber.

"He's a pharmacist."

"Street pharmacist?" replied Amber anxiously.

"No, Amber. He's not a street pharmacist, not a drug dealer."

"Girl, don't listen to Amber. I think it's wonderful."

"Hey, I was just making sure. You never know these days. You know I'm happy for you, been trying to hook you up with someone for months."

"Yeah like that mama's boy I went out with on Valentine's Day."

"Hey, he is a sweet guy." replied Amber.

"Yeah, if you're looking to raise and support a grown man, but thank goodness your hook up services are no longer needed."

"I'm hungry." stated Gabrielle. "You wanna go get something from the concession stand?"

"I'll go." said Jillian. "I want to stop by the ladies room."

"I'm going to stay and try and cheer my man from the bench, but bring me a large pretzel and a coke back."

Gabrielle stood in line at the concession stand as Jillian made a dash for the ladies room. The arena was crowded as people waited in line to place their food order. Their was about six people in front of Gabrielle as she looked and searched for Jillian's return. Before looking up at the menu board, Gabrielle did notice only two people left before she was the next up in line. She was debating on a bud light or not, then takes a step up closer to the people in front of her. Gabrielle checks the menu board again. Jillian finally appears when the people in front of Gabrielle were leaving.

"Good, you're back, didn't know what you wanted."

"May I help whose next." said the young female concession attendant.

"Yes, we will have two pretzels, a large coke, a diet coke for me, and what did you want Gabby?"

"I'll have a hot dog and a bud light."

"Will that be all?" asked the concession attendant. "Yes."

"$27.50, hey Keith I need a bud light!"

Gabrielle hands Jillian some money. "I think I have some change." she said.

As Gabrielle dug around in her purse for change, she glances over and notices a strong sexy brown arm that sits down her beer. Her eyes followed the arm up to the shoulder, then to the head and face. Both of their eyes meet. It was an instant, mesmerizing attraction. Both had a certain song on their mind as they stare at each other, for him, "Moments in Love" by Art of Noise; and for Gabrielle, "When I Saw You" by Mariah Carey. He smiled, spoke and asked would there be anything else. Gabrielle eyes were locked inside his eyes with a hypnotically strange enchantment. Staring into his eyes, she sees his soul. His soul was warm, gentle and very familiar. "Gabby, did you have the fifty cents? No, that will be all sir." Gabrielle found the change, but kept her eyes on the charmingly enticing black man. He carried on working, but did find it hard to do so. Gabrielle's soul spoke to him as well.

"Can I help whose next." said the female concession attendant.

"Well are you going to help me with this stuff Gabrielle?"

"Yes, I just-"

"Tell me later, after you stop drooling."

After getting some distances away from the concession stand, Jillian picked up where they left off. She noticed how Gabrielle kept looking back there.

"Stop looking back there. I saw you checking that fine brother out."

"I got this strange feeling we've met before."

"Well the way you were staring at him, I think he would remember."

"He's handsome." said Gabrielle with a smile.

"Girl, handsome is not even the word, try scrumptious."

When Jillian and Gabrielle finally made it back to their courtside seats, Jillian shares with Amber, Gabrielle's love interest in a whisper.

"It's about time you guy's returned. You missed Trey play for about a hot five minutes."

"Sorry, Gabrielle was busy meeting the man of her dreams."

"What, so where's Mr. Right?"

"Working the concession stand." replied Jillian.

"Working the concession stand, oh no. Gabrielle I've told you, when it comes to adult men, they must be at our level or above financially."

"Well what about a close second financially?" asked Gabrielle.

"That's fine, but sounds like he's far from that, working the concession stand at a basketball game."

"Gabrielle, you have your own mind. Don't let Amber's opinions miss-direct you girl."

Twenty minutes later after her hotdog was gone and Gabrielle was still sipping on the last of her beer, thoughts of that brief encounter played over in her mind. She definitely knows him from somewhere, but where. All Gabrielle knew was, she finally felt her heart beat repetitiously for the first time in ten years. Not even Bryce made her heart skip; he may have given her butterflies, but nothing overwhelming as making your heart flutter. All this time, Gabrielle felt her heart was in a coma and only beats for itself, then she sees someone that shocks her vital organ and gives it rhythm and life again. Something as abundantly magnificent as this doesn't come around too often, about as often as Halley's Comet.

"I've gotta got to the ladies room!" said Gabrielle as she stood up.

"Oh good, me too." said Amber.

"Damn!" thought Gabrielle.

"Not me, I'll catch the next run." stated Jillian.

On the way to the ladies room, Gabrielle thought about how she could lose Amber, so she can go find that guy. As they walked to the restroom, Amber was making small talk, but Gabrielle couldn't tell you for a million dollars what Amber was speaking about. Her mind was still on Mr. Wonderful. When Amber did walk out of the bathroom stall to wash her hands, she didn't see Gabrielle. After washing her hands and drying them off, she still didn't see Gabrielle. Amber said Gabrielle's name aloud, but there was no answer. Just as Amber began calling Gabrielle on her cell phone, Gabrielle was putting her cell phone on silent. Gabrielle appeared a little nervous as she waited in line at that exact concessions stand. She didn't know what exactly she would say to him, but honestly needed to know if he could make her heart skip again. Amber left Gabrielle a message on her cell phone and made her way back to their seats.

"I think I lost Gabrielle while I was in the restroom." Jillian gives a clever smile.

"You don't say?"

"What are you smiling at? What's so amusing?"

"I could have told you before you left, that you would come back alone and I'll bet you five dollars, Gabrielle is back at that concession stand."

"That heifer!"

"One bud light please."

Gabrielle had step up as the next customer, but disappointingly did not see the light of her life. "I need a bud light!" yield the young concession attendant. This time unfortunately, an older white male places the beer down in front of her. He thanks Gabrielle and walks away. As Gabrielle began to walk away with her beer, she kept looking back at the concession stand, hoping he would reappear, but he didn't. In somewhat of a desperation miracle moment, Gabrielle thought she would give one more look back before returning back to her seat. She did and still, no sight of the handsome gentleman. As soon as she turned back around and looked in front of her, there he stood. All the noise around her became silent as her heart gave a small involuntary jolt to skip a beat. Gabrielle took a small breath gazing into his eyes as the noise around her slowly came back in circulation.

"I'm sorry, did I frighten you?" he asked.

"No no, I think I was having a mild heart attack."

"Do you need a doctor?" he appeared concerned.

"No." Gabrielle smiled. "This is actually a good heart gesture."

"Okay, I hope you don't mind me coming over here like this, but I was about to spend my entire break searching for you."

Gabrielle gives a bashful smile and he smiles back.

"No, no I don't. I might have a beer every once in a while and this just so happens to be my second once in a while."

"Have we met before?" he asked curiously.

"I was thinking the same thing, but I think I would have remembered."

"How do you do that?" he asked.

"Do what?" Gabrielle replied.

"Make your eyes and teeth sparkle simultaneously."

Gabrielle began to blush.

"Hello, my name is Keith, Keith McNair and you are?" He offers his hand for her to shake. "Oh, hello Keith, my name is Gabrielle Michaels."

Gabrielle gently takes his hand and shakes it. With a single touch, their souls began to breathe, taking in air of felicitous vibes of a magical lasting impression. Yes, their minds were attracted to each other subconscious, but this aureole surrounding them was by all means different from the norm. Gabrielle couldn't put her finger on it at the moment, but it was something about his eyes that keep her attraction to him attentive. "I have twenty minutes left on my break; I would like to spend it with you, if you don't mind?"

"Not at all, I would like that."

Gabrielle and Keith walked, talked, and couldn't keep their eyes off each other. The twenty minutes went by so fast that it was hardly enough time to really communicate. They both were over whelmed and anxious to know more about one another, so naturally numbers were exchanged. When Gabrielle did return back to her seat, the Chicago Bulls were beginning third period of the game. Gabrielle returned to her seat with a glowing smile.

"Thanks for ditching me heifer."

"I'm sorry Amber."

"Girl forget Amber, did you find what you was looking for?"

"I did." said Gabrielle cheerfully.

"I sure hope you know what you are doing Gabrielle?"

"Leave it alone Amber, not everyone can marry a pro basketball player who rides the bench."

"Oh ok, ya'll laugh, but if it wasn't for my bench sitting husband, you all wouldn't have great seats and Gabrielle wouldn't have met the concession stand man of her dreams."

"He's helping out a friend, not his profession."

"And just what does Mr. Concession stand helper do for a living?"

"Actually, I don't know." said Gabrielle shockingly.

"Then just what the hell have you been doing all this time, getting a quickie in the restroom?"

"No, just talking Amber."

"Girl, pay Amber no mind. She needs to be trying to bribe the coach for more playing time for Trey."

As the three friends carried on jokingly with one another, they enjoyed the rest of the game. However, the only person on Gabrielle's mind was Keith and same as for Keith. As he continued to volunteer his time, the only one person on his mind was Gabrielle. That night when Gabrielle did get home, she received a call from Keith and they talked until almost one o'clock in the morning. Keith told Gabrielle that he was off today and would like to see her and talk more over dinner. Gabrielle was delighted and gladly accepts his invitation. With not much sleep to absorb, Gabrielle did lay down to rest. This time however, the picture of Percy did not accompany her to bed. Maybe she was too tired to realize that, who knows. All Gabrielle did know when she did drift off to sleep, that she was happy.

That next evening on a Thursday, Gabrielle found herself driving over to Prairie District Lofts. When Keith mentioned dinner, she thought they would be going out for a bite. What Keith was referring to was cooking her dinner. Gabrielle's high expectations of him were now getting mixed reviews. Honestly, most men don't cook and second, when a guy is trying to get you over his place on the first date, he's most likely trying to have sex. 1727 South Indiana Avenue was the address Gabrielle was in search for. After parking, she caught the elevator up to his loft apartment. When Keith opened his door, he graced her with a warm smile and wearing a black apron. There, you see, he did it again. Did you hear it this time? Keith gave Gabrielle a little rush, made her heart skip a beat. It was an intense rush, but Gabrielle had to admit, she liked it. She returned the smile given, spoke and entered his home.

"Wow, rooftop deck, fireplace, hardwood floors and high ceilings. Your place is a knockout."

"Thank you, you look wonderful."

"Why thank you. I brought wine."

"I see, and thank you again. I'll take that."

He escorted the bottle of wine into his kitchen. That gave Gabrielle a chance to really look the place over. It wasn't your ordinary guy's pad, his place complements him well. He actually has nice taste. Plus, there was smooth contemporary Jazz playing, which scored more points for him.

"Gabrielle?"

"Yes."

"Would you like to join me in the kitchen?'

"Certainly."

"So tell me Gabrielle, were you hesitant about coming over for dinner?"

"A little, man I love this kitchen. It's huge and you have an island."

"No kitchen is complete without one. As you can see I have unprepared meats lying out with vegetables."

"Yes I see."

He opens a bottle of wine and pours her glass. Gabrielle takes a seat on a bar stool next to the island. After receiving a glass of wine, she takes a sip. Keith then hands her a printed out piece of paper.

"This is what's on the menu tonight. I can cook everything you see, just need to know what interest you the most."

"Well this is different. I know you said you are in the restaurant business, so you must be a chef."

"That's correct."

"Really, which restaurant?"

"TRU on North Saint Clair."

"No, get out! That's a great restaurant."

"So you've dined there before?"

"Yes, with my good friend, rap recording artist Tru."

"Really, you know Tru?"

"We went to high school together."

"But wait, he doesn't own that restaurant right?"

"No, he wish. The restaurant was in business before he became famous."

Keith pulls some plastic wrap off a small bowel of strawberries and offers Gabrielle one. She kindly accepts one and takes a bite.

"Now, I know what you are thinking, I invited you up to my place to butter you up in hopes of a night cap right?"

"Well, the thought did cross my mind."

"Gabrielle, this is my home and you are welcome here anytime, free from negative stereotypical conceptions of men's intentions. I am good people, as I think you are. You are a lady and I was taught to always respect a lady."

Gabrielle blushes with a smile tenderly to his honest words. "Thank you."

"Now, with that out of the way, maybe I can get down to business of cooking. Have you decided your entrée for this evening?

Gabrielle looks over the menu again. "I must say, the Ginger Orange-Bourbon Salmon with Vegetable Corn Salad sounds tempting, but the Garlic Shrimp and Steamed Rice seem like a good idea, then again, the

Garlicky Teriyaki Steak with Herb Sugar Snap Peas could be tasty and delightful. I think I'll go with the Garlicky Teriyaki Steak."

"Well done, I was thinking the same thing. Let me wash my hands and I'll get started."

As soothing contemporary Jazz played through out his home with surround sound, Gabrielle watched as Keith prepares their meals before her eyes. She had to admit to herself, she was impressed. Gabrielle never had a man to cook for her before. In a strange way, she feels she's known Keith for years. They got along well, felt extremely comfortable around each other.

They conversant moderately in good spirits during the course of the meal preparation, but still it was something about Keith's eyes that kept Gabrielle positively attentive in everyway. Twenty minutes later, dinner was served outside on his rooftop deck.

"This is lovely. I usually get this type of treatment in a restaurant."

"It standard, but I do go out of my way to please."

"I see, and why are you single again?"

The smile on Keith face would dissipate slightly, but when he looked up from his plate into Gabrielle's eyes, his attractive smile returned tenderly.

"Yes, I am single and have been single for a year now, because she stopped loving me."

"Excuse me for saying this, but was she on crack?"

"Yes she was." he said sadly.

"Oh dear, I didn't know. I'm sorry."

'Well you should be, however, that was not the real reason for her departure."

said Keith with a smile.

"Man, you had me going." she said with a smile of relief.

"Well, we were engaged, but I soon found out she still loved her ex boyfriend."

"How did you find out, if you don't mind me asking?"

"No, I came home; this is when I lived in New York. I came home to find a Dear John note that said, I can't marry you, I love someone else."
"Keith I'm sorry."

"Don't be, what she did was, saved us problems and a divorce in the future. Ok my turn; why on earth are you single?"

"Because I caught my ex cheating on me with his ex girlfriend, who is now his girlfriend."

"Ouch, that's gotta hurt."

"Tell me about it, but I'm glad I found out, she would have caused problems with the relationship in the future."

"Then lets toast to new beginnings." he suggested with a smile.

"To new beginnings." she replied also with a cheerful smile.

After enjoying a lovely meal, Gabrielle insisted that she help Keith in the kitchen to clean up. When they were done in the kitchen, they had dessert in the living room, a slice of strawberry cheesecake. Smooth contemporary Jazz continued to play on their evening together, which only improved their chances of their own new beginnings.

"So you are a great chef who knows other great chefs like, Marcus Samuelsson, Michelle Jean, Melba Wilson and you were friends with the late Patrick Clark."

"That's correct."

"Do you know Emerial?"

"Not personally no, but he's great, Bam!" They both laughed briefly. "Tell me more about you."

"Well, I studied at New York's Technical College. I have a passion for cooking and for teaching."

"Oh, so you teach as well, what do you teach?"

"I teach African-American history part time at Richard Daley Community College."

Gabrielle ears grew closer to Keith words as he revealed more about himself.

"As a teenager, I really didn't know where I was headed in life. I mean, I use to dabble in the kitchen and consider becoming a chef, then one day I woke up out of the blue and wanted to teach African-American history. I received my Bachelors degree in history from the University of Alabama then moved to New York and studied culinary there."

"Wow, two different skills you're blessed with. You're twenty-six right?"

"Right and I will be twenty-seven in July."

"July what?"

"The seventeenth."

"Hummmm." Gabrielle thought. "One day after Percy's." "Do you enjoy contemporary Jazz Gabrielle?"

"Do I, it soothes my soul. I can't imagine life without contemporary Jazz or Hip Hop."

"I'm a fan of both myself, more wine?"

"No thank you. This is fine?"

"I noticed you staring at my chin."

"I apologize."

"It's quite alright. It's not a dimple, but a small scar, my past."

"Please explain."

"Well when I was sixteen years old, I got hit by a car walking home from my best friend house."

"Goodness, hope it wasn't too serious?"

"Banged me up pretty good, it was a hit and run. When I was struck, I landed funny, hitting my head and chin. I was out for a couple of days in a coma, but I survived."

"Did they ever catch the person responsible?"

"Yes they did, and I never will forget, every April 19th I remember how I cheated death."

Gabrielle thoughts quickly became raveled around the date of his accident. "You were sixteen when this happen?"

"Yes."

"So the accident happened April 19, 1990." "Yes, that's right."

Gabrielle thoughts circled around that date once again. "Do you, maybe recall the time of the accident?"

"Well let's see, my mom had called me home for supper and that's usually around six, but I left an hour later. I'll say around seven or seven thirty."

Gabrielle eyes fell to her lap, as her thoughts continued to put the misfortunate revelations together.

"Why, did something happen to you on that day as well?"

Gabrielle's eyes rushes up to meet his question, but appeared uncertain. "You can say that, and you said you were in a coma?"

"For a couple of days, gave my family a scare, but when I did wake up, I remember telling my mother that I wanted to teach African-American history."

Gabrielle eyes grew wider and her thoughts became unsettling.

"Finding work as a chef wasn't a problem. I still don't know how, I would wake up wanting to teach after being struck by a car, but a rare position opened up at the community college that moved me to the windy city. I guess you can say, the accident changed my life."

"I must go!" Gabrielle stood up in a hurry. "Are you alright Gabrielle?" he asked.

Gabrielle's heart was really racing. Her thoughts were now flooded with Percy. "I hate to rush out, but I must leave."

"I'm sorry to hear that. I was enjoying your company."

Gabrielle goes to walk, but stumbles a little and Keith moves closer to help her. Gabrielle grabs his arm and looks up in his face, directly into his eyes. She froze, staring helplessly into his familiar sight. Then it hit her, that's why his eyes seemed so peacefully secure. Gabrielle's attentiveness to Keith's eyes was so strong because when Gabrielle looked into Keith's magnetic eyes, she saw the soul of an old friend."

"You ok, can you drive?"

"Yes, Keith I'm sorry, I have to go, but I will call you later."

Gabrielle grabbed her keys and purse and rushed out of Keith's place. On her drive home, Gabrielle kept expressing the words, it couldn't be and that's impossible. Her confusion and mild hysteria caused her to run only one red light, but she did make it come safely. Gabrielle rushed inside her apartment, straight to her bedroom to the picture that sat on her nightstand. She lifts up Percy's black and white picture and stares at it carefully. Her eyes met his eyes, but she didn't have to stare too hard because once she saw Percy's eyes, she also saw Keith's eyes. "That's impossible, she said. I mean, it couldn't be humanly possible, unless Keith died when he was hit by that car and now has Percy's soul."

Gabrielle stares at Percy's picture harder before slowly looking up.

"Oh my God, Keith is really Percy!" Gabrielle eyes rolled back some as she fell backward on to her bed. She fainted.

A few moments later, Gabrielle regained consciousness with Percy's picture lying across her chest. She sits up and takes another look at Percy's picture, but this time tenderly. Tears formed in her eyes as reality sets in from her absurd thinking. Gabrielle couldn't believe she actually thought Percy was now Keith. Keith popped into her mind.

"Keith!" she said before grabbing the phone.

"Hello."

"Keith, I apologize for running out like that."

"It's okay, are you alright? That's my concern."

"Yes, you must think I'm crazy?"

"No, but you did look like you seen a ghost. If you hated my cooking, that's all you had to say."

Gabrielle released her serious state of mind with laughter.

"No, that definitely wasn't the case. I thought I left my iron on."

"Ok, I'll accept that fib, but only if your dash in a flash wasn't because of a possible disinterest in me."

"Absolutely not."

"Good, because I would like to see and know more of you Gabrielle Michaels." "I would like that."

Gabrielle talked with Keith for about an hour. A bubble bath was calling her name, so she did her mind and body a favor. Recaps of tonight's dinner date accompanied her into the warm bath. Hunting thoughts of her silly assumption also visited her thoughts. When Gabrielle did lie down for the night, Percy's picture accompanied her to bed. She held his picture close to her. It was no use denying her real thoughts. To think what she thought wasn't sensibly normal. Although, those thoughts alone could be quite pleasing, even reassuring, Gabrielle was no fool. As she lay with her arms around Percy's picture, Gabrielle couldn't help but think as she drifted off to sleep, that ten years after losing her true love; she just may have witnessed the reincarnation of love.

CHAPTER TWENTY-FOUR

Your Prejudice Becomes You

Friday night of the same week, the ladies happy hour gathering would be dinner and a movie. Gabrielle had spent most of their dinner speaking about her date with Keith. Standing in line at the concession stand for snacks, Gabriele brought up the subject of her hopeful romantic interest again. Amber however, wasn't convinced of Gabrielle's newfound happiness.

"If Mr. Wonderful is all that and a bag of chips, then why did you leave in such a stir crazy hurry? You never told us why you left so soon."

Gabrielle's face promptly showed a hint of embarrassment before smiling.

"I got nervous, couldn't breathe, along with a touch of diarrhea I might add." She hated to lie.

"You mean he scared the shit out of you?" whispered Amber.

"Amber please, spare us. It's ok Gabrielle; I get that way some times." "May I help you?" asked the female concession attendant.

"Yes, I will have a medium popcorn with butter, a medium coke, and whatever else my friends want." Amber hands Gabrielle a twenty-dollar bill.

"This treat is on me, I'm going to run to the ladies room."

"Ok, thanks. I'll eat on Amber's popcorn. I'll have a medium coke and some Raisnets. What you want Jillian?"

"A medium diet coke and some Twizzlers." "Will that be all?"

"Yes."

"That will be $18.50."

Gabrielle hands the twenty-dollar bill to the cashier and the teenage Caucasian female snatches the money from Gabrielle's hand. The smile on

Gabrielle's face shrunk some at the cashier's unpleasant attitude. The cashier closes her register and hands Gabrielle her change, but draws her hand back after touching Gabrielle's hand. Jillian began grabbing their snacks.

"May I help whose next?"

Gabrielle just shakes her head pitifully and began helping Jillian. Sadly, the cashiers rude behavior has happened to Gabrielle before. I'm sure many black Americans have experienced this type of ignorance before. Gabrielle has noticed the same behavior with a bank teller where she does her banking. This incident made Gabrielle think of her. As Gabrielle and Jillian walked away from the concession stand, Gabrielle had a few words for that cashier. She was about to turn around and give that cashier a piece of her mind, but changed her mind, didn't want to make a scene.

"You ok Gabrielle?"

"Yeah, hey I wanted to ask you something." "Why do I have a feeling it's about Keith?" "Well not really, sort of."

"What Gabrielle?"

"Jillian do you believe in reincarnation?" "You mean like being reborn, coming back?" "Yes, the rebirth of a soul."

"Well you know I'm a spiritual person. So naturally, I feel that spirits can be reborn again and come back, as what, I have no idea. Why you ask?"

"No reason."

"Wait, I hope you're not thinking, what I'm thinking?" "Forget it!"

"No, I'm intrigued. We'll talk later cause here comes your girl." "You guys are ready?"

"Just waiting on you princess Amber." replied Jillian.

Saturday afternoon, Gabrielle and Jillian did talk while shopping the Magnificent Mile shopping district. Gabrielle spoke about her possible encounter of reincarnation freely without sounding as if her mind was on vacation at a psych ward. If it was anyone she could talk to about this, it had to be Jillian. "So that's why you left in a stir crazy panic, you believe because Keith was struck by a car on the same night Percy died, that Keith maybe Percy spiritually?"

"Is it insane to think that?" "No, is it possible? Possibly."

"And he said as soon as he woke from the coma, he wanted to teach African- American History and you know that was Percy's dream."

"True, but any healthy minded person especially a psychiatrist, will tell you it's just a coincidence."

"Do you think it's just a coincidence Jillian?"

"Most likely, but maybe not, either way, it's a big freaking coincidence."

"My thoughts exactly."

"My advice to you is, don't pressure yourself about it. Let nature take its course. See him, see Keith. Get to know him. Don't build your hopes up on thinking that Percy has come back to you. It will be an over whelming disappointing let down, that may scar you emotionally."

"You're right."

"You obviously like him and he seems to like you, just see where it goes, without living in the past."

Sunday evening the prospective pair tried this getting to know one another again. Keith was invited over to Gabrielle's place in which she would attempt to prepare one of only few meals she could pull off.

"This looks great, I love Chicken Fettuccine."

"Thanks, it's one of my favorite's foods, so I had to learn how to create it."

"I can't get over your place. You have exquisite taste."

Gabrielle couldn't help but melt into his eyes with a smile. "Thank you, I try."

"That song playing, isn't that "Bella" by Special EFX?"

"Why yes it is."

"And we just so happen to be drinking Bella Sera wine. That's somewhat of a coincidence, don't you think?"

"A little, its good wine and I like the meaning of it." "Well I too, believe it's going to be a beautiful evening."

Gabrielle smiled and Keith returned the favor before they toasted to his words.

After their delightful meal, they got comfortable in her living room to watch a movie. No up and running out in a hurry tonight, Gabrielle was already home. Jack seemed to take alikeness to Keith susceptibly. Usually Jack will come out just to see who is visiting, but this time instead of retreating back to the bedroom, he got relaxed beside Keith's feet.

"My mom is a cat person, she has two. My dad is a dog lover. He has adopted the family dog as his own."

"What about you, I didn't see any pet's at your place."

"I love all pets and can't wait to get a dog."

"What's keeping you?"

"Marriage."

"Excuse me?"

"Well, I hope to get a puppy someday and hopefully I will be married, that way we both can start out with a significant connection to the puppy and watch it grow as our marriage grows."

"Oh, that's sweet. I never really thought about it like that."

"I still can't believe Phillip Michaels is your father and that you are GABRIELLE."

"Well, I don't like to brag."

"I have all his CD's. I also enjoy the sounds of Marion Meadows, Paul Taylor, Boney James and Chris Botti. What about you?'

The name of that last artist mention, made Gabrielle think of Malcolm.

"I have several; I also favor the artist's you mentioned along with Kim Waters, Najee, Hiroshima, Herbie Hancock, Herb Alpert and Grover Washington, Junior."

Gabrielle got lost in his eyes again just from staring too long.

"Finally, the end of the previews." Keith declared. "I heard about this movie, people say its good."

"That's what I heard, I'm sure it will be."

As the move began, Gabrielle found it hard not to observe Keith. She stared at his physique, his brown skin tone, his facial features and of course his eyes. The view of his loving eyes was at a disadvantage, but that didn't keep Gabrielle from trying. Keith looks over at Gabrielle and she tries to pretend as if she's watching the movie and smiles. "You ok Gabrielle?"

"Oh yes, they say it suppose to be a sequel to the Matrix." They both resume watching the featured presentation, but as soon as Gabrielle thought Keith was occupied by the movie again, her eyes went exploring again. She tried to see Keith as himself, but all Gabrielle thought of was Percy. In her mind, she believed he was Percy, her heart says he's Percy and until proving otherwise, she will treat Keith as the love of her life that has come back. Just one thing though, why the hell doesn't Percy remember her?

Three days later on her lunch break, Gabrielle had to stop by the bank. As Gabrielle waited in line for the next teller, she hoped she didn't have to deal with the older Caucasian woman, the narrow-minded one.

Unfortunately she was out of luck. Once again, after Gabrielle completed her business transaction, the older woman slightly draws her hands back so she wouldn't have to touch her. The teller thanked Gabrielle in a dry way before sending her on her way. Gabrielle was about to leave, but turned back around with some words. "Just thought you should know, your prejudice becomes you."

"I beg your pardon?" said the teller.

"I said, your prejudice becomes you."

The supervisor walks over concerned. "Is there a problem ma'am?" he asked.

"Yes, too bad she doesn't know what it is." Gabrielle then walks away.

"You did right Gabrielle and I know who you are speaking about. That old white skank has done the same thing to me." stated Jasmine.

"Um-um cause, after I would have finished with her, she would have been drawing unemployment." replied Amber.

The next night was margarita night and everyone was over to Jillian's place off Glenwood Drive in Bloomingdale, Illinois. The book of the month was a novel by Eric Jerome Dickey and because they were over to Jillian's place, they had to discuss the novel for at least a half an hour. With that already out of the way, the ladies could get down to some real business of card playing, drinking and discussing the other race. The topic of race and racism got a little heated tonight and was quite a doozy.

"What, do they think if they touch us, that our skin will rub off on them or something?" asked Carman.

"Hell I hope not, cause if that was the case, black skin would scream and go running away like a wounded puppy." said Tationna.

Everyone shared a laugh.

"Gabrielle, everyone can say they have experienced that type of ignorant prejudice." said Jillian. "I know I have trying to buy coffee."

Most all the woman agreed they have experienced that type of ignorance. "It just isn't very nice." said Gabrielle.

"Isn't nice." replied Amber. "Let me tell you what isn't nice. The fact that Black Americans are still not receiving the RESPECT that is owed to us. White folks walk around all day with their nose up in the air thinking they are still superior over us, as if they are doing us a favor by allowing us to live here in America and be free."

"Amen." Jasmine testified.

Jillian brings in a tray of snacks from the kitchen.

"Well I say people are people until they prove otherwise." said Gabrielle. "And don't so many go out of their way to do so." stated Tationna.

"Absolutely, the KKK isn't someone with a stammering problem." replied Carman. "Now you know you can't stop racism, that's like trying to get every Republican to switch political parties. Furthermore, as a teacher I have heard white children say their parents hate black people because someone in their family got killed or murdered by one."

"Well it's a good thing the whole world doesn't think that way." replied Amber. "Because if that's the case, every black person in America with slave ancestors, have more than enough reason to walk around with a lifetime of hate."

"The other race is so quick to say, go back to Africa and my response to that is, when they go back to hell." replied Jasmine.

"Ladies you know the other race is still threaten by us, afraid of blacks." Gabrielle stated.

Amber was about to take a sip of her margarita, but volunteered to respond to that. "Scared of blacks for what, or should I say of what? Thugs, gangs, crime, murder, hell that comes from all races."

"That among other things." Jillian added. "Like our intelligences, our mind. Knowledge is power."

"Well I don't think whites are that afraid of our minds." replied Amber. "A random killing is one thing and let's talk murder. Everyone knows, most serial killers are white males, white middle-aged men particularly. Black men might be angry, but some are out trying to make a dollar, while white men are trying to make your ass holler."

"You tell it girl!" replied Jasmine.

"And another thing." Amber adds. "If we are really going to talk murder and taking lives, let's go back to the era of lynching. Lynching, where many of our people and ancestors lives were snatched away, men, women and children. The biggest crime whites ever got away with was slavery. You say murder without justifiable consent, I say white folks!"

"W E L L!" stated Jasmine, as Amber continues preaching.

"Today blacks are judged and convicted of crimes they haven't committed yet, another word for that, racial profiling. We should be the one walking around scared. We should be cautious and on alert, because we really just don't know what groups or organizations are plotting or conspiring."

"True, go on girl!" replied Jasmine.

"We as black folks should be afraid, afraid to walk the streets wondering which white person is walking around with a noose in their back pocket!"

"Amen Amber, Amen!"

About fifty miles north of Chicago in a secluded wooded area, another illegal dog-fighting event was taking place. Jasper, Demarco and another Black Panther member, Alex Rice were all present and witnessing the current match taking place.

"Hey man, I'm glad you guys invited me again to this dog fighting event. I thought you forgot about me."

"Is that right?" said Demarco with a counterfeit smile. "Yeah my hands have been burning to bet this ten grand." Moments later you heard a dog cry out from defeat of death. "Looks like that's it, a winning around for us." stated Jasper. "Told you Cujo don't play."

"Demarco go collect our winnings and have it for us tomorrow." "My pleasure, oh and Alex, great doing business with you again." "With my winnings, I look forward to doing this again." he replied. "Let's go Brother Rice." insisted Jasper.

On their drive back to Chicago, Alex tries to make small talk with his fellow Black Panther member. However, the only thing on Jasper's mind was correcting things between him and Aaron.

"Hey, why don't you ever collect your money at those events?"

"Because Brother Rice, the less you can connect yourself to this illegal sport, the better off you are."

"So I'll have my winnings tomorrow?" "Would you relax, you can trust Demarco."

"Jasper, why have I been excluded from weekly Black Panther meetings?" "You haven't been excluded Brother Rice."

"For the last month, every time I try to be present for one, it's been canceled or they have already adjourned. What's up?"

"You got me; all members are notified about upcoming events and meetings through e-mails."

"I mean, I feel left out and all."

"Damn, I knew I should have gone to the bathroom before we left. It's about twenty miles to the next gas station."

"Yeah."

"Looks like I'm going to have to pull over and take a leak."

Still deep down a long secluded highway far from the next town, Jasper pulls his car over on the side of the road. Jasper gets out of the car into the dark night. He began walking toward the passenger side over near the woods when Alex's cell phone rings. As Brother Rice reaches into his jacket for the phone, the passengers door opens and a gun was placed to his head.

"You might want to let voicemail get that." "Brother Ware what the hell!"

"Shut up and give me your gun, don't make me ask you twice." Alex Rice slowly reaches for his gun and hands it to Jasper. "Now kill the engine and lights."

With Jaspers gun still pointed to his head, Alex Rice did what Jasper said. "Get out of the car."

"Can you tell me what's this all about?" "Another word and it will be your last." Jasper tells Alex to shut the door.

"Now start walking."

Less than a half of a mile into the woods, Jasper orders Alex Rice to stop walking and turn around. "Anything you want to tell me about yourself?"

"Like what man?"

"Cut the bullshit. I know what you are."

"Brother Ware, I have no idea what you are speaking of."

Jasper throws a hard left and punches Alex Rice in the face. "Ok, ok, ok. You found out I'm an informant."

"Is that all you are, or are you a fucking cop."

"Just an informant, just an informant." Alex replied.

"Strip!"

"What?"

"You're probably wearing a wire and I really don't want to touch you, so strip. Take off your clothes, leaving on just your underwear."

"Man, I'm not wearing a wire."

Jasper points his gun at Alex's forehead and Alex began to undress. "Did you really think we wouldn't find out?"

"It's not you they want, it's Aaron. Work with us, they can make you a deal. You won't see any prison time."

"Do you think I believe that?" "It's the truth, there! No wire." "Good!"

Three shots were fired into Alex Rice as he fell to the ground. He was shot with his own gun. My children, were the last words he spoke before he closed his eyes in death. Even with gloves on, Jasper still wipes the gun off and tosses it beside Alex Rice. He kicks the dead body, calls him a traitor then walks away. From a distance, you could still here Alex Rice's cell phone ringing.

The next afternoon, Jasper was on the roof of the Black Panthers Party Urban Headquarters building, explaining Alex Rice's outcome.

"I really wish you would have discussed this with me first Jasper." "You said take care of it, I did."

"Without repercussions, how long do you think before the cops find him and bring hell on us?"

"They can question us as much as they like, they are not going have anything to connect us."

"Us, surely you mean you Brother Ware, but unfortunately you mean me." "Why are you worried, you have an alibi. You was with your receptionist right?" "That's none of your business and why that area? State police busted a dog fighting ring five miles from there."

"It was a secluded area. How did you hear about some dog fighting ring bust?" "It was in this morning's local paper." Aaron shows Jasper the front page.

"That son of a bitch!" Jasper thought.

Jasper looks over the paper for a second.

"I haven't heard and didn't see anyone around for miles."

"Did he have anything to say Jasper?"

"Yeah, that the cops are after you."

"Still trying to bring me down after all this time. Did he say about what in particular?"

"No, he didn't say."

Aaron cells phones rings.

"Just a minute Jasper, Hello Gabrielle, how are you?" Jasper gives a distasteful stare at his caller.

"Listen Gabrielle, I'm in a meeting right now, I will have to call you back. Ok, you know I will, bye."

"Doesn't she have something better to do than bother you?"

"My conversations with Dr. Michaels don't concern you. You just be ready for any eventualities when they come our way. I will contact you if new information comes about."

Brother Ware wasn't even out the Black Panther building good when he immediately called Demarco. "Where are you?"

"Waiting on you at the spot."

"You have my money?"

"Yes, your boy tried to take us down last night huh?"

"Well unfortunately for him, he was the one put down last night. When did you leave?"

"Fifteen minutes after you."

"We'll divided his winnings and split it in half."

"Sounds good to me."

"Now we can carry on with our dealings in peace."

Jasper Ware is a man who one might say, has no regards for human life. One reason for that is because he loathes people. Jasper Ware is a man with few emotions unexpressed. He is a racist, a lothario, a sexist and a misogynist. Hatred, also a good friend of his, seem to pump his heart with disdain blood. Remorse was something Jasper Ware wiped off his shoes on a doormat before entering any place. His appreciation for life is dark and limited from despair of no conscience. Hell, was something he carried in his eyes and didn't mind inflicting it on others. You may know someone or group of individuals of this nature. Jasper Ware was death walking. He is well aware of that and it doesn't seem to bother him any. Karma, was something he drank to and always kept an eye out for with open arms. If you are familiar with the saying, what goes around comes around, then you will have no problem relating when I say, when Jasper Ware's day does come, he will catch it six ways from Sunday.

CHAPTER TWENTY-FIVE

Third Time Around

Through the words of Lauren Hill, after winter, comes spring, everything is everything. Spring in Chicago is like three weeks of the four different seasons playing tug of war. Ahhh, but when summer does arrive, the complicated Elnino version of the dominate split personality of winter subsides. Gabrielle and Keith met in May and after two weeks of dating; Chicago was blessed with warmer weather in the lovely month of June.

Gabrielle and Keith relationship was as normal as most, yet intriguing enough for constant anticipation. Although Gabriele felt her fondness of Keith was mostly based on her past true love, she focused on the real true aspects of their involvement. Her and Keith have so much in common. They enjoy each other's company, got along with each other, communicated well intelligently, very attracted to each other and last but not least, their kisses were compatible. Keith is a great kisser. Each kiss was a love potion of romantic divine; it was like opening a present on Christmas day. One thing however, Gabrielle couldn't figure out was, ever since her and Keith have been dating, Percy presences has yet to make an appearance in her dreams.

It was another lunch date with her sister in the sophisticated surroundings at the Capital Grille restaurant, also time for Gabrielle to tell Ivy about Keith.

"Oh now you tell, after you are ready to walk down the aisle. Wedding anyone?" Gabrielle laughs briefly.

"What, girl please. It's only been two weeks, not two years."

"So, I don't remember when the last time I've seen you so happy."

"Thanks, but there's something else."

"What? Don't tell me, he's short and bald?"

Gabrielle smiled nervously.

"No, you know I like my men tall."

"What then?"

"He has eyes like Percy. That's what attracted me to Keith."

"So, long as he isn't, oh, how did someone else put it? As long as he isn't locked away, gay, strung out, unemployed, or messed up in the head, sound like a winner to me."

Gabrielle debated for a second on if she should tell Ivy the rest of her crazy assumption, but decide not to, didn't want to risk Ivy trying to commit her in some institution. "Good I'm glad you approve."

"So when do I get to meet him?" "Soon."

"When the last time you heard from Malcolm?"

"A week ago, he said he misses me."

"Do you miss him?"

"Yeah sure, a little."

"Well, he had his chance, focus on Mr. Right."

"How are the girls?"

"Better now that I'm home more, and since you mentioned Percy. I remember for months after he died, how you would go to bed with his 8x10 black and white picture. Boy, I was glad when you stopped."

Gabrielle thoughts went straight to Percy's picture sitting on her nightstand. "Yeah, I was still trying to let go."

"Percy just knew he was going to marry you, always called me sister in-law. Anyway, I'm sure he would be proud of you."

"You think so?"

"I know so, just don't let him down from not giving your all to another." "What are you saying Ivy?"

"Gabrielle, you are my sister and I love you. I also know you better than you know yourself. I hear it in your voice; you still have love for Percy. Hell, I mentioned his name and your eyes lit up." Gabrielle looks away from Ivy and her eyes falls to the table. "Why do you say that?"

"Because it's true Gabrielle, am I lying?"

Silence took a seat at the table as Gabrielle takes a sip of her ice tea.

"Am I lying?"

"No."

"Ok then. To look into Keith's eyes and see Percy is one thing, but to mislead your feeling because of a strong love in the past is wrong and I hope is not the case Gabrielle."

"I'm not misleading my feeling, I like Keith very much."

"Yes, you like Keith, but still love Percy."

"Yes, I still have love for Percy, I always will, but Keith and Percy are two different people and I recognize that and will love accordingly."

"I hope so little sister. I certainly hope so."

June 15, 2000 1:30 pm

Aaron receives a call from his receptions that a couple of detectives were here to speak with him. He tells her to send them right in and she does.

"Good afternoon detectives, how can I help you?"

"I'm detective Dan Cross with Chicago police, this is detective Stephen Peterson. We are investigating the murder of one of your Black Panther members, Kelsey Alexander Rice."

"Officer Peterson, it's been a long time, you've been promoted. Don't I have a restraining order on you?"

"Now you go run and call anyone you like, but I'm just doing my job and yes, I've made detective. That way the reward will be even better when I see you rotting in prison."

"Stephen, I got this. Mr. James, did you not hear what I just said?"

"I did, one of my members has died."

"Murdered!" uttered Detective Peterson angrily.

"Murder, well, that's new to me. So he was murdered?" asked Aaron.

"That's correct Mr. James and detective Peterson and I would like to know when the last time you spoke with Alex Rice?"

Aaron sits back in his seat and reflects on detective Cross question.

"Well let's see, about two maybe three months ago."

"You haven't spoken with Mr. Rice prior to those months?"

"No detective Cross, I believe the last time I spoke with Alex Rice, was after he was sworn in as a new Black Panther member."

"His wife reported him missing on May 19th 2000, were you not aware of his absence from weekly meetings?"

"We notify all members about future events and meetings through e-mail and yes, it was brought to my attention that Mr. Rice has been absent, but we assume it was because of work. We had no reason to be concern."

"Didn't his wife call you Mr. James?"

"Yes, his wife did call me on May 18th to ask was there a special event we were having that her husband might be, and I told her no."

"The remains of one of you dedicated and loyal members were found yesterday, out in the middle of no where, not far from a dog fighting ring bust. What you know about that James?" asked Detective Peterson.

"Absolutely nothing." "He's lying!"

"Stephen, chill. What about a Black Panther member by the name of Jasper Ware?"

"What about him?" Aaron asked candidly.

"Do you know where we can find him?"

"At work possibly, why?"

"We have reason to believe Jasper Ware was the last person to see Alex Rice alive." stated Detective Cross.

"Does that bother you Aaron?"

"No, it doesn't detective Peterson."

Detective Cross walks forward some, closer to Aaron's desk.

"Mr. James, you just loss one of your men, shouldn't your group be out protesting or something?"

"People grieve differently detective Cross. The loss of one of my men is painful, but we are letting the police do their job. We will be having a memorial services for him in a few days and you and detective Peterson are welcome to attend, if it would make you feel any better about the way the New Generation Black Panther Party Organization handles grief."

"You think you have won, don't you wiseass, but it's far from over!"

"No, I don't think I've won anything detective Peterson, but if this is some type of game for you, then I say to you through the words of Chess, Knight to Bishop, I've taken your man, your move."

Detective Peterson snatches open the office door and walks out angrily.

"Mr. James, here's my card. Call me if you can think of anything and you already know, we will certainly be in touch."

"I will, good day gentlemen."

As soon as the two detectives were on the elevator, Aaron grabs his cell phone and makes a call. He waits for the person on the other line to pick up. As soon as the person receiving the call picks up, Aaron relay some words.

"Keep your eyes on the prize."

Twenty minutes later, detectives Cross and Peterson were pulling up to Security Services of America, 1440 Webster's Ave.

"Like I said Detectives, Alex Rice was supposed to pick me up that night to go shoot some pool, but he never showed."

"Do you have reason to believe that Mr. Rice was apart of this dog fighting ring?" asked detective Cross.

"Honestly, I can't say, but from what I've known personally, Brother Rice was a law abiding citizen. He will be missed."

Detective Peterson was steady observing Mr. Ware's office.

"Does this suppose to be some small replica of Aaron James office?" asked detective Peterson.

"Not exactly, his office is magnificently outstanding."

"Well maybe you can have his office, after we nail his ass for good."

"Stephen chill, I told you, I've got this."

Jasper Ware draws a hard unpleasant stare at detective Peterson. Jasper sees himself putting a gun inside detective Peterson's mouth and pulling the trigger. "You have to excuse my partner. Here's my card. Call me if something else comes to mind. You enjoy the rest of your day Mr. Ware."

"You men do the same."

That Friday the next day June 16, 2000, was Jillian's birthday. Instead of girl's night out, Jillian would spend her birthday with her new man Caziah the pharmacist. Gabrielle and Amber however, did take Jillian out for lunch that day bearing gifts. Amber and Trey would catch a flight later to South Carolina to visit his folks and since Keith was off tonight, him and Gabrielle was having dinner at Geja's. The last time she was there, Bryce was proposing to her. Gabrielle gazed around the restaurant reminiscing on old times. Geja's was great place to pop the question, too bad it was more of an ultimatum.

"Are you ok Gabrielle?"

"Oh yes, just trying to shake the past."

"Hope it wasn't all bad?"

"This is one of my favorite restaurants to dine in and well, the last time I was here, I was being proposed to."

"You're ex Bryce."

"Yes."

"And if you are sitting her with me, I can assume your answer was no."

"Exactly."

"Do you regret the decisions?"

"God no."

"Then the past is the past and tonight will be the start of new and prosperous memories."

Gabrielle humbles Keith with a heartfelt smile. He always knows how to establish a declaration of the best is yet to come.

"I guess I should have asked this on our first date, but I was getting to know who you are, not what you want. No time like the present, so what are you looking for in a man?" The question sort of caught her off guard. Gabrielle takes a sip of her wine trying not to appear insecurely nervous.

"Uh well, that will take all night."

"We have all night."

"What I'm really looking for is in a list that is quite long, but I can narrow it down and give you an idea."

"Ok, but that's not really necessary."

"I know, but for my sake it is."

"So give me an idea then."

"I'm looking for an intelligent, decent looking, heterosexual, mature and God fearing man, who is loving and has a good true heart."

"Is that all?"

"No, there's more. I'm looking for a responsible, honest, charming, kind-hearted, confident and considerate man who has somewhat of a sense of humor. I'm looking for a HIV negative, strong, affectionate man that appreciates me, someone who makes me happy and tries to keep me happy. This man must always have respect for me. I'm looking for a real man who has my best interest at heart."

Keith himself had to take a swallow of his wine before responding. "And this is the short version?"

"Somewhat."

"So there's more?" he said with a smile.

"Yes there is. To put it all in perspective, basically, I'm looking for the one that makes you better than you are alone."

"I like that."

"So do I. I forget who said that though."

"Well Gabrielle, I believe I'm all those things, even more and I think I can help you with your search, if you allow me."

"You are allowed; let's just see if you will be around for the yearly evaluation."

"I look forward to it."

"So what about yourself? What are you looking for in a woman?"

"It's quite simple really, but simple is something she is far from."

"Oh really, what kind of woman are you looking for that wouldn't have to steal your heart, but someone you would just gift wrap the key?"

Keith looks deep into Gabrielle's eyes before responding. "You."

Gabrielle is not bashful, but his response was most surprising and she had to look away. She began to blush. Her heart began to jump rope, releasing good sensations of flourished feelings. Now with regained confidence, she stares into his eyes. They both compliment each other with a smile. Still staring into his eyes, Gabrielle sees joyfulness, youthful innocents, potential love, but most of all, home. Sadly however, happiness wasn't something that filled the pair of hateful and watchful eyes from the person outside staring upon Keith and Gabrielle's cozy evening. Those pair of jealous eyes has witnessed enough and has now graduated to anger.

Later that same evening when Keith was driving Gabrielle home, he noticed her occasional quietness and after she asked him would he like to come up for a little while, he agreed and would go on to ask her about that.

"You've been quiet most of the way home Gabrielle, are you ok?" "I'm sorry what?"

"How are you *feeling* Gabrielle?"

Gabrielle smiled as if he would never ask.

"Oh, I'm feeling the sounds of Brian McKnight with a Mai Tai."

Keith gave a bizarre, what did you just say smile.

"You're feeling w h o? with what?"

Gabrielle gave a small giggle before answering.

"I'm feeling the musical sounds of Brian McKnight with a drink, which is a Mai Tai. It's my little habit, my actual mood to feelings."

"Oh righty then, long as you are alright."

"I'm good." she said with a smile.

"Good then, sit please. I would like to talk to you for a moment."

Gabrielle walks over and takes a sit beside Keith on the couch.

"Ok, I know you said you've had two long term relationships. You didn't say much about the first one, but the second one was a failure."

"True."

"Are you ready for another serious relationship?"

Gabrielle was taken aback, actually blown away by the question. She smiles calmly to easy some of her speechless tension in the room.

"Listen Gabrielle. I know because of Bryce, I've missed out on being the second one in your life and that could have been like the song, "Second Time Around" by Shalamar type of beginning. I'm the possible third and it has been said, third times the charm. So what I want to know is, are you ready for another long-term relationship, the third time around?"

Gabrielle smiled again briefly before clearing her throat.

"Well, I am. I've dated quite a few men, possible boyfriend type material. A couple of them got serious, but never really worked out."

"Why is that?"

"Everyone seemed to be on their best behavior on the first couple of dates, but who they really are will eventually show."

"And they were not right for you?"

"Right."

"Am I right for you Gabrielle? I mean, we have been dating for almost a month now, surely you have some idea?"

Gabrielle face carried a serious expression, but then it slowly melted away. "Keith, we've seemed to have established a good relationship, however, neither myself nor this relationship comes with instructions, so please, handle with care. And yes, I honestly believe you are right for me."

"Well I honestly feel the same way about you Gabrielle."

Keith leans over and kisses Gabrielle tenderly. After their warm kiss, Gabrielle emerged with a question.

"If you could think of any song, what song would describe our relationship now and six months from now?"

Well, that was a question Keith certainly wasn't expecting, but he relaxed into it by placing an arm around Gabrielle and pulling her closer to him.

"Let me see, a song that would describe our relationship now and six months from now."

"Yes, if it's too soon to know, I'll understand."

"No, this is quite interesting, different, but good. Any song huh?"

"Yes."

"Then I would definitely say Brian McKnight's song, "Back at one"."

Gabrielle breathes in a deep breath and releases a comforting smile of happiness as she laid her head down on his chest. She has never felt so secure. "Well, did I pass? How was my answer?"

"Good, very good for my third time around."

Three days later on that Monday evening, the New Generation Black Panther Party Organization held a memorial service for their fallen brother, Alex Rice. The memorial service was held at Mount Pilgrim Baptist Church. All members that could attend did which was most of their society, along with news reporters looking for worthy statements. Detectives Cross and Peterson took it upon themselves to accept Aaron's invite. Aaron did settle the herd of hungry reporters by giving them a brief statement regarding the death of one of their members, before making his way inside the church. Not wasting anytime speaking on Alex Rice's behalf, Aaron let members and other guest know that a special account has been set up at Bank America for Alex Rice's children college fund. Aaron himself, donated one hundred thousand dollars.

In the middle of his speech, Aaron noticed Brother Ware entering the church and watches him take a seat in the back row. Soon after that, Aaron concluded his speech and allowed Pastor Wright to speak. Aaron walks down from the stage passing most of the members in attendance and walks inside another part of the church. Shortly after that, Jasper Ware gets up and follows Aaron. Once Brother Ware was inside the pastor's office, he closes the door and a discussion began.

"Where are our good friends the police?" asked Aaron. "Still sitting in their car."

"Are you sure they can't connect you to this murder?"

"With all do respect sir, if they could, I would be trying to post bail by now." "Don't ever under estimate their means to find someone accountable Jasper." "Everyone thinks Alex Rice was part of this dog fighting ring that somehow went wrong."

"Well if Peterson is working the case, then Alex Rice was possibly his informant." "Now there's someone that has too much time on his prejudice hands."

"Yes, said Aaron with a smile. I see he still have a grudge on me and still mad as ever."

"They have pills for someone like him." Jasper suggested.

"This I know, however, an accidental over dose will be his bitter end if he continues on this path."

"Suicide is susceptible to me." replied Jasper.

"For you and I both, but still, you must keep your eyes and ears open until this blows over. Now, if you will excuse me, I must return back to the memorial service of one of our dedicated and loyal members, as detective Peterson put it." Aaron gets up from behind the desk and walks to the door.

"Do I have to stay?" asked Jasper.

Aaron opens the door and turns around.

"Yes, yes you do. This is the bed you've made and you will lie in it."

To officially kick summer off right in the windy city, Taste of Chicago is an annual event that commands the attention of your taste buds. Taste of Chicago is usually held between the dates of June 24 through July 4, a ten-day period in Grant Park. We are talking three million people, free concerts, cooking demonstrations, area restaurants representing their best, fashion shows, and talent shows. Everyone who is anyone in Chicago attends and if you don't, it's like missing a parade marching right down your own street.

This is one event Gabrielle and her friends always attend. So that Saturday afternoon, Gabrielle and her two friends were in the mist of all the activities, soaking up as much fun in the sun as possible. Each one of the lovely, educated and well to do sista's seem to be content with their current situation in life. Ever notice how the word *s e e m,* seems to make everything in your life better or worst than it really is. Seem, is a word hardly seen to its true potential because most women place that particular word when referring to the condition of their life in a girdle for support. Now men, I have no idea where they put their *s e e m,* of maintaining great expectations of assurances in fronting on reality. I guess that's why so many of them wind up putting their foot in their mouth. Either way, seem is, is what seem does, and if any of these ladies real life seem not up to par, let them speak now or forever hold their peace.

"Damn, I knew I shouldn't have worn these shoes."

"Amber you do this every year." stated Gabrielle. "It supposes to be summer casual event, no one told you to wear those stiletto heels."

"That's right; Gabrielle and I are not leaving early if they become a discomfort."

"Well it's a good thing I drove then huh? How about I leave both of you here with your insensitive ass attitudes."

"Now you see, I knew I should have drove."

"Jillian pay Amber no mind. Amber will play nice if she wants a birthday gift next weekend."

"That's right, next Saturday is July 1st. In that case, another rude word and my gift goes to the homeless."

"Jillian you wouldn't dare!"

"Gabrielle, Amber doesn't know me very well, does she?"

"Amber, you should know by now, Jillian don't lie."

"Jillian, have I ever told you, you're my best friend in the whole wide world?" Amber said with a smile.

"Yes, the last time you wanted to borrow my car on one of your private eye investigations to try and catch Trey cheating."

"Oh shut up why don't you!" "Ahh she got you Amber."

"Hey, what time is it?" asked Amber. "I want to catch the fashion show, but we seem to be stuck at Eli's Cheesecake World booth."

"It's one thirty." replied Gabrielle.

"Now I want to taste everything, stop the press, who is that? It's moments like this that makes me wish I didn't say I do."

"What are you talking about now Amber?" asked Jillian.

Gabrielle and Jillian turns around to see whom Amber is speaking about highly.

"That fine specimen headed this way."

Gabrielle smiles and acknowledges his presence by waving. "Gabrielle you know that fine brother?"

Jillian smiles because she already knows who it is.

"Why yes Amber, I do know him. That fine specimen is Keith." "That's Keith, I be damn!"

"Quiet, and close your mouth."

"Well hello ladies, how is everyone on this beautiful Saturday afternoon?" Everyone spoke.

"Hope I didn't keep you waiting long?"

"No Keith, you're right on time. I would like you to meet my best friends, Amber Hudson and Jillian Asbury."

"Now I saw you Ms. Asbury at the basketball game, nice to meet you and I've heard a lot about you Amber, nice to finally meet you."

"All good I hope?"

"I have never heard Gabrielle speak an unkind word about anyone."

"Good, because if she did, I would say divide that information by two, multiply it by three and subtract it by one, then depending on my month's horoscope reading, it may or may not be true."

"And there it is, this is what makes you, you." replied Keith.

"Keith you don't know the half of her and please don't get her started." Stated Jillian.

"Ok ladies, give me and Keith a few seconds and I will join you momentarily."

Jillian and Amber both said it was nice to meet him and Keith said likewise. Gabrielle pulls her man along as they began to walk and talk.

"I like your friends."

"Thanks, they are something else, but I love them."

"You will have to meet some of my friends soon."

"Anytime you are ready."

"You know I work tonight until ten."

"Yes I do."

"Would you like me to stop by later?"

"If you're not too tired."

"Not at all, it's good to have something to look forward to when I get off of work." "Then I will see you later." After a small kiss goodbye, Keith says bye to Gabrielle's friends before leaving.

"You heifer! Why do you always get the good ones?"

"Not really, Bryce started out good, but spoiled in the end." "Oh Amber, it's not like Trey isn't good looking." said Jillian. "Yeah, but I think it's time for a new coat."

"Trouble in Paradise?" asked Gabrielle.

"I'm just tired of beating off hoes to prove my love. All this playing detective is getting old."

"Amber, Gabrielle and I are not taking you seriously. You and Trey are not going anywhere; you're like Bobby and Whitney."

"Why on earth would you use them as a inspirational couple?"

"Because, if they can make it work, so can you and Trey."

"Speaking of couples, why haven't Gabrielle and I met your man, the street pharmacist yet?"

"Yeah Jillian, why haven't we?"

"Amber, he is not a drug dealer and you both will soon, just not today."

"Well we understand if he can't be seen for house arrest reasons."

"See, there you go again Amber, he's not a drug dealer!"

Later that night, Keith did stop by Gabrielle's place. He was even kind enough to bring Gabrielle a snack from work. After enjoying a late snack and DVD, Keith said goodbye for now. As Gabrielle walked happily into the kitchen to straighten up, she notices Keith cell phone on the kitchen table. He had just left and if she hurries, maybe he would still be out there. When Gabrielle walked outside the doors of the apartment building, Keith had just drove off. She waved at him even though she knows he probably didn't see her. Gabrielle looks over at her car and sees a beer bottle sitting on the trunk of her car. She walks over and takes the empty beer bottle off her car. She looks around oddly before making her way back to the building entrance. Once she reached the front doors, a loud crashing sound of breaking glass was heard as if someone smashed a bottle on purpose. It startled Gabrielle as she turned around in a panic and sees a car she didn't recognize pull off in a hurry and drives away.

CHAPTER TWENTY-SIX

Know Thy Enemies

The following weekend when Amber was away with her husband for her birthday, in a tropical climate I might add, Gabrielle and Jillian just chilled back home in Chicago with their new mates. That Sunday afternoon, Aaron was invited over to Gabrielle's place for tea and a little competitive power play of chess. Gabrielle invited Aaron over to meet the new man of her dreams, Keith. This time, Aaron was aware of company that would come knocking and even more pleased to know that Gabrielle's current desired interest is a black man.

"Aaron James, I would like for you to meet my boyfriend Keith McNair. Keith, this is my dear and good friend, Aaron James."

Aaron gives Keith that special Black Hand shake where they lean forward to touch shoulders.

"Good to meet you brother." said Aaron.

"Same here man."

When Aaron really got a solid look at Keith in his eyes, it made Aaron space out for a second in thought.

"You alright man."

"Yes, seem as if I may have known you from somewhere."

"No, I can't say I remember ever meeting you."

Gabrielle knew the reason for Aaron's soul-searching distraction. He see's the same thing she see's, Percy's soul.

"Aaron teaches Ethics & Society in Philosophy at Chicago State University."

"Oh really, I teach African-American history at Richard Daley Community College."

"Really, I taught their for a year, good school."

"Excuse me for asking, but aren't you the President of the New Generation Black Panther Party?" Aaron gave a rather large smile with pride.

"Yes, that I am." "You're a busy man." "Yes, that I am as well."

"Gabrielle is in company of many famous people."

"Now I wouldn't say that Keith." said Gabrielle.

"I see someone is losing in chess."

"Guilty." replied Gabrielle.

"Do you play?" asked Aaron.

"A little, but not in a while."

"Well we will have to play sometime."

"I would like that, but don't leave on my account."

"Not on your account at all, like you said, busy man."

"Ahh, that's right."

"McNair, where do I know that name? Where are you from?"

"I'm from Macon Georgia. You may recognize the last name from my great uncle, Chris McNair."

"So there is some history in your name during the Civil Rights Movement?"

"Yes it is."

"You never told me that Keith." said Gabrielle surprisingly.

"I know, forgive me. He's my father's uncle, sometimes people connect the name, most of the time they don't."

"Well Keith, it was a pleasure meeting you. We must talk sometimes." Aaron offers his hand and Keith shakes it.

"Likewise, I would like that."

Aaron would sneak another stare into Keith eyes.

"You're alright man, you're alright." said Aaron.

"Thanks."

"Gabrielle, call me when you get a chance."

"Oh you know I will."

Aaron would see his way out, but not before stopping and relaying more words to Keith. "Keith, Gabrielle is a rare gem Nubian Princess, you take good care of her, you hear?" Gabrielle smiled with pure innocents.

"Yes I know, and will." Tuesday July 4, 2000, 2:17 pm

While most Americans were outside barbecuing and celebrating our nation's birthday, Aaron receives a call from one of the remaining partners of Project Hope. Harold Stokes didn't go into details of his call, only that there was a problem onsite of the project. Aaron did notice that Harold didn't quite sound like himself, but agreed to meet him there at once. When Aaron did arrive on the construction site of Project Hope, he sees Harold's car, but no sight of him. Aaron get's out of his car and began making his way toward the future building site. Aaron tries Harold on his cell phone and the call went to voicemail.

The entrance to the unfinished building was open and Aaron walked inside. There was still much work to be done on the building before the opening in spring of next year. Aaron called out Harold's name as he made his way further in the building. A noise was heard that got Aaron's attention and he calls Harold name out again. While walking into an area sectioned off in thick plastic, Aaron tries Harold on his cell phone once more. The call went straight to voice mail. This time Aaron began to leave a message. "Harold, this is Aaron, you call me and asked me to meet you here. Where are you? Call me back." Observing his surrounding, Aaron kicks a soda pop can in frustration. He was about to leave, when he noticed another part of the wing in the area sectioned off in plastic with a divided wall. Aaron walked over and entered the open entranceway. Birds immediately flew up and away in a fluster with manic anticipation of fear. When the birds did clear their path in every direction, Aaron eyes grew enormous in disbelief of what his sight sees. Dangling from a metal beam ten feet in the air was the body of Harold Stokes, with a large note attached on his chest that read, I Owe You.

Aaron suddenly felt ill as he stared up at Harold's body hanging from a noose. He stumbles back trying to leave and falls. Aaron leaps up to his feet and runs out of the construction site. Once outside, he try's to regain his breath then makes a phone call. Five minutes later police pulled up at 2119 Heritage Lane, an area five miles from the Magnificent Mile shopping District off of North Michigan Ave. Aaron was explaining to detective John Mackey with the Chicago police his reason for being there, when Detectives Cross and Peterson enters the crime scene with probable cause. Detective

Rodney Watts, John Mackey's partner stops the two detectives before they could get into the crime scene good.

"What's up fellas, out sight seeing on this Fourth of July holiday?"

"You can say that." said detective Cross.

"Well try not to ruffle our feathers here boys, because this here is our crime scene."

Detective Cross gives a big smile of acknowledgement.

"Hey, we wouldn't dream of it." said detective Cross.

"The Bastard struck again!" stated detective Peterson.

Aaron glances over at detectives Cross and Peterson, but continued to speak with detective Mackey. Peterson walks over closer to the body and stares up at the victim with more words.

"I sure hope you guys can catch this lowlife, but I do believe you wouldn't have to look far, just around the room perhaps."

Aaron tries to ignore Peterson's talk, but found it difficult. "Go ahead Mr. James." replied detective Mackey.

Still staring at the victim hanging by a noose, detective Peterson delivers a final blow of words. "Looks like strange fruit to me."

Now, the words Strange Fruit in reference of a black person that has been lynched, is an insult and as racist as the word Nigger. Aaron eyes leaps over at Peterson with a reaction of, you Motherfucker! Aaron heads over to Peterson in anger and detective John Mackey tries to stop him. Peterson also headed in Aaron's direction in response to his attempt, but detectives Cross and Watts stopped him. "Come on Aaron, I've been waiting to mop the floor up with your ass!" Aaron starts in his direction again and detective Mackey tries to hold Aaron back. "Oh yeah, well that will be the day your dead nephew come back!" Peterson face turned red in anger. "Why you son of a Bitch!" More tension and scuffle escalated as more cops tries to break up the commotion. Detective Cross and Peterson were ordered to leave the premises, as detective Mackey tries to calm Aaron down.

"Calm down Mr. James, would you calm down please!"

"Man, I am calm. You need to get that asshole out of here!"

"He's gone alright, you want a cigarette? Do you smoke?"

"No, I don't smoke."

"Ok, just a few more questions for my report. What does I owe you mean?"

Aaron shakes his head trying to regain knowledge of the situation.

"I, I don't know, don't have a clue."

"And the victim, did he call-"

"His name is Harold Stokes."

"Yes the victim Harold Stokes, did he call you first to inform you of a problem with Project Hope?"

"Yes, I explain that already."

"Just making sure my report and your statement is accurate."

"Are we done?"

"Yes Mr. James for now, but we will be in touch."

"Then I'm sure you know where to find me."

Aaron makes his way out of the crime scene to his car. Once outside, reporters forces microphones in Aaron's face with questions.

"Professor James, what happen here?"

"No comment."

"Was a crime committed here?"

"No comment."

Aaron makes his way through the mob of reporters and safely takes refuge in his car before leaving the scene.

Gabrielle was at a cookout over at Keith's place with some of his friends, when she receives a call from Aaron.

"Hey Aaron, what's up?"

"Harold Stokes is dead."

Silences circulated the phone call as Gabrielle's smile melts away to sadness. "Gabrielle I must speak with you as soon as possible."

"Do you want to meet somewhere now?" she asked.

"No, I hear the holiday gathering in the background."

"Ok, what about tomorrow evening?"

"I will see you then."

Gabrielle ended the call with grieving disbelief. Keith noticed her sadness.

"What's wrong Gabrielle?"

"Someone I know has died."

"Oh I'm sorry to hear that, is there something I can do?"

"No, I'll be fine."

"Do you need to leave?"

"No, I don't want to be alone."

"Ok, I'm sorry honey."

Keith comforts Gabrielle with a hug. Gabrielle's thoughts couldn't help but wonder, just what the hell is really going on.

That evening, breaking news of city councilman Harold Stokes murder was being broadcasted on different local stations. Aaron sat at home watching coverage of this tragic developing story in which once again he has found himself right in the mist of things. The only other partner, Kelvin Mc Donald tried calling Aaron several times, however, Aaron wasn't accepting any calls at the moment, but knew eventually he would have to speak with him. Aaron stares out his window and naturally, a few reporters were on stand by along with a pair of detectives posted up in an unmarked car. This was turning out to be a very bad holiday for Aaron. Aaron takes a sip of his Hennessy then closes his window blinds.

Wednesday, the next evening when Gabrielle came home, she had just entered the apartment building to find Aaron standing by the tenant's mail receptacles bearing takeout. "Forgive me, but in risk of reporters finding me, I entered the building when someone was leaving."

"It's quite alright, let me just get my mail and we can go up."

Gabrielle enters her apartment and decodes the alarm. She was greeted by Jack, but when Jack sees her company, he retreats back to another room.

"I guess Jack is not in the mood for company." said Aaron.

"He's usually friendly. I've been watching the news."

Gabrielle's home phone rings and she walks over by the bar to answer it. Aaron takes the food into the kitchen. Once Gabrielle says hello, the person on the other end hangs up. She looked at her answering machine and there were no messages. She then joins Aaron in the kitchen.

"Chinese, smells good."

"So with the news version of what happen, what do you know so far?"

"That Harold was murdered and you found him hanging at Project Hope's site." Aaron thoughts went back to the moment he found Harold dead.

"I'm sorry what?"

"I asked would you care for some wine Aaron?"

"Yes please, I've talked to Kelvin. The remaining money for Project Hope is missing. Harold withdrew the money out of the special account the day before." Gabrielle appeared concerned.

"So does this mean Project Hope is on hold?"

"I'm afraid so, because of the crime scene and missing funds." "Aaron, what were you doing there?"

"Harold called me, said there was a problem on site and needed me to come down there."

"And when you got there, you found him that way?" "Yes, most horrible thing I've seen in my day."

Once again, Aaron thoughts traveled back to the moment he found Harold. "Aaron not only was you the last person to speak to Harold, you were the one that found him."

"I know, I believe I'm being setup." "By whom Aaron?"

"I honestly don't know, but have reason to believe Peterson may be involved." Gabrielle's memory went in search for a second.

"You mean Officer Stephen Peterson; I thought he was kicked off the force?" "No, I wish. That racist moron somehow made detective."

"He still believes you killed his nephew Rodney Peterson and his partner, Kenneth Harris?"

"Let the record show, I was out of town when those homicides took place." "Are they trying to pin you for this murder?"

"It looks that way, Peterson and I were about to break grounds of physical reckoning. Besides, their precinct is not even investigating these murders."

"That's right, murders. Ross Thomas's case has yet to be solved. Man! I can't believe both of them are gone. Do you think these murders are connected?"

Aaron takes a sip of his wine before responding.

"It's very likely; someone doesn't want Project Hope to come to pass."

"You said the remaining funds for Project Hope are missing right?"

"Yes, but once this situation is cleared, I may replace the rest. It's all tax deductible."

"Aaron do you believe your life is in danger?"

"I can't be for certain at this point. It is however, important to know thy enemies." "Do you know all of yours Aaron?"

"Of course, and I play my enemies like a game of chess, never knowing they will be the one laid to rest."

"Aaron, please don't say things like that."

"I'm just keeping it real. Get them before they get you."

"I don't like all this talk of violence."

"Well you need some advice. You carry mace for protection right?"

"Yes."

Aaron stands up from his seat and faces Gabrielle.

"Ok it's only natural for me to carry protection as well. My gun is a registered lethal weapon in which I have no problem in putting it to use."

"Aaron please, put that gun away. You are making me uncomfortable."

"I'm sorry, but you need to look into purchasing one for yourself."

"No thanks. So what are you going to do about all this Aaron?"

"The only thing I can do, wait, wait and see what develops."

"When is the funeral?"

"As soon as the autopsy is complete."

"Man, I can believe this is happening again."

"Well wake up and believe it Gabrielle, because unfortunately the worst is yet to come."

Two weeks later, funeral services were held for the late councilman Harold Stokes. There were many people in attendance including Gabrielle and her closest friends. The autopsy ruled the cause of death to be blunt force trauma to the head. So Harold was already dead when he was hanged. That didn't stop some citizens of Chicago from given mixed emotions and Aaron hard stares. Aaron still stood his ground and kept his head up. Gabrielle and Amber finally got to meet Jillian's man Caziah, the pharmacist. They didn't like the fact that they had to meet under these circumstances. After Harold's funeral, the three couples went out for a bite to eat. Gabrielle was pleased to see all the couples getting along so well, looks as if these current mates will have a lasting impression for possible years to come. Trey, Amber's husband did ask Caziah was he a street pharmacist in humor and he assured everyone that he is a real licensed pharmacist. With that finally cleared up out of the way, the lasting bond of a tight friendship began to evolve. They could look to Keith for great meals, look to Trey for great seats at the Chicago Bulls games, and look to Caziah for OxyContin. Just kidding, but it was great that these couples can come together knowing they had each others back and a toast was given to friendship.

Friendship was not the mood or topic of discussion in the area of Elmwood Park, Illinois, where in that shady commercial building another distinguished high status poker game was taking place. Members of the World Church of Masters Creator society anted up for this special request. Patrick Reddick was definitely in on this go round. With Patrick and another member left to put up or shut up, cards were revealed. The member up against Reddick lays out a two, three, four, five and six of clubs for a straight flush and Reddick lays out four ace's and a joker for his five of a kind.

"Goddamn you Patrick, no one is that lucky!"

"It isn't luck."

"He cheated."

Reddick throws his cigarette down.

"Are you calling me a cheat Steve?"

"Yeah I said it, what of it?"

"Well I ain't no cheat; you should learn how to play."

"Are we done? Patrick, bring your cheating ass over here and get this folder."

ordered the supervisor.

Patrick steps on his cigarette and makes his way over to the supervisor.

"He thinks he's the shit because Mark is his cousin."

"I heard that." stated Patrick.

"Good, I wanted you to."

"Patrick get over here, what are you doing huh?"

"I'm winning Sam."

"You've read over this folder before."

Patrick opens and looks over the information in the folder.

"Oh yeah, nice to see you again."

"You know what to do, no fuck ups alright?"

"No problem, hey any of you sore loser want second chair?"

"Blow me Patrick!" said one member.

"Fuck you Steve!"

"I'll take second chair Patrick."

"Jason you pussy." said Steve.

"Hey thanks Jason."

"No problem."

Three weeks later, now in the month of August, Gabrielle was enjoying a romantic dinner over to Keith's place. Keith would wine and dine her like no man has done before and Gabrielle was more than grateful. It was about that time to show Keith just how grateful and appreciative she is of him. Ladies if a man is willing to wait for loving at least one month or more, then you can rest to sure he's interested in a long term serious relationship. Plus, the longer you both wait, the more you will make it, how the musical artist Aaliyah says it, hot like fire.

Standing outside on his roof deck staring at the stars a million miles away, Keith walks up behind Gabrielle and embraces her with a tender hug. He kisses her cheek and she smiles. "How are you *feeling* Gabrielle?"

Without hesitation, Gabrielle gives her answer.

"Oh, I'm feeling the sounds of Marvin Gaye with a glass of Hennessy."

With that catch phrase, Lets get it on, in mind, they began to kiss. The next morning after a night filled with lovemaking, Gabrielle awakens beside Keith with him smiling at her. He leans in for a kiss, but she covers her mouth with the sheets, morning breath she foretold.

"I've made breakfast."

Gabrielle removes the sheet and looks over at the nightstand to find a lovely tray of food with one red rose.

"So you are a morning person?" she asked.

"No sense of letting the day pass."

"What time is it?"

"Seven thirty."

Gabrielle throws the covers away from her in a hurry.

"Hold on there." he suggested.

Keith grabs hold of her, pulling Gabrielle back down on the bed.

"I gotta go home, get ready for work."

"You have time and you must promise me you will eat something before you go, deal?" She nods her head.

"Deal." He kisses her cheek and Gabrielle walks over in his bathroom to freshen up. "Gabrielle?"

"Yes Keith?"

"Who is Percy?"

Oh boy! Hearing Keith say Percy's name, was not what Gabrielle was expecting the morning after.

"What?" she said with hesitation. "Who is Percy?"

Gabrielle spits out some mouthwash into the sink, then runs the water for a few moments. "How do you know that name Keith?"

"You said that name a couple of times before you woke up."

Gabrielle comes out of the bathroom, slipping her blouse over her head. "Look Keith, I'm really press for time, can we talk about this later?"

"What about breakfast?"

Gabrielle walks over to the tray of food and places a piece of toast in her mouth. "There!" she said in a mumble.

Gabrielle takes a bite of the toast, lays the rest down, and finished getting dress. "Is there something you need to tell me?" he asked.

"No, I mean yes, well, we will talk about this later okay?"

Gabrielle rushes over to Keith who was still lying on the bed and gives him a tender kiss, before trying to depart company.

"I think sister in-law likes me."

Gabrielle stops in the middle of his bedroom doorway and turns around. "What did you just say?"

"I said, I think sister in-law likes me, your sister Ivy."

"I've gotta go!"

Gabrielle lit out the door in her delayed morning, which despite the jitter circumstances, was good.

Gabrielle pulls up into the parking lot of her mid-rise apartment as if she just raced the Daytona 500. With no time to waste, Gabrielle bolts from her BMW. After a few hurried steps, she realized she forgot her purse. After retrieving her purse, Gabrielle also realized she was going to be a little late for work, so no use of running around like a chicken with its head cut off. She closes her car door, puts her best foot forward and began walking her way to the apartment building. Then out of nowhere came a black Camaro pulling in front of her. A white male on the passenger's side gets out and grabs Gabrielle. Gabrielle began to scream and fight as if her life depended on it. The white male began dragging Gabrielle over to the car. Gabrielle kept screaming and fighting, all along trying to grab a hold of her mace. The man tries to force Gabrielle inside the car and the driver lunges out for her. Gabrielle kicks at the driver while forcing her self back, still fighting the man who has a hold of her. She finally locks hold of her mace and sprays the man in the eyes and face. "You Bitch!" he yelled.

He turns Gabrielle loose, but not before knocking her down. The white male on the driver's side gets out the car and Gabrielle screams loud enough to awake the dead. A tenant from the apartment building walks outside and sees the commotion. The driver sees the tenant as he goes for Gabrielle and stops in his tracks. Gabrielle screams once more as she tries to get up. The driver tells his accomplice to get his dumb ass in the car as he rushes back to the driver's side. The male tenant rushed over to help Gabrielle as the two men jumps back inside their vehicle and takes off. Once the tenant reaches Gabrielle, he tries to help her up. "Are you alright?" he asked.

Out of breath, Gabrielle tells him to get the tag number. The speeding car stops and began to backup. The driver was headed straight for them and the tenant pulls out a gun from his waist and fires shots at the approaching car. The driver quickly put on the breaks, resumes the drive gear, and blazed out of the parking lot within seconds.

Waiting in a room in the inside the ER, Ivy brings Gabrielle a cup of water. With only a few scrapes and bruises, including a bump on her head, Gabrielle was all right, just shaken up. There was a knock on her door and Bryce enters the room. "Hi Gabrielle, Ivy, I saw your name on the board, just wanted to see if you were ok?"

"I'm okay." The cup of water in Gabrielle's hand trembles some.

"Bryce can you check to see if she can be discharged."

"Sure Ivy, I can do that."

"Thanks."

On Bryce's way out, detectives were on their way inside the room.

"Ms. Michaels, I'm detective John Mackey and this is detective Rodney Watts. Do you remember me?"

"You're the detective investigating Ross Thomas murder."

"Right."

"She has spoken with the police already." Ivy stated.

"Yes ma'am and you are?"

"Ivy Jackson, her sister."

"Oh yeah, the Walsh Case. Well we need to speak with your sister further."

"Concerning?" asked Ivy.

"Concerning, the threat on her life ma'am."

"The What!" Ivy replied.

Gabrielle immediately felt ill and very afraid.

"Dr. Michaels, last night we received word that a threat was put on your life. We tried to contact you at home, but you were not there."

"That's right; I was over my boyfriend place."

"Anything else you can remember about the attempted abduction?"
"Only what I've told local police already and that a tenant saved my life."

"That was no tenant, that was an undercover detective put there by me. Do you remember what these men look like?"

"Not really, they were wearing a ski mask over their heads."

Detective Mackey opens a folder and shows surveillances pictures of some men. "Do you recognize any of these men?"

Gabrielle stares at the pictures, but was uncertain.

"Take your time honey." advised Ivy.

"Maybe this guy, judging from his eyes, but I'm not for certain. They both were white males."

Detective Mackey picks up one of the pictures and hands it to Gabrielle.

"What about this guy?"

Gabrielle stares at the picture, but seem to be having a hard time with it. "Like I said, they were wearing ski masks and it happened so fast."

"Do you believe this has something to do with Ross Thomas and Harold Stokes murders?" asked Ivy.

"We don't know, just following some leads ma'am."

"Well I want twenty-four hours detail on my sister."

"Ivy no."

"What do you mean no! Someone just tried to kidnap you and if these detectives are concern, then you should be too."

"I don't want that."

"How about just for a couple of days and nights then?" detective Mackey suggested.

"Sure, but only for a couple of days."

"We need you to come down to the police station and look at more pictures."

"Gabrielle I hope you reconsider longer protection." advised Ivy.

There was a knock at the door and Keith enters the room. Tears began to form in Gabrielle eyes when she sees him. Keith speaks to everyone then walks over to Gabrielle and hugs her tight. "Are you okay?"

"Even better, now that you are here."

"And you are?" asked Detective Watts.

Another knock at the door and Bryce enters the room.

"I'm Keith McNair, her boyfriend." he replied.

Bryce walked in to see Keith arm around Gabrielle.

"Gabrielle, you have been discharged and ready to go. Take the prescribed prescription for any pain you may have."

"Thank you Bryce."

"Anytime, hope you feel better." Bryce closed the door on his way out.

That evening all of Gabrielle friends were over to her place with a guarded police detail outside on the premises. Keith had to work, but would come over later. Aaron was the first guest there and the last to stay until Keith arrived, even then, Aaron didn't want to leave her side. Gabrielle thanked Aaron and assured him she was in good hands. When Aaron did close the door to Gabrielle's apartment, he thanked God she was all right. He was angry though, because he wasn't sure what this kidnapping attempt was all about, but now more than ever, he was going to find out.

Back inside Gabrielle place, Keith and Gabrielle gets comfortably close to one another. "I almost lost you today."

"Keith please, I don't want to talk about it." "Ok, but we do have a lot to discuss."

Gabrielle rests her head on his chest and tries to relax. Relaxing was something far from her mind because like Aaron, Gabrielle has enemies of her own to be concerned with.

CHAPTER TWENTY-SEVEN

Unfortunate Circumstances

The next day Gabrielle did feel brave enough to go back to work. The police followed her there and made sure she was safely inside the building, one detective would remain on the premises outside. Many of her colleagues were happy for Gabrielle's return, but didn't want to make her feel uncomfortable about it. They re-laid their sincerity without bringing up what had happened and Gabrielle appreciated that. After a full day of work, Gabrielle walked to her car and began her after work ritual. It was sort of hard to breath in positive thoughts after yesterdays life threatening attack, but she knew it was by the grace of God, that it just was not her time to go.

Gabrielle pulled out of the parking deck with a white Chevy Lumina following her. She didn't have to guess, Gabrielle knew it was the police detail making sure she gets home safely. Girls night out was canceled and Keith was glad of that. After what had happened, he didn't want Gabrielle going out anyhow. While Keith worked, Ivy and her children kept Gabrielle company over at her apartment. When Keith did arrive for his night shift watch, their talk began. Keith stared at the 8x10 black and white picture of Gabrielle's first true love.

"I guess we do have similar eyes."

"He was my first love."

"All what you have told me Gabrielle, is that the reason you left my home in a panic on our first date?"

"I'm afraid so."

"Percy and I both experienced traumatic incidents on the same night. He died and I lived. Gabrielle do you honestly believe I am Percy?"

Gabrielle takes a seat beside Keith on the couch. She stares at him sincerely. "Much as I would like for it to be so, I don't. My sanity won't ever allow me to believe that."

"I'm sorry about your friend, but I'm the same person I've been since the day I was born. This abnormal coincidence is highly out of the ordinary, but may have happened for a reason."

"That's what I keep telling myself, this coincidence happened for a reason, I just don't know why?"

"Well don't worry yourself about it, just know that who I am is real, that my feelings for you are real, not someone else's."

"I know Keith, I know."

Keith takes Gabrielle gently by the hand.

"Question." he said.

"Yes?"

"What song describes your feelings right at this very moment."

"Honestly." she said.

"Yes."

"I would have to say, "Happy" by Mary J. Blige."

"I feel you on that; do you see a future for us Gabrielle?"

"Absolutely, but what song describes your feelings on that?"

"I thought you would never ask, the song "Baby I'm for real" by After 7." Gabrielle smiles and smothers him with a hug and kisses.

"You were waiting to present that one."

"Maybe, but hopefully one day both of our songs in mind will be on the same page."

Even though Gabrielle has cleared the air with Keith about Percy, deep down inside, Gabrielle feels a connection lies between the two men. Gabrielle's feelings for Keith is strong and very real and her sanity helps her identify between the two relationships. Love for Keith is close in the air. She just hopes when love presents its self, she won't allow the past lingering potential feelings to confuse the two souls. Still, since Gabrielle and Keith have been dating, Percy has yet to welcome a visit in her dreams.

The month of August ended without any more deaths or incidents. September 1, 2000, things seem to be getting back to normal or so it *seemed*.

Gabrielle was leaving work that Friday headed to her car when a man in the parking deck stopped her. Before the man could get two words out, undercover cops was all over him like white on rice.

"Stop! Please stop! He's is a friend of mines!"

Cops released the man and pulled him up from against his car.

"Sorry, just doing our job ma'am."

"I told police that I didn't want anymore protection."

"Then you need to speak with your sister ma'am. You both have a good evening now." The police walked away and returned to their cars.

"Trey, I'm sorry. I'm so sorry."

"That shit was deep. Are you in some type of Witness Protection Program?"

"No, what are you doing here anyway Trey?"

"Wasn't sure what time you got off and was on my way in to talk to you."

"About what?"

"Amber, she hasn't been herself lately, distance. Now I know I've been good, haven't done anything wrong. Maybe you know something?"

"Actually I don't Trey. Amber has been the same old Amber, God help us all."

she said with a smile.

"Well listen, do me a favor. Tonight is happy hour or girls night out right?"

"Right."

"Would you talk to her and find out what's going on?"

"Gee Trey, I don't know."

"Please, it's like she don't care anymore. I don't want to loose her."

"Ok, I'll try to talk to her, but I can't guarantee anything."

"Thanks, here's my cell number and put a leash on those German shepherds of yours."

"I will and I apologize once again."

"Glad you are okay."

"Thanks."

Happy hour started out at Webster's Wine and Bar on Webster's Ave, the ladies were enjoying drinks and chatting about the latest gossip when in walks the company of Fletcher and Reese.

"Good evening ladies, mind if we join you?" asked Fletcher.

"Don't we always." replied Amber.

"Hey Fletcher, Reese, not at all, come join us." Gabrielle insisted.

"You already know to pay Amber no mind." suggested Jillian.

"Thanks Jillian, some friend you are."

"No mind, yes we know Amber has no mind." said Reese.

"And how are you Amber?" asked Fletcher.

"Fine, even better when you leave."

"Winter is gone my darling, must you keep bitter cold isolated forget—me—not's, as a reminder." Fletcher replied.

"If icy cold is my mood, then I would blame you, not the food."

"Cute Amber, did you learn that in college?" asked Reese.

"Four years of Jeopardy."

"Ah I see, looks like you're low on your drink?" "Why yes I am, can you help me with that Reese?"

"I sure can, waitress, a Prozac cocktail for my friend."

"Forget you Reese!"

Everyone except Amber shared in Reese's humor.

"Excuse me ladies and gentlemen." said Jillian. "I have to make a trip to the ladies room."

"You're excused, need any help in there?"

"Reese please!"

"Hey, doesn't hurt to ask?"

"So what are you guys up to tonight?" asked Gabrielle.

"Bout to hit the clubs, are you ladies interested?" replied Fletcher.

"I think I speak for all of us when I say, Hell No! We Won't Go!"

"Ella!"

"It's cool Gabrielle, we just stop by. Glad to know you are safe and ok."

"Yeah, we are." said Reese.

"Thanks Guys."

"And as always, this round is on us."

Fletcher lays two twenty dollar bills down on the table. Before both men got up to leave, Reese tries to confiscate the money and Gabrielle slaps his hand. "Alright, alright." he said.

"Have a good evening ladies." said Fletcher.

Gabrielle wishes them the same and Amber just ignores them.

Once the guy's were out of sight and Jillian was still in the ladies room, Gabrielle began to question Amber.

"Amber, what has gotten into you lately?"

"What do you mean?"

"Why must you treat Fletcher so mean? I can understand about Reese."

"Fletcher has done enough all ready."

"What does that mean? Is everything alright with you and Trey?"

"No!"

"Well what's wrong now?"

"I'm late."

Gabrielle expresses a smile of congrats.

"You mean your gonna have a baby, but wait, your drinking."

"I know, I said I'm late, not with child."

"That's wonderful, so what's the problem?"

Amber looks around suspiciously before answering.

"If I am, the baby may not be Trey's."

"What!"

"Would you keep quiet please."

"Well who else could it be, I mean—oh hell no. Please don't say who I think it is." Amber appeared a little embarrassed.

"Fletcher, I'm afraid so."

Gabrielle stares at Amber shockingly surprised.

"What! Don't give me that look; I never said I was Jesus Christ's sister."

"Amen to that, what ya'll talking about?" asked Jillian.

"Nothing that a trip to confession and a few Hail Mary's can't solve."

"Fletcher and Reese gone?"

"Yes." said Gabriele. "They bought the next round."

"That Fletcher is so sweet, I guess he's still hung up on you Amber."

Amber quickly places a hand over her mouth in references to Jillian's statement. "I think I'm going to be sick!"

That same evening on Chicago's Southside, Black Panther member Jasper Ware met with Aaron's cousin Demarco to discuss future business plans.

"Longtime no hear from man, where you been?" "Laying low until this Alex Rice mess blows over."

"Cops haven't come around questioning you anymore, have they?"

"No, but you can never tell when they're gonna pull a warrant out of their ass."

"Ain't that the truth? So what's up, when are you going to start betting again?"

"Soon, you said the men involved are ready to start back up, this time with tighter security I'm sure."

"Yeah no doubt, those men who are really behind dog fighting were pissed."

"Well that problem is gone; I'll be ready to bet again soon."

"Oh yeah, the Mallory brothers wants to know are you really serious about being apart of this action to become a main distributor?"

Jasper draws slowly off his cigarette and blows the smoke out from his nose before responding.

"I'm weighing my options, but definitely serious."

"A big shipment of the finest commodities is on its way to Chicago. Two other buyers want in. They have plenty of dough. You know, Donald Trump worthy ends."

"When is this deal going down?"

"Not exactly sure of the date, cause the Mallory brothers are trying to shake a couple of rats in their entourage, but most likely at the end of the year."

"Good, that gives me plenty of time to generate more funds."

"How is my cousin?"

"He's good, just trying to balance some priorities."

"I hope Aaron's not killing those dudes and taking their money."

"You know man, Aaron was right about you."

"What?"

"Your lack of intelligences, blossoms in stupidity with each breath you take."

"He said that?"

"Yes he did."

"I'm touched."

"A, Aaron don't kill his own people and 2, he has money like Donald Trump remember?"

"A and 2, are you trying to fit algebra into this, cause I don't do algebra."

"Why am I not surprised."

Before the weekend could run off, the three couples spent the rest of their weekend at the Chicago's Jazz festival. This free annual festival is held at Grant Park. In sponsor with a tribute to Duke Ellington, there is a host of events, food, an extensive art and craft fair. It was the ladies first Saturday night outing with their men in a while. Several months ago, Jillian and Gabrielle's love life was on hiatus. Now, they both have a steady man in their life, two for Amber, but they have someone to love and to receive love and that's what really matters.

Three weeks later, Gabrielle sat over to Amber's place waiting for her to come out of the bathroom with her pregnancy test.

"Well, should I start planning a baby shower?" "It reads negative."

"Good, close call. Now you just have to set things right with Trey."

"Wait, but why haven't I got my period yet?"

"Stress, hormones, I don't know. Go see your gynecologist."

"And what do you mean set things right with Trey?"

"Trey has been worried about you lately. He came to talk to me at work three weeks ago."

"He did what!"

"Calm down, he has been worried that you were seeing someone else and he was right. Hell, you had me and Jillian both fooled."

"I'm not proud of that okay. It just happened that's all."

"Don't mention to Trey that I told you about his visit, but do you still love Fletcher?"

Amber puts the pregnancy test back inside the box then places that box inside her pursue. "What?" Amber replied.

"Girl, I know you heard me."

"I don't know. Him and Emerald are still together and it's a chance he may move to Atlanta with her."

"Fletcher said that?"

"Yes, so it wouldn't make a differences if I do or don't."

"Actually it does. You know Fletcher still loves you and would dump Emerald in a second if he thought you both could be together again."

"Trey has been so sweet. I mean he has really come around, fully focused on our marriage now."

"Do you love Trey?"

"Girl, much trouble I went through to snag him, you know I do."

"Okay, do you love Fletcher?"

Amber thought seriously for a second, but finally exhaled out the truth.

"Yeah I do, but differently. I don't know what to do?"

"It's simple, you must choose, little Miss. Adulteress. Through the words of LL Cool J song, "Lounging" who do you really love. Will it be Trey or Fletcher?"

This year for Gabrielle's birthday, everything went as scheduled. That weekend before her birthday, the ladies went out and did everything they were suppose to do on the day before her big day last year. They went shopping, got their hair and nails done, and enjoyed a lovely day at the spa without the threat of a cheating heart. Keith made reservation at Narcisse restaurant, the playground for the beautiful. The last time she was there was last winter with Malcolm. The warmer season is even lovelier at Narcisse. Her birthday evening was going well with hint of love in the air, but Keith had some news to share with her.

"Are you enjoying yourself Gabrielle?"

"I am, I love this place. They make you feel so special here, like everyone is a celebrity."

"Well good. I have some good new and bad news."

"Will the bad news ruin my birthday?"

"I hope not, I guess it depends on how you look at it."

"I'm ready, fire away."

"The good news is, next summer I will be opening my own restaurant in Chicago."

"Wow, that's wonderful Keith. Any names in mind so far?"

"A few, but the bad new is, I have to go to Birmingham, Alabama to teach a culinary class for a semester."

"Birmingham, Alabama, when?"

"The position just came available, so I leave this weekend."

Gabrielle felt like her man was deserting her. "Oh Keith, do you have to?"

"It's just a semester. Plus, it would be good for me. The Culinard Institute in Birmingham, Alabama is a great school." "How long is the semester?"

"My course is from October through December."

"Less dreadfully cold weather in Alabama, what about your classes here?"

"Yes, less dreadfully cold, but my class will still be taught online."

"Oh okay, well do you promise to visit me when you can?"

"Yes, I will."

"And do you promise to be back in my arms on Christmas Eve?"

"God willingly, absolutely."

"Okay, but I'm going to miss you." She appeared a little sad.

"Don't worry love; ask me what song can prove my devotion to return back to you?"

"Ok and what song would that be?"

"Freddie Jackson's song, "We've only just begun.""

Gabrielle's brief sadness faded to an over flowing joy, which was only natural because the particular song running through her mind when it came to her overwhelming feelings for Keith was, "You Bring Me Joy" by Anita Baker.

Saturday afternoon Gabrielle would see her man off at O'Hare airport. She appeared strong, but silently her heart was suffocating inside. That night, Gabrielle wasn't up for going out with friends, nor did she want any company. She chilled at home with some DVD's and fixed up some of her favorite treats, which included some messy nachos and a chocolate shake. It wasn't long before the TV was watching her. With Jack comfortably by her side, the evening wasn't too bad. Gabrielle woke up as the end of the movie credits were playing. Five minutes later, she received a call from Amber.

"You busy?"

"No, what's up diamond girl?"

"I got my period."

"That's good Amber." said Gabrielle with a sigh.

"Don't be feeling sad that Keith is gone, he's coming back to you."

"I know, I miss him already."

"What are you doing?"

"I was watching a DVD, now I'm watching a movie on TV."

"What are you watching?"

"Girl, the Golden Child with Eddie Murphy is on."

"I remember that movie, who knew that the kid playing the Golden Child would grow up to become a famous professional golf player."

"He did?"

"Yeah, Tiger Woods is one of the best pro golfers of all time."

Amber's silliness did put Gabrielle in a better mood before she finally decided to call it a night. Her and Jack got settled in bed and looked forward to a good nights rest. Ten minutes late, Gabrielle would fall peacefully asleep. Twenty minutes later, without the company of his picture on the other side of her, Percy appeared in her dreams without warning. Before this visit, one reason for Percy's presences in her dreams was because of a certain song. The song "Come back to me" by Janet Jackson was usually on Gabrielle's mind when she did fall asleep. However, tonight without any songs on her mind, a song did emerge in her dream when Percy appeared. For some reason the song "Again" by Janet Jackson begin to play when she laid eyes on Percy. Yes, he appeared without warning, but a warning was something not needed. Percy has always been with her in spirit. She smiled at him heavenly with an expression of, hello dear friend, where have you been.

Back in East Peoria, Illinois, Mark Hale received a phone call on a clear line from one of his members in Elmwood Park, Illinois.

"Where is he Sam?"

"Mr. Hotshot is laying low, sight seeing in Toronto."

"Did he say what happen?"

"Yeah, he fucked up. Well, Jason fucked up." "Well we all make mistakes."

"They went in half cocked with their dicks in there hands. That's what usually happens when you fuck up."

"When is he due back?"

"Soon and our customer is pissed. He wants his money back."

"That's not happening. The contract is signed and there are no cancellations." "That's what I told him."

"Have the Feds been by for visit?"

"Sure, they stopped by to fuck with us, but if they really had any probable cause, those two geniuses would be on CNN Headline News by now."

"We need to turn up the heat a little, complicate some priorities, that will make things interesting. If our customer calls back, tell him we will fulfill our contract. These things take time, but no refunds. Tell him if he can do a better job, he's welcome to try."

"I'll do that."

The next morning Gabrielle woke with a blissful smile of happiness. The world as she knows it was all-good. Percy's presence in her dreams always made her feel exceptionally over joyed with life. Gabrielle honestly believes life stands still when Percy is in the presences of her dreams. Unfortunately, we know the real world stands still for no one, but God. Fall arrived then winter and in between those times, Keith came home to visit her on some weekends. Gabrielle even made a trip down south a couple of weekends. Their potential love for one another made a lasting impression that stayed strong and anew, with a chemical bond of attraction they found irresistible. Just as Keith promised, he was right back in her arms Christmas Eve. However, he had more delaying news. As they sat comfortably on his loveseat, in front of a fireplace, you could her Nat King Cole Christmas songs playing in the background. They had cups of eggnog close by as they both found serenity in the moment. Have you ever noticed that the world maybe at its quietest peak on Christmas Eve.

"Do you believe this election Gabrielle? This re-count, is one for the record books."

"No doubt and it looks like the courts found a ruling suitable for their victor. "Gabrielle after New Years, I must return back to Birmingham a little while longer."

Gabrielle felt sad all over again.

"No Keith, why?"

"Don't look so sad Gabrielle. I may, that's may, need to teach another semester, but the real reason, my great uncle wants me to help him with his new Art Gallery."

"That's great, but are you sure there isn't something else you need to tell me?" "Like what?"

"Like you secretly have a wife and children there."

Keith nearly spits out his eggnog before laughing. She laughs at the sight of him. "That I have what?"

"A wife and family in Birmingham."

"Gabrielle, I've never been married, nor do I have any illegitimate children." "It's possible, just checking that's all."

"That my dear, you won't ever have to worry about."

Gabrielle smiled with reassurances.

"So I have you for a week?" she asked.

"At least that, do we have plans for New Year's Eve?"

"Yes, my friends and I usually attend the New Year's Eve Odyssey Cruise."

"Really, my friends were there last year. They usually attend that."

"Great, now my friends can meet your friends."

"See, I knew you were the one for me. I love you."

Those three words certainly caught Gabrielle off guard. She wasn't expecting to hear those words so soon. She looked Keith in the eyes sincerely surprised. "What did you just say?"

"I said, I knew you were-"

"The last part."

"Oh, that part."

"Yes."

"I love you."

Her heart skipped a beat and felt those words in more ways than one, given her a rush of splendid happiness with a sense of calm.

"You love me?"

"Yes, I do Gabrielle. I am afraid to ask, but do you think you could ever love me?" Gabrielle placed her eggnog down and moved closer to Keith. She stares him in the eyes with the deepest sincerity.

"Maybe in about twenty years."

Keith grabs Gabrielle playfully and pulls her on top of him and they laugh. "I love you too." she said.

"You do?" "Yes."

"I mean, I want you to feel comfortable and secure to say that, but only when you-"

"Keith, I love you. I don't have to think about it, nor are they someone else's feelings."

"Then I couldn't have asked for a better Christmas gift."

December 31, 2000, 6:30 pm

Aaron had just left the Black Panthers Party Urban Headquarters in route home for the evening. Once he pulled up to his home, he finds Kelvin McDonald waiting on his front steps. Aaron hadn't firmly established a reason for his uninvited guest, but just the sight of him gave Aaron a bad feeling.

"Kelvin, what are you doing here, is something else wrong concerning Project Hope?" Kelvin walks down from the few steps.

"Aaron I got a call that I should meet you here, what's this all about?"

"Your guess is as good as mine. I never called anyone and told them to tell you to meet me here, and for what?"

Chicago police suddenly rolls up in three different set of cars.

"What the Hell!" said Aaron.

"Aaron, I don't believe you are behind the murders of my partners, but when I got word that you needed to meet me, I called the police, they already had me under surveillances."

"It's alright Kelvin, I understand."

"Aaron James, we have a warrant to search your premises." stated detective John Mackey. He hands Aaron the papers.

"Do you want to do the honors or shall we?" asked detective Watts.

Aaron walks up the few steps and unlocks his front door. He then stepped aside to allow the police to enter his home. Once Aaron entered his home, he noticed his home security did not give a signal to disarm. Aaron looks closely at his alarm system. He pushes one button and the entire front panel falls off. It had been tampered with.

"Hey detectives, we need you down stairs in his weight room."

Aaron joined detectives Mackey and Watts on their way down stairs to observe there findings. Lying on a bench were two Polaroid pictures of each prior victim hanging in their crime scene. Also beside the pictures, was a noose with a note that read, Project Hope is cursed.

"Mr. James, do you always have pictures of dead guys and a noose lying around, or is this for show?" asked detective Watts.

"Aaron James you are under arrest for the murders of Ross Thomas and Harold Stokes." stated detective Mackey.

Detective Watts began reading Aaron his rights as Chicago police takes him into custody. Aaron remained silent; he knew he was being setup. Kelvin McDonald just stared at Aaron strangely as they brought him out of his home in handcuffs. Aaron was placed in the back seat of a cop cruiser and was taken away. If the police had searched Aaron's place thoroughly, they would have found his back door unlocked and tampered with.

8:30 pm Aaron had already placed his one phone call to his attorney Robert Lee. Their attorney was out of town, but was on the first flight back to Chicago. All that was left to do was wait. Wait indeed; due to the fact that it was New Year's Eve and felony charges of murder against him, Aaron was looking at a possible seventy-two hour hold. Just the thought of that made Aaron's soul ill, but he somehow was trying to keep a strong composure with an optimistic outlook. Sitting alone in a jail cell, he wonders just how Gabrielle's evening was going.

"Swell! I'm having a marvelous time." Gabrielle professes to Keith.

Her and Keith were cutting a rug on the dance floor at the New Year's Eve Odyssey Cruise Spectacular. Gabrielle and Keith friends did meet, adding a touch of color to the grand party. When the clock struck twelve to ring in the new year of 2001, a rush of future blessings came over Gabrielle. All past misfortunes of bewilder burdens, heartaches, regrets and life-threatening incidents all seem to disappear from her life. It was a new year, which technically means everyone can start anew and yes, even you. As confetti poured down and kisses were taking place, Gabrielle had no idea that her dear friend Aaron James was braving the night behind bars.

January 1, 2001, 9:05 am New Year's Day

An older man in appearance wearing eyeglasses, who is originally from India, looks at the clock on his wall. He knows it isn't like his first appointment to be late. When Aaron was brought some food, he asked the police officer the time and the police officer told him it was 9:05 am. Aaron had spoke with his attorney face to face, but there wasn't anything he could do until after the forty-eight to seventy-two hour hold in which he will be arraigned. Aaron wasn't hungry, he was worried, worried because his soul was not safe. Unfortunately, Aaron had to force himself to come to terms with the inevitable. He will miss the ritual act to preserve and re-bless his soul on the specific day ordain.

This sacred ritual to re-bless Aaron's soul, allegedly keeps his soul safe from karma, negative forces and misfortunes that may linger or carry forth from the past year. Aaron's yearly ritual once performed, is good for the entire New Year. Instead of eating, Aaron got on his knees and prayed. He prayed that God would have mercy on his soul and most importantly, that the possible curse on his family was notional, not real in any way, shape or form. As he continued to sit and wait for his arraignment, Aaron did much thinking. He thought about his enemies, being setup and all the probabilities that had led him to where he is now. The only demanding thought that continues to circle his mind was, this was all a tremendous misunderstanding of unfortunate circumstances.

Early noon on New Year's Day, Keith was watching a bowel game on TV. Between the commercials and halftime, he would find himself channel surfing and this time he landed on a local station which was broadcasting the news. To his surprise, he did not think he would see a story about Gabrielle's friend.

"Hey Gabrielle?" "Yeah?"

"Your friend, Aaron James is on the news."

Gabrielle walks out from his kitchen with a plate of sandwiches and smiles. "Oh, he's probably about to start some protest."

"No, I don't think so. The story on him just stated that he was arrested last night for the murders of Ross Thomas and Harold Stokes."

The plate of sandwiches Gabrielle was holding, would soon fall to the floor. "Wait a minute Gabrielle, where are you going?"

"I've gotta go!"

"Now hold on, hold on a second. I'm sure he is innocent, but the last time you hurried out of my place, your life was in danger."

"They're wrong! Aaron didn't commit those murders. I have to go see him." "Well I'll go with you, but I think he's still being held in jail."

"I can't believe this is happening. Aaron said he thought he was being setup. Oh I hope he sues the city for entrapment and bankrupt their ass for life!" "Remind me not to ever get you mad at me."

CHAPTER TWENTY-EIGHT

In the Black Pot,
the Past Surfaces and Runs Overed

On their ride to the police station, Gabrielle tried calling Aaron at home, but there was no answer. She tried his cell phone and after one ring, it went to voicemail. She leaves a message in references of his arrest. Gabrielle was angry; upset that detective Peterson could be behind Aaron's unfortunate circumstances. When Gabrielle and Keith did reach the police station, they arrived only to be turned away. Aaron could not receive any visitors except from his attorney. Luckily, Robert Lee was there and was leaving out when he see's Gabrielle and her friend. They talked briefly and he assured Gabrielle that Aaron was fine and that there was nothing anyone could do until his arraignment.

That evening, Aaron did receive a visitor. This visitor did not come for Aaron's best interest or assistances, but to gloat and breathe happiness of his misery. "My Christmas gift came late, but was well worth the wait."

Aaron looks up from his reading material to find detective Stephen Peterson standing in front of his jail cell. He continues reading.

"You see, it all works out. You may not rot in prison for the murders of my nephew and his partner, but you will rot for these murders."

"You think so?" Aaron replied.

"Oh I know so boy."

"Well, maybe I would have reason for concern, if you were the judge and jury, but you're not. So I would say a dismissal is in my favor."

Detective Peterson walks closer to the jail cell and grabs hold of the bars.

"That's unlikely, you see I've become quite chummy with the D.A. and he's ready to put these murders to bed. With my persuasion, I plan to make sure you get a needle in that black arm of yours."

"Is that right?"

"Yeah, that's right, but either way, you're going down. You see, I firmly believe in what goes around, comes around and judging from your missed appointment today, I would say all bets are off!"

Aaron looks up from his reading material abruptly.

"Oh yeah that's right boy, bet I have your attention now. You see, I know all about your sacred ritual. Your soul is without protection, but don't worry, it's going where it's suppose to, straight to hell."

Anger slowly fills Aaron's eyes.

"Oh and your King is in check, looks like I've won. See ya around Aaron, hopefully not for long."

Wednesday January 3, 2001, 8:30 am

At Aaron's arraignment, he pleads not guilty to two chargers of first-degree murder and was barely released on a two million dollar bond. The first thing Aaron did upon his release was visit his Hindu priest. Despite the delaying circumstances, Aaron soul was re-blessed. Whether the late ritual to preserve his soul helped his chances of regaining immunity or not, still remains to be seen. At this point of on going drama, filled with puzzling ecstasy that includes the ingredients of murder, lies, and plots, Keith did not want to leave Gabrielle, but needed to return back to Birmingham, Alabama. He made Gabrielle promise not to get herself tangibly involved. He wasn't sure if Aaron's potential setup had anything to do with Gabrielle's kidnapping attempt. He also promised Gabrielle that he would return as soon as he possibly could.

1:55 pm that same day of Aaron's release on bond, Gabrielle tried to will work along as fast and as humanly possible. She plans to stop by and visit him after work. Aaron seemed to occupy her mind all day. Ivy had to miss lunch yesterday, but made up for it today. If her sister's opinionated put downs of Aaron's circumstances at lunch wasn't enough, Gabrielle would become a little more aggravated after returning back to work when a nosey physician of anesthesiology stop by to question her.

"Hey Dr. Reynolds, what's up?"

"Hello Gabrielle, word is, you're friends with the accused murderer of the Project Hope partners?"

"Yes, Aaron James is a close friend of mine."

"Do you think he's guilty?"

"Absolutely not, and the police and media are going to eat their words."

"I guess Project Hope will have to forfeit its future business plans without the funds of your friend."

Gabrielle gives the anesthesiologist a displeasing stare.

"No Dr. Reynolds, the clinic will open sometime this spring, just as planned."

"Oh really, then I'm sure the only partner left is glad to know that." "This is all a big misunderstanding. The truth will come out."

"I'm most certain it will Dr. Michaels. Your friend and O.J. Simpson have much in common."

"And what exactly does that mean Dr. Reynolds?"

"Their version of the truth has a wealthy friend."

5:45 pm Gabrielle was ringing Aaron's doorbell and bearing takeout. Gabrielle was aware of the plainclothes undercover cops parked a block away from Aaron's place. "Gabrielle, come in. I'm glad you could stop by."

"Looks like you have surveillance set up about a block away."

"Yes, I know and don't mind. Please come in."

Once inside, Gabrielle observes the disarrange condition police left Aaron's home. "Oh Aaron, they broke your statue of Ganesha."

"Yes, when I saw Kelvin McDonalds standing outside my front steps, along with watching my statue of Ganesha slowly come crashing down, I knew I was in for a bad evening."

"I'm sorry Aaron; I know that was your favorite Hindu Deity."

"It's alright, my place isn't so bad. I've cleaned up the worst of it. What do you have there?"

"Some of Mama Pearl's famous chicken with the works."

"Great, I'll fix us something to drink."

Gabrielle found it hard to consume Mama Pearl's original recipe with all the information Aaron has shared with her. Just the thought of someone gaining access to your home without your knowledge is frightening. If you can't feel safe in your own home, then just what Secret Service Security should we invest in for protection?

"So not only did someone break into your home, they planted pictures of Ross and Harold's crime scene."

"Don't forget the noose, accompanied with a note."

"Aaron someone is really making an effort to stop the development of Project Hope."

"Yes well, for some reason I honestly believe this goes beyond Project Hope." Gabrielle appeared even more concerned.

"You think so?"

"I'm not sure. I obviously have an enemy unaware of."

"You mean you don't think it's that prick Peterson that may have set you up?"

"It's hard to say at this point, but no. Whoever is really behind this, wants me to believe its Peterson."

"I may have already asked you this, but do you believe my attempted kidnapping and these murders are connected?"

"I don't want to frighten you Gabrielle, but it's possible."

"Too late, that kidnapping attempt has already successfully accomplished that. I think my sister still have private eyes on me from a distances."

"More Cran-apple juice Gabrielle?"

"Um, no thanks."

"My case looks stable with a very strong fighting chance, thanks to my home security services."

"So they can verify that your alarm was tampered with?"

"Yes, they had reason to believe that the fire alarm was performing a self check test, but actually that was someone disabling the arm."

"Did the police find evidence that someone broke in your home?"

"I have no idea, but after my arrest I had my attorney and a few other Black Panther members return to place to gather evidence and he did."

"What kind of evidence?"

"Well for one, Robert found evidence that someone entered my home through my back door and left it unlock."

"See there, I knew you were innocent, people are going to eat there words."

"I'm sure people have had much to say."

"Of course, but the truth will speak louder. You just carry on with your normal everyday life like you always do."

Aaron sat his Cranapple juice down with a somewhat low expression.

"Easily said than done my darling."

"Why do you say that Aaron?"

"I was placed on paid administrative leave from Chicago State University."

"Oh Aaron no!"

"Yes, but its ok. Depending on the outcome of the trial, that will consider my chances of returning."

"In other words, you will be reinstated?"

"Of course. The police did however, has frozen my bank accounts."

"Will you be okay, do you need to hold something?"

"No, but thank you. I have a special stash in a personal safe that holds more money than some people make in ten years."

"Okay, you let me hold something then?"

They both laugh.

"Certainly, how much do you need?"

"I'm kidding Aaron, but is there anything else I can do for you?"

"You have done plenty. Thank you for the meal."

"My pleasure."

"Well, looks like it's going to be a bad year for me and a bad year for the people of this nation, possibly for the next four years, now that Bush succeeded in the recount. Anyway, it's dark out and I don't want you going home late."

"I could stay and help you straighten up, if you like?"

"Thanks, but that won't be necessary. I have to check this place thoroughly. I wouldn't be surprised if the police are listening to our conversation." "You really think so?"

"At this point of them trying to bring me down, it's possible."

"Ok Aaron, I will call you when I make it home."

"You do that, and thanks again."

"Don't mention it; you just keep your head up."

"Oh I intend to because through the words of Billy Joel, I am an innocent man." Gabrielle gave a proud smile.

"Now that's what I like to hear."

Aaron watched Gabrielle make it to her car safely and returned back inside of his home. He put up the remaining food and tried to finish straightening up. Not long in his effort, he stops to make a phone call. Aaron stares at the broken picture frame of him, his brothers and mother. He waits for the person on the other end to pick up. "Brother Ware, I need you to come over to my place as soon as possible."

Gabrielle did make it home safely. She sat in her car a few moments observing her surrounding. With her mace firmly in hand, Gabrielle proceeded to get out her car and walk to the apartment building. Once inside the building, she collects her mail. She always felt safer inside the building, but as Gabrielle catches the elevator up to the fifth floor, she wasn't safely aware of the black Lexus with an out of state license plate that pulled up once she entered the building. When the person in the Lexus sees the lights to Gabrielle's apartment switch on, they slowly drive away.

"Well I'm glad you made it home safely Gabrielle. I will give you a call tomorrow, alright bye."

Aaron hangs up his phone then stares at his guest. Jasper had picked up one of his golf clubs and swings it playfully.

"How come you don't play golf anymore Aaron?"

"I do, Tyrone and I still do."

"They don't play golf in prison."

"Well it's a good thing I don't have to worry about that, do I?"

"When is your trial?"

"Don't worry about that, listen. I was glad to know that all the Black Panther members came down to the police station New Year's Eve and stood in the streets with a clinched fist salute. I appreciate that, but starting a possible riot wasn't going to help me any. That's why I gave word to Brother Hampton to send you men home."

"We all were willing to stay until your release."

Aaron walks over and places his cordless phone back on the base.

"I know, but there wasn't anything anyone could do, but there is something you can do for me."

"What's that?"

"I need you to keep an eye on detective Peterson."

"Isn't that the asshole that set you up?"

"Maybe not."

"Then why do you want me to watch him?"

"Because I said so."

"What about the eye I have on your valuable asset."

"Jasper I will handle that, just keep an eye on Peterson and where were you today? I couldn't get a hold of you."

Brother Ware places the golf club back into the golf bag.

"Taking care of some personal business. What does the Black Panther Society have to say about your arrest?"

"Don't try to change the subject, that is none of your concern!"

"My apologies, just concerned about your up coming trial."

"Every member knows that if for some reason I must step down from acting President, that Vice President Tyrone Hampton will have full control."

"Man I hope not, he seems to give me a hard time."

"Don't worry about that, Tyrone is a good man, been with me since day one. I've talked to the Chairman and other board members of the Black Panther Nation and they are behind me one hundred percent. Just contact me with any information on Peterson."

"Why don't you let me do you a favor and off this racist asshole?"

"No, detective Peterson will die of natural causes of his own free will, not by us."

"The sooner the better."

"Well God has a plan for us all and it just so happens the word abomination wasn't placed in the dictionary by accident."

The remainder of that week, Aaron stayed pretty much out of sight from the media. He didn't appreciate the fact that his name and life was constantly being broadcasted on the news as if they were promoting a new product. Aaron did stop by his office at the Black Panther Urban Headquarters a few times. Vice President Tyrone Hampton assured him everything was fine. Splendid, now if his life could resume that same status, all would be well. With Aaron's office on the top floor, watching from his window, he could see a few reporters out lurking around like some homeless person in search for their next meal. Vultures, he expressed.

Now since Keith was out of town again, Gabrielle had nothing to do that Saturday, her and Aaron both, so Aaron was forced over to Gabrielle's place by a chess challenge. From all what was going on in Aaron's life, it must have been on his mind because for once in almost two years, Gabrielle was finally crowned the victor again. In the mist of her excitement, Gabrielle receives a call from a friend out of the blue.

"Hello Malcolm, it's good to hear your voice."

"Guess whose back in town?"

"You're joking right?"

"No, but I can fly back home if you like?"

"Don't you dare."

"Are you busy?"

"Aaron is over."

"I didn't mean to disturb you."

"Oh no, no, I just beat Aaron in a game of chess."

"Congratulation."

"Are you coming over?"

"Well, if you like."

"Of course, see you then."

Aaron stands up and began putting his coat on.

"Wait, wait, wait, where are you going?"

"Just want you to know, I let you win."

"Did not, I know how you play, you don't even make it easy for little Percy. I know you Aaron; you stay strong until you've won."

"Fine, take advantage of me and my circumstances."

"Oh Aaron don't go."

"I over heard, Malcolm's back in town."

"Yes he is, hey let's all go out to a dinner and a movie."

"I don't think so."

"Why not Aaron."

"I would, but I have some business I must attend to about little Percy's future. Plus, I'm sure you and Malcolm have a lot of catching up to do."

"Well ok Aaron, tell little Percy I said hello. You sure I can't change your mind?" Aaron gives a brief smile.

"I'm sure, but I want a rematch."

"Most definitely and you can best to believe I will gloat until then."

Enjoying dinner at Meritage Café and Wine Bar, Malcolm couldn't believe all the tabloid worthy information Gabrielle was sharing. Gabrielle couldn't tell, but Malcolm appeared a little disappointed that she was seriously involved with someone.

Gabrielle spoke highly of Keith and for once, was able to share what she really feels about him.

"I think I'm in love."

"Gee Gabrielle, I leave and come back to find your life turned upside down with love and chaos of suspenseful drama. Where do I sign up?"

"Trust me, you'll find more joy in getting your wisdom tooth pulled. You don't want to be apart of this on going madness."

"I'm just glad you are all right. I think I've seen some of Aaron's story on CNN Headline News."

"I didn't know it made national coverage, but they are usually the first to know anyway."

"Despite all this hoopla, you seem very happy Gabrielle."

"Thanks, like I said, I think I'm in love."

"Looks like you have your very own personal chef now; I must meet the lucky guy."

Gabrielle smiled briefly as she thought about it.

"Yeah I guess you're right, I would like that. How long will you fill this position at the museum?"

"A month, maybe two."

"Keith is Alabama right now."

"Alabama, for what?"

"He is teaching a semester at Culinard the Culinary Institute."

"Good, that gives me time to steal you away from him."

Gabrielle blushes with an alluring smile. Malcolm also smiled, but meant every word. "He tries to come home every other weekend. I'm so glad you are back Malcolm. Now I have someone to spend my time with when Keith is away."

"It will seem like old times."

Tuesday January 9, 2001

Now with a little more time to kill, Aaron went to visit his brother at a State Corrections Institute in Terre Pekin, Illinois. It was a complete surprise to his brother because after spending twelve years in prison without as much as a letter from Aaron, he didn't think Aaron gave a damn.

"You look good Aaron, real good. You and Percy always looked more like dad anyway."

"How have you been holding up Jesse?"

"As well as to be expected for someone on death row. I'm getting by, plenty of money on the books no doubt."

"You really beefed up Jesse from pumping that iron."

"Yeah well what else can you do?"

"Maybe get an education."

"Education won't do no good for a dead man walking. Now what's the real reason for your visit Aaron after all this time?"

"I guess you've heard I'm in some trouble with the law?"

"Yeah, I've heard. You checking out your future environment?"

"Not at all, had some free time to kill that's all."

"That's right; you have plenty of money to buy yourself freedom."

"I don't have to buy my verdict. I'm innocent."

"Well if it helps, I believe you, but I'm not the one you have to convince. How is little Percy doing?"

Aaron eyes lit up to hear his brother mention his son's name.

"Percy is brilliant, thanks for asking. Mom said Jesse Jr. and Tyoune are doing well."

"Yeah, thanks to their step dad."

"Sonya did get remarried didn't she?"

"I hate it, but it was out of my hands. I tell you something else, these young dudes going out getting these girls pregnant and thinking it's cool, that they are a man. Well, it's no joy to watch another man raise your children and it sums up just how much of a man you really are."

"Your children still carry the James last name don't they?"

"No doubt, he may have adopted them, but they still carry our name."

"Jesse Jr. graduates from high school next year don't he?"

"I know, he's gonna turn out better than I did for sure."

"And you know their college education will be taken care of by me."

"Yes, mom told me. I wanna thank you for that."

"Don't mention it, we are still family."

"That's hard to tell from the long absent from my life, but Demarco has been keeping me well informed."

"I can imagine."

"When was the last time you seen our not so bright cousin?"

"It's been a while Jesse and I'm not looking for him either."

Aaron and his brother both laughed.

"Well when you do see him again, tell him to come holler at a brother."

"I thought you guys were tight?"

"We are, but business has changed hands. He's hanging with the Mallory brothers trying to come up."

"The Mallory brothers of all people."

"Yeah, but Demarco is making some good ends in other illegal practices, if you get my drift."

"Must be the old, but new game."

"Right, and with his new partner, I think he said his name is Ware. They are-" That name suddenly commanded Aaron's attention.

"Wait a second, you said his new partner Ware?"

"That's right."

"Jasper Ware?"

"Yeah! That's that cat's name. No sense of humor. Him and Demarco are about to run things on the Southside."

Aaron draws a very low look of disappointment.

"You know that dude?"

"Unfortunately for him I do."

"I keep forgetting your means to know just about everyone in Chi Town. Hey, you leaving so soon?"

"Jesse I'm sorry, I must go, but hang in there and I will come back to visit you as soon as possible."

"Aaron."

"Yes?"

"Thanks for coming, it means a lot."

"We will always be brothers Jesse, no matter what."

As soon as Aaron was off the property of the corrections facility, he makes a call to Vice President Tyrone Hampton.

"I have disturbing news about Brother Ware. I am on my way back to Chicago and to the office to discuss a change in command among other things."

"I'll be waiting."

6:00 pm that same evening, Gabrielle was sitting uncomfortably in a room at the First District Police Station. Detective John Mackey and his partner detective Watts enters the room and Gabrielle immediately stands up from her seat with questions.

"Why did you have the police personally escort me down here?"

"I apologize Dr. Michaels, but it was necessary. Please sit down."

Gabrielle calmly takes a seat and listens.

"Dr. Michaels I know you didn't want anymore surveillance, so I made sure a detective would check your surroundings at your apartment, once in the morning and once in the evening before you came home."

"You did what?"

"Believe me, you will thank me. This evening as my plainclothes detective was doing his job, he spotted a 2001 black Lexus with New York license plates near your apartment building."

New York license plates somehow made Gabrielle very concerned. "Go on detective Mackey." she insisted.

"Well the person was not inside the vehicle. My detective called in the license plate number and found it was registered to Ethan Roberts. Does that name ring a bell?"

An uneasiness of restless fear came over Gabrielle. A haunting name from the past surfaces as if it was washed ashore. In the black pot, the past surfaces and runs overed. "Yes, I believe it does detective Mackey."

"My detective went inside the building to make a normal sweep of your floor and found Ethan Roberts lurking in the stairwell."

Gabrielle eyes grew exceptionally large.

"He was in my apartment building on my floor?"

"Yes ma'am, when my detective tried to confront him, he ran. He was caught and arrested. How do you know this Ethan Roberts?"

Gabrielle's thoughts were forced back to her first years of college.

"From Cornell University. We dated very briefly."

"Dr. Michaels, do you believe this Ethan Roberts has reason to try to harm you?"

Tears began filled Gabrielle eyes as she thought about her attempted Kidnapping.

"Yes I do."

Gabrielle looks up at the glass wall as police brings the suspect inside the room across from them. Gabrielle becomes very nervous.

"He can't see or hear us Dr. Michaels, but is this man Ethan Roberts?"

Gabrielle stands up slowly and draws her attention to the clean cut gentleman with light blond hair in handcuffs. A little older than he appeared in college, but he was a senior at New York University then anyway. His piercing blue eyes stared hard through the mirrors, a stare so disturbingly deep and focused, that he seemed to be staring directly at Gabrielle.

"Yes, that's Ethan Roberts."

"We think he maybe a person of interest in your attempted kidnapping. So we are going to need to know everything about this guy, starting from the day you both met."

That same night Aaron gives the New Generation Black Panthers Party Chief of security a call. Brother Ware was at a local pool hall with Aaron's cousin Demarco. Jasper sees the incoming caller on his cell phone and takes the call outside.

"Brother Ware?"

"Yes Brother James?"

"I need to speak with you, are you busy?"

"Not really, what's up?"

"Well, the police have frozen all my bank account pending the trial. There's no telling how long this will be, so I am forced to other alternatives. I'm in search for some under the table action."

"Continue Brother James."

"Well, I do have some money stashed away for a rainy day, but will need more. I remember my cousin Demarco has some connections to the underworld of dog fighting among other things."

"Sounds like his illegal trade, so will you be giving him a call then?"

"No, Demarco knows my crooked ways in the past. I don't want him thinking I've gone back to my old ways. Maybe you can contact him and discuss possible business ventures without directly involving me."

"It's possible, I think he hangs out at Crimson's Pool Hall a lot."

"Good, I have a half million dollars to put toward this trade if it will generate more funds for me."

"With that kind of money, I'm sure it could. I think I'll head down that way now to the pool hall to try and find him."

"Oh and Brother Ware?"

"Yes Aaron?"

"Not a word about my involvement. You will be the middleman in this under the table action, okay?"

"No problem, I understand completely."

Demarco walks outside as Jasper ends his call.

"Hey man, are you done playing pool or what?"

"Good news, Aaron wants in on our dog fighting bets."

"BULLSHIT!"

"I just got off the phone with him. Cops have frozen his bank accounts."

"I knew something could pressure him back into the old trade."

"He told me to contact you, but don't want you to know he's apart of this."

"Yeah no shit, then I would be proven right and he can't have that."

"If Aaron is really serious about this, then it's possible he will commence to our new Southside connection?"

"Don't push it, Aaron was never apart of the drug business. He knew the people and the connections, but never did any drug business with them. He despises drug dealers. His brother Jesse is proof of that. Now back in the day, Aaron was apart of the dog fighting trade. Hell, when the New Generation Black Panthers started up, they were more of a gang where some neighborhoods and businesses paid for protection. Aaron is really a gangster, you know that, and his good friend Vice President Tyrone Hampton, he was Aaron's bookie."

"That dude was Aaron's bookie?"

"Yeah, still is in some sense, more like the Black Panthers accountant, but don't ever test or cross him, he would literally rip your heart out and send it to your mother."

"Well with Aaron being pressured to generate more money, there's no telling what he would consider adapting to."

"Hell I don't know, maybe. I do believe the old Aaron is coming around."

Outside about a block away, Tyrone Hampton is parked in a black Lincoln Continental with his eyes directly on the two men standing outside Crimson's pool hall. Brother Hampton answers his cell phone on the first ring.

"I have sight of Brother Ware and your cousin in view."

"Good, then it's all coming together as planned."

CHAPTER TWENTY-NINE

Coming Full Circle

When Gabrielle made it safely home, she made calls to her sister and Amber. They were the only two people besides the police that knew the circumstances behind Ethan Roberts. Gabrielle sat down on her bed and thoughts of the past seem to circle her head. It was no escaping it, she might as well bring an extra blanket to bed because this lingering pervious history that has invaded her thoughts, will accompany her. The stipulating events of what has happen to Gabrielle in the past was vivid and as clear as if it happened yesterday. Not once, did Gabrielle ever believe that circumstances from that particular past would come back for vengeances. It was now very clear to Gabrielle, just who her enemy is.

It all began when a fraternity brother dared his cousin on a sexual conquest to score with Gabrielle within a week. You see, that fraternity brother, Todd Hartman was the cousin of Ethan Roberts. Todd Hartman who attended Cornell University asked Gabrielle out on a date two weeks prior and she turned him down. His cousin Ethan, was not in a fraternity and attended New York University. Ethan was visiting his cousin when the bet came about. Ethan accepted the challenge, which meant befriending Gabrielle. After almost a week of deceitful charm and socializing on brief dates, Ethan invited Gabrielle to a fraternity party. Gabrielle was hesitant in going, in fact only stayed thirty minutes. Gabrielle didn't feel comfortable there and told Ethan she was leaving. Todd brought the bet up to Ethan again as he was leaving the party. Ethan assured his cousin with confidences that he had everything under control and left the party to catch up with Gabrielle walking.

"Hey Gabby, wait up." Ethan yelled.

Gabrielle stops walking to allow Ethan to catch up.

"Why you left the party so soon, it was just getting started?"

"Well your friend Todd Hartman needs to be hitting the books studying than partying."

"He's a good guy, his dad is a doctor. So Gabby, did you enjoy the full thirty minutes of the party?"

"Well Ethan, spending the evening at a frat party eating on chicken wings and drinking beer from a keg wasn't the kind of evening I was trying to get into."

"But you did enjoy yourself right?"

"Uh well, at least it gave me a break from my studies."

Ethan runs and leaps on a park bench.

"It was a blast!" he hollers with enthusiasm.

Gabrielle laughs at the sight of him and continues walking. Ethan walks back up beside Gabrielle with a sexy yet slick smile. He places his arm around Gabrielle shoulders.

"Are you tired Gabby?"

"No, not so much."

Ethan slowly lowers his head for a kiss and Gabrielle stops walking and allowed Ethan to innocently kiss her, beer breath and all. Ethan's kiss alone, from all the alcohol he had consumed could have gave her a light buzz, but she didn't mind. He really *seemed* like a nice guy. When Gabrielle reached her dorm room, she thanked Ethan for walking her there, but he wasn't in a rush to leave just yet. "Aren't you going to invite me in for a minute?"

"Ethan, I still have more studying to do."

Ethan goes for a hug, but instead lifts Gabrielle up over his shoulders and opens the door. "I am caveman, hear me roar!"

"Quiet, and put me down. You are going to wake my roommate."

Ethan walks in the dorm room and closed the door with his foot then places Gabrielle back down on the floor. Gabrielle went to check her roommate room as Ethan walked into hers. "Great, of all nights, she decides to go out this night." Gabrielle does an about face and walks over into her bedroom.

Gabrielle walked into her room and found Ethan staring at a picture of Gabrielle and her sister. He looks up at Gabrielle as she takes her jacket off and Gabrielle laughs. Ethan was wearing some reading glasses.

"Ok Ethan, it's been a minute, time to go."

"Hey things are just getting started."

He takes off the reading glasses and walks directly up to her.

"Are you ready to become my lady tonight?"

"Ethan what are you talking about?"

Ethan places his arms around Gabrielle and stares into her eyes. He smiles briefly as he gently kisses her. His kiss was warm and felt good. Gabrielle got lost in his kiss as they fell onto her bed. Ethan began to kiss her harder as Gabrielle tried to catch her breath. His hand began to wonder below her waist, but Gabrielle stops his hand. Ethan continued to kiss her as she tried to speak.

"Ethan it's time for you to go."

Ethan grunts before forcing his tongue inside her mouth. A shot of tequila seems to swarms Gabrielle's head with a light buzz from a mouthful of his tongue. He began to kiss her neck.

"Ethan you gotta go."

"Come on Gabby." he whispered.

"Ethan are you high?"

He kisses her in the mouth again while trying to feel between her legs.

"Ethan stop! This is not going to happen."

He didn't listen as he tried unzipping her jeans.

"Ethan NO!" she screamed.

"Would you shut up? It's time you gave up that black pussy to me."

He held her down with his body and she tried to scream, but he put his hand over her mouth. Gabrielle struggles to get up, but he was too strong. He forces her legs apart then tries to remove her jeans. Gabrielle manages to bite his hand. He hollers, calls her a bitch and slaps her. He continues with his effort and Gabrielle continues to fight and tries to stop him. Her Jeans were half way down when he unzipped his jeans. With one hand now across her throat in a choke position, Ethan reaches inside his pants as Gabrielle begs him not to do this.

As Ethan reached inside his jeans to pull his penis out, within seconds a group of unidentified black male's charges inside Gabrielle's dorm room and snatches Ethan up off her. They knocked Ethan to the floor and began kicking and stomping on him. Gabrielle pulled her pants back up yelling for them to stop, but her cries went unheard. She grabbed the phone to call campus police. Those boys beat on Ethan, which seemed to be five minutes or more before running up out of there. Students were now in the halls, but didn't recognize the men running pass them. Gabrielle tries to help Ethan up, but he pushes her away and curses at her. Ethan barely could walk, but found strength enough to leave Gabrielle's dorm room.

An incident report was written up by campus police, but Gabrielle didn't know any of the black males that jumped Ethan. They were not friends of hers or her roommate because her roommate was from the Brazil and she didn't really know anyone in New York. Ethan had managed to leave the property before campus police arrived. Needless to say, Gabrielle thought that was the last she seen of Ethan Roberts crawling out of her dorm room that night, sadly she was wrong. After rare luck landed her residency back home in Chicago, her first year residency ended with papers being served to her unexpectedly. Gabrielle was being summons back to New York to testify against non other than Ethan Roberts. It would appear that Ethan's criminal behavior finally caught up with him.

Gabrielle spoke on the phone with the prosecuting attorney that summons her. All she needed was her testimony of her former acquaintance that she dated briefly. Gabrielle didn't want any part of it, but was being forced to testify. Gabrielle left for New York and would stay gone almost two days. Heaven knows she didn't want to drag up the past history of Ethan Robert's violent behavior, but knew her voice needed to be heard. On the morning of her court appearance, Gabrielle remembers being a little worried and feeling a lot of anxiety. Gabrielle waited patiently in the hallway of a federal court building. The courtroom doors open and a deputy requested her presence inside. As Gabrielle quietly enters the courtroom, she could hear the prosecuting attorney addressing the judge.

"Your Honor the prosecution would like to call our next witness. Prosecution calls Dr. Gabrielle Michaels to the stand."

The defense attorney grabs his witness list and quickly looks over it. Ethan Roberts slowly turns around in his seat and he and Gabrielle's eyes would soon meet.

"Objection! Your Honor, defense knows nothing about this new witness." "Neither did we Your Honor. The prosecution was not aware of the existence of this new witness until yesterday. Full details of this witness and crucial new evidence, just came to our attention late last night. The defense will find her name on this morning up dated witness list that I have provided for them."

"I will allow it, Dr. Michaels, please take the stand."

Gabrielle is sworn in and takes a seat on the witness stand. Ethan Roberts's piercing blue eyes slowly expanses but subsides to a brisk cold stare. He leans over and whispers something in his attorney's ear. Gabrielle's testimony was the low blow for the defense team. She was the key witness to Ethan Robert's conviction to second-degree assault and attempted rape of a former girlfriend. Ethan never threatened Gabrielle formerly, but who says threats comes with a personal invitation. That night at home alone and with Keith still away, Gabrielle have never felt so afraid.

The next day on his lunch break, Jasper Ware stopped by the Black Panthers Party Urban Headquarters to speak with Aaron. Once he stepped off the elevators, Jasper was met by two Black Panther members. He speaks to them and they speak back. One of the members looks at Jasper strangely while the other shakes his head as they step aboard the elevators. Jasper thought their encounter was odd, but brushed it off. The receptionist stands from behind her desk and asks Brother Ware was Aaron expecting him and he says yes, he had just spoke with him on the phone. Jasper knocks and enters Aaron's office. Aaron hangs up his phone and Vice President Tyrone Hampton stands from his seat.

"Brother James."

"Brother Ware."

"Bother Hampton."

"Brother Ware."

"Aaron I have some information on what you have inquired about."

"Oh good, Brother Hampton would you excuse us."

"Of course."

Once Brother Hampton closes the door, Jasper shares his information.

"Aaron, I did run into your cousin last night. He is still apart of that underground dog fighting ring."

Aaron smiles. "I figured he was."

"He is willing to place bets for me, if you are serious?"

"Oh I am quite serious. When can I get started?"

"Tonight, if you like."

"Sounds good. Now what else has my cousin been up to these days?"

"Well I'm not sure. He didn't discuss other business ventures."

"Is that right?"

"Yes, and you were right. Your cousin isn't too bright, shit for brains."

Aaron smiles briefly before drawing a serious firm face.

"Are you sure, you don't know about other dealings with my cousin?"

"Yes I'm sure, why do you keep asking?"

"Because I just got off the phone thirty minuets ago with one of the Mallory brothers and he told me riveting details about Demarco, his new partner and their new Southside venture."

Suddenly Aaron's office door opens and Vice President Tyrone Hampton enters with his gun drawn.

"What the hell?"

Aaron stands from his chair.

"You're lying Brother Ware; in fact you have been lying to me for quite sometime."

Brother Hampton removes Jaspers gun from his side holster.

"Aaron, wait. It's not what you think."

"Well why don't you explain it to me Jasper."

"I was just moonlighting to make a few extra dollars, that's all."

"You were there that night before cops raided that dog fighting ring, weren't you Jasper?"

"Yes, but-"

"But Nothing! You would jeopardize the future of the New Generation Black Panthers Organization by getting involved in this corrupt world of illegal tender that includes dog fighting and drugs!"

"It was a misjudgment on my part."

"You damn right! You over step your bounds once, I may give you a pardon, you cross me twice, you're over ruled and shit out of luck!"

"Aaron I'm sorry."

"You caused this whole problem with Alex Rice and now this. It has come to my attention, that you just don't have the New Generation Black Panthers Organization best interest at heart anymore."

"Aaron wait!"

Jasper takes a step forward and Brother Hampton cocks his gun.

"Not another step." advised Brother Hampton.

"Brother Ware, you have been suspended from active duty with the Black Panthers Party." "What!"

"You are being forced to step down from your position. David Duckworth will assume Chief of Security and Robert Burton will be Captain."

"Please don't do this."

"Brother Hampton and I have to present this evidence and information to the board. You will have a reinstatement hearing in six weeks to decide if you are allowed back in our organization. Do I make myself clear?"

"Aaron, I'm wrong, guilty, but please don't take away my position."

"Do I make myself clear Mr. Ware?"

Jasper hangs his head down before he nods yes.

"That is your gun and it will be given back to you once you are out of this building and we need your access card and keys."

Jasper hands his access card and keys over to Brother Hampton. Brother Hampton lays the keys and access card on Aaron's desk then proceeds to open the office door and escorts Jasper out of the office.

"Tell Demarco, my brother Jesse said to give him a holler."

Jasper turns back around with an apology. "Aaron I'm sorry."

"Get out of my sight."

Gabrielle was on her lunch break and decides to drop by Aaron's office. She has just walked through the doors of the Black Panthers building. She speaks to their security guard and pushes the button to the elevators to go up stairs. When the elevators doors open, Brother Hampton and Jasper were inside.

"Hey Tyrone, Jasper, just stopping by to see Aaron." "Go ahead on up Gabrielle and I will be back shortly." "Ok, see you around Jasper."

The former Black Panther member just stares at Gabrielle with vague and malice filled eyes. Brother Hampton continues to walk Jasper out of the building. Once Jasper was outside the doors of the building, Brother Hampton empties out his gun clip and hands Jaspers' gun back to him with words. "If you're smart, you'll go home, cool off, and think about how to get yourself out of this mess, but don't let me catch you around the building or Aaron's place, or I will personally rip your fucking head off and ship it to your mother."

When Gabrielle stepped off the elevator, she wasn't greeted by the receptionist. The receptionist was away from her desk. Gabrielle began walking toward Aaron's office, but heard arguing. As she got closer, she sees Aaron and the receptionist in an ongoing argument. Aaron turns his back on the receptionist and she grabs his arm to get his attention. Aaron turns around with quickness and strikes her across the face. Gabrielle immediately froze in her tracks. She hadn't quite made it in range view of the office door. Aaron said in reference, that she was not to ever touch him. He continues to argue with the receptionist, consumed with the moment. Gabrielle quickly turns around, walks back to the elevator, and catches the elevator back down. When Gabrielle stepped off the elevators, she sees Brother Hampton speaking with their security guard.

"Did you speak with Aaron Gabrielle?"

"No, I got an important call and I have to go, but tell him I stopped by."

"Ok, you be careful now."

"Thanks I will."

When Gabrielle crosses the street, Aaron sees her from his window and calls her cell phone. "Gabrielle. I didn't know you were here?"

"Yes, for a second before I got an important call and now I have to go."

"Well was there something you needed to talk with me about?"

"Yes, maybe later."

"How about you stop by after work?"

"Um, you will probably be busy."

"Nonsense, please stop back by after work."

"Ok, I'll see you then."

5:30 pm that evening, Gabrielle was seen riding the elevators back up to Aaron's floor. Images of what happen earlier stayed on her mind. She have never witness Aaron betray such violent behavior before, especially on a woman. When the elevator doors opened to Aaron's floor, once again there was no sight of his receptionist. She had already left for the day. So Gabrielle escorted herself down to Aaron's office. She knocks before entering.

"Gabrielle, I'm so glad you stopped back by."

"Hello Aaron, are you busy?"

"Not at all. Please, have a seat."

Aaron takes a seat back down in his chair. Gabrielle smiles at him, but was staring with different eyes at what seem to be a totally different Aaron. Aaron's behavior earlier really opened Gabrielle's eyes up to just who Aaron really may be.

"So young lady, what can I do you for?"

"I wanted to call you last night, but I talked with Keith until very late."

"Is he coming home this weekend?"

"Maybe sooner than that. Aaron I was at the police station yesterday evening for hours."

"What on earth for?"

"I know who my enemy is and who's behind my kidnapping attempt."

Aaron sits up in his chair and pays close attention to Gabrielle.

"Who Gabrielle?"

"Ethan Roberts, a guy I dated very briefly at Cornell University."

"Ethan Roberts, the police know this for certain?"

"They are investigating this matter further, but yes, it looks that way. They have him in custody. Aaron, he was at my apartment building, hiding in the stairwell on my floor."

"He was what!"

Aaron stands from his chair and walks over to Gabrielle.

"Yeah, my feelings exactly."

"Gabrielle are you alright?"

"No, not really. If it wasn't for detective Mackey having a plainclothes detective there doing a sweep of the place, there is no telling what may have happened." Tears began to fill her eyes.

"Oh Gabrielle."

Aaron bends down on one knee and gives her a hug. Gabrielle needed that relief hug, it felt real and warmly sincere. It also let her know every little thing was going to be all right.

When Aaron releases Gabrielle from his hug, he smiles and wipes a tear from her eye before standing.

"There, you okay?"

"Yes." she smiled.

"Have you eaten yet?"

"I suppose to meet Malcolm in an hour."

Gabrielle stands from her seat as Aaron makes his way back around to his desk. "Well I am certainly glad the police have this Ethan Roberts in custody. I never understood what you saw in him anyway."

Gabrielle froze, she literally froze because that is when she experienced the most unkindest cut of all, the cut of deceit, of a trusted friend and God only knows what else. She stares at Aaron ever so strangely.

"Aaron, I never told you anything about who I dated in college. How do you know about Ethan Roberts?"

Aaron quickly tries to grasp thoughts with a bit of nervous confusion.

"I don't. I mean I assume."

Aaron's words become silent as he gave a fragile smile with guilt in his eyes.

Suddenly darkness of terror fell over Gabrielle. It became very clear just how Aaron knew Ethan Roberts. Fear filled Gabrielle's eyes.

"It was you." she whispered. "You were responsible for the attack on Ethan. It was your Black Panther members."

"Attack on Ethan, you were the one being attacked Gabrielle."

"Don't come near me! Stay where you are Aaron!"

"Calm down Gabrielle. Yes, it was me. I was only protecting you."

"Protecting me, with a personal eye on my life!"

"You should thank me Gabrielle; I saved you from being raped."

"Aaron how could you do that? How long have you been watching me huh?" A timid form of quiet guilt came over Aaron. "How long Aaron!"

"My surveillances stopped when you graduated."

"Your surveillance!"

"Gabrielle you don't understand. I did it to protect you."

"I don't know who you really are anymore Aaron and frankly, I don't wanna know."

"Gabrielle please, don't leave like this."

Gabrielle stops and turns around.

"Makes me wonder about the circumstances around the death of those police officers. Now I'm not so sure anymore."

Gabrielle hurries out of his office to the elevators. Aaron walks over to his bar and pours himself a drink. Gabrielle runs out of the Black Panthers building to her car. Once inside her car she locks the doors and allows both hands to clutch the steering wheel. She was breathing heavily, almost to the point of hyperventilation. In an effort to pull herself together, Gabrielle began to take deep breaths through her nose, trying to collect her thoughts in the process. After a minute, she starts her engine and leaves. Looking down from his office window with a particular song in mind, Aaron watches as Gabrielle drives away. Sadly, that particular song heavy on Aaron's mind was, "Kiss from a Rose" by Seal.

An hour later, Gabrielle was having dinner with Malcolm at Dragonfly Mandarin restaurant on N. State Parkway. Gabrielle was still shaken from the information encountered, but tried to conceal her protective layer of appearance with a less tense mood. She shared Ethan Roberts's information with Malcolm without getting into specific details. After consuming that bit of information, Malcolm was even more afraid for her. Malcolm could however, tell something else was bothering her. Gabrielle's cell phone rings unexpectedly and Gabrielle sees that it is Aaron calling.

She let the call go to voicemail. Malcolm asked Gabrielle did she need some privacy and she said no. Gabrielle was relieved that Malcolm was back in town, but desperately wishes Keith were home. After they enjoyed dinner, Malcolm personally made sure that Gabrielle made it home safely. Gabrielle had three different massages waiting on her answering machine from her sister, Amber and Aaron. She hadn't even made herself comfortable at home when her home phones rings.

"Hello."

"Dr. Michaels, its detective John Mackey. How are you?"

"You mean besides being afraid for my life?"

"I know ma'am, just needed to keep you posted with some information."

"I don't think I can stand anymore tonight."

"It's vital that you be informed. Now, Robert's attorney came down and we really don't have too much of anything to hold him on."

"You mean he has been released?"

"I'm afraid so."

"I'm dead."

""Please don't say that Dr. Michaels. I will have police on duty for your protection and we will personally see to it that Ethan Roberts is out of Illinois."

"That's some relief."

"We are still working on leads to the possible kidnapping connection, so don't worry. We believe Roberts is our man."

Friday's happy hour was canceled and Gabrielle stayed at home and waited for Keith's return. Before Friday's evening was gone, Gabrielle was explaining the entire current situation to Keith. He was now worried more than ever. Gabrielle even told Keith aspects surrounding her attempted rape her freshman year, but did not dare tell him about what Aaron had done. In fact, she didn't tell anyone about what Aaron had done. Gabrielle knew if she breathed a word of it to Ivy, then Aaron's life just might be the one in danger, but who could she tell? It was all so dark and twisted, stalker potential even. Gabrielle just didn't know how to allow things to settle with Aaron. Maybe this is why all these years, Gabrielle felt that someone was watching her? Did Aaron kill detective Peterson's nephew and partner? It was all still unclear. Lying peacefully in Keith arms, thoughts of lies, plots, betrayal and murder continues to circle Gabrielle's mind. It appears that this thing of the unknown is coming full circle, but just the tip of the iceberg and like stated before, all circles must end sooner or later.

That Saturday the two men in Gabrielle's life met for the first time. Gabrielle, Keith and Malcolm had lunch together. Both men hit it off well, neither of the men felt threaten by one another. They both found mutual likeness fill with respect, esteem and regards to one another's impressive career, male bonding also played a huge factor. Gabrielle now has two men to keep her safe. Sadly, she wasn't sure if those watchful eyes she still feels, were from the police or Aaron. Gabrielle and her two men had a fun filled day that included a trip to the museum, the movies and later that evening, dinner and a concert at The House of Blues with special guest, Diana Krall. Gabrielle enjoyed her company. It was a good time had by all, something she really hasn't had since her troubles began. Troubles usually lingers as long as you entertain them, but for now she would enjoy Keith while she could, because tomorrow, he must leave her again.

That same night, Jasper Ware kept avoiding calls from Aaron's cousin. Jasper was at home alone where he has been since his suspension from the Black Panther Party Organization. He tried calling Aaron a few times, but Aaron wouldn't accept his calls, not to mention Aaron's own problems he had to address. Jasper could have made things worst for Aaron by going to the police, but he would only incriminate himself for Alex Rice murder. Jasper is already aware of the kind of person Aaron James truly is and just what organization he stands to be up against, which had many members. Jasper didn't fear God, but fears Aaron. Besides, how could he fear something he didn't believe in? Jasper wouldn't dare help the police, he despise them more than anything. No, Jasper wanted back inside his home with the New Generation Black Panther Party. He wanted things between him and Aaron right again. As Jasper sits at home smoking pot and drinking, one person was on his mind. This is the one person that would make things right between him and Aaron. What he needed to do was already thought through and waiting on him. Time for redemption.

Also, that same evening over in Elmwood Park, Illinois, someone was welcomed back with open arms along with a generous amount of teasing.

"Hey Sam, have Mark called?"

"He sure has Patrick, call him tomorrow and welcome back."

"Well if it isn't Mr. Royal fuck up himself."

"Screw you Lou, talk to Jason about fuck up's ok."

"Don't have to, WGN News told me everything."

"Sam, was it on the news?"

"Yeah, not much, just a mention of a possible kidnapping attempt."

"Goddamn it!"

"Don't worry about it, shit happens."

"Where is Jason anyway?"

"Don't worry about it or fuck with him."

"Hey the man let a hundred and twenty pound female kick his ass that caused my fuck up. I just want to shake his hand that's all."

"Sure you do Patrick, that's why you need to call Mark tomorrow."

"Yeah, leave Jason alone; don't blame him on your team effort."

"Shut up Lou, or I swear to God, I will hit your ass so hard, you'll re-digest your food!" That particular member stands from his chair.

"Yeah, well when ever you feel greater than God, go ahead Rambo."

"Oh Yeah Lou?"

"Yeah!"

Patrick heads toward Lou's direction and the supervisor stops him.

"Patrick, get the hell out of here and go cool off! Go see your girlfriend and slap her around. I don't care, just go!"

Patrick calms down and grabs a smoke.

"Yeah, I'll go, but I will say this much. I will finish my job without the help of any of you morons!"

"Oh no, really?" said Lou. "I think I might cry."

Patrick throws down his cigarette and heads over in Lou's direction again before the supervisor grabs a hold of his shoulder.

"Let it go Reddick, and just go!"

That Sunday afternoon Gabrielle said Goodbye to Keith with a sad face. She didn't want to let him go or hear any more promises, she just wanted him back home for good. Keith was going to do everything humanly possible to grant that request. He spoke practical safety habits to her and advised Gabrielle to be extremely careful. Curious to know what particular song that expressed her mood at the moment, he asked her and she told him, "Wonderful" by Ella Fitzgerald. Gabrielle then inquired the same question and he replied, "Have You Ever Really Loved a Woman" by Bryan Adams. She felt pleased with the song, but asked why that particular song? Keith places a hand underneath her chin and lifts her head up some while gazing into her eyes. He replied, because I see our unborn children in your eyes. Now, if that didn't seal their future together, then I don't know what will. Keith did manage to turn Gabrielle's sad face around after all.

4:00 pm on that same Sunday, Jasper makes a call from a payphone to detective Peterson; he tells Peterson that he has some information he would like to share and would like to meet with him. He gives detective Peterson the address while advising him to come alone. Thirty minutes later, detective Peterson enters an old factory warehouse near Clarke Junction. As detective Peterson makes his way further inside the warehouse, he notices that electricity still powers the building. It wasn't long before Peterson walked up on Jasper dark presence.

"I thought this building was condemned?"

"It is detective and privately own."

"I must say, I was rather pleased that you agreed to meet like this."

"And why is that detective Peterson?"

Detective Peterson draws a fake smile before continuing.

"Well, I've been meaning to contact you for a little while now and this just gives me the opportunity to lay it all out."

Jasper wasn't exactly sure what detective Peterson was speaking of, but remained apprehensive and cool.

"I did call you down here with information on Alex Rice's case."

"You know what? That won't be necessary."

Jasper slowly draws a gun on detective Peterson. Peterson didn't appear to be worried or afraid, not even in the least bit. In fact, he began to laugh. Jasper views Peterson and his humor with caution as he removes detective Peterson's gun away from him.

"Boy, I sure hope you know what you're doing Ware?"

"I like to think so."

"Well like I said, I'm ready to lay it all out now."

"Lay what out asshole?"

"How things are going to be. You see, you may have that gun drawn on me now, but after I tell you what I know, you will be placing my gun into my hands." Jasper gives a rare smile.

"Is that right?"

"Oh yes, absolutely. See your life is in my hands and right now, you're looking at life in prison, but if you kill me, automatic death sentences."

"Who said anyone will connect me to your death?"

"I say they will genius! Let me tell you what I know and have. I know Alex Rice was my informant. I know you picked up Alex Rice from Webster's Wine and Bar the night he was killed. I also know you killed Alex Rice."

Jasper was surprised and appeared concerned, but still in control.

"Oh yeah, how you figure that?"

"Because I've been watching you boy. I was the last call made to Alex before you killed him in that wooded area. I have pictures in my car with you leaving Webster's Wine and Bar with Alex that night. I have a lot of pictures of you both together."

"If this is true, then why not arrest me the day you and your partner came to question me?"

"You see that last call to Alex was to let him know that we had the exact location of the dog fighting ring and was ready to proceed with arrest. That is when I was going to bust you and with the charges against you, make you come work for me."

Jasper bucks his eyes in disbelief to detective Peterson's last statement.

"I, would come work for you?"

"That's right. What this is all about, is what I've been after for six years, Aaron. I want Aaron rotting in prison."

"Jasper began to do what detective Peterson did earlier, laugh. Peterson didn't share his humor.

"This is all its ever been about with you. You are obsessed with Aaron."

"Call it what you want, but I have all the proof I need to convict you for illegal dog fighting practices and for the murder of Alex Rice. See, Alex wasn't wearing a wire. He refused to, but on his set of car keys was a small flashlight with a recording device and camera. I have you, Alex Rice and Aaron's lowlife cousin in pictures together."

The smile on Jasper's face began to fade. What detective Peterson was saying could bring him down if it's the truth.

"Alex Rice was your informant, but you let him lay wasting away for almost a month before the body was found?"

"I don't give a fuck about that bastard! I didn't need him anymore when I knew I had Aaron's right hand man. Like I said, I want Aaron and you are going to help me. You are going to tell me everything you know about Aaron's involvement in my nephew and his partner murder."

"I am?"

"Yes, don't be stupid. You kill me; my trail will lead the police right to you. Now give me the gun."

Jasper shakes his head in confusion trying to figure a new plan to optimize, but found it difficult due to Peterson's ongoing chatter.

"Come on buddy, give it up. My way is better."

Jasper walks up closer to Peterson and places the gun to the side of his head. "Naw, I believe my way is just fine."

"Man is you crazy! You want to go to prison? I want Aaron! I know that son of a bitch killed my nephew!"

"Would you stop bitching that Aaron killed your punk ass nephew! Aaron was no where around in town when your nephew was killed!"

"Oh yeah, well if Aaron didn't kill them, then who did?"

"I did!"

Peterson's face irrupts with astonishment and Jasper strikes him over the head with his gun. That hard blow to the head drops Peterson to the floor rendering him unconscious. Jasper grabs detective Peterson's handcuffs, rolls him over and cuffs his hands behind his back. Jasper stands up and stares down at Peterson lying unconscious on the floor.

"All these years your dumb ass has been trying to finger Aaron for your nephew's murder. You were after the wrong man! You wanna know something else? I killed that prick, Stuart Elliott too. That's right, I'm minding my own business trying to have lunch when that asshole congregates with friends and implies that slavery was the best thing that ever happen to America. That motherfucker had the audacity to speak that. Well, since he was so much for slavery, I thought he should die like a slave. Now at least before you die Peterson, you will have some closure."

After thirty minutes of conducting his original plan, Jasper walks out the condemned warehouse alone. Night had fallen, but Jasper wasn't quite through just yet. Although Jasper may have walked out that building alone, someone else however, was out that night cruising the area for potential locations, and spots Jasper. Taking detective Peterson's information into consideration, Jasper enters Peterson's car. Pictures of Alex Rice and Jasper, their illegal connection were in a folder inside Peterson's car just as he stated. Jasper wasn't aware of the loathing eyes upon him, but knew his next stop was over to Peterson's home. Lucky for Jasper, Peterson's wife and children left him three years ago over his obsession with Aaron. Breaking and entering detective Peterson's home was a breeze. There, Jasper found all he needed to clear his name from possible connections to Alex Rice murder. He also found a disturbing shrine of pictures and newspaper articles of Aaron James on a wall. Sick, Jasper professed. After collecting what was needed and leaving, all Jasper had to do now was wait.

Around 7:30 pm that same evening, Gabrielle receives a call from Aaron. She couldn't avoid him forever, so she answered his call just to hear what he had to say.

"Gabrielle please don't hang up."

"I'm not, just curious to know what exactly could you possibly say to me, after finding out the truth."

"Gabrielle on Percy's grave, I apologize for what I did."

"Don't, don't you dare mention Percy's name in an effort to excuse what you did Aaron."

"You're right, it's wrong to mention his name, but it wasn't in an effort to excuse what I've done. Percy was however, the reason for my watchful eye."

"How could you say that? My personal life before and after Percy's death was none of your business."

"You don't understand Gabrielle."

"Please Aaron, explain it to me."

"You won't believe me if I tried."

"Oh at this point, you probably could spit on my shoes and make me believe it raindrops."

"Gabrielle, after Percy died I received a message from him."

Silences was all Aaron could here over the phone line. In fact, it was so quiet, that you could hear Gabrielle's heart beating.

"What did you just say?"

"I know, it sounds crazy, but the truth."

"What are you talking about Aaron?"

"Maybe we can discuss this over coffee?"

"Nice try Aaron, but I'm not falling for that."

"It's nothing to fall for Gabrielle, just because I dip my hand in the bowl with you, does not mean I will betray you. I think we need to talk."

"Well that's what we are doing Aaron."

"No, I mean face to face."

"I'm not ready for that."

"Please Gabrielle."

"You have already betrayed my trust, but I will think about meeting with you to discuss this, but definitely not tonight."

"Ok, I understand, but hopefully soon."

"We will see, I have to go."

"Gabrielle?" "Yes Aaron?"

"Until then, may I say this, to err is human, to forgive, divine."

Monday January 15, 2001

On Martin Luther King Jr. day at twelve noon, Aaron receives a call from A-1

Security about a security alarm that has gone off. Aaron didn't want to involve the police and told them he would check it out, possible false alarm and would report back to them. Twenty minutes later, Aaron pulls up to an old factory warehouse near Clarke Junction, a condemned building where most of the windows were boarded up from vandalism. Aaron went inside the building through the front entrance and checks his alarm system. It didn't appear to be tampered with. Moments later to Aaron's surprise, Gabrielle walks through the same door.

"Gabrielle, what are you doing here?"

"I received an urgent message at work stating to meet my father at this address, that it was a life or death emergency. Now what's this all about Aaron? You got me out in this freezing weather."

"I don't know. I got a call from A-1 Security about a possible alarm."

"Here, why?"

"I own the property."

Some noise was heard from inside the warehouse. Aaron pulls his gun out and Gabrielle becomes very frighten. "What are you doing Aaron?" "Stay here, while I have a look." "I'm calling the police."

"Fine, just stay here."

Aaron makes his way further inside the warehouse. He enters the production floor area and switches on the lights. Aaron's jaw drops at the sight before him. Aaron stares up at detective Peterson hanging from the ceiling. Aaron heard footsteps approaching and turns around with his gun drawn.

"Aaron, don't point that gun at me! Jesus Christ! Is that Peterson?"

"I'm afraid so." Aaron said disappointingly.

"I finally got a signal on my phone; the police are on their way."

Gabrielle and Aaron both walk closer over to the body.

"I don't believe this. I think I'm going to be sick."

"Maybe you should go back to the front Gabrielle."

"Aaron, I need to know did you do this?"

Aaron looks away from Peterson body hanging in the air to face Gabrielle. "No, I was here only moments before you arrived."

An uninvited guest up stairs, who was watching Gabrielle and Aaron, now has his subject in view. He aims his gun down and Aaron eyes rushes up and sees him. Aaron lunges over and pushes Gabrielle out of the way as two shots was squeezed off, hitting Aaron in the shoulder and stomach. Aaron also managed to fire a shot off at the intruder up stairs, but misses his target. The man runs from view. Standing in a quiver of tremendous darkness of fear, Gabrielle watches Aaron go down in slow motion. She screams in the mist of sure horror in which there was no sound. Her eyes wonder in every direction, trying to grasp hold of the circulating moment of terror in silences. When Gabrielle visual and preliminary sound regain caption, she heard Aaron calling her name. She rushes over to his side.

"Aaron you've been shot, hold on for the police."

"My gun." he whispers. "Take my gun."

Gabrielle heard footsteps approaching and grabs Aaron's gun from his bloody hands. The electricity goes out, leaving very little light in the dark warehouse. Gabrielle stands up and began firing off shots in panic. The footsteps she heard faded out upon its departure. You could hear Aaron's gun begin to click from having no more bullets. After a few moments, Aaron calls Gabrielle's name again and she drops the gun as if it was hot. She hurries back over to him by his side. She checks both areas where he was shot and removes her coat then applies pressure to his stomach.

"You have to get out of here." he said.

"No, I'm not going to leave you. Where the hell are the police?"

"Don't worry about me, go. I will be fine."

"No, I'm not leaving you. Just hold on Aaron, hold on."

"When I said I wanted to talk to you face to face, I didn't mean like this."

Gabrielle tried to spare a brief smile, but was more concerned about her friend.

"Quiet now Aaron."

"There's something I must tell you Gabrielle."

"Not now Aaron, later."

"Later is out of the question."

"Don't say that."

"The truth is, I didn't kill officers Peterson and Harris, but, but."

Aaron grunts from pain.

"Don't worry about that now."

"No." he whispered. "I must clear my conscience and soul. I didn't kill those police officers, but I. I did order them to be killed."

Gabrielle looked down at Aaron's fading existence with tears and compassion in her eyes. "You're going to be fine Aaron, hush now."

"I'm sorry for everything Gabrielle."

"I forgive you Aaron. I forgive you."

Aaron smiles through the pain, trying to stay conscience of his surroundings.

"You still want to know the meaning of life?"

"Aaron please, save your strength for me. Don't worry about that."

"Gabrielle, I love you, but this is farewell."

"Aaron don't you dare leave me, *Please*!"

"My soul is well and at ease, it praises holiness of higher good, it rest like love and is at peace-"

CHAPTER THIRTY

Red Rum Comes To Light

*N*ot all nor nearly all of the murders done by white men during the past thirty years in the South, have come to light. A Red Record, by Ida B. Wells

If all inhabitants of Africa, not just former slaves, but all African-Americans, man, woman and children of color, from soldiers to civil right activist, all black folks who has died or was brutally murdered because of the color of their skin, the unjust, vile and cold blooded fate that was bestowed forth on their most precious fiber of being, their very souls sealed and sacrificed for the future race of our people. If those very souls was to stand up all at once from graves and speak out of their own mouths, it would emancipate forth an over whelming cry that would spread like a tsunami that could be heard all over mankind. That over whelming cry of evolution would multiply only to awake other souls of any and all races, past or present that has passed on due to hate or the pure fact of an unrighteous death of murder and they too, all of mankind would cry out for justice and with one voice say, no more, no more.

Red was the color of Gabrielle's palms as she slowly rose to her feet and stared at her hands. Her emotions were running high. She wasn't sure if she was in shock or just delusional. He was dead, but she couldn't understand why. There were other unreasonable deaths from people in her life, but this one appears to be personal and voluntarily cold. There was a loud crash behind Gabrielle that startled her weak, which brought more daylight into the condemned building. The police had knocked out some of the boarded up windows, as law enforcement officials enters from other parts of the building. Tears in her eyes, Gabrielle turns away from the bright light that was focused on her. She stumbles as she tries to walk, but didn't get far. Detective John Mackey rushes up to Gabrielle, catching her before she falls. "Dr. Michaels, what happen? Are you hurt? Get EMS in here now!" he yells. The room was spinning and she couldn't breathe. Gabrielle tries to pull away from detective Mackey in rage before letting out an emotional, soul-draining outcry. She then blacks out in his arms. Detective Mackey stares at the body of Aaron James on the floor, then his eyes gradually rises up at the body of detective Stephen Peterson hanging from the ceiling.

Gabrielle awakens from a sedative in the hospital with her sister Ivy by her side. Gabrielle hoped it was all a bad dream, unfortunately it was not. "Aaron's dead isn't he?" she asks Ivy. Ivy takes a seat on the hospital bed next to her sister. "I am so sorry Gabrielle." Tears filled Gabrielle's eyes and began to fall. Ivy consoles her with a hug. It didn't seem real, it just didn't seem real, and no matter how hard she cried, Aaron was not coming back. "Gabrielle, what happen? What were you doing there?" Gabrielle sobs harder in Ivy's arms as reality snatches another friend from her life. There was a knock on the door as detective Mackey enters the room. Ivy throws up an arm stopping him at the door. "Give us a minute." Detective Mackey nods his head and steps back out of the room. Ten minutes later, detective Mackey returns back to the room with questions for Gabrielle. Phillip Michaels was now also present and very concerned.

"Dr. Michaels, I know Aaron was a close friend and you have my sympathy. I have a few questions." Gabrielle nods her head.

"Dr. Michaels, why were you at that building?"

"I received an urgent message at work to meet my father there, that it was a life and death emergency."

"Oh my God." expressed Ivy.

"Did you leave that message Mr. Michaels?" asked detective Mackey.

"No, I was busy recording in my studio."

"What did Aaron have to say when you arrived?" asked detective Mackey.

"Aaron owned the building, said he received a call from A-1 Security of a possible alarm."

"So Aaron wasn't the one that left the urgent message for you to meet your father?"

"No, he didn't know anything about it. I tried calling my dad, but got his voice mail."

"Was detective Peterson already dead when you got there?"

"Yes, from what I could tell."

"Dr. Michaels, who shot and killed Aaron James?"

"I don't know. I remember Aaron rushing in front of me when shots were fired. A man up stairs ran from view when Aaron fired back at him."

"Did you get a look at him?"

"No, not really. He was a white male."

"So shots were being fired at you Dr. Michaels?"

"Yes, Aaron saved my life." said Gabrielle grief-stricken.

Tears began to fill Gabrielle's eyes as Ivy walks over and put her arms around her. It was still hard to believe that Aaron is gone.

"Well we are going to need a full statement from you when ever you are discharged."

"Not today she won't. She's staying over night for observation. I will make sure we both come down sometime tomorrow."

"That will be fine ma'am. Dr. Michaels, I apologize about my detectives, they wasn't on their job and didn't even see you leave the premises. Again, I'm sorry for your loss."

"Thank you." Gabrielle whispered.

"Oh and I have two new detectives standing guard outside your door."

"Good!" replied Ivy. "Keeps me from making a call."

Full details of the homicides at the warehouse over near Clarke Junction were sketchy as newsrooms receive bits and pieces of information as it comes in. That evening the two unidentified men names were released with complete details of the story. Jasper Ware had just arrived home that evening from work and looked forward to viewing the news. He was waiting for the news to announce the death of detective Stephen Peterson. After all, Jasper did pay a some teenager to go by and set off the alarm at that old warehouse, but by the time that boy made it there, the police and paramedics were already on the scene.

As the news story came into play, Jasper eyes lit up with joy when the death of detective Peterson was announced. Sadly however, he wasn't expecting the name of his hero to follow with words in death and murder. It was a tremendous blow to his chest that knocked the breath right out of him.

That part of the story couldn't be right, wasn't true. How could the news broadcast such fabrication. Aaron was only supposed to go there and find detective Peterson's body. No no no no, he thought. A news anchor woman then mentions another name associated with these mysterious murders. The name of Dr. Gabrielle Michaels was given. They also mentioned she was taken to Northwestern University hospital where she is in stable and guarded condition. Red lining slowly began to fill the upper right side of Jasper's right eye. Jasper had just busted a blood vessel in his right eye. He then throws a beer bottle at his TV screen and the bottle smashes into pieces.

Also watching the news down at the local pool hall was Aaron's cousin, Demarco. When his cousin's name was released in death, Demarco flipped out. He literally went mad, started busting up the joint and was eventually carried out of the place. Aaron's mother was the first next of kin notified. When detectives told Mrs. Mavis James of Aaron's death, she seemed to be lost in another place and time. Mrs. James just sat in her rocking chair rocking, staring a million miles into the past. She thought of the threat made to her on that bright moonlit night. It was the curse, she thought and it seems to be staying true to its word. As detectives left her home, a relative closed the door behind them. Mrs. James continued rocking in her chair. She thought if given the chance to do it all over, she would choose the same. She would definitely choose the same. Aaron's mother may have been the next of kin notified first, but word of Aaron's death had already circulated at the State Prison in Terre Pekin, Illinois. When Aaron's brother Jesse received word of Aaron's death, he broke down in the prison yard. Actual word of his brother's death was truly unbearable, but he also knew at that very moment that he was the only remaining living child of his mother and unfortunately for him, not for long.

8:00 am the next morning; Gabrielle was released from the hospital only to be bombarded by news reporters for a statement. Cameras and microphones were shoved in Gabrielle's and Ivy's face as snap shots circled them both. Gabrielle was rolled outside in a wheel chair where she was seen entering her sister's Mercedes. Ten minutes later Gabrielle and Ivy were sitting inside the police station. After giving her full statement and accounts of what happened, the FBI enters the room. Ivy was proud to know that a brother will be running things.

"Dr. Michaels, this is Special Agent Wiley Gibson with the FBI. They are taking over this case."

"My case or Project Hope murders?" asked Gabrielle.

"Both." stated detective Mackey.

"That's right ma'am. We believe your case and Project Hope murders have a possible connection."

Special Agent Gibson shows Gabrielle a picture of a man of interest.

"Do you recognize this man?"

Gabrielle stares at the picture, but wasn't sure who she was looking at.

"Kinda favors the man who shot Aaron."

"We need a positive ID ma'am."

"I really didn't get a good look at the guy."

"It's quite alright ma'am."

"Who is he?"

"Patrick Reddick, the cousin of Mark Hale, a white supremacist leader."

"Oh dear God!" Ivy expressed.

"I know who that is." said Gabrielle. "He is the one behind those deadly rampage shootings in 99 and possibly responsible for the murders of that federal judge and her family."

"That you are right ma'am." stated Special Agent Gibson.

"Do you believe he's behind these murders or the attempt on my sister's life."

"That we don't know for certain Mr. Jackson."

"Well do she needs to go into hiding or-?"

"Ivy, let the FBI do their job. Should I be worried?"

"Concerned, Dr. Michaels. We will keep guarded men on you as long as you want?"

"Good!" declared Ivy.

"Well, can you do what detective Mackey did? He had a detective perform a sweep of my apt building, once that morning and before I come home."

"Is that what you want?"

"No, she doesn't." stated Ivy.

"Ivy, it's my decision. Yes, that's what I want."

"Then it's done. However, we will have surveillance on you for the next forty-eight hours."

"Thank you!" expressed Ivy.

When Gabrielle and Ivy walked out of the police station, Gabrielle walked right into Keith's arms. She had spoke with Keith on the phone and told him he didn't have to come right back, but that was out of the question. That evening at her place, Gabrielle had the company of Keith, Malcolm, Amber and Jillian to comfort her. It was unimaginable for any of the woman to believe that Aaron was really gone. It was hard to believe, it was just hard to believe. Later that night after everyone was gone except Keith, Gabrielle found it difficult to keep her composure. Before she knew it, Gabrielle broke down in tears. Memories of a dear friend she will never see again have finally sunk in. Keith put her to bed where she cried herself to sleep beside him.

On Tuesday the next day, board members of the New Generation Black Panther Party Organization were in town. The CEO and Chairman of the Black Panther Party were discussing matters with Tyrone Hampton in Aaron's office. Tyrone Hampton would now assume head President of Illinois New Generation Black Panthers. The CEO and Chairman are both pleased with Tyrone Hampton and does not plan to assign another member as President. Timothy Walker, a local member will assume the Vice President position. Brother Hampton was proud of his new position, but was devastated over Aaron's death. He appeared brave and very much in control of business proceedings in front of his superiors, but silently inside lachrymose, sad and very hurt. The death of his close friend was heavy on his heart; Brother Hampton truly felt he has lost a brother.

Saturday January 20, 2001 1:00 pm

Funeral services for Dr. Aaron James were held at Mount Pilgrim Baptist Church. It was a huge turn out, a little over a thousand guests in attendance. The CEO and Chairman of the Black Panther Organization along with all four hundred local Black Panther members were in attendance, and yes, even suspended member Jasper Ware. Jasper Ware attended as a civilian not as a member. Each President of the New Generation Black Panther Party in each of the twenty states operating was also in attendance. Gabrielle and all of her friends were in attendance to say farewell to a dear friend. Ivy and Aaron had their differences, but she did attend Aaron's funeral to show her respect. Ivy was also silently thanking Aaron for saving her sister's life. Aaron's mother took it the hardest. Gabrielle couldn't hold back her tears, especially when she seen Aaron's son Percy, with tears streaming down his face. As they laid Aaron body down to rest beside his father and brothers, Gabrielle gave her condolences to his mother. Despite the kind of life Aaron James lead, a human life was taken. It was a sad day for all who knew him.

Resentfully, not everyone cared that the leader of the New Generation Black Panther Party Organization is dead. No, not everyone shared the mournful feelings of loss over Aaron James, people like, most of Chicago's police department. One person in particular who didn't sympathize or share any grief was detective Dan Cross, detective Peterson's partner. What about his death. A cop was murdered and police officers of Chicago wanted justice. Two other people, who also didn't share a mournful heart over Aaron's death, spoke over the phone with a joyful heart and bias opinions.

"Do you believe this shit Mark! The whole fuckin' town is weeping over this self-righteous nigger."

"Patrick you killed a man, show some respect."

Mark Hale laughs at his own words.

"Yeah the day I show some nigger respect, will be the day you become President of the United States."

"Hold on now, there still hope for me."

"Yeah, you and Adolf Hitler both."

"But seriously Patrick, I want you to abort you last job."

"No fucking way!"

"I mean it, I help you set up this brilliant opportunity and you fail."

"I can do it, I swear I can."

"I think I want Sam to assign someone else out of state."

"No, Mark Please. I won't fuck up again. I promise."

"Where are you Patrick?"

"Springfield."

"You better not be at our Rolex location."

"Where else am I gonna go Mark?"

"Not there, you may have eyes on you."

"Not to worry, police don't suspect a thing. I'm good, we're good."

"Well do me a favor, take what you need and hide out somewhere else alright?"

"Fine, but I'm going to finish this job."

"You have a week."

The first day of the workweek started out well for Gabrielle even though a big part of her life was forever taken away. Keith returned back to Birmingham, Alabama although he didn't want to. He did look forward to returning back to Chicago for good in a couple of months and getting his own restaurant up and running. Even though her first day back to work was going well, Gabrielle found it hard to think of anyone else. She wished she had met with Aaron that night before his death. Most of all, Gabrielle wanted to know what Aaron meant when he said that Percy had sent him a message after he died. There was one person who possibly has some answers to her questions and Gabrielle knew just where to find him, because if he didn't know, then it probably isn't so.

After work, Gabrielle found herself riding the elevators up to the top floor of the Black Panthers Party Urban Headquarters. When she stepped off the elevators, she noticed the receptionist had already gone for the day. Approaching Aaron's office felt strange because she knew Aaron would never be seen there again. The office door was closed so Gabrielle knocked, but there was no answer. She knocked again and waited. Just when she was about to leave, the office door opens with a face she wasn't expecting.

"LaTiera, is that you?"

"The one and only."

"Longtime no see girl."

"Well I've been busy, still working at the GM plant."

"Ok then, is your brother here?"

"Yeah, but he really don't want any company now."

"Ok, but I really needed to talk to him, it's important."

"Sorry, the Presidents orders."

"I understand, tell him I stopped by and I really need to speak with him."

"I'll do that Gabrielle."

Gabrielle turns to walk away when LaTiera volunteered to share more words with her.

"Hey uh Gabrielle?"

Gabrielle stops and turns back around.

"If you really need someone to talk to, I'm available."

As soon as she said that, Gabrielle remembered her teenage days hanging out with Aaron and the Black Panthers. She remembered LaTiera being three years older than her and hanging out there with them. An uneasy feeling settles over Gabrielle with discomfort. Gabrielle also remembered LaTiera's sexual preferences of the same sex. Gabrielle smiled politely with a response. "LaTiera, not even if Jesus turned me away."

Before Gabrielle could turn around to leave, President Tyrone Hampton opens the office door up wider.

"LaTiera, why don't you go start a Gay Rights campaign or something."

"When you give me the funds to back it."

"Gabrielle, I apologize. Latiera, just go, please."

"I'll be back in an hour."

"Fine, search for a rainbow while you're gone. Gabrielle, come on inside." Gabrielle enters Aaron's office to find everything pretty much the same, everything except the new name on the door and desk, plus there was another picture on the wall. It was a black and white picture of Aaron and Tyrone back in the day when the new Panthers were just getting started.

"I apologize again Gabrielle about that. Sis just broke up with her girlfriend."

"Oh I know how she is, so you are running things now at headquarters?"

"Looks that way. I still prefer Aaron to be sitting in this chair."

"I know, I miss him too and the reason why I am here."

"Are you sure you can be here, with the police and all?"

"Yes, but I don't doubt they have their eyes on me."

"I'm sure, how can I help you?"

"The night before Aaron's death, he told me that his brother Percy sent him a message after he died. What was Aaron talking about?"

The office became quiet with no response.

"Come on Tyrone, I know you know what I'm talking about. If anyone knows, its you."

"How can you be so certain?"

"Because I know about the surveillance on me at Cornell University."

"Aaron told you?"

"I figured it out myself when Ethan Roberts came by for a visit."

"I'm really sorry about that whole surveillance thing."

"So what was Aaron talking about when he said Percy sent him a message?"

"Ok, here's the deal. When Percy died, Aaron took it harder than their mother did. He felt partly responsible. Do you remember the day they buried Percy?"

"Yes I do."

"You walked over and gave Aaron a hug right?"

"Yeah, I also gave their mother a hug, just as I did Saturday."

"Well Aaron would swear on a stack of bibles that he felt Percy's spirit come through you in that hug. Do you recall encountering an overwhelming intense rush of energy in that particular hug?"

"Something like that, with a holy ghost nature. It was kinda weird because Aaron didn't seem to want to let go."

"Right. That night, Aaron dreamed that Percy came to him with a message. Percy's message was that your life was somehow in danger and that you would need Aaron's protection."

Gabrielle stares at the New President of the Black Panthers Organization with an open mind, but with doubtful eyes.

"Ok, my life is now somehow in danger, but come on."

"I know I know, sounds far-fetched."

"I want to believe this, but I don't."

"You know I was Vice President for a longtime, master of secrets and orders, so to speak. Come on now Gabrielle, you mean to tell me, you don't believe in spirits, that spirits can't speak to you, warn you even?"

That question made Gabrielle think for a moment, because she dreams of Percy all the time and he did try to warn her about Bryce.

"Maybe, I don't know."

"Well surveillance was set up and sure enough, that punk tried to rape you."

"Tyrone, Aaron said surveillance on me stopped after I graduated and came home, is that true?"

Tyrone became quiet at first before continuing with the truth.

"I'm sorry Gabrielle, but no. I even thought that Aaron was a little obsessed with you. I already knew he was in love with you."

"In love with me!" Gabrielle was shocked and greatly surprised.

"Yes, you mean to tell me after all this time, you never knew Aaron was in love with you?"

"No, I guess I was blind, but no. I always thought of him as a big brother."

"Well he was, and surveillance been off and on periodically, but was never cancelled. He had Brother Ware handling that."

"You mean Jasper Ware?"

"Yes, but don't worry about him. He is no longer a Black Panther member."

"What about other members and surveillance?"

"When Aaron died, so did his surveillance on your life."

"Well that's good to know, but I still don't know about all off this."

"Despite others opinions of him, Aaron was a good man. His only problem was letting go. Now Gabrielle, you know if you ever need me for anything just say the word, come by anytime. I wish you and your life well and God bless." Gabrielle and Tyrone both stand from their seats.

"Thank you Tyrone, for the truth."

Gabrielle left the Black Panthers Headquarters and met Amber at a bar for an after work drink. All this information was dangerously too much to keep to herself. Gabrielle had to talk to someone about all of this.

"Out so soon? Would you care for another?"

"No, not another rum and coke." said Gabrielle. "Give me something with a very low risk of side effects."

"One Shirley Temple coming up."

"Keep my vodka martinis coming."

"Sure thing."

"So Aaron had surveillance on you all this time?"

"Yes, and I always felt someone was watching me."

"I can't believe that chick was trying to push up on you."

"Yeah, tell me about it."

"You know me, I would have hollered, repent bitch, repent! And threw some holy water on her ass."

Gabrielle laughs at her friend wildly outrageous sense of humor.

"Girl you crazy."

"Girls night out on this Friday?"

"I don't know, we will have to see. I'm really not ready Amber."

"Gabrielle, all this sadness and sorrow, I've had enough. We have to get our life back."

"I know. Speaking of getting our life back, who did you choose?"

"Next question please."

"Come on now. I was glad to see the both of you at Aaron's funeral."

"Well, unlike my mother and father, I don't believe in divorce. I choose Trey."

"Good. I'm happy for you. How did Fletcher take it?"

"He understood. He's going to move to Atlanta."

"Really?"

"Yeah, but I told him not to leave on my account."

"Girl you know it will always bother him to see you and Trey together."

"He has a job offer with Sprint anyway."

"I'm glad, you did the right thing. It will be hard I know, but I'm sure Fletcher will get over you one day."

"Well, I do have that lasting affect on people." Amber said with a smile.

"You sure do Amber, the overdose effect."

FBI agent's surveillance saw Gabrielle home that night and to work the next morning, whether she was aware of it or not. Those protective eyes also saw Gabrielle have lunch with her sister and would see her home after her workday. The FBI agents assigned to her, called in their where a bouts every hour on the hour. Around 6:30 pm that evening, FBI agents watched a black Acura pull up to Gabrielle's apartment building with a Caucasian male inside. What those on alert agents wasn't aware of was, also out braving the cold air were a pair of eyes watching them.

"Relax Paul; it's her white lover coming to pick her up."

"That guy from the museum is not her lover Nick, the black guy who favors Shemar Moore from the Young and the Restless is."

"You watch the Young and the Restless Paul?"

"Yeah so."

"Something else you wanna tell me Paul?"

"He's a good actor."

"You're sad.

The two agents followed Malcolm and Gabrielle to Blue Water Grill, a classy and upscale seafood restaurant on North Dearborn Street and called in their where a bouts for the next possible hour. Parked about a block away from the restaurant, FBI agents watched Gabrielle and Malcolm walk inside the restaurant. Ten minutes later, a man walks up to the FBI agent's car and knocks on the window. The agent on the driver side rolls down the window. "Hate to bother you gentlemen, but do either of you have a light?"

"Sure."

The agent goes for his lighter and two shots were fired into the car by a firearm silencer, hitting both agents in the head. The man walks away and waits for a particular guest to return back outside.

An hour later Malcolm and Gabrielle was seen walking outside of the restaurant to Malcolm's car. As soon as they reached his car, Gabrielle froze in fear from the sight of the man that walked upon them.

"Jasper, what are you doing here?" asked Gabrielle terrifyingly.

Jasper slowly draws his gun on Gabrielle and her guest.

"Get in the car, you drive, Gabrielle and I will sit in the back."

After being forced into Malcolm's car at gunpoint, Jasper gives Malcolm an address to drive them to.

"Jasper what's this all about?"

"Not another word Gabrielle." He then points the gun at her side.

The ride to Jasper's requested location was dreadfully quiet. Gabrielle had a rather qualm feeling she may be riding to her death. She didn't understand what this was all about and it had nothing to do with Jasper. Gabrielle remembered Tyrone saying that Jasper was the Black Panther member handling her surveillance, but gave his word that surveillance had ended. Gabrielle became very afraid when Malcolm pulled up to the condemned building where Aaron was shot and killed.

Jasper orders them both out of the car at gunpoint. Disregarding the police yellow caution tape and warning signs to stay away from the crime scene, Jasper makes Malcolm unlock the entrances doors with his keys. Once inside the building, Jasper flips on some lights. Pushing them both forward, he orders Malcolm and Gabrielle to walk further inside the warehouse. Tears began to fill Gabrielle's eyes when she was forced to the area Aaron was shot and killed. Gabrielle stared at the bloodstained chalk line were Aaron laid and died on that floor. Memories of that sad day came rushing back to Gabrielle's mind, but was quickly interrupted.

"You wanna know what's this all about Gabrielle?"

"Yes Jasper, I think I deserve an explanation." She stares at the red blotch in Jasper's upper right eye from the burst blood vessel.

"This is about you, what it has always been about for the last ten years."

"Look Jasper, you and I don't have any beef. I know about the surveillance, you watching me, but that's over now."

"Oh I beg to differ Gabrielle. You have no idea the kind of man Aaron was or just who we lost."

"I loved Aaron like a brother Jasper, but Aaron made choices that brought consequences."

"The man could have been the first black president of the United States, but the death of his brother Percy and you somehow altered that. I tried to bring him out of the past, but he refused to let go and was lost, and for the last ten years, Aaron was more concerned about you than his own future."

"Jasper I can't help or be responsible for Aaron's downfall of regrets and obsession, but that's over now. Let the man rest in peace."

Jasper shakes his head at Gabrielle statement with disagreeable approval.

"Peace, do you honestly think his soul has found any peace?"

"Sooner or later everyone must answer to God, but yes, he has peace now."

"Wrong! Aaron place was here on earth. His soul was put here for a reason, but you ended that dream and purpose."

"Jasper would you listen to yourself, you can't blame other people for Aaron's own faults in life."

"He was the smartest man I ever known, with the most unusual display of words and quotes and believe me, I listen to every word. Tell me Gabrielle, have your taste buds ever had the pleasure to experience Red rum?"

Gabrielle looks at Malcolm then back over at Jasper oddly confused.

"Red-rum, no, I didn't know such a flavor existed."

"Oh yes, a rare selective liquor of molasses that many people unwillingly had the pleasure to wet their souls."

It was coming quite clear to Gabrielle that the words Jasper was speaking, were not his own, but of Aaron's. She knew only one true meaning of Red Rum and wondered will it be her outcome.

"Although I never sat and pondered the thought of the taste of death, however, the taste of death can set your soul free."

"The taste of death?" expressed Gabrielle sadly.

"Yes, Red rum. Red rum is the taste to die for, the most unlawful and malicious acts of death."

"Jasper you're not making any sense. This is all-"

"Furthest of days, shadows of spite, death to them all, may their souls regain sight. A time for all things, crimes enlighten from graves take flight, time to drink and savor the taste of delight. Please tell me my friendly foe; will you be able to handle the truthful reckoning, when *red rum comes to light?*"

Gabrielle and Malcolm both stared at Jasper, helplessly drawn to his miraculously strange words of criminal intent, but were still somehow clueless and for their sake, remained confused.

"Murder Gabrielle! Red-rum as one word spelt backwards is, *Murder*. You murdered Aaron Gabrielle and now, you must die."

Jasper lifts the gun up and points it directly at Gabrielle.

"You won't get away with this!" said Malcolm hastily.

"That's where you are wrong Mr. White Man. Thanks to those men already after Gabrielle, police will assume they are responsible. I must say Gabrielle, after all this time, I won't be sad to see you go."

Jasper's eyes then quickly ascends up stairs to an uninvited guest, a gun shot was fired, hitting Jasper in the chest. He falls backwards to the floor. Gabrielle and Malcolm turned around and looked up at the person up stairs. This person face was now clearly visible. Jasper manages to sit up on the floor and looks up at the man that shot him.

"See boy, told you I had your number and now, your number is up."

Another shot was fired, striking Jasper in the forehead as he falls backwards to the floor dead. Now getting a good look at the man that just killed Jasper, Gabrielle whispers the name, Reddick.

"Now you little lady, you almost cost me my career. I would have liked to have had a little up close and personal physical contact with you, but time is of the essences, so I'll take my credit now."

Patrick Reddick aims and fires, but the gun misfires. Gabrielle and Malcolm take off running, but before they could reach the corner of exit, another shot was fired hitting Malcolm in his left shoulder. He falls down between the doorway and Gabrielle hides behind a wall. Reddick began making his way down stairs. "Malcolm are you hurt bad?"

"Go Gabrielle, run!"

Gabrielle takes off toward the entrance doors and Malcolm gets up running in an effort not far behind her. More shots were fired as they ran out the entrance doors of the building. Gabrielle and Malcolm race towards

Malcolm's car with no seconds to waste and jumped inside. Gabrielle starts the engine and speeds off in seconds with shots still being fired behind them. The back window to Malcolm's car was shattered into pieces from the hale of bullets, but Gabrielle managed to drive them away unharmed.

"Goddamn it!" said Reddick. Reddick then runs on foot from sight.

Malcolm was bleeding from his gunshot wound to the shoulder, but calls the police from his cell phone as Gabrielle drives them to the nearest Emergency Room. As Malcolm was being treated for his gun shot wound, Gabrielle was giving the police a full statement of what happened and just who tried to kill them tonight. Gabrielle called her sister from the hospital and shared disturbing news of another attempt on her life. Gabrielle had to beg Ivy not to come out there, but soon found herself the only one on the phone line. Gabrielle also called the president of the New Generation Black Panther Party, Tyrone Hampton. She shared information to Brother Hampton that the man that shot and killed Jasper Ware tonight, was the same man who killed Aaron. Brother Hampton kindly thanked Gabrielle for that bit of information.

Malcolm would stay over night in the hospital for observation and Gabrielle and her sister was escorted over to Ivy's home by FBI agents. When Gabrielle did lay down in her sister's guestroom for the night, she already knew she wouldn't be able to sleep. Gabrielle felt her life may forever be in danger. As Gabrielle lay in bed wide awake and very frighten, little did she know, Special Agent Wiley Gibson with the FBI and his team were putting their information and plan into effect. 11: 30 pm that same night, Mark Hale receives a call from his cousin with bad news. "Mark, I have to leave the country, I'm hot. The target got a look at my face."

"What does that matter, if she's dead?"

There was a brief moment of silence on the phone.

"The target got away." said Patrick disappointingly.

"Then why am I wasting my time on the phone with you?"

"Mark I need your help–"

The phone line went dead.

The next morning after only an hour at work, Special Agent Wiley Gibson comes to Gabrielle with important turn of events and life relieving news. Dr. Michaels watch as anesthesiologist Dr. Richard Reynolds is taken away in handcuffs. Also arrested in New York was Ethan Roberts.

Dr. Reynolds ordered and paid for contract killings on the partners of Project Hope. Ethan Roberts ordered a contract murder on Gabrielle. Those contract killings were affiliated and connected to the World Church of Masters Creator Organization. FBI agents found all this information out when warrants was issued at two places, the shady commercial building over in Elmwood Park, Illinois in which arrest were made and at Mark Hales Rolex location in Springfield Illinois. FBI agents had just missed Patrick Reddick minutes before arriving at the Rolex location late last night.

There at the Rolex location was the stolen money from Project Hope and 250 thousand dollars of other money from already paid contract killings. Also at the Rolex location, was a thick black notebook of past and present contract murders. There was also an envelope with a list of twenty-five names of the most powerful, successful, and influential African-Americans that would possibly be sought out as a target and assassinated, names of well-known public figures and leaders and entrepreneurs of this great nation. Money, plots and murder for hire, all confined in one space connected to the World Church of Masters Creator Organization. However, once again, none of the evidence found and confiscated pointed to, nor could it be connected to Mark Hale the white supremacist. He was becoming Mr. Untouchable.

With Patrick Reddick still on the run and now placed on the FBI's most wanted list, Gabrielle still required secured protection by the police. She did go home that evening from work with a better and hopeful outlook of her future. Sadly, it took the unreasonable deaths of some of her closest friends for the truth to come to light. Late that same night, gassed up in a brand-new Chevy Trail Blazer paid for with cash, Patrick Reddick stops at a local convenience store one hundred and seventy-five miles south of Chicago to buy some cigarettes. Reddicks walks outside the store and lights up a smoke. After closing the SUV door, he makes a call on his cell phone to his cousin Mark Hale. The recording stated that this cellular phone was no longer a working number. Reddick eyes then glances over at the rearview mirror to find someone sitting in the backseat. Two shots were fired to the back of Reddicks head with a silencer, as blood splatter decorated the windshield. The black man in the backseat of the SUV gets out as another vehicle pulls up beside him. The unidentified black male opens the car door then takes a seat in the passenger side of a late model black Cadillac. He shuts the passenger door and the car drives away. Police and the FBI would soon find Patrick Reddick's body, but would never know that the person associated with Patrick Reddick murder, could be traced back to members of the New Generation Black Panther Party Organization.

CHAPTER THIRTY-ONE

There's A Divinity That Shapes Our Ends

People are people until proven other wise and just who decides such judgment, no one other than Jehovah God himself. Although many juries and judges inflict such powerful decisions everyday, judgment for the fate of ruthless individuals that justify their liberty and take it upon themselves to commit such heinous and vicious crimes without as much of a drop of compassion or ounce of conscience. Just what exactly drives these individuals to believe they are greater than God and have the ordain right to take another life, snatch another soul from existences. The United States Government of great debtors can argue this topic for the sake of cruel and unusual punishment regarding the death penalty for hours on end, which basically all comes down to an eye for an eye. If this is the true case, then what required equal principle of justice, fate or punishment, should the forefathers of slavery bear.

When you speak of our great nation past, it is very hard to over look slavery. If you know your history, then maybe you have read about the Trail of Tears or the Holocaust. The Trail of Tears was a march of suffering from Native Americans and the Holocaust was the destruction of six million Jews. Native American, Black Americans and Jews all suffered tremendous hardship and loss, leaving each group of people with only moderate amount ancestors to regroup, redefine and to re-establish their culture or themselves as human beings, only to be consider as minorities. When it comes to Native Americans, Black Americans and Jews, the mistreatment of each group of people during their great depression period of physical and mental torture, should not have to be compared; there is enough cruel and unusual punishment to go around and to last a lifetime. Although, there are some people willing to debate the cruelty and mistreatment of their race out exceeds any other race, any day of the week, including holidays.

For those who wish to debate their race mistreatment of the past, there is no contest or actual winner. However, allow me to say this without any bias feelings of comparison. Slavery, was an inhuman birth of exposed bondage filled with grief and pain in which suffering, is a too kind of word to acknowledge. Throughout the nearly 380 years the transatlantic slave trade was in operation and I quote, "It is estimated that at least 12 million slaves were imported into America and that an additional 1.3 to 4 million people died aboard ship. The 12 million figure represent those people who survived not only the slave ships but also the initial capture, forced marches to the African coast and imprisonment in Barracoons; for every slave loaded aboard a slave ship, three or four others died before ever reaching the African coast."

When you calculate the slaves that died before ever reaching the African coast, the 1.3 to 4 million that died aboard ship and all the countless other people that sacrificed their lives during slavery in the United States, these numbers are too staggering to over look. African-American ancestors produced enough anguish tears to form another entire ocean, an ocean to join the history of other great oceans such as, the Pacific Ocean, the Atlantic Ocean, the Indian Ocean, the Arctic Ocean and yes, the *Enslavement Ocean*. We've all heard the saying, what goes around comes around and that history repeats itself. Does that apply to the Trail of Tears, Slavery or the Holocaust? Let's pray not.

Yes, the murders of this story comes to light with a fictional twist of fate, leaving our world, a reality state of mind with a hangover of appalling crimes of the past, that still even today have not changed closed minded white Americans. In a Red Record, a comprehensive report on lynching, by Ida B. Wells stated, "The wrongs of two centuries can not be righted in a day." However, many of days have passed, yet that day is still long over due. Crimes speak for themselves, but not all crimes are equal in justice. No representation is made that the quality of present racially motivated crimes and murders to be tried, is greater than the quality of past racially motivated crimes and murders that has not been tried and yet to fully come to light with equal justice.

Many people of color way back in the day, black souls of the past rest, but cannot honestly say they have found unconditional peace. What about the forgotten justice of Thomas Moss, Calvin McDowell and Henry Stewart, the three friends of Ida B. Wells who were murdered in 1892 because their grocery store competed successfully with a nearby white owned store. What about the forgotten justice of the 1955 kidnapping and brutal slaying of Emmett Till, what about the unequal justice of the Four Little Girls, victims of the 1963 Alabama church bombing or the racism victim, Virgil Ware? A great many of souls thriving from slavery, unwillingly sacrificed their lives, but wasn't given credit for justice. When will they souls be blessed with the peace of equal justice, or should we just forget the past and continue to turn the other cheek? Many white Americans campaign for this outcome, just wanna sweep the past and all its unjust tales under the rug. I speak with the voice of the present and future, for myself and possibly every other black American or person of color when I say, Hell To The Naw! That's just not going to happen.

Slavery, their struggles, depression, grief, tears and the countless numbers of unreasonable deaths that speak m u r d e r, will forever be burned in the minds of those people who were truly affected and so many others of the future who promote change of racial equality; sadly, which for the black American race is still on lay-away. Can our great white nation buy our silence? That's what some white Americans hope to establish in slave reparation. Ask any white member of Congress about slave reparation and their reply just might be, welfare aid should qualify as amendable compensation and all is welcome to apply for their share. Talk on the subject of slave reparation draws mix reviews and opinions, but what if the American government did pay blacks what is justly owed. Will that restitution remove the scares from the many of lashes our black ancestors received from their masters, or undo the noose around the necks of so many of our sisters and brothers in which they hung from? No, it cannot. That is why it is so important to educate our children of the past, never letting anyone forget what once was. These words do not only apply to my race, African-Americans, but to all races from Jews to Latino's, from Native Americans to Asians, blue, black, red or green; anyone and I mean anyone, that may be considered a minority.

There's a divinity that shapes our ends, a divine power that influences human affairs. No soothsayer could have predicted this outcome of revelations. The pair of powerful eyes guiding Gabrielle's fate was one of a heavenly supreme. Dr. Michaels was given the news the next day of Patrick Reddick's death. The news of Reddicks death came with an over whelming relief of anxiety, releasing that shadow of a potential threat hold on Gabrielle's life. Mark Hale also received word of his cousin, Patrick Reddick's death in which he showed no remorse or sympathy. Unfortunately and technically, Mark Hale could not be connected to the conspiracy contract murders for hire. From what was stated by Hale, Samuel Shelton was the leader of this independent ring, which Mr. Shelton contrived and set up under Mark Hale's World Church of Masters Creator Organization, in which Mark Hale allegedly had no knowledge of this. In fact, with Hale awareness of being in the clear, undercover FBI agents stated with surveillance, that Mark Hale could be found at his home in East Peoria, Illinois laughing about the whole thing.

Mark Hale was the enemy Aaron James was not aware of or gave any reason of a potential threat. Hale apparently had a hovering eye over Aaron James since his career as the president of the New Generation Black Panther Party began. Mark Hale was the enemy that set Aaron up for those Project Hope murders. Little did Aaron know, the home security service he did business with, had employees affiliated with the World Church of Masters Creator Organization. Although there was no record on paper to state it, police and FBI officials assumed Stuart Elliott and detective Stephen Peterson death were plots set up by the World Church of Masters Creator Organization to frame Aaron James. Alex Rice murder would go to the cold case files in which it will remain unsolved due to the fact that the police only suspect Jasper Ware, had been murdered.

Dr. Richard Reynolds the anesthesiologist, was arrested and brought up on charges of conspiring to commit murder. His name was on the list of clients that paid for contract murder services through the World Church of Masters Creator Organization. His reason, four years ago his twenty-two year old daughter who volunteered her time at the Meals on Wheels program, was kidnapped, raped and murdered by two black men. At that point, even after the two men arrest and conviction, Dr. Reynolds remained bias of all African-Americans. Not only did Dr. Reynolds didn't want

Project Hope to come to pass, but voted against it and its zoning location. The location for Project Hope, which Dr. Reynolds voted against, was near the area of the Magnificent Mile district. Unbelievably to Northwestern University Hospital surprise, the staff had no idea that Dr. Reynolds was already being investigated for the potential deaths of four out of five African-Americans in the last two years who under his anesthesia care, never regain conscience and Dr. Reynolds may be responsible for their deaths as well.

Also arrested and on the clients list that paid for contract murder services was Ethan Roberts. Ethan Roberts sits in a New York Jail waiting trial for attempted kidnapping and conspiracy to commit murder charges. This time, Ethan Roberts will serve time for the charges, which has been brought up against him. Sometime people can hold a grudge as long as air breaths through their body. You can't blame other people for the wrongs or crimes you subject your own self to and commit. There is always a price to pay and no, not the price you pay others to do your dirty work, but consequences of your unlawful actions. Let's just say, Dr. Reynolds and Ethan Roberts will have a long time of prison confinement to think about what exactly they did wrong.

That same day after receiving word of Patrick Reddicks death, Gabrielle went to visit Malcolm and shared the good news. The first thing Malcolm expressed, was that when he spoke of signing up for all this exciting drama, he was only joking. Malcolm Reid would go on to finish his month assignment at the museum and was on his way back to California in which he looked forward to gladly. On a Sunday before he left, him and Gabrielle had brunch at Jane's where their friendship began. It was nice for a change, sharing friendly leisure time without a harmful threat or watchful eye, but it wasn't long before Malcolm had to say goodbye. Standing before Gabrielle with his heart and eyes filled with joy and love, Malcolm expressed a warm lovingly hug goodbye. He asked that her and Keith come out for a visit sometimes and she agreed.

Malcolm also had a song in thought that he kindly shared with her. That particular song in mind was, "Three Times a Lady" by the Commodores.

Fortunately, life went on as normal for Dr. Gabrielle Michaels as far as getting back into the routine swing of things. Happy hour/ girl's night out resumed its Friday evening weekly schedule. Margarita night continued with more talk of the actual novel and less talk of the other race. Sipping on margaritas and playing cards will always be the highlight and main event. Dr. Bryce Whitney would go on to accept a position at a hospital in Maryland. He is moving away to Prince George's County Maryland, one of America's wealthiest black counties. Dr. Jennifer Lyndon will also accompany Bryce, word is, they are engaged to be married and that's all good. Love is love no matter the color. Regardless of others opinions, don't fight or deny yourself happiness and what's true in your heart. If you can do that without hurting others in the process, God and your conscience will be most appreciative.

As far as Gabrielle's career, she will go on to be successful in her field. There will still be good and bad days when it comes to the screening of the *beast*. Gabrielle's advice to the women that are diagnose with breast cancer, veto it, reject cancers uninvited invasion of your body, fight and give the *beast* hell every step of the way to your recovery. Mrs. Bayer came in for her annual check up at Lynn Sage Breast Cancer Center and cancer could not be found. She is one of many brave women that is considered a survivor.

Another survivor is Percy James, Aaron's son. Percy James is one of the luckiest and wealthiest black children in America. He has a substantial trust fund to receive when he graduates with a college degree in law and political science. His mother, a well-educated black woman has specific instructions and guidelines to follow concerning Aaron's son. Right now, Percy is attending Sidwell private school in Washington D.C. and is expected to go on to bigger and better achievements in life. He is under surveillance at all time, twenty-four seven. Little Percy receives the type of secured protection as the man in the white house. Speaking of the white house, Percy James future outline left by his father Aaron James, expressed a keen interest in that field. Percy James could very well be one of America's black Presidents.

Hours filled days, days flourish weeks, and week's blossoms into months. On May 7, 2001, there was a ribbon cutting ceremony for the new Percy R. James Health Clinic grand opening. It was a proud day for the only remaining partner, Kelvin McDonald. Gabrielle was the first of several speakers. She began her brief speech quoting the words of a dear friend who she will always admire and remember.

"I am not going to stand here before you today and give a lecture, because this is not my show. This completed project through endless effort will do more for our black community than the assuring fortified words coming forth from

my mouth. I will however, say this much. If we do not strive to help our people, then just who will? Those were some words of a dear friend, one of three that could not be her today, but I'm sure they are with us in spirit and send their blessings and approval from above."

That afternoon Gabrielle went home to put another dear friend to rest. She opened her armoire cabinet and pulled out the 8x10 black and white picture of Percy from its safe haven. She stares at his picture ever so tenderly. Gabrielle quietly walked that picture up front to the living room. She placed Percy's picture beside another 8x10 picture of her and Aaron. Those two souls were a great significant part of her life, her past and their spirits will forever remain apart of her. That night Gabrielle had a dream. She dreamed her and Keith were walking in the park. In distances, not far from them, Percy appeared. Percy smiled and raised his hand to speak. Gabrielle smiled, releasing a breath of happiness before returning the gesture. As Percy and Gabrielle smiled and stare at each other lovingly, a particular song seems to flow from him. That particular song, "I'll be there" by The Escape Club." Then without notice, a bright light from above came down over him as Gabrielle watched Percy fade away with a loving smile on his face and rejoicing tears in her eyes.

If you follow this particular rhythm of lively colored, radiate rays of the sun, it will probably lead you to the roof of Gabrielle's apartment building. There, you will find those sunrays flourishing all around Gabrielle, where they have made themselves comfortable. Gabrielle stares out beyond the clear blue skies, thinking of her life and just how fortunate she is. There was a certain song playing all around her in her mind. That particular song was "I Can See Clearly Now" by Jonny Nash. Gabrielle was happy and she knew it. She had everything in life that mattered most, and that is good health, friends and most importantly, family. Her sister Ivy continues to be successful as a partner with Lambert, McGhee, Hewitt and Jackson. Her father Phillip Michaels, released his seventh album entitled GABRIELLE II and once again it struck gold selling 750,000 copies its first week.

Gabrielle takes a deep breath and releases some happiness into the air for others to breathe. "My soul is well and it ease, it praises holiness of higher good, it rest like love and is at peace." she said with a smile. It was at that moment Gabrielle knew that the only eyes watching her, were of God, and those eyes are always welcomed in her life anytime. The door to the roof opened and Keith walks outside. Their eyes meet and they smile. He walks over to Gabrielle and blesses her with a hug. As they both stare out among the blue sky, it was at that particular moment they both had the same song on their mind. For once, both of their songs on their minds were on the same page. That particular song was "Always" by Mr. Stevie Wonder himself. Gabrielle suggests a game of chess and Keith says sure, why not, and they began their walk back inside the building with their arms around each other. Keith however, stops her along the way with a question. "So Gabrielle, *how are you feeling*?" Gabrielle stops walking for a moment, thinking of her life and their future. "Fine, I'll be just fine."

The End